MAD ABOUT
MADELINE

Dear Julia ~
May you enjoy Madeline's
travels and journeys!
Happy Birthday
Love
Aunt Kristyn & Uncle Brad
1996

MAD ABOUT
MADELINE

THE COMPLETE TALES

LUDWIG BEMELMANS

VIKING

Viking

Published by the Penguin Group,
Penguin Books USA Inc., 375 Hudson Street, New York, New York 10014 , U.S.A.
Penguin Books Ltd, 27 Wrights Lane, London W8 5TZ, England
Penguin Books Australia Ltd, Ringwood, Victoria, Australia
Penguin Books Canada Ltd, 10 Alcorn Avenue, Toronto, Ontario, Canada M4V 3B2
Penguin Books (N.Z.) Ltd, 182-190 Wairau Road, Auckland 10, New Zealand

Penguin Books Ltd, Registered Offices: Harmondsworth, Middlesex, England

Library of Congress Cataloging in Publication Data
Bemelmans, Ludwig, 1898–1962.
   [Selections]
   Mad about Madeline : the collected tales / story and pictures by Ludwig Bemelmans.
       p.   cm.
   Contents: Madeline–Madeline's rescue–Madeline and the bad hat–Madeline and the gypsies–Madeline in London–Madeline's Christmas.
   ISBN 0-670-85187-6 (set)
   1. Children's stories, American. [1. Paris (France)–Fiction. 2. Boarding schools–Fiction. 3. Schools–Fiction. 4. Stories in rhyme.] I. Title.
PZ8.3.B425Maac 1993
[E]–dc20   93-14663
                                              CIP
                                              AC

Printed in the United States of America

CONTENTS

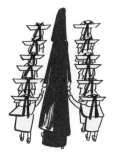

Introduction by Anna Quindlen   9

Madeline   13

Madeline and the Bad Hat   61

Madeline's Rescue   115

Madeline and the Gypsies   169

Madeline in London   227

Madeline's Christmas   283

The Isle of God (or Madeline's Origin)   313

With a selection of original sketches of Madeline
from Ludwig Bemelmans' notebooks

Introduction

During the years that our three children were growing from babyhood to youth, *Madeline* was not considered as much a book in our household as it was a language and a way of life. When Maria, our youngest, broke her arm and her brothers were grousing about the tucking up on the sofa and the public allure of her fuschia cast, it seemed perfectly natural to turn to them and say, "Boohoo, we want to have our arms broken, too."

When I was trying to describe Maria's character to a friend long distance, I finally resorted to the simplest way of evoking little girl feistiness: "To the tiger in the zoo / Madeline just said, 'Pooh-pooh'." And occasionally all three of my children must tire of my tendency to move through their rooms from time to time in the dark moments after the light has just been turned off, saying softly, "Good night little girls! / Thank the lord you are well / And now go to sleep!" / said Miss Clavel."

I can recite *Madeline* by heart, as my children know well. But it's likely that, in small chunks, they can recite it, too. In fact, it would not be too much of a stretch to say that most of the people I know know *Madeline* by heart.

This is curious. Amid a childhood full of children's books, amid glorious pictures and imaginative plots, it is worth wondering why this story is among a handful of books that now-grown children can declaim without a text, that now-grown children invariably buy for their own more than half a century after Ludwig Bemelmans began writing it on the back of a restaurant menu.

Why would three American children who go to a day school, have never visited Paris or worn a uniform, and who are still flummoxed by why Miss Clavel wears a veil be almost instantly and consistently en rapport with twelve little girls in two straight lines being led by their boarding school nurse in flat sailor hats and identical coats through the Place de la Concorde and past Notre Dame?

The answer, I think, can be contained in one word: attitude. And the attitude, of course, belongs to Madeline, "the smallest one." Through the other books—*Madeline's Rescue, Madeline's Christmas, Madeline and the Gypsies,*

Madeline and the Bad Hat, *Madeline in London*—we never even learn the names of the eleven other girls, who are barely discernible from one another except for variations of hair.

But we know of Madeline all we need to know of anyone's character: that she is utterly fearless and sure of herself, small in stature but large in moxie. Not afraid of mice, of ice, or of teetering on a stone bridge over a river. It's a mistake to stretch childhood associations too far—and also a mistake not to take them seriously enough—but it would not be stretching it too far to say that, for little girls especially, Madeline is a kind of role model. That "pooh-pooh" rang enduringly in the ears of many of us. Translation from the French: Stand back, world. I fear nothing.

The role of gutsy girls in children's literature should never be discounted, from Anne Shirley of the *Green Gables* series to Jo March in *Little Women*. When I was a girl, girl characters who were outspoken, smart, strong, and just a bit disobedient were the primary way I found to define and discover myself and all the ways in which I felt different from standard notions of femininity.

But for younger children, the girls in storybooks have, until recently, most often been princesses spinning straw into gold or sleeping their lives away until a prince plants the kiss of true love on their compliant lips. Perhaps the best known exception is Kay Thompson's Eloise, a little girl with untidy hair and manners who lives—and writes on the walls—in the Plaza Hotel.

Truth to tell, I have always found Eloise's chaotic existence and her self-protective little asides about her mother shopping at Bergdorf's a bit pathetic and lonely, a decidedly grown-up version of the madcap child. When I think of Eloise grown up, I think of her with a drinking problem, knocking about from avocation to avocation, unhappily married or unhappily divorced, childless.

When I think of Madeline grown up, I think of her as the French Minister of Culture or the owner of a stupendous couture house, sending her children off to Miss Clavel to be educated. Perhaps they have apprehended all this, but while my children like Eloise, they *live* Madeline, which makes all the difference.

For those of us who believe that children feel secure with structure, part of the enduring charm of the books surely must be that Madeline's confidence and fearlessness are set within a backdrop of utter safety. While Eloise's nanny, for instance, is always at her wit's end, Miss Clavel is concerned but competent, and life is safe within the "old house in Paris / that was covered with vines."

In their two straight lines the children march predictably through life, with Madeline the admired wild card who reforms the rambunctious Bad Hat and runs away with the gypsies. Even when she has what has become the best known emergency appendectomy in literature, the surgery becomes simultaneously an adventure and a school routine, the kind of combination of the scary and the safe that is alluring when you are trying to become yourself.

It's a combination of the masterly and the simplistic that makes the drawings so successful, too. I hope it would not offend Bemelmans to say that the illustrations are in many ways quite childlike: the simple, almost crude lines of the interiors; the faces with dot eyes and U-shaped mouths; the scribble quality to much of the detail work. The rendering of the Eiffel Tower as a Christmas tree in the holiday Madeline book is wonderful and yet sensible to children, who might well embellish the landmark in exactly the same way.

Rich picture books are wonderful, but when you are little they often make you feel rather incompetent. *Madeline* is different. Of course the simplicity of the drawings is quite deceptive; the one in which Madeline stands on the bed and shows the other girls her scar after the appendectomy is perhaps as good a rendering of carriage-as-character as I've ever seen outside of Holbein's portraits. But the best children's illustrators have a good deal of the child in them, and Bemelmans is no exception. "He colors outside the lines," my oldest child said approvingly.

Classics are always ineffable: why does *Goodnight Moon* appeal for generation after generation, despite changes in mores, manners, technology, and television fare? Why do children as different as Abbott and Costello agree completely about the indispensability of *The Cat in the Hat*? Why does *A Wrinkle in Time* speak as clearly to my sons as it did to me three decades ago? What is it that Sendak has that lesser lights just do not?

The answer, I think, is that there are certain books written out of some grown-up's idea of children, of who they are and what they should be like, of what we like to think absorbs and amuses them. And then there are the books that are written for real children by people who manage, however they do it, to maintain an utterly childlike part of their minds. They understand that children prize both security and adventure, both bad behavior and conformity, both connections and independence.

Madeline charms because of rhyme and meter, vivid illustrations and engaging situations. But the Madeline books endure because they understand children and epitomize what they fear, what they desire, and what they hope to be in the person of one little girl. A risk taker. An adventurer. And at the end, a small child drifting off to sleep. "That's all there is— / there isn't any more."

Anna Quindlen
November 1993

MADELINE

In an old house in Paris

that was covered with vines

lived twelve little girls in two straight lines.

In two straight lines they broke their bread

and brushed their teeth

and went to bed.

They smiled at the good

and frowned at the bad

and sometimes they were very sad.

They left the house
at half past nine
in two straight lines

in rain

or shine—

the smallest one was Madeline.

She was not afraid of mice—

she loved winter, snow, and ice.

To the tiger in the zoo
Madeline just said, "Pooh-pooh,"

and nobody knew so well

how to frighten Miss Clavel.

In the middle of one night
Miss Clavel turned on her light
and said, "Something is not right!"

Little Madeline sat in bed,

cried and cried; her eyes were red.

And soon after Dr. Cohn

came, he rushed out to the phone

and he dialed: DANton-ten-six—

"Nurse," he said, "it's an appendix!"

Everybody had to cry—

not a single eye was dry.

Madeline was in his arm

in a blanket safe and warm.

In a car with a red light

they drove out into the night.

Madeline woke up two hours

later, in a room with flowers.

Madeline soon ate and drank.

On her bed there was a crank,

and a crack on the ceiling had the habit
of sometimes looking like a rabbit.

Outside were birds, trees, and sky—
and so ten days passed quickly by.

One nice morning Miss Clavel said—

"Isn't this a fine—

day to visit

Madeline."

VISITORS FROM TWO TO FOUR
read a sign outside her door.

Tiptoeing with solemn face,

with some flowers and a vase,

in they walked and then said, "Ahhh,"
when they saw the toys and candy
and the dollhouse from Papa.

But the biggest surprise by far—

on her stomach

was a scar!

"Good-by," they said, "we'll come again,"

and the little girls left in the rain.

They went home and broke their bread

brushed their teeth

and went to bed.

In the middle of the night
Miss Clavel turned on the light
and said, "Something is not right!"

And afraid of a disaster

Miss Clavel ran fast

and faster,

and she said, "Please children do—
tell me what is troubling you?"

And all the little girls cried, "Boohoo,
we want to have our appendix out, too!"

"Good night, little girls!
Thank the lord you are well!
And now go to sleep!"
said Miss Clavel.

And she turned out the light—
and closed the door—
and that's all there is—
there isn't any more.

HERE is a list for those who may wish to identify the Paris scenes Ludwig Bemelmans has pictured in this book.

On the cover and in one of the
illustrations
THE EIFFEL TOWER

In the picture of the lady feeding
the horse
THE OPERA

A gendarme chases a jewel thief across
THE PLACE VENDOME

A wounded soldier at
THE HOTEL DES INVALIDES

A rainy day in front of
NOTRE DAME

A sunny day looking across
THE GARDENS AT THE LUXEMBOURG

Behind the little girls skating is
THE CHURCH OF THE SACRE COEUR

A man is feeding birds in
THE TUILERIES GARDENS FACING
THE LOUVRE

MADELINE AND THE BAD HAT

To

Mimi

In an old house in Paris
That was covered with vines
Lived twelve little girls
In two straight lines.
They left the house at half-past-nine
In two straight lines, in rain or shine.
The smallest one was Madeline.

One day the Spanish Ambassador

Moved into the house next door.

Look, my darlings, what bliss, what joy!

His Excellency has a boy.

Madeline said, "It is evident that
This little boy is a Bad Hat!"

In the spring when birdies sing
Something suddenly went "zing!"

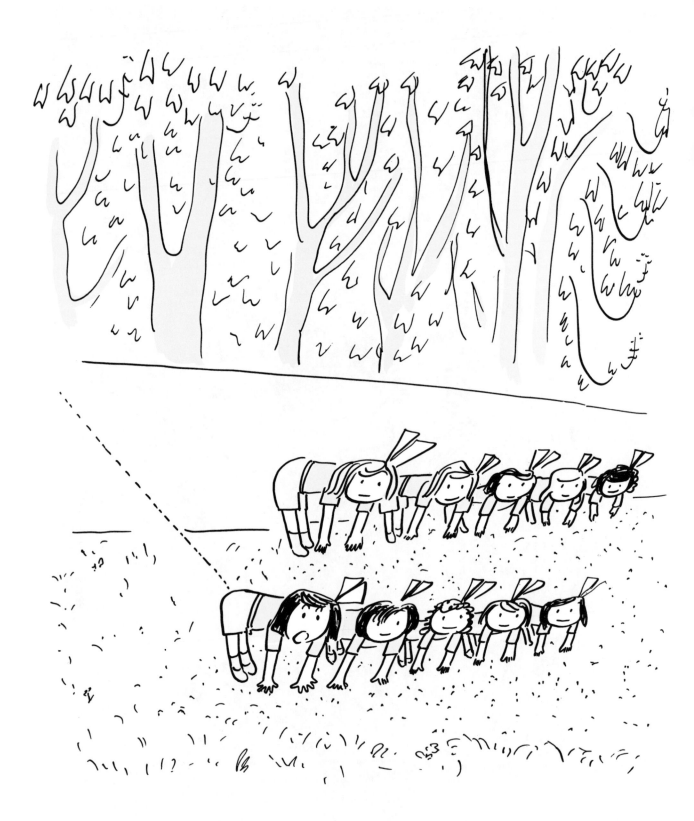

Causing pain and shocked surprise
During morning exercise.

On hot summer nights he ghosted;

In the autumn wind he boasted

That he flew the highest kite.

Year in, year out, he was polite.

He was sure and quick on ice,

And Miss Clavel said, "Isn't he nice!"

One day he climbed upon the wall
And cried, "Come, I invite you all!
Come over some time, and I'll let you see
My toys and my menagerie—
My frogs and birds and bugs and bats,
Squirrels, hedgehogs, and two cats.
The hunting in this neighborhood
Is exceptionally good."

But Madeline said, "Please don't molest us,
Your menagerie does not interest us."

He changed his clothes and said, "I bet
This invitation they'll accept."

Madeline answered, "A Torero
Is not at all our idea of a hero!"
The poor lad left; he was lonesome and blue;
He shut himself in—what else could he do?

But in a short while, the little elf
Was back again, and his old self.

Said Miss Clavel, "It seems to me
He needs an outlet for his energy.

"A chest of tools might be attractive
For a little boy that's very active.

"I knew it—listen to him play,
Hammering, sawing, and working away."

Oh, but that boy was really mean!

He built himself a GUILLOTINE!

He was unmoved by the last look
The frightened chickens gave the cook.

He ate them ROASTED, GRILLED, and FRITO!
¡Oh, what a horror was PEPITO!

One day, when out to take the air,

Madeline said, "Oh, look who's there!"

Pepito carried a bulging sack.

He was followed by an increasing pack

Of all the dogs in the neighborhood.

"That boy is simply misunderstood.

Look at him bringing those doggies food!"

He said, "Let's have a game of tag"—
And let a CAT out of the bag!

There were no trees, and so instead
The cat jumped on Pepito's head.

And now just listen to the poor
Boy crying, "AU SECOURS!"
Which you must cry, if by any chance
You're ever in need of help in France.

Miss Clavel ran fast and faster
To the scene of the disaster.

She came in time to save the Bad Hat,
And Madeline took care of the cat.
Good-by, Fido; so long, Rover.
Let's go home—the fun is over.

There was sorrowing and pain

In the Embassy of Spain.

The Ambassadress wept tears of joy,
As she thanked Miss Clavel for saving her boy.

"Nothing," said the Ambassador,
"Would cheer up poor Pepito more
Than a visit from next door.

"Only one visitor at a time,
Will you go in first, Miss Madeline?"

So Madeline went in on tiptoe,
And whispered, "Can you hear me, Pepito?
It serves you right, you horrid brat,
For what you did to that poor cat."

"I'll never hurt another cat,"
Pepito said. "I swear to that.
I've learned my lesson. Please believe
I'm turning over a new leaf."
"That's fine," she said. "I hope you do.
We all will keep our eyes on you!"

And lo and behold, the former Barbarian

Turned into a Vegetarian.

And the starling and turtle, the bunny and bat,

Went back to their native habitat.

His love of animals was such,

Even Miss Clavel said,

"It's too much!"

The little girls all cried "Boo-hoo!"

But Madeline said, "I know what to do."

And Madeline told Pepito that
He was no longer a BAD HAT.
She said, "You are our pride and joy,
You are the world's most wonderful boy!"

They went home and broke their bread
And brushed their teeth and went to bed,

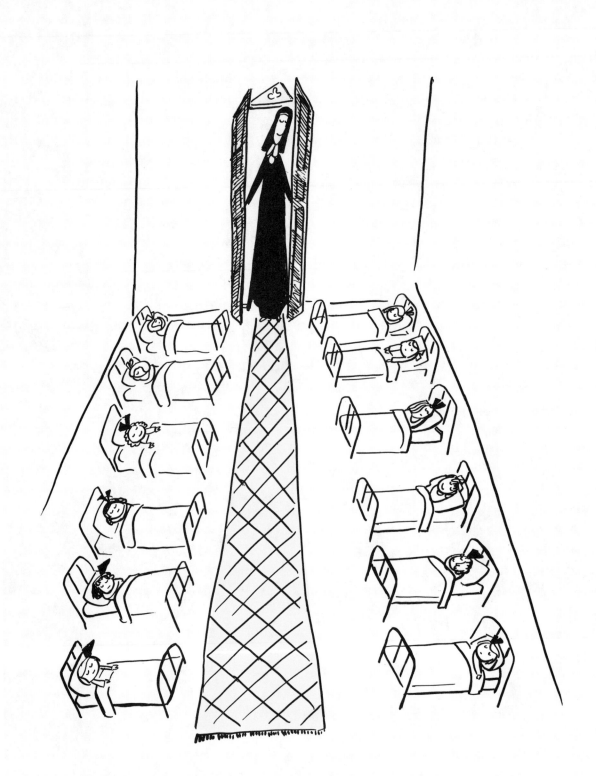

And as Miss Clavel turned out the light
She said, "I knew it would all come out right."

MADELINE'S RESCUE

MADELINE'S
RESCUE

In an old house in Paris that was covered with vines
Lived twelve little girls in two straight lines.
They left the house at half past nine
In two straight lines in rain or shine.
The smallest one was Madeline.
She was not afraid of mice.
She loved winter, snow, and ice.
To the tiger in the zoo
Madeline just said, "Pooh pooh!"

And nobody knew so well
How to frighten Miss Clavel—

Until the day she slipped and fell.

Poor Madeline would now be dead

But for a dog

That kept its head,

And dragged her safe from a watery grave.

"From now on, I hope you will listen to me,

"And here is a cup of camomile tea.

"Good night, little girls—I hope you sleep well."
"Good night, good night, dear Miss Clavel!"

Miss Clavel turned out the light.

After she left there was a fight

About where the dog should sleep that night.

The new pupil was ever
So helpful and clever.

The dog loved biscuits, milk, and beef
And they named it Genevieve.

She could sing and almost talk

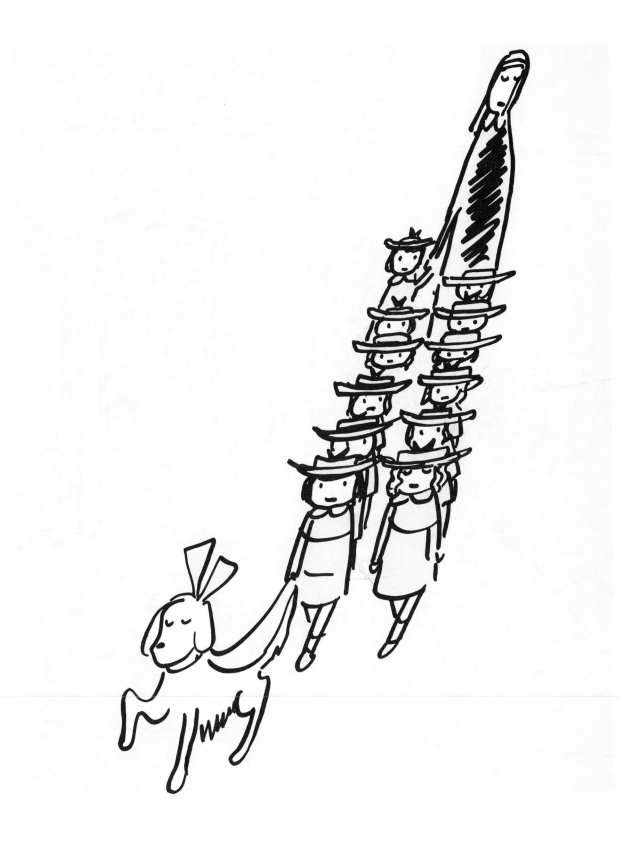

And enjoyed the daily walk.

Soon the snow began to fly,
Inside it was warm and dry
And six months passed quickly by.

When the first of May came near
There was nervousness each year.

For on that day there arrived a collection
Of trustees for the annual inspection.

The inspection was most thorough,
Much to everybody's sorrow.

"Tap, tap!" "Whatever can that be?"

"Tap, tap!" "Come out and let me see!

"Dear me, it's a dog! Isn't there a rule

"That says DOGS AREN'T ALLOWED IN SCHOOL?"

"Miss Clavel, get rid of it, please,"
Said the president of the board of trustees.
"Yes, but the children love her so,"
Said Miss Clavel. "Please don't make her go."

"I daresay," said Lord Cucuface.
"I mean—it's a perfect disgrace
"For young ladies to embrace
"This creature of uncertain race!

"Off with you! Go on—run! scat!
"Go away and don't come back!"

Madeline jumped on a chair.

"Lord Cucuface," she cried, "beware!

"Miss Genevieve, noblest dog in France,

"You shall have your VEN-GE-ANCE!"

"It's no use crying or talking.

"Let's get dressed and go out walking.

"The sooner we're ready, the sooner we'll leave—

"The sooner we'll find Miss Genevieve."

They went looking high

and low

And every place a dog might go.

In every place they called her name

But no one answered to the same.

The gendarmes said, "We don't believe
"We've seen a dog like Genevieve."

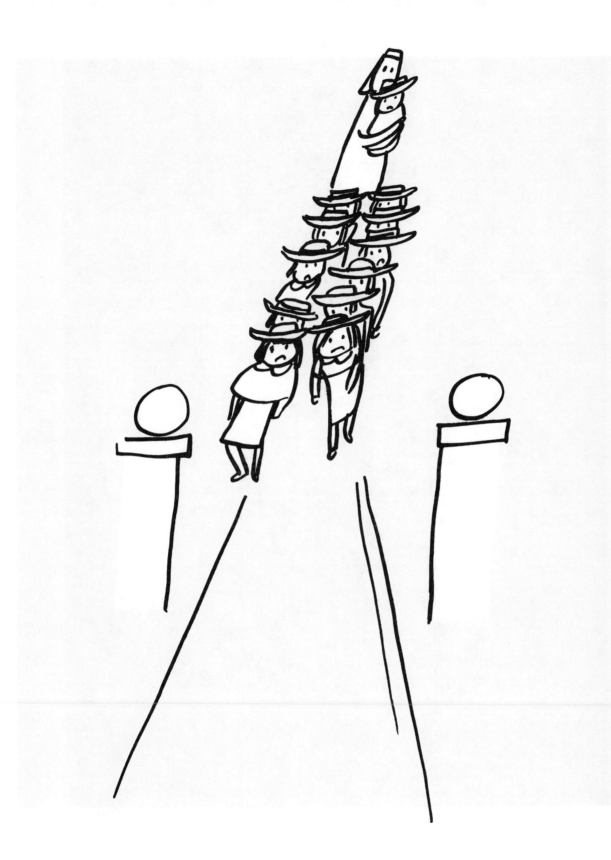

Hours after they had started
They came back home broken-hearted.

"Oh, Genevieve, where can you be?
"Genevieve, please come back to me."

In the middle of the night
Miss Clavel turned on the light.
And said, "Something is not right."

An old street lamp shed its light
On Miss Genevieve outside.

She was petted, she was fed,
And everybody went to bed.

"Good night, little girls, I hope you sleep well."
"Good night, good night, dear Miss Clavel!"

Miss Clavel turned out the light,
And again there was a fight,
As each little girl cried,
"Genevieve is *mine* tonight!"

For a second time that night
Miss Clavel turned on her light,

And afraid of a disaster,
She ran fast—

And even faster.

"If there's one more fight about Genevieve,
"I'm sorry, but she'll have to leave!"

That was the end of the riot—
Suddenly all was quiet. .

For the third time that night
Miss Clavel turned on the light,

And to her surprise she found

That suddenly there was enough hound

THE END

To go all around.

MADELINE AND THE GYPSIES

MADELINE *and the* GYPSIES

Ⅰn an old house in Paris that was
   covered with vines
Lived twelve little girls in two
   straight lines.
In two straight lines they broke
   their bread
And brushed their teeth and went
   to bed.
They left the house at half-past
   nine—
The smallest one was Madeline.
In another old house that stood
   next door
Lived the son of the Spanish
   Ambassador.
He was all alone; his parents were
   away;
He had no one with whom to play.
He asked, "Please come, I invite
   you all,
To a wonderful Gypsy Carnival."
And so—

   Dear reader—

Here we go!

Up and down and down and up—
They hoped the wheel would never stop.
Round and round; the children cried,
"Dear Miss Clavel, just one more ride!"

A sudden gust of wind,
A bolt of lightning,

Even the Rooster found it frightening.

The big wheel stops; the passengers land.

How fortunate there is a taxi stand!

"Hurry, children, off with these things!
You'll eat in bed."
Mrs. Murphy brings
The soup of the evening; it is half-past nine.

"Good heavens, where is MADELINE?"

Poor Miss Clavel, how would she feel
If she knew that on top of the Ferris wheel,
In weather that turned from bad to rotten,
Pepito and Madeline had been forgotten?

Pepito said, "Don't be afraid.
I will climb down and get some aid."
It was downpouring more and more
As he knocked on the Gypsies' caravan door.

The Gypsy Mama with her umbrella went
And got some help in the circus tent.
With the aid of the strong man and the clown,
Madeline was safely taken down.

The Gypsy Mama tucked them in
And gave them potent medicine.

The big wheel was folded, and the tent.
They packed their wagons and away they went.
For Gypsies do not like to stay—
They only come to go away.

A bright new day—the sky is blue;
The storm is gone; the world is new.

This is the Castle of Fountainblue—
"All this, dear children, belongs to you."

How wonderful to float in a pool,
Watch other children go to school,

Never to have to brush your teeth,

And never—never—

To go to sleep.

The Gypsies taught them grace

And speed,

And how to ride

The circus steed.

Then Madeline said, "It's about time
We sent dear Miss Clavel a line."

Poor Miss Clavel—a shadow of her former self
From worrying, because, instead of twelve,
There were only eleven little girls—
Stopped brushing their curls
    And suddenly revived
      When the postal card arrived.
"Thank heaven," she said, "the children are well!
But dear, oh dear, they've forgotten how to spell."
She studied the postmark, and then fast and faster

They rushed to the scene of the disaster.

The Gypsy Mama didn't like at all
What she saw in her magic crystal ball.

The Gypsy Mama said, "How would you like to try on
This lovely costume of a lion?"

With a curved needle and some string
She sewed both the children in,
And nobody knew what was inside
The tough old lion's leathery hide.

A circus lion earns his bread
By scaring people half to death.

And after doing that, he's fed.

And after that, he's put to bed.

A lovely dawn and all was well;

The lion roamed through wood and dell.

He smelled sweet flowers; he came to a farm;

He frightened the barnyard—

Intending no harm.

They saw a man and said, "Please help
Us to get out of this old pelt."

The man was a hunter; he took his gun;
He got to his feet and started to run.

Said the lion, "We'd better go back, for if we're not
In a zoo or circus, we'll surely be shot."

They got to the tent
In time for the show.

"Look," said Madeline,

"There in the first row—"

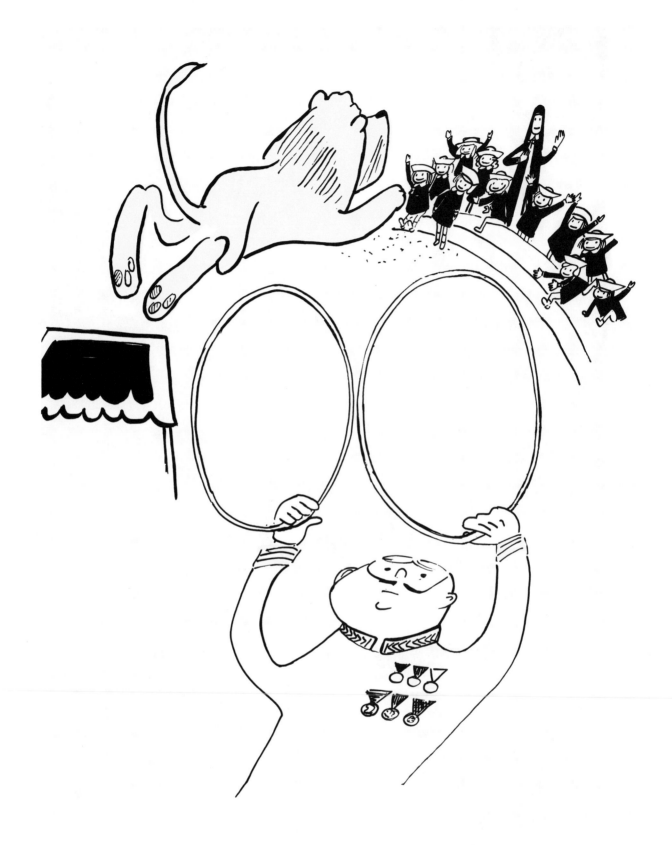

"Oh yes," said Pepito,
"There are people we know!"

"Dear Miss Clavel! at last we found you!
Please let us put our arms around you."

The Gypsy Mama sobbed her grief
Into her only handkerchief.

The strong man suddenly felt weak,
And tears were running down his cheek.
Even the poor clown had to cry
As the time came to say good-by.

The best part of a voyage—by plane,
By ship,

Or train—

Is when the trip is over and you are

Home again.

Here is a freshly laundered shirty—
It's better to be clean than dirty.

In two straight lines
They broke their bread
And brushed their teeth
And went to bed.

"Good night, little girls, thank the Lord you are well!
And now PLEASE go to sleep," said Miss Clavel.
And she turned out the light and closed the door—

And then she came back, just to count them once more!

Scenery in

MADELINE
and the Gypsies

	PAGE
Notre-Dame in a storm	178-179
Château de Fontainebleau	186-187
The pool at Marly-le-Roi	188
Chartres, with the Cathedral	189
Mont-Saint-Michel	190-191
Carcassonne	194-195
A Normandy farm	206-207
The seacoast at Deauville	211
Gare Saint-Lazare in Paris	218-219

MADELINE IN LONDON

In an old house
in Paris

that was covered
with vines

Lived twelve little girls
in two straight lines.

They left the house

at half past nine.

The smallest one
was Madeline.

In another old house
that stood next door

Lived Pepito,
the son of

the Spanish Ambassador.

An Ambassador doesn't
have to pay rent,
But he has to move
to wherever he's sent.

He took his family
and his hat;

They left for England—
all but the cat.

"I'm glad," said the cat.
"There goes that bad hat.
Let him annoy some other kitten
At the Embassy in Great Britain."
The little girls all cried: "Boo-hoo—
We'd like to go to London too."

In London Pepito just picked at his dinner,
Soon he grew thin and then he grew thinner—

And when he began to look like a stick
His mama said, "My, this boy looks sick.
I think Pepito is lonely for
Madeline and the little girls next door."

His papa called Paris. "Hello, Miss Clavel,
My little Pepito is not at all well.

"He misses you; and he's lonesome for
Madeline and the little girls next door.

"May we request the pleasure of your company—
There's plenty of room here at our embassy."

"Quick, darlings, pack your bags, and we'll get
Out to the airport and catch the next jet."

Fill the house with lovely flowers,

Fly our flags from all the towers.

For Pepito's birthday bake
The most wonderful birthday cake.

Place twelve beds in two straight lines.
The last one here will be Madeline's.

"Welcome to London, the weather's fine,
And it's exactly half past nine."

"Good Heavens," said Miss Clavel, "we've brought no toy
For his excellency's little boy!"
Said Madeline, "Everybody knows, of course,
He always said he craved a horse."
In their little purses and in Miss Clavel's bag
There wasn't enough money to buy the meanest nag.

But in London there's a place to get
A retired horse to keep as a pet.

And when they went to the place, they found
A horse that was gentle, strong, and sound.

Some poor old dobbins are made into glue,
But not this one—

Look, he's as good as new.

"Happy birthday, Pepito, happy birthday to you.

This lovely horse belongs to you."

Just then—"Tara, tara"—a trumpet blew
Suddenly outside, and off he flew
Over the wall to take his place at the head

Of the Queen's Life Guards, which he had always led
Before the Royal Society for the Protection of Horses
Had retired him from Her Majesty's Forces.

"Oh, dear! They've gone. Oh, what a pity!

Come, children, we'll find them in the city."

"Careful, girls, watch your feet.

Look right before you cross the street."

Oh, for a cup of tea and crumpets—

Hark, hark, there goes the sound of trumpets.

These birds have seen

all this before.

But they are glad

of an encore.

And so are the people—on ship...

and shore.

And now it's getting really grand.

Here comes the mascot and his band.

The people below are stout and loyal,

And those on the balcony mostly Royal.

The show is over, it's getting dark
In the city, in the park.
Dinner is waiting; we must be on time.
Now let's find Pepito and Madeline.

Well, isn't it lovely—they're standing sentry
Right here at the Whitehall entry.
That is the power and the beauty:
In England everyone does his duty!

Visiting is fun and gay—

Let's celebrate a lovely day.

Everyone had been well fed,

Everyone was in his bed.

Only one was forgotten, he'd been on his feet
All day long, without anything to eat.

In a cottage that was thatched,
Wearing trousers that were patched,
Lived the gardener, who loved flowers,
Especially in the morning hours,
When their faces, fresh with dew,
Smiled at him—"How DO you do?"

The gardener, who was never late,
Opened up the garden gate.

The gardener dropped his garden hose.

There wasn't a daisy or a rose.

"All my work and all my care
For nought! Oh, this is hard to bear.

"Where's my celery, carrots, tomatoes, my beans and peas?
And not an apple on my apple trees!"

Everybody had to cry.
Not a single eye was dry.

Oh, look who is lying there,
With his feet up in the air.

"I feel his breath, he's not dead yet.
Quick, Pepito, get the vet."

The vet said, "Don't worry, he's only asleep.
Help me get him on his feet.

"As a diet, there is nothing worse
Than green apples and roses for an old horse."
"Dear lady," said Miss Clavel, "we beg your pardon.
It seems our horse has eaten up your garden.

"A little sunshine, a little rain,
And it all will be the same again."
Pepito's mother said, "Quite so, quite so!
Still I'm afraid the horse must go."

Then Madeline cried, "I know what to do.
Pepito, let us take care of him for you."

"Fasten your seat belts, in half an hour
You will see the Eiffel Tower."

"Madeline, Madeline, where have you been?"
"We've been to London to see the Queen."

"At last," sighed Madeline, "we are able
To sit down without being thirteen at table."

They brushed his teeth and gave him bread,

And covered him up

and put him to bed.

"Good night, little girls,

Thank the Lord you are well.

And now go to sleep," said Miss Clavel.

And she turned out the light and closed the door.

There were twelve upstairs, and below one more.

MADELINE'S CHRISTMAS

MADELINE'S CHRISTMAS

In an old house in Paris
That was covered with vines
Lived twelve little girls
In two straight lines.
They left the house at half-past nine
In two straight lines, in rain or shine.
The smallest one was MADELINE.

She was not afraid of mice

She loved winter, snow and ice

And to the tiger in the zoo

Madeline just said...

"POOH, POOH!"

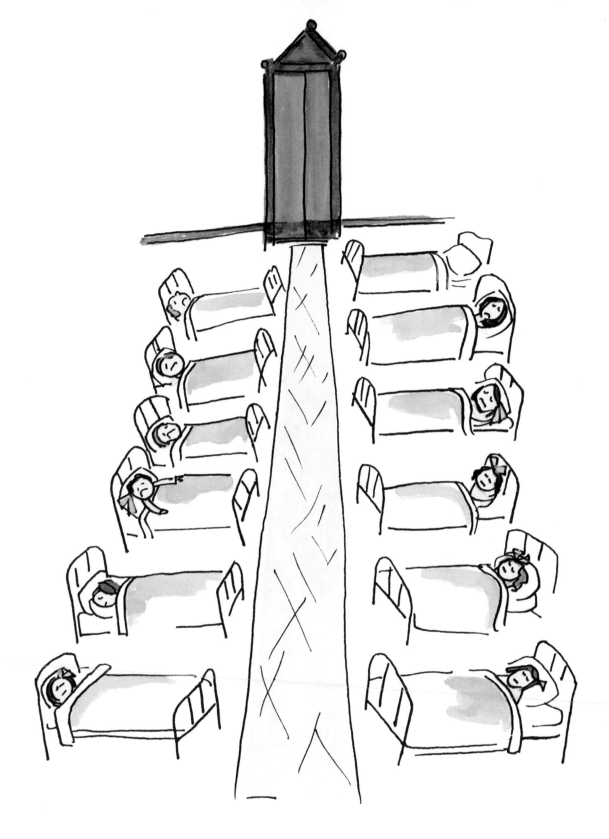

It was the night before Christmas
And all through the house
Not a creature was stirring
Not even the mouse.

For like everyone else in that house which was old
The poor mouse was in bed with a miserable cold.

And only
Our brave little Madeline

Was up and about

And feeling

Just fine.

Suddenly came a knock
Which made her pause—

Could it perhaps be Santa Claus?
But no...

A rug merchant was at the door.

He had twelve rugs, he had no more.

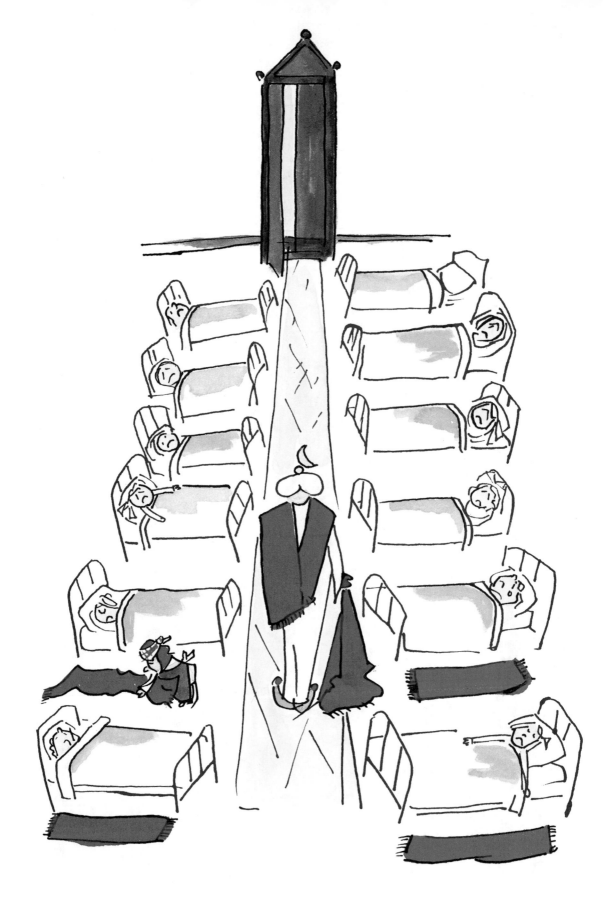

"Why, these," said Madeline, "would be so neat
For our ice-cold in the morning feet."

"It seems to me," said Miss Clavel,

"That you have chosen very well."

Madeline gave him a handful of francs,
"Here they are with all our thanks."

Without the rugs
Which he had sold
The rug merchant got awfully cold..

"To sell my rugs," he cried, "was silly!
Without them I am very chilly."
He wants to get them back—
But will he?

He made it—back to Madeline's door—
He couldn't take one footstep more.

And little Madeline set about
To find a way to thaw him out.

The merchant, who was tall and thin
(And also a ma-gi-ci-an)
Bravely took his medicine.

The magician, as he took his pill, said
"Ask me, Madeline, what you will."
Said she, "I've cooked a dinner nutritious,
Will you please help me with these dishes?"

"If you'll clear up
I'll go and see
If I can find
A Christmas tree."

His magic ring he gave a glance
And went into a special trance—
The dirty dishes washed themselves
And jumped right back upon the shelves.

And then he mumbled words profound—

"ABRACADABRA"
BRACADABR
RACADAB
ACADA
CAD
A!"

That made the carpets leave the ground—

And twelve little girls were on their way—

To surprise their parents on Christmas Day.

Miss Clavel again quite well
Thought it time to ring her bell
Which quickly broke the magic spell.

And now we're back, all twelve right here
To wish our friends a HAPPY NEW YEAR!

The Isle of God
(or Madeline's Origin)

With original sketches of Madeline
from Ludwig Bemelmans' notebooks

Ludwig and Madeleine Bemelmans

When Barbara was two, we spent the summer on the Île d'Yeu, which lies in the Bay of Biscay, off the west coast of France. I have forgotten why we decided to go there. Most probably somebody told us about it.

The Île d'Yeu is immediately beautiful and at once familiar. Its round, small harbor is stuffed with boats; the big tuna schooners lie in the center; around them are sleek sardine and lobster boats. One can walk around in the harbor over the decks of boats. Only between bows and sterns shine triangles of green water. Twice a day there is a creaking of hulls and a tilting of masts; all the boats begin to settle, to lean on their neighbors; the tide, all the water, runs out of the harbor, and the bottom is dry.

The first house you come to is a small poem of a hotel. It has a bridal suite with a pompom-curtained bed, a chaste washstand, pale pink wallpaper with white pigeons flying over it, and three fauteuils, tangerine velvet and every one large enough for two, closely held, to sit in together.

The five-foot proprietor rubs his hands, hops about, glares at employees, smiles at guests. Madame sits behind an ornate desk in the dining-room, her eyes everywhere. The kitchen is bright and smells of good butter, the linen is white, the silver gleams, the waiter is spotless. Outside, under an awning, behind a hedge of well-watered yew trees, overlooking the harbor, are the apéritif tables and chairs.

The prospectus states besides that the hotel has "*eau chaude et froide, chauffage central, tout confort moderne*"—all this is of no consequence, because you can never get a room there. The hotel has but twenty-six rooms, and these are reserved, year after year, by the same people, French families.

Further down is the Hôtel des Voyageurs, sixty rooms, the same thing, the bridal suite in green, the prices somewhat more moderate, the *confort* less *moderne*, but also all booked by April. "Ah, if you would only have written me a letter in March," say the proprietors of both places several times a day from June to September.

Walking down the Quai Sadi-Carnot, you turn right and go through the rue de la Sardine. This street is beautifully named; the houses on both sides touch your shoulders and only a man with one short leg can walk through it in comfort, as half the street is taken up by a sidewalk.

At the end of the Street of the Sardine is the Island's store, the Nouvelles Galeries Insulaires. Its owner Monsieur Penaud will find a place for you to live. Île d'Yeu should really be Île de Dieu, Monsieur Penaud explained, "d'Yeu" being the ancient and faulty way the Islanders spelled "of God." He established us in a fisherman's house, at the holiest address in this world, namely: No. 3, rue du Paradis, Saint-Sauveur, Île d'Yeu.

Our house was a sage, white, well-designed building. Through every door and window of it smiled the marine charm of the Island. The sea was no more than sixty yards from our door. Across the street was an eleventh-century church, whose steeple was built in the shape of a lighthouse. Over the house a brace of gulls hung in the air; there was the murmur of the sea; an old rowboat, with a sailor painted on its keel, stood up in the corner of the garden and served as a chicken coop.

The vegetables in the garden, the fruit on the trees, and the chicken eggs went with the house; included also was a bicycle, trademarked "Hirondelle." It is a nice thing to take over a household so living, complete, and warm, and dig up radishes that someone else has planted for you and cut flowers in a garden that someone else has tended.

The coast of the Island is a succession of small, private beaches, each one like a room, its walls three curtains of rock and greenery. There is a cave to dress in. Once you arrive, it is yours. On the open side is the water, little waves, fine sand; and out on the green ocean all day long the sardine fleet crosses back and forth with colored sails leaning over the water.

There seem to be only three kinds of people: sailors, their hundred-times-patched sensible pants and blouses in every shade of color; children; and everywhere two little bent old women dressed in black, their sharp profiles hooked together in gossip. Like crows in a tree they are, and, rightly enough, called "*vieux corbeaux.*"

Posing everywhere are fish and the things relating to them. The sardine is the banana of the Île d'Yeu: you slip and fall on it. It looks out of the small market baskets that the *vieux corbeaux* carry home; its tail sticks out of fishermen's pockets; it is dragged by in boxes and barrels. Other fish, the tuna predominating, wander by on the shoulders of strong sailors, tied to bicycles, pushed by pairs of boys in carts.

* * *

One day I bought four lobsters and rode back to the rue du Paradis and almost ran into Paradise itself. Pedaling along with the sack over my shoulder, both hands in my pockets and tracing fancy curves in the roadbed, I came to a bend, which is hidden by some dozen pine trees. Around this turn raced the Island's only automobile, a four-horsepower Super-Rosengart, belonging to the baker of Saint-Sauveur. This car is a fragrant, flour-covered breadbasket on wheels; it threw me in a wide curve off the bicycle into a bramble bush. I took the car's doorhandle off with my elbow.

I asked the baker to take me to the hospital in Saint-Sauveur, but he said that, according to French law, a car must remain exactly where it was when the accident occurred, so that the gendarmes could make their proper deductions and see who was on the wrong side of the road. I tried to change his mind, but he said, "Permit me, *alors*, monsieur, if you use words like that, then it is of no use at all to go on with this conversation."

Having spoken, he went on to pick up his *pain de ménage* and some croissants that were scattered on the road, and then spread aside the branches of the thicket to look for the doorhandle of his Super-Rosengart. I took my lobsters and went to the hospital on foot.

A doctor came, with a cigarette stub hanging from his lower lip. With a blunt needle he wobbled into my arm. "*Excusez-moi,*" he said, "*mais votre peau est dure!*" I was put into a small white carbolicky bed. In the next room was a little girl who had had her appendix out, and on the ceiling over my bed was a crack that, in the varying light of morning, noon, and evening, looked like a rabbit, like the profile of Léon Blum, and at last, in conformity with the Island, like a tremendous sardine.

I saw the nun bringing soup to the little girl. I remembered the stories my mother had told me of life in the convent school at Altötting and the little girl, the hospital, the room, the crank on the bed, the nurse, the old doctor, who looked like Léon Blum, all fell into place.

I thought about where Madeline and her friends should live and decided on Paris. I made the first sketches on a sidewalk table outside the Restaurant Voltaire on the quai of that same name. The first words of the text, "In an old house in Paris / that was covered with vines," were written on the back of a menu in Pete's Tavern on the corner of Eighteenth Street and Irving Place in New York. *Madeline* was first published in 1939.

It took about ten years to think of the next one, which was *Madeline's Rescue*. One day, after that was finished and in print, I stood and looked down at the Seine opposite Notre Dame. Some little boys were pointing at something floating in the river. One of them shouted: "Ah, there comes the wooden leg of my grandfather." I looked at the object that was approaching and discovered that in my book I had the Seine flowing in the wrong direction.

—Ludwig Bemelmans

HE WAS SURE AND QUICK ON ICE—

ONE NEVER KNOWS HOW A FIESTA ENDS.

ITS TIME
TO TAKE STEP.
TO TEACH
A LESSON
TO THAT
BOY PEP

AND MISS CLAUEL SAID
"ISNT HE NICE"

FIRST CAME
SOUP- THEN
FISH THEN
STE AR- Chowlut
SALAD-
ICECREAM
ALMOND CAKE

Barbara, Madeleine and Ludwig Bemelmans
Bedford Village, New York, 1940

Ludwig and Barbara Bemelmans
Gramercy Park studio,
New York, 1941

PLACE DE LA

Dressing The Bride

Dressing The Bride

written and photographed

by

Larry Goldman

Crown Publishers, Inc., New York

To my mother,
Re Vera,
and to my daughters,
Rachel and Kate

Published by Crown Publishers, Inc., 201 East 50th Street, New York, New York 10022. Member of the Crown Publishing Group.

Random House, Inc. New York, Toronto, London, Sydney, Auckland

CROWN is a trademark of Crown Publishers, Inc.

Manufactured in Japan
Design by Lauren Dong

Library of Congress Cataloging-in-Publication Data
Goldman, Larry.
        dressing the bride/Larry Goldman.
        Includes index.
        1. Wedding costume—United States.   I   Title.
    GT1753.U6G65 1993   92-17995
    392'.54--dc20   CIP

ISBN 0-517-58552-9

10   9   8   7   6   5   4   3   2   1

First Edition

FRONTISPIECE: When released, these rosettes and ruffles, bustled into a floral burst, fall along a gracefully trailing cathedral-length train.

Acknowledgments

The first person to thank is my editor and friend, Jane Meara, for her clear thinking, accurate observations, and enlightened guidance as well as her patience and monumental faith. I also wish to publicly acknowledge that without her support, I could not have orchestrated or accomplished the photographs illustrating this book. I am grateful to Crown Publishers' superb staff, including Ken Sansone for his insightful art direction, Lauren Dong for her inspired design, which unites text and pictures, Christine Pilla and Elizabeth Kelly for innumerable details accomplished quickly and efficiently, and to Andrea Connolly and Laurie Stark for production editing my book. I am also grateful to Miriam Hurewitz for copyediting with a fine-toothed comb.

I remain forever indebted to James Stevens for his enduring dedication and continuous encouragement during months of twenty-hour work days, for reading and commenting on each manuscript page, for his quick wit, for his help in pinpointing qualified resources, for his awesome ability to interpret information and facts, and for his assistance—all along the way.

Nor will I ever underestimate the dedication or the advantage of Myraslawa Prystay's fashion editorial assistance. It was her incredible sense of style, organizational and production talent, as well as her resourcefulness that enabled so many appropriate models, actresses, location settings, and background environments to be captured by my camera. In particular, I wish to express my sincerest gratitude to her for combing the bridal-wear market, and for participating in the decision about how each bridal ensemble could be presented to its best advantage.

I then would like to acknowledge the enormous contribution of Julius Scheck (aka Mr. Butch) and his unsurpassed knowledge of women's clothing styles, from couturier ball gowns to casual ready-to-wear outfits, as well as the intricacies of fabrics, laces, and passementerie, which he explained item by item; without these clarifications and corrections, I would have been lost.

This volume benefited from and, in fact, its very existence is due to the willingness of bridal-wear designers and manufacturers, retailers and suppliers, commentators and editors, to share their insiders' knowledge and vast creative energy. Their cooperation, contribution, and incalculable effort, often including their staffs' time, brought this book to fruition. Particularly notable was the help of three pillars of the bridal-wear industry: Hedda Kleinfeld, Monica Hickey, and Barbara Tober. My sincerest gratitude to Najma Kahou Beard for arranging the very first interviews; to Millie Martini Bratten of *Bride's* magazine for her cheerful resolution of hard-to-solve problems, accomplished in an exacting and practical manner; and to Rachel Leonard for all her resourceful suggestions. I am indebted to each bridal-wear fashion publicist, especially to Cindy Starrer of Jim Hjelm, Deborah Hughes of Carolina Herrera, Bob Miller of Victor Costa, Pat Steel of Vera Wang, Michael De Cuollo of Christos, Barbara Tanner of Jody Donohue for being the conduit to Scaasi, Barbara Iscart of Alfred Angelo, and Brian Bantry; and to Gloria Starr Kins for her excellent suggestions and level-headed advice on many small details as well as her much-needed encouragement and support. I wish to thank Diane Silver for general understanding and comfort; Dean Lauren for researching fabrics, lace, and bridal passementerie; Erica Seidman for proofreading the manuscript; the F.I.T. reference librarians and the Brooklyn Museum, Metropolitan Museum of Art, and Stonybrook Museum, Long Island, costume curators; and finally, to Paul Goldberger, whose seminal guide to New York City's architecture, *The City Observed*, was a constant resource and inspiration for environments in which bridal gowns could be appropriately set off.

Contents

PREFACE *9*

INTRODUCTION: WEDDING STYLES AND FORMALITY *11*

Part One: For Today's Bride 17

TRADITIONAL, PERIOD, AND CONTEMPORARY BRIDAL GARB: UNIVERSAL SYMBOLS *19*

Holding to Traditions *20* ∽ Retrogressive Dressing *23*
A Contemporary Mood *25* ∽ Color...All Dressed in White *27*

YOUR WEDDING DRESS: FROM ULTRAFORMAL TO INFORMAL *31*

Elements of Style: The Silhouette Right for You *32*
Defining Formal Regalia and Semiformal Garb *39* ∽ Informal and
Contemporary Directions—The Experts' Broad-based Assessment *54*

ATTENTION TO DETAIL: FABRIC, LACE, AND EMBELLISHMENTS *63*

Fabrics—The Goods' Hand *65* ∽ Laces—A Long-standing Tradition *70*
Trimmings—Fabric and Lace *75* ∽ Enhancements—Flickering Finery *81*
Notions—The Closing Story *86*

FINDING YOUR GOOD PROVIDER: RETAIL BRIDAL WEAR *89*

Something Old…Restoring an Heirloom or Choosing an Antique *92*
Something New…Something Borrowed…*94* ❧ Something (Windsor) Blue…*103*

Part Two: Completing Your Ensemble *109*

THE CROWNING TOUCHES: WHERE TO BEGIN AMONG
RELATED ELEMENTS *111*

Starting at the Top: Your Hairstyle *113* ❧ Finding the Right Accompaniment:
Headdresses and Ornaments *115* ❧ A Lustrous Touch: Your Jewelry *126*
The Crowning Glory: A Bride's Mantle *131* ❧ Customized Headdress *139*

FLORESCENCE: CARRYING AND WEARING FLOWERS *141*

Personal Preference: The First Guideline in Selection *142*
Flower Varieties *142* ❧ Color, Texture, and Shape *145* ❧ Determining an
Appropriate Bouquet Design and Style *146* ❧ Design Principles and
Concepts *148* ❧ Alternative Formal, Semiformal, and Informal Floral Uses *152*

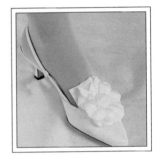

ADDING ACCENTS: THE FINAL FLOURISHES *155*

Necessary Niceties: A Story Goes on Beneath *156*
The Bottom Line: Shoes *160* ❧ A Bride's Patina: Her Makeup *163*
The Functional Necessities *166* ❧ Pampering Yourself:
Achieving a Total Look *169* ❧ When Your Big Day Arrives *171*

*Part Three: Dressing the Bride…and
Bridegroom* *173*

L'ENVOI: REVIEWING YOUR SITUATION *175*

A SAMPLING OF BRIDAL SALONS AROUND THE COUNTRY *185*
OTHER PURVEYORS *197*
PHOTOGRAPHY ACKNOWLEDGMENTS *199*
PHOTOGRAPHY CREDITS *201*
INDEX *203*

$\mathcal{P}$reface

Brides have spared no effort and little expense adorning themselves for their wedding. *Dressing the Bride* guides you through each facet of contemporary and traditional bridal garb—outfits, dresses, gowns, or suits—and introduces you to bridal-wear experts who share their insider's knowledge and experience. You'll discover where and when to begin planning, how to isolate the wedding style attire that is right for you and where to find it, how to choose a bridal consultant, and how to evaluate the silhouette or design line that is appropriate.

From world-renowned bridal-gown designers, wedding-dress manufacturers, fashion commentators and editors, milliners, jewelry designers, beauty experts, and the consultants themselves, you will learn how to pull together the bridal ensemble of your dreams. Every detail—from the commonly used notions and fastenings, to trimmings (bows and borders, just to name a few) and enhancements (reembroidered lace with pearls and the like)— is enumerated, categorized, and visually depicted.

Dressing the Bride is for all brides-to-be as they pursue their fantasy, whether sophisticated, innocent, understated, grand, classic, or romantic; for those looking for advice and hints on fashion and beauty; for professional women who may need a quicker route; for the fashion conscious and the budget conscious. If the big question has been popped, your answer given, your families advised, and the time and place decided—now is the time to start.

The arena in which to begin your quest is photographs: visual information is communicated in books on fashion, costume, and design, in bridal magazine editorial spreads, in the bridal section of sewing pattern books and fashion catalogs, and in fashion manufacturer and designer advertisements. There are many other fertile grounds for ideas—old films, new videos, works of art, department stores, out-of-the-way shops, fashion runways, manufacturers' displays, seamstress's workrooms, family and friends' photo albums, an aunt's attic, or, of course, your local bridal salon. Each suggests elements to be gathered together for your ensemble; a lace hanky, kid gloves, a cameo heirloom, or flowers as a remembrance of summers past in Aunt Leonie's Combray garden help project the image you want walking down the aisle, on your receiving line, or while dancing, eating, or mingling with your guests.

Every bride deserves to be beautiful on her wedding day. Since this is the one moment in your life with a 100 percent guarantee that you will be the center of attention, every aspect of your appearance should be a compliment, from your flowers to the wedding party. Your bridal ensemble not only expresses your personal style, emotions, and sentiments, but it projects how you and your bridegroom view each other as individuals and as a couple, as you publicly acknowledge the responsibilities and obligations of matrimony.

addressing

your

proposal

OPPOSITE: The bride's pale blue, silk supercotehardie with an English net overgown and five-point diadem is paired with the bridegroom's lustrous, black barathea wool tailcoat without closure, matching trousers with two silk stripes down the outside seams, double-breasted white piqué waistcoat, silk top hat, white kid gloves, and a silver-handled cane.

Introduction

As the twentieth century draws to a close, more brides-to-be than ever before have come into their own as older, better-educated, actualized career women with a well-developed sense of who they are. The "anything goes" statement has exploded as women have refused to fit into a single mold. Along with big traditional weddings, other types of wedding attitudes are now appreciated throughout the world: small, delicate chapel weddings in Germany; afternoon garden teas in New England; an intimate gathering aboard a yacht in the Pacific; 2,500 friends at a country club in the Midwest; a carefully selected group of fifty in a London restaurant. Any wedding direction, traditional, period, or contemporary, civil or religious, can be planned for Grandma's suburban house, beside a waterfall or stream, in an underground cave, around the swimming pool in St. Tropez, within the expanse of a grand cathedral, or in the quaint confines of a country church with a horse-drawn carriage waiting. There is a wedding dress for each ambience. Could the same dress be worn at each type of ceremony? Of course not.

Most brides-to-be begin with something concrete and tangible: they have shopped for enough clothing to know what suits them; they know their best features, and what works with their complexion. They have been to enough weddings and browsed through enough bridal magazines to have a vision of what is special to them. Most brides-to-be know the spirit they wish to convey as a bride.

By definition, having a wedding ceremony means adhering to order, rules, and conventions. The character with which the bridal couple treats the event is a conscious decision that dictates the wedding's formality. There was a time when the fabric, silhouette, neckline, and train's length rigidly differentiated style: what distinguishes a formal bridal gown from a wedding dress. For today's bride-to-be, there are fewer hard-and-fast rules beyond acceptable taste and good sense when considering your bridal gown. A certain bareness may not be appropriate in church or morning ceremonies, but everything else is left up to the bridal couple and their family's personal discretion. When age or financial independence are factors, very often the bridal couple's wishes come more into play.

There are two well-defined wedding style directions. More brides-to-be—young, older, first-time, or remarrying—are deciding to be contemporary on their wedding day by choosing bridal attire close to their everyday selves, though more often dressy than casual. As the fashion industry realized there was a wide, new, and delicious avenue for its imagination, clothing designers, from haute couture to those around every corner, jumped into the contemporary bridal market, ready to please fashion-conscious brides-to-be. After all, why

wedding styles and formality

OPPOSITE: *A simple drop waist defines the flowing handkerchief-hem skirt on this fluid, classic semiformal allover-lace wedding dress.*

wouldn't a bride-to-be with personal style and a fashion sense want that same flamboyance to be present on her wedding day?

Then, of course, there are the traditional bridal gowns, dresses, and outfits in three distinct degrees of formality. Formal regalia—the look of a fairytale fantasy—is characterized by the grandest ball-gown styles with long trains, body-hugging bodices (waistline to neckline), a trailing hem-length tulle (transparent net) veil treatment, and elaborate enhancements. When the use of the elements becomes extremely lavish and the scale is overly exaggerated, the gown is ultraformal. Semiformal approaches—less extravagant—are familiar classic silhouettes with a shorter hemline, train, and veil; and informal attire—everyday silhouettes—means using the same fabrics, bridal laces, and motifs, such as floral designs and bows, but with minimal embellishments or reembroidery, and for a smaller, more personal setting. A traditional informal bridal presentation reinterprets conventional bridal elements such as lace, a headdress, flowers, and pearls, whereas similar fabrics and motifs—floral designs and bows, for example—are used on semiformal and formal gowns in either a comfortable, tailored (constructed, sculpted, and built up) suit or a current dressmaker (cut on a pattern and sewn) silhouette. The train is eliminated and the veil is shorter and smaller.

Every bride, regardless of her wedding-dress direction or its formality, selects harmonious accessories, including a hairdo, headdress, jewelry, and veil (or no veil), and coordinated accents, such as gloves and wrap, and holds a bouquet or wears flowers to complete her ensemble. The bridal ensemble's function is to make a bride feel important, beautiful, and magical. Without a doubt each component can do its part when it follows the gown's lead; therefore,

the gown is selected first, except in special situations. If your mother's veil fills your every desire, or when a memento you want to wear at the altar has a distinct style, then this special part of your ensemble is taken into consideration before deciding on a style of gown.

Defining Your Statement

America is a two-hundred-year-old nation with an accumulated heritage melded from the cultures and mores of many nations. Today's urbane, first-time, or remarrying bride-to-be amalgamates herself, her bridegroom, and her favorite sports or business interests, too. Whether she lives at home or alone, she has a better sense of herself, but at the same time she isn't willing to scrap everything from the old country; she is looking at her roots and saying, Where do I come from, what am I melding, how many generations can I please? This individualism carries over to each decision she will make regarding her wedding-day attire.

Before a bride-to-be can actively look for her wedding dress, an initial wedding plan must be in place. It will reflect how the bridal couple wants to celebrate their joining, and it is a necessary preliminary to finding a wedding dress in the style and with the detailing that is called for. A bride-to-be mistakenly shopping for her wedding gown first, without the overall budget, character, and spirit of the event mutually agreed upon, risks falling in love with a gown and being disappointed if a compromise needs to be made further down the line.

This is a very stressful time in the engagement period as both families begin to express their wishes. While working in conjunction with your father and mother, and your bridegroom and his family, hold on to the event

behind the wedding plan: you are marrying the man you love. If you keep this uppermost in your mind, all your decision making will be easier and you will derive more pleasure by keeping a stressful time happy.

A bona fide wedding plan defines seven points that will govern your wedding-attire selection. It sets a tentative wedding day that firmly dictates a schedule for deciding on your wedding dress, as well as looking for the many other elements to complete your ensemble; a preferred time of day, which will affect the dress's spirit; the intended site for the wedding ceremony and for the reception and their scale (large or small) and ambience (simple to lavish); and finally, most important of all, the overall budget and the price range allotted for your wedding dress.

As the wedding budget is being discussed,

it is helpful to visit local shops and department stores as well as to jot down whatever possibilities struck you at the weddings you have attended. You can look through bridal magazines and tear out the pages that interest you. Try tracing the dresses you like freehand, sketching any trim changes you would want, and deciding on a color. Get a general sense of the costs involved from the editorial section, which includes the gown's price (advertisements do not). By all means share your thoughts with your relatives. Relive a recent bride's experiences, if you wish. A few cautionary words are appropriate here: limit the number of people who will be accompanying you as you search for a gown. If the number is too large, you will be frustrated by too many opinions; all the bridesmaids would be too many people,

When lace is placed near skin, the association benefits both; the contrast plays into a youthful and innocent spirit.

A fitted, formal, flamenco-style ruffled-tulle skirt balances an elongated torso, while an equally sheer, satin-edged puffed-sleeve treatment adds neckline drama.

∾

OVERLEAF: *An upturned Queen Anne collar frames a modern, street-length ensemble's dressmaker organza jacket.*

this early stage it is wise to think of the cost of your entire ensemble—including your bouquet. The dress, including alterations, will consume approximately 70 percent of the total.

As you are deciding what is comfortable for you, further refinements in the wedding plan, as well as how you want to look during the four distinct portions of your wedding day, will become clear. You will know where the ceremony (religious or civil) will be held. This indicates what your procession (your first presentation) to the altar will be: Is it long? How long? Will you be escorted by your father and attendants? Will you meet your bridegroom at the altar? Where is the guests' vantage point? How importantly will you treat your back (your second presentation) during the ceremony? Once the number of guests to invite has been decided and the caterer or hall confirmed, you will know where your bridal party procession ends and your receiving line begins (your third presentation). Whether you're mingling with thirty, sixty, ninety, or three hundred people, at a champagne breakfast, luncheon, cocktails, or a seated dinner (your fourth presentation), the bride's situation continually changes. The bride's initial presentation with each change is important. Just as your bridal ensemble allotment is finalized, these considerations and how they affect the details of your bridal ensemble come into play.

You'll be encouraged to know that each bridal gown silhouette and every wedding dress style—any ensemble possibility to be married in—is available within every bride-to-be's budget. A formal bridal gown is not necessarily more costly than a short, informal wedding dress. What is more, the enormous selection, availability, and over-abundance of bridal wear makes your selection far easier once you are headed in the right direction.

but just your mother might not be enough. Consider wisely whom you ask to accompany you because there is little doubt your advisers will have an impact on the dress you select.

Although the amount each bride-to-be can spend on her bridal ensemble differs, finding a wedding dress within the wedding budget is an issue common to all. Your dress price range is determined by its priority within the wedding budget, and its importance must be weighed against estimable considerations other than attire. So even at

Snug sleeves and a pointed hip yoke with heavy beading on a silky, chiffon handkerchief-style skirt.

Part One

For

Today's

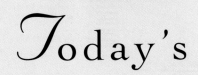

Bride

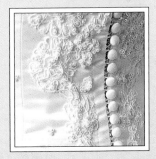

*Un*iversally, bridal garb demonstrates purity and fertility while it provides an opportunity to display wealth, taste, and the bride's social position. Wearing one's finery to taste with accessories—such as a headdress with a veil, adorned with flowers—has endured as an integral part of the bride's ensemble down through the ages. These universal symbols have evolved village by village, passed on from one generation to the next, and are shared by all cultures.

As bridal garb revises itself, many design elements and motifs become customary before turning into traditions. Though fascinating as lore, the bridal symbolism and tradition extends beyond merely knowing that Egyptians included important necklines, that silk finery was introduced by ancient Greeks,

Traditional, Period, and Contemporary Bridal Garb

that the pearl's purity was revered by the Romans, that lace was adopted by medieval brides, as if by decree, that a medieval brooch of innocence evolved into the cameo wedding-collar neckline, or that in Renaissance France, symbolic and sentimental trimmings were reembroidered onto a bride's garb: double-looped sashes cut and tied into bows symbolized the couple's joining in nuptial vows, hearts represented chivalrous romance, and church bells ensured the bridegroom's fidelity.

The value of symbolic traditions is in the understanding that a common bond exists between you and each bride before you. While there is no longer a right or wrong way to include tradition when assembling a bridal ensemble, knowing how bridal motifs and elements came to be included gives each bride-to-be an additional perspective on her wedding day.

universal symbols

OPPOSITE: Renaissance retro-dressing.

The cotton crepe Mexican-style wedding dress by Fred Leighton was bought by the bride's mother ten years before the wedding.

Holding to Traditions

Lace, one of the oldest Western bridal traditions, has endured five hundred years, ever since Italian and French sumptuary edicts, as they were called, banned ostentatious displays of wealth by the new merchant class. An exception was made for brides, though, and the union of weddings and lace has lasted ever since. But from time immemorial, an agrarian bride wore a wreath, circlet, or garland of earth's bounties to ensure her fertility and the well-being of her community-at-large. At first the bride's crown was fashioned from roots, leaves, and herbs, but soon stalks of rye, wheat, myrtle, or olive were added. The earth's abundance was soon proclaimed by its sweet-smelling flowers as well. Crowns later expanded into veils and headdresses: southern Arabian brides tucked garlic into their white, wrapped turbans; Armenians wore red silk with feathers on their heads; Caucasus brides bore headdresses of gold and silver coins. A bridal crown intrinsic to a clan became common, and still is in Scandinavian, Eastern European, and Russian Orthodox communities.

While the bride's headdress has evolved, vestiges of far-flung ancient predecessors have remained as universal symbols. An Egyptian bride wore an elaborate cloth headdress with flowing ends and jewels, gold serpentlike coils, or fresh flowers; a Greek bride wove an intricate hairdo, beginning high on the forehead and incorporating a carved or engraved crown (stephane) in back of the hairline. A Roman bride (in her vernacular, the *nova nupta*) parted her hair six times with a spear and entwined flowers and sacred plants among her braided locks, which were left draped across her bodice.

During Europe's early Dark Ages unbraided, shoulder-length rippling hair was a bride's sign of rank as well as her virginity, and in medieval Germany, colorful wildflowers with entwined baby's breath sprigs or myrtle fashioned into wreaths were made for the bride to wear, further glorifying her hair. In the fourteenth century, a pointed chaplet of leaves, called a crespin, and a cagelike mesh adorned with pearls and flowers worn over the ears encasing braids, called a caul, were popular as a bridal headdress, though fashionable brides wore a turban, reminiscent of the Orient.

During medieval times, the age of chivalry, came bridal headdresses in the form of a steeple-shaped toque with flowing tulle, called a hennin, and a close-fitting Juliet cap, or ferronière, which was a ribbon or band holding a pendant, wound about the head. An Elizabethan bride wore roses or colorful ribbons streaming from her hair. By the end of the seventeenth century, most European bridal headdress consisted of a wreathlike floral headdress with a thin veil of hair covering the bride's face, or very elaborately draped lace, called the mantilla.

Flowers of all varieties continued to be carried or worn as personal adornment to symbolize true love, faithfulness, and fecundity—in short, a lifetime together. Entwined floral garlands and sheaths of gathered white flowers were substituted as a symbol of innocence, and purple flowers were added to represent Christ's blood. Moorish Spain introduced orange blossoms. Priceless red tulips came to be carried in rural Holland, and a white rose was attached over the bride's heart in Italy. At various points during medieval times, the bride carried a handheld arrangement, called a corsage, and the bridegroom wore a boutonniere. Later, in England, the posy, a corsage composed of meaningful flowers, appeared as a Victorian concept.

Layers of sheer veil were an ancient device to protect the bride from both outsiders and the evil eye. The ancient Semitic tribes held up a tent and the Anglo-Saxons a "care cloth" over the bride's head to serve as gift wrapping with virginity guaranteed. The ancient Chinese wrapped the bride and included her father's shoes as a disguise as well. A Roman bride exchanged her everyday *ricinum*, or veil, for a flame-colored net veil, called a *nubere*. The early Christians adopted the bridal veil, sanctified it, and covered their brides at betrothal through the wedding ceremony; medieval bishops later banned the practice as a pagan rite, except for nuns (Christ's brides). The tulle veil, a coverchief, was substituted and worn throughout the Middle Ages; then during the Renaissance period, a Madonna-like veil found favor again, and different versions have been used ever since.

From the late eighteenth century through the end of the nineteenth, brides wore net, lace, or gauze attached to a bonnet or hat. Outside of her home, a Victorian woman always wore a veil that extended to her chin; a bride, however, chose a length of white net or silk illusion worn over her face and reaching to her waist, hips, ankles, or the floor in back during the ceremony as a symbol of her purity. The net or tulle was turned back after the ceremony; this remains a bridal tradition.

During the Renaissance, a houppelande, the precursor of the modern bridal gown, with a high-button, standing neck developed into a large Elizabethan ruff. The short-waisted, V-shaped bodice with puffed sleeves, often including a cyclas or surcoat reaching to the hips, was introduced in the fifteenth century. By the sixteenth century, the houppelande's bodice was corsetlike with a huge heart-shaped or square neckline and a collar or ruff. The sleeves were stiff, puffed, and slashed and the skirt, supported by a farthingale, was bell-shaped; or it was a straight supercotehardie with a petticoat underneath, fastened by a single button at the waist. Most sixteenth-century dresses were worn long, but without a train, which was added as court attire.

The ebb and flow of fashion silhouettes, waistlines, sleeves, and skirts expanded from

Breastplate bodice with silk brocade, cord braid, and medieval-style dropped tear-shape pearls are reminiscent of a long-gone courtly age.

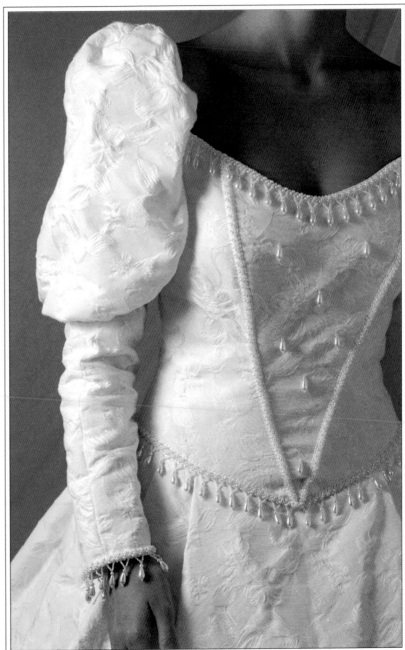

long and narrow to full and bouffant throughout the seventeenth, eighteenth, and nineteenth centuries brought recurring design elements: draped and snug bodices; large puffed, pagoda-style bell and balloonlike sleeves; fussy, feminine furbelows, such as hoops, panniers (side cages at the hips), bustles, and apron effects added to gored (tapering triangular panel), gathered, full, and overskirts; or high to plunging necklines with additions, like the fichu, a triangular kerchief. And trains continued to be used for ceremonial occasions. The spirit moved from the sophisticated high-waist, square-neckline Empire dress to romantic billowing crinolines (stiff horsehair and linen buckram) under large skirts, to effulgent imitation pastoral laced bodices, such as the Velasquez-immortalized Basque lines, to riding clothes, especially the Directory-style redingote (from "riding coat") jacket—the forerunner of the tailor-made dress.

Historically, the white wedding dress can be traced to the birth of chivalry, although fickle fashion fads dictated blue, brown, and black as well. Brides continued to wear their best dress (purchasing a specific bridal gown is a twentieth-century concept) with bridal headdress, and carried flowers that held chivalrous sentiments or had significance as fertility symbols. Around 1820, the traditional white wedding dress concept emerged as we know it. Then in 1840, Queen Victoria of England married her cousin Prince Albert in a white wedding dress—instead of silver, a royal tradition—and marrying in a white wedding dress instantly became an English bridal tradition. Few American brides wore white wedding dresses during the nineteenth century; black, in fact, was quite popular. Nevertheless, Victorian practices have become lasting bridal traditions. Since the age of chivalry no period has had as lasting an impact on bridal customs.

Evoking the court of Tsar Nicholas II.

Opposite: A Victorian confection with full skirt is held in shape by a soft-pleated tulle swag and large silk roses; the rose motif randomly trims the skirt and creates the drop-shoulder sleeve detail.

Retrogressive Dressing

As the twentieth century opened, brides-to-be throughout Europe and America were beginning to select white wedding dresses specifically for their wedding day. At first, their style was in keeping with the fashions of the times. But as the century moved on and hemlines moved off the floor, bridal wear reverted to the grandest design elements of Victoria's reign, such as off-the-shoulder ball gowns and low-cut heart-shaped bodices, the stomacher (an inverted triangle beginning at the breasts) and the thinner cuirass (breastplate) bodices adapted from the medieval houppelande, and, of course, a long, flowing train. Intricate laces, including the Honiton lace Victoria wore, fringed flowers, and crystal or bronze beads were also adopted.

American brides-to-be of the period sought to celebrate their suffrage, growing independence, and newfound prosperity in their

Matching silk bra, skirt, and turban and heavy gold passementerie dress up an oriental-style jacket to become an informal bridal ensemble approach.

OPPOSITE: Three-piece dressing consisting of dressmaker camisole and skirt contrasting with a tailored jacket.

upcoming matrimony, while invoking their heritage and traditions. This was accomplished by incorporating heirloom laces along with important design elements, such as pannier-style side hoops, into bridal garb. Larger-than-life bridal regalia was designed to exaggerate, accentuate, and enlarge the bride's size. At big weddings, a long dress creates drama, and its fullness has a sophisticated aura that allows a bride the psychological edge to fill up her space beyond the structure of that dress. Brides-to-be also embraced the style of the royal Tudor weddings, whose brides were dressed in big and elaborate garb for their nuptials, often completed with a tissue-thin pure silk English net blusher over the virgin princess's face. Henry VIII's six wives, for instance, built themselves up with puffed shoulders and crinolines; Catherine the Great of Russia—already large—adorned herself in huge capelike raiments with fur trim; even in Asia, an emperor's bride wore an exaggerated kimono flowing around her body to emphasize stature and create an image of largesse.

Any bride-to-be selecting a period wedding dress, a recurring and appealing theme for a meaningful wedding celebration, is recalling a romantic time or a statement of the bride and groom's mutual interests, such as a shared fondness for the period's literature, music, or fashion. This sentimental direction can also reflect a desire to connect with your heritage and tradition. Both the 1920s and '30s seem to evoke a more recent romantic past, but European eighteenth-

and nineteenth-century dress continues to have an everlasting fantasy aura.

If you and your bridegroom lack the time needed to properly view museums and costume collections, to do research in libraries, to contact theatrical, ballet, and opera costume designers, or to track down costume rental houses for the fashion styles of the period, hiring a wedding planner or consultant who is enthusiastic about working with you is an excellent way to discover authentic mores, customs, and rites. "Early America and colonial themes, such as a Williamsburg wedding, are popular," says the New York Metropolitan Museum's Costume Institute restorer Francesca Bianca. "If there is to be a religious ceremony, the right site or house of worship must be secured early, such as an eighteenth-century church or synagogue. Appropriate invitations, perhaps of parchment, can be found. The particular ambience, such as period dishes, music, and flower arrangements, can be duplicated—as closely as time and money allow. An ancient Roman wedding not only requires a yellow or blue *stola* for the bride, but rice for the bridal couple to walk on, and sweetmeats to break over their heads."

The bride-to-be working with her consultant or designer will get advice on the wedding-dress style, whether to include panniers for the seventeenth century or hoops for the Victorian era. The bridegroom-to-be sets out to find a period frock coat or have it made. "A costume budget, if you will," Bianca advises, "must be set aside first. This is important since the additional costs—over and above those of a conventional ceremony and reception—that establish the period's spirit are varied. Completing the ensemble accurately with the appropriate hairstyle, wig, and headdress, along with accurate jewelry, popular flowers, and musical arrangement, is crucial.

"There are ready-to-wear wedding dresses that jump out at you as from a particular period, such as hoop and tier, lace antebellum dresses. Recently, for instance, a bride-to-be who wanted to be a thirteenth-century Medici princess asked me to style her wedding gown. I designed a green velvet gown with white fur and twisted pearl trim. It coordinated with a festive atmosphere that included a roast boar banquet with jugglers and bards performing in a rented castle. Another bride-to-be asked me to copy the imperial court of Tsar Nicholas II. The bride appeared luxuriously dressed in an all-white satin gown embroidered with hand-cut pearls, white mink muff at her wrist, and a crown of white mink and pearls. After the ceremony she just wore the pearl diadem, but continued to carry her white orchids."

A Contemporary Mood

There have also been definable fashion currents from within America influencing its twentieth-century bridal ensembles. They mirror economic cycles, political fortunes, and shifting social mores, and include fashion-forward, everyday street clothes such as Edwardian high-neck, jabot-ruffled blouses; the '20s flapper style with dropped-waist, loose tea-length skirts; '40s bias-draped, Hollywood glamour-queen sheaths, and '50s Givenchy-inspired Audrey Hepburn bows.

It was during the 1960s that a more independent, free-thinking generation of designers drastically changed bridal attire. Betsey Johnson, Zandra Rhodes, Fred Leighton, Giorgio Sant' Angelo, and then some, translated the most hip European and American fashion trends into bridal wear. Informal turned quite casual and non-traditional with unpredictable flourishes, including the use of paper and vinyl, patch-

work-quilted bodices, feather borders on handkerchief hemlines, and even unbleached muslin dresses, double-knit jersey pantsuits, and denim jackets.

Beautiful bridal garb and elaborate celebrations replaced the slinky mermaid silhouette of the 1970s as excitement rose in anticipation of Prince Charles's marriage to Lady Diana Spencer. Her traditional regal gown style inspired atavistic contemporary bridal ensembles. All marriages, even remarriages (customarily at-home, civil-ceremony weddings), embraced the big wedding celebration concept with gusto, including remarrying brides adorned in formal veil presentations but without a virginal blusher. Other changing social mores, moreover, necessitated a new, hybrid look for weddings that melded seemingly incongruous elements, such as a short, strapless minidress and train at a religious ceremony, a high-neck, unenhanced cashmere sweater with a full taffeta skirt in a New York ballroom, or a serious, crepe gown at a beach wedding.

The allure of nineteenth-century design lines did not lie dormant either. Arnold Scaasi, dean of American couture designers, began creating haute-couture wedding dresses in 1964. To this day, he regularly travels to bridal salons across the country consulting with brides-to-be regarding their bridal ensembles. "The phrase that I first heard from every bride-to-be," Scaasi says, "was the same I hear today: 'It's a very special day in my life. I want to look like a fairy princess.' I therefore create a storybook, fairy-princess look for brides—though each wedding gown will be of today as well. Traditional innocence combines with femininity and glamour as the style ingredients of a modern bridal gown. A truly timely gown changes with the proportions of each decade. As clothes will change, our eye changes too."

Perhaps what Balenciaga, possibly the greatest couture bridal gown designer of the twentieth century, suggested in the 1950s will always hold true: "Every bride hopes her wedding portrait—in retrospect—won't look awkward, so I search for purity of line." Adding to these words of wisdom is Pat Kerr, one of America's foremost lace bridal gown designers: "My bridal gowns evoke the past rather than trends, because my goal is a sense of timelessness. On a woman's tenth wedding anniversary, her wedding dress should still be her first choice in which to be married."

Color...All Dressed in White

In each culture and religion one color is closely associated with innocence, purity, and virginity. One color is also set aside for different ceremonial uses and life's special occasions, especially birth, marriage, and death. The color, however, varies from culture to culture, even region to region, which means that white is not universally reserved for a bride. Thus in China, the Caucasus, and Armenia, the bride wears red; in Switzerland, black is common for both bride and groom; Indian bridegrooms wear a yellow brocade; in Japan, white is worn by a widow.

In most Western cultures, for the past 150 years, a young, virginal bride all dressed in white has been the celebratory choice. Pastels are reserved for older, remarrying women. Although white is no longer chosen exclusively, it remains predominant, because no superstition or negative connotation surrounds it. Off-white to pale ivory and even pink, especially shades of blush, are perennial alternatives, whereas various shades of green are not, because they have become associated with envy and wantonness. The perfect bridal pink, the experts

aver, is not achieved with pink fabric, but a blush lining. Even under a large, heavy satin gown, the hue comes through.

Pastels, vibrant colors, even languid gold lamé, have often been introduced on white wedding gowns. This can take many forms, from dimensional embellishments, such as a garden-flower appliqué and iridescent crystal-beaded accents, to textural fabrics and overlays, which soften an all-white wedding dress.

If your decision to wear white has been reached, then only one thought is necessary to keep in mind: all whites are not the same; there are differing degrees of purity. A pure white silk is warmer, richer, and softer than polyester white. It serves to envelop the bride. A cotton, for instance, is different from a cotton blend, and each manmade fabric is different still, even when woven to simulate satin. Be aware of the color differential each fabric possesses when deciding on your wedding-dress white.

Apply the knowledge you have accumulated regarding the different colors—their

A formal gown created from yards and yards of pale pink silk lends an eternally youthful aura to the bride.

OPPOSITE: The sophisticated ensemble—ribbon lace reembroidered with cellophane in both dress and coat.

variations, their brightness or intensity, and their saturation or purity—that look best on you. Research color experts' advice on the effect of colors on each other and on your overall mood. This has been written about extensively in magazines and books. Take into account the lighting that will surround you. Think about the overall coloration of the chapel, reception area, groom, and wedding party. Then, when deciding on an accenting color to use with your choice of white, choose one that is most complimentary for you and your surroundings.

A bride all dressed in white will always look special, yet very, very fair brides-to-be should be wary of a pure white washing them out. The combination of hair, eyes, and skin will not necessarily be flattering. "I recommend staying away from blue- or gray-white," says Hedda Kleinfeld, proprietor of a popular bridal salon in Brooklyn, New York. "They are equally difficult to wear. The hue depends on the fabric, and many dresses are available in several different fabrics. With ivory, there is far greater range and variation, since each fabric takes a dye differently.

"Also, if your wedding date is set for the spring, summer, or fall, keep in mind how you tan. Will you have a golden, reddish, or dark skin tone? This should be calculated into both your choice of white and an accenting color, because ivory looks decidedly better with most suntans."

In a white wedding dress, a bride is conforming with tradition, while in pale ivory and pink, she is less so. A gray or mauve for an Art Deco dress, for instance, would be a more eccentric choice, and a vibrant silver creates a decidedly avant-garde aura. Wearing a black wedding dress, however, is exotic, but not necessarily a fashion statement. "It sounds great, but we wear black every day," says Barbara Tober, editor-in-chief of

Bride's magazine. "I just think a woman with a black veil looks funereal, and there are now opportunities to wear a color other than white for a bride-to-be who is fashion-conscious. Standing in front of a mirror, a bride-to-be should look at herself to see the difference between a white and a black dress."

Many young, sophisticated brides-to-be are selecting a stylish wedding dress adapted to contemporary tastes. Their experience dressing and coordinating their everyday, cocktail, and dressy outfits has taught them a crucial lesson: the role color can play. This includes contrasting or emphasizing their skin, hair, and eye coloring. Many older, remarrying brides still prefer a simple light-colored dress or suit with tasteful traditional or contemporary details, such as jewel buttons that sparkle with crystals or colorful stones; for evening, the fancy buttons can be replaced with a richer bullion (gold- or silver-covered thread) and aurora borealis beading, which look better in candlelight than in sunlight. An older woman also has had experience playing with the accessories on hand and may know where to find a new, appropriately colored piece.

"The same style dress can be turned into something altogether different with the color treatment," says Vera Wang, a former *Vogue* magazine editor, and more recently a bridal salon owner on Manhattan's prestigious Madison Avenue. "When designing my collection, I occasionally use an accenting color, such as a blue satin sash, to tie an ensemble together; it can add a very definite dressy aura to every ensemble whether a short, tea-length, or long dress. How color is used, its intensity, and the environment it will be seen in are all key.

"A second-time bride will select her gown and color treatment to reflect her individual tastes rather than those of family, religion, or strict tradition. As twists and turns have

OPPOSITE: A blue sash and self-fabric cabbage rose define the natural waist while flat stitched and unstitched pleating form controlled soft shaping for the drop-waist silhouette. The design-line changes are made by an overskirt with hip-high release pleats, and again by a floor-length pleated panel flounce that echos the neckline.

updated traditional gowns, independent-minded fortyish brides are selecting formal wedding gowns; however, they don't feel comfortable looking like a 'cake bride'—symbolized by a traditional, figurine-form bride dressed in a layered, full-skirted, white gown. White tulle and seed pearls are the antithesis of how they see themselves.

"Instead, a professional woman often decides to look sophisticated with her taste coming through, but she also wants to imply celebration, ceremony, and the specialness of her wedding day. She often aspires to appear as though she was attending an evening party, but as a bride. And the right color treatment does just that. She might feel more comfortable in a custom-made gown that has little rapport with traditional garb. One example is a very sophisticated, pared-down, sleek and narrow, bias-draped sheath with an illusion (transparent) chiffon top, and a matching train that goes on and on.

"She would create a column with not one bead, bow, or appliqué flower; it could be off-white or ivory, or she may see herself in a pale candlelight, blush color that would make her glow."

Ultimately, the color—or hue of white—of your wedding dress should be calculated according to personal considerations, not what others dictate. Susan Lane, the fashion designer for Country Elegance, a large ready-to-wear bridal house, and owner of a Los Angeles bridal salon, agrees: "Since many second-time brides-to-be do not wish to wear pure white, all my wedding dresses are lined in off-white, rose, and blush to create a glow. On the hanger, the blush liner looks peach, but on your body it takes on a flattering, warm skin tone." And world-famous couturier Bob Mackie's thoughts concur with this: "For big, second weddings, I love flattering, pretty, and romantic wedding dresses in ivory and pale evening shades."

*Y*our wedding dress has everything to do with the overall wedding statement. Its style directs your entire ensemble as well as what the bridegroom, wedding party, and ultimately the guests will wear. The silhouette, fabric, and lace—and the bridegroom's attire that accompanied it—at one time rigidly differentiated a formal bridal gown from less formal wedding dresses.

Such specific, hard-and-fast wedding-dress style codes are no longer always applicable and most formality rules are considerably looser than ever before. What now distinguishes the somewhat antiquated categories of informal (scaled-down), semiformal (moderately scaled), formal (larger), and ultraformal (very large) wedding dresses is largely a matter of opinion and degree. Essentially, the only hard-and-fast rule that must be followed is consistency of purpose—and that purpose is to create a beautiful bride. Therefore, today's bride-to-be freely picks and chooses from among whatever traditional components or employs any contemporary elements that create a personal statement.

Perhaps the quintessential illustration of an ultraformal initial presentation was engineered by Charles James, who was renowned for his inventive fashion designs. When commissioned to design the wedding ensemble for an important client's daughter, James began by creating a stunning bridal gown.

He fashioned a basic but meticulously fitted, shaped, and sculptured ball gown of heavy silk faille. He then proceeded to cover the entire dress with tiny slits in a continuous swirling pattern. The evening before the wedding, hundreds of minute vials filled with water were inserted into the openings. At midnight, a thousand closed gardenias were carefully placed in the vials. By nine o'clock the next morning each bud began to open. At precisely noon, the gown was ready for the ceremony to begin: every flower had opened and was at its peak of fragrance. As the

*Y*our *W*edding *D*ress

from ultraformal to informal

OPPOSITE: A modern ribbon motif is paired with a traditional headpiece and a cascading tulle veil to balance the ball-gown skirt.

OVERLEAF: An informal hemline, sleeve, and neckline lace treatment.

bride walked down the aisle, the scent cascaded over the congregation. James's bridal gown can only be construed as ultraformal, yet very contemporary!

There are a few relatively simple guidelines that help determine what is appropriate for the occasion. Your wedding dress should relate to the ceremony and reception ambience, including its lavishness, number of guests, time of day, place, and formality. Every bride, moreover, should be perfectly set off from—never in competition with—her environment. There are endless statements and options available. Every aspect of the surroundings, even the church steps and aisle, must accommodate the degree of formality: an ultraformal bride, after all, should first be seen in an imposing cathedral rather than walking down a side chapel aisle. At a garden ceremony a bride might emulate the flowers' lightness and beauty, and wear a short, ivory off-the-shoulder wedding dress with a floral back treatment rather than an overly stiff gown. The receiving line outside a grand hotel ballroom with its ornate tapestries and bejeweled guests is different: a long, white, full-skirted, off-the-shoulder ball gown might seem more appropriate. And in front of a university library or in a home, a miniskirt, off-the-shoulder wedding dress with detachable train for dancing at the reception might be just right.

Elements of Style: The Silhouette Right for You

The right wedding dress makes you feel important and presents you at your best. Each aspect should be considered in relation to your overall statement, direction, and spirit—whether innocent or vivacious, understated or grand, romantic or sophisticated. Certain wedding-dress and bridal-gown silhouettes (the overall outline, ranging from short and straight to long and full) harmonize with your personality. Some components (the parts, such as the neckline) and design elements (additions, such as a train) complement your body's proportions better than others, highlighting advantages (perhaps a beautiful chest and throat), drawing attention away from flaws (large hips), and camouflaging imperfections with a proportionate and balanced design line from the shoulder to the hemline. The right silhouette requires the proper shape, perfectly combined components, and coordinated design elements; this must be carefully thought out and planned.

A beautiful bride always emerges when each aspect is selected in relation to another, to flatter and compliment, to blend with but not overwhelm the whole, and to create overall harmony and balance. No detail should be considered in a vacuum, but rather in its turn, and each decision should be based on an understanding of wedding-fashion concepts and language.

Every dress, both long and short, and any gown's outline consists of an upper and lower portion. The upper part, the bodice, covers the torso, and includes such basic elements as a neckline, shoulders, sleeves, and waistline. Technically, the waistline joins the bodice and the lower portion, the skirt, though it may not be where the body nips in. The skirt hangs from the waistline down, ending in the hemline at the thigh, knee, calf, ankle, or floor. An optional extension, a train, can be included as well, and in some instances trousers cover each leg separately.

Though researching bridal magazine photographs for the wedding dress of your dreams will give you a direction, and tracing your choice with changes or deletions or sketching it freehand will refine your statement, the

A lace and taffeta formal bridal gown can be varied by wearing both the bell-shaped taffeta overskirt and narrow lace skirt, or removing either; the train also extends, bustles, or detaches, making nine possibilities in all.

SILHOUETTES

The three traditional bridal silhouette classifications include a long evening gown silhouette, ranging from narrow to full; a classic or currently fashionable dress style—a bodice and skirt as either one unit or two separate units; and a suit jacket with coordinated skirt (in rare instances a trouser).

The classic gown silhouettes include the *ball gown*, consisting of a yoke sharply nipped into a natural waist that continues into a full skirt; the *basque* style, a ball gown–like form with a dropped waist and V front; the *Empire* gown, which has a cropped bodice, high waist, and a flared skirt; the *princess* version, with vertical seams flowing from the shoulders down to the hem of a more flared skirt; the *A-line*, a snug bodice and a gradual flare beginning at the bust line and graduating until it reaches the hemline, like a letter A; and the *sheath*, a body-hugging style without a waist and with a straight skirt (the *mermaid* variation has a trumpet skirt below the knee).

Skirt widths range from *slim*—slightly tapered down to the hem; *straight*—from the hips to the hem; *flared*—a gradual spreading out; *trumpet*—flared only below the knee; *circular*—smooth at the waist but forming a complete circle at the hem; *full*—gathered at the waist and continuously spreading to the hem; *bubble*—which is any addition to the hemline, such as gored (tapering wedge-shaped panels) or a ruffle that forms a full skirt; *three-tiered*—which are overskirts or layered panels falling in graduated lengths; and *bouffant*—the most exaggerated a full skirt can be. An *underskirt*, which is designed to be seen, has a fancy lace, ruffle, or stitched hem.

There are optional design elements worn as additions over the hips, to alter a silhouette as well, including a *flounce*—strips of gathered, pleated, or braided fabric attached as a decorative trim; a *peplum*—a short overskirt from a 1½-inch fringe to a 10-inch-wide ruffle; or *panniers*—exaggerated fabric-covered cages worn at the side of the hips. The design options, worn over the shoulders, can change the silhouette line drastically or not at all, and include a bolero-style short *jacket*; a longer-line and flared *princess*; a *redingote* (an open coat revealing a dress or petticoat beneath, descended from an Englishwoman's riding costume); a long, sleeveless *theater coat*; a *cape* or short cloak; a *shawl* or wrap; and *panels* or exaggerated draping bands.

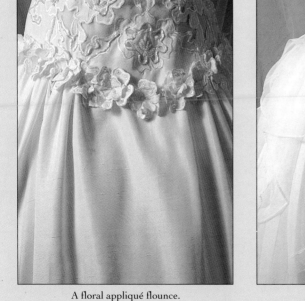

A floral appliqué flounce.

A modern pannier effect.

OPPOSITE: A formal, traditional bridal ball gown and train silhouette are modernized by a dramatic open décolletage and shoulder treatment.

actual selection process should begin with determining the right outline and proportions for you. After becoming familiar with each silhouette, it is crucial to consider its potential advantages, to understand the possible liabilities, and to weigh each. It is useful to remember that the silhouette can be either slightly modified or radically changed for you, depending on the basic components and elements employed and how they are combined. Exploring all these possibilities is the estimable domain of the bridal-fashion designer.

Don't fall into the trap of falling in love with a particular outline without trying it on. Only a bride-to-be with a model's figure can wear any silhouette and look just as good; certain design lines simply look better on certain figures. Also, a wedding dress is not a "hanger dress"; its size and weight are designed to be filled out. Therefore, you must approach each with an open mind.

Any combination of neckline, shoulder/sleeve treatment, and waistline is feasible, though unfortunately each does not work equally well on every body shape. So as a practical matter, after choosing the overall silhouette and skirt (straight, flared, or full) the next step is to consider any design element—a back treatment, train, overskirt, and so forth—which serves to further balance your proportions. This is followed by the components and scale best suited to your size and figure.

The outline in which you look best can be objectively determined by trying on each basic silhouette and skirt shape while standing in a dimly lit room with a bright light behind you. The shadows will fill in the outline to create a solid figure. Look at the mirror and turn in every direction. The shape that most pleases you is the one to begin with. One invaluable cautionary note: if you are inexperienced, attempting something

Long lace-trimmed panels transform a spare dress into a regal presentation.

completely new, or have a disproportionate (short and ample) or extreme (tall and thin) body shape, a second, experienced opinion may be desirable.

Good proportions—width in relation to length and balanced curves—cannot change a basic body shape, but they can create the illusion of length by eliminating horizontal lines or maximizing existing vertical lines—by adding shoulder-to-floor panels, for instance. Graceful curves can be shaped and formed if needed with a peplum, or better balance achieved with an overskirt; essentially this means that a more triangular or classic inverted wedge shape is created by the illusion of broader shoulders and a narrowing to the hips. Good proportions also ameliorate bulky areas by deemphasizing them; for example, the long-waisted, princess-line jacket paired with a straight skirt elongates a wide torso by skimming the body and flaring just below the hips. Similarly, the Empire silhouette balancing a shorter skirt creates its horizontal line high at the bust line, whereas the effect of a blouson design or of draped fabric does not always improve the proportion and balance of a wide torso.

About length: To create length rather than width, the volume of a ball gown silhouette's full skirt should be scaled down. The general rule of thumb is that a petite bride looks better in a full skirt and a tall bride in a sleek, draped dress, but the right fullness depends on the bride-to-be's shape. A more voluminous skirt, especially one that is more than 6 yards around the hemline, envelops any short bride because a wider waistline is needed for balance, which causes the overall silhouette to appear heavier. A slightly flared skirt camouflages more figure flaws, such as a pouchlike stomach; therefore, a better overall figure is required as the skirt becomes narrower. Furthermore, very full skirts work better on a good figure. The

ABOVE: *Contemporary convertibility is epitomized in a street-length allover-lace sheath dress with puffy satin sleeves and detachable train.*

LEFT: *For versatility, a short jacket can change a gown's overall design line.*

A short satin-stripe organza jacket worn over a strapless, drop-waist, princess-shaped bodice.

princess, A-line, Empire silhouette, and fuller bodice are wonderful for petite or ample brides wanting a longer, leaner, graceful look, because there are no vertical breaks—every line goes up and down. Dior, Balenciaga, and Charles James, for example, created enormous size by employing minimal A-line skirts with raised Empire waists, but not bouffant skirts.

About height: To appear taller requires a smooth, flat design, whereas a bulky, heavier touch makes you look shorter. Any slim silhouette also creates the illusion of height for a short bride; a straight sheath works as well for a very tall, size-12 or over bride with a wonderful waistline, bust line, and narrow hips. While a sheath is an ideal silhouette for an average figure, only a size 8 or 10 bride can wear a mermaid without looking like Mae West. Adding a higher flounce, peplum, or pannier on a tall, thin bride's gown creates a curve at the hipline to balance the sheath's severity or to create a dramatic break or a needed focal point. A mermaid effect accomplishes this below the knee; but it has to be carefully considered because its exaggerated

form-fit makes walking down a long aisle and moving around or dancing at a reception awkward or uncomfortable. Also, the appropriateness of a body-hugging line from shoulder to knee at a religious ceremony should be carefully weighed.

About slimness: Flowing, larger sizes for an ample woman who wants to look more feminine are appealing when the shape is broken up with vertical lines down the center. "Allowing those lines to realign with the bride-to-be's movements focuses more attention on the changing shapes, not the overall size," advises Reuben Cruz, chief designer at Joelle Bridals in New York City. "It's as if another, thinner dress exists within the bigger dress. A light, airy skirt demands attention, creating an illusion of gracefulness. Likewise, the embellishing design details should not be too heavy. A bridal jacket, whenever included, has to create the impression of a beautiful body underneath the dress."

Depending on your figure and the fullness you desire, crinolines can be sewn on from your waist to your hipline, then thinned on the left or right for balance; even more crinolines can be added at your knee for extra fullness, which facilitates walking.

Fifty years ago, when Priscilla Kidder, also known as Priscilla of Boston, began her illustrious career, variety in bridal wear did not exist; in fact, most bridal gowns were quite dull. Not only were fabrics, laces, appliqués, and trimmings limited, but the styles were not as innovative. By the time she dressed the 1960s Johnson and Nixon White House brides, Kidder was the undisputed queen of bridal wear. "Today's bride-to-be is unwilling to make compromises," she has observed, "so she assumes control of her wedding day and her wedding gown. Every bride-to-be has a very specific idea of each element she wants on her wedding dress.

And she is willing to go to any lengths to find it. If her search proves unsuccessful, she has it altered and made to her liking.

"A young bride-to-be is not interested in the etiquette of which style to wear when or where, either. If she wants an informal dress, I suggest several silhouettes, even strapless with a jacket, that make a fashion statement. However, it often turns out that what is an informal scale to her is more suited to a large cathedral. But if that is the wedding dress she wants, I suggest that she might want to have it all."

One sure method for achieving different presentations is detachable design elements that create pageantry walking down the aisle, more-traditional quality viewed from the back during the ceremony, but when eliminated make your wedding dress appear quite contemporary on a receiving line, and then very fun-loving at the party. For example, a long-sleeved, short jacket and a wide, long train forming an overskirt effect create a very striking and different look by going from a demure high-neck, floor-length sheath to a bold, strapless sheath. A short bride-to-be, however, must be careful that her jacket does not create an additional unwanted horizontal line with a foreshortening effect.

Defining Formal Regalia and Semiformal Garb

Every wedding dress—whether retrogressive through traditional or very contemporary in direction—is an expression of the bride's taste, the occasion, and conforms to the body within the fashions of the day. Common to every ultraformal or semiformal traditional bridal presentation is the low hemline and important back treatment as the second presentation at the altar. "The long train returned as a design element of a bridal look after Prince Charles married Lady Diana," says Monica Hickey of Saks Fifth Avenue. "But when they came they came with a bang. A long, wide, white satin surface became every bride-to-be's dream. Only a graceful sweep extension from the hemline is intended to trail slightly behind the bride throughout her wedding day. The courtly chapel through cathedral trains, whether at the hips or shoulders, must either be detachable or bustle. Often, a bride-to-be doesn't realize this until the fitting is taking place, however."

Most components and design elements work on ultraformal, formal, semiformal, and informal presentations. While the more exaggerated components, especially a

This demure, three-piece, duchess satin ensemble adds a new dimension to formal bridal garb convertibility. The heavy pearl trim on a long-sleeved bolero over a snug bodice is enhanced by an overskirt with a formal train. In a pared-down version, a contemporary vampish bride emerges in a strapless sheath.

A heavy duchess satin
gown and extended train
with pearl-enhanced lace
appliqués for the ultimate
traditional ball-gown
silhouette.

décolletage (cleavage-exposing) neckline, are more appropriate at large, formal evening weddings, others, such as a shorter skirt and illusion scoop neckline, are suitable for smaller, semiformal weddings. Strictly speaking, a formal bridal presentation—a full or slim floor-length skirt with a substantial train and a lace or tulle veil to the hem or trailing extravagantly behind—always has a sophisticated or innocent fantasy aura. A floor-length, ankle-length, or even high-in-front, low-in-back skirt, scaled down with a somewhat modest train and characterized by a less rigid or airy and more up-to-date feeling, is a semiformal presentation.

At various times in every bride-to-be's life, she has imagined herself to be a fairytale princess on her wedding day. Little else conveys that spirit better than a long, full skirt and a train. The important design aspect for a train is a proper shape—long, point, ellipsoid, or round—and proportion—length to width—to properly reflect the gown and your size. For instance, a slim sheath or small bride needs a narrow or elliptical train, and a large bride or ball-gown skirt wants additional fullness and length. Most of all, trains should never be either too skimpy or overpowering, but should flow from your shoulders or waist or hipline as a graceful extension.

The skirt's fullness and length also directly affect a bride's illusion of height and overall stature. The best break for both short and heavy brides is at one extreme or the other—ankle or mini length. A hemline nearer the knee tends to condense a short frame and expand a wide one. A petite bride-to-be should always consider a narrow skirt first, because a full skirt can make her look squat rather than lean.

Over the years, Bob Mackie's couture, bridal-wear, and ready-to-wear collections have dictated worldwide fashion trends.

He often persuades many brides-to-be seeking a "hip" or glamorous gown to try a full-length traditional style—whether pretty or feminine, romantic or sophisticated, off-the-shoulder or a high wedding-collar neckline with a well-proportioned ball-gown skirt and train. "With delight, I watch as she melts," Mackie remarks. "But a bride-to-be who looks and feels better in scaled-down clothes should stick with that look—which could be called semiformal—because a snug bodice, bouffant skirt, and cathedral train are not going to work as well for her. Espe-

Youthful, textured point d'esprit dramatizes a high/low ruffled-hem semiformal presentation.

HEMLINES AND TRAINS

A hem is the folded-under, finished-off, or trimmed edge ending a skirt. Since the 1960s, all hemlines above the knee are referred to as *mini* and the shortest variety are called *micromini*. Below-the-knee hemlines ending above the floor in descending order are *street-length* hemlines, which stop just above, at, or below the knee as dictated by current fashion; *midi* and *intermission*, which fall between the knee and midcalf, the latter longer in back; and *tea-length* and *handkerchief*, which end midcalf, the latter's longest tapering points ending at the ankle. Hemlines that stop just above the floor and swirl about the ankle are *ankle-* or *ballet-length*. A full skirt that reveals the ankle beneath is a *ballerina* hemline, and any hem that barely touches the ground is *floor-length*.

A train is any swath of material suspended from behind a gown and trailing behind it. There are eight lengths of trains and three places from where they can extend: a continuation of the gown's finished edge in back — a *sweeping train*; draping from the *waist*; or hanging at the shoulders — a *Watteau* train. Without exception, the longer the train the more formal the look. A *royal* or *extended cathedral* train consists of 3 yards of fabric; a *cathedral* train, of 2½ yards; a *chapel* train, 1⅓ yards; and a *court* train, more than 1 foot. A *sweep* or *brush* train is any token fabric trailing behind. The nontrailing train lengths in ascending order are *ballet* — at the ankle; *intermission* — midway between the knee and ankle; and *street* — falling just below the knee.

The extension can be sewn directly onto the gown or can be detachable (a practical solution if you will need freedom to eat and dance at the reception) or be bustled (bunching waist-high with a hook, snap, or button to form a flowerlike burst and allowing the remainder to drape).

cially for a younger bride-to-be with limited experience wearing a formal gown, I begin by trying a simple silhouette in a lovely shape rather than one covered with complicated details and elements. In too much dress, she may feel foolish or uncomfortable walking, talking, and dancing.

"On a full-skirt traditional gown with a train, I prefer embellishments to move the eye, perhaps flowers, lace, or tiny diamonds," Mackie continues. "A detachable train is important, especially if long, so it does not inhibit the bride's movement during the reception. Normally, my bridal gowns are constructed to be full and are worn with only panties and pantyhose underneath. How-

ever, if an additional underpinning is going to be included, it should be fancy, of the finest materials, and designed to look very feminine. On the right dress, I think a fringed or lace-trimmed petticoat looks great when picked up to climb a stair."

Beginning in the Middle Ages, bustles were shelflike cages worn to extend the feminine line in back, creating fullness just below the waist. They were a design element. Although trains were included from time to time, a bustle was not meant merely to lift a train off the floor. Their size, shape, position, and very presence ebbed and flowed with fashion, decade by decade. One hundred years ago, bustles became extinct, but through the twentieth century, vestiges, such as a peplum or flounce, reappeared. Because a long train that looks magnificent going down the aisle and back to the guests during the ceremony, and trailing during the bridal party's procession to the receiving line, must remain a showpiece the remainder of the day, modern brides often opt for the bustled back treatment as an alternative to holding or looping the strap around the wrist to lift the train off the floor and out of the way during the wedding reception.

As trains reentered every bride-to-be's dream, they entered designers' minds, including that of neophyte Lora Van Lear. After designing for several companies that she felt were too staid, she opened Van Lear Bridal House with her sister, Lisa, who had followed her to New York from Cincinnati, Ohio. Because long trains were being bustled by the bridal salon fitter, a designer never saw how it bustled, or where the hooks, loops, or buttons were being integrated into their designs.

"But we all heard afterward that the bustling did not hold fast; with the first mishap, out it came," says Van Lear, speaking for her peers. "I felt there had to be a better way. I thought to myself, the bustle should somehow be incorporated into the design in a manner to look as pretty throughout the day as during the ceremony.

"A convertible bustle that could be pulled up in back, looped, and fastened to hold in place came to me in a dream. I got up and wrote it down. The following morning, I thought about it some more and did a sketch. I was afraid everyone in my showroom might laugh me out the door. But they didn't. Several days later, *Modern Bride*'s editor-in-chief, Cele Lalli, was in the showroom and I mentioned my convertible bustle concept. She did not pass it off either. 'Nobody has done a drawstring bustle before!' she said. I had given birth to a good idea!

"My successful convertible bustle styles are decorative and a functional option to a detachable train—for instance, exaggerated tuckings to resemble a shirred waistline with the remaining fabric forming a floor-length, A-line silhouette or a floral cluster, whose petals are skirt and train trimmings concealing the drawstring channel that bustles these appliqués into individual flowers."

An ideal bodice includes a neckline, shoulder treatment, and waistline that are well balanced, in good proportion, and the right complement for that bride's figure and size. The components of the bodice, their scale, and how they are combined govern both the overall effect and its impression up close, and can be used in formal, semiformal, or informal presentations. The first step to selecting the bodice parts that fit your body, personality, and wedding ambience is to recognize and understand its properties, and then to remember that most silhouettes work with several component combinations.

OVERLEAF: A Watteau train falls from a self-fabric rose garland.

Bustle back treatment releases a formal train on this slim Edwardian gown with lace portrait neckline.

The silhouette and bodice outline is also influenced by the midriff shape—the chest-to-waist section—and its construction, ranging from a snugly fitted form to a soft, generous draping. The midriff section can reaffirm an overall mood as well—for example, romance by a gently dropped V waist or innocence through a cinched bodice, like a milkmaid in a laced corset. The more open and the less fabric a bride is swaddled in, such as a wide and low portrait collar, the less risk of appearing overwhelmed.

Vertical lines always create length and horizontal lines, width. But it does not necessarily follow that a covered-up heavy bride looks wider, unless a bodice's lines are predominantly horizontal. The princess or Empire lines, for instance, are especially wonderful for a thick bodice, because they skim rather than hug, creating a longer, leaner look. Likewise, a shorter bride-to-be wishing to elongate her look can do so by creating interest up high, and wearing an Empire or a princess line with a flared skirt—as full as proportion allows.

No combination on the neck, shoulder, or waist is absolutely right or wrong, and almost any combination will work if the scale, proportion, and balance are coordinated for your particular body shape. When standing in front of a mirror, nothing should seem exaggerated; for example, if you see only sleeves or hips, something is probably unbalanced.

As hemlines move up and down the leg and as skirts expand and contract from bouffant to slim with fashion trends, the neckline, shoulder treatment, and waistline—front and back—remain three important focal points that can, with only slight modification, affect the spirit of a wedding dress. They are usually considered simultaneously, but what an array of shapes, sizes, and combinations from which to choose!

A deep-squared V neck.

A heart-shaped keyhole.

A Watteau-style draping swag.

BUSTLES AND BACK TREATMENTS

Back presentations form from a design element at the shoulder, waist, and hips. The bunched or bustled train is an alternative method to the train strap for lifting the fabric.

Bustled shapes today include very narrow to wide *panels* draped and bursting from a floral-like gathering; geometric designs giving a *pillow* or saddle effect; a gathered fabric forming a *pouf* or a larger yet graceful fullness; cascading ruffled *tiers*; wide to oversized *bows* with ribbons or streamers; or a series of *cones*, which are formed by tucks, pleats, or ruching buttoning along the waistline to hike the train to the hemline or trail slightly behind. Bustles also include enhancement borders, cutouts, and embroidered beading. Trimming details, such as a fringe or appliqués on the skirt, can be bustled to further coordinate with the gown.

A bride-to-be wishing to avoid additional width at the hips can choose from many other *back treatments*, including a *keyhole* back—the generic term for any cutout shape, such as a heart, circle, or diamond, latticework line, or bows fastening a graceful, V-, U-shape, or deeper *scoop*; the see-through illusion or complete bareness of a *backless* design to the waist; a plunging *neckline*; fabric draping from the shoulders; or a simple yet important row of *buttons* from the neckline to the waistline. Each creates the desired focal interest.

Along with the above-the-waist and waist-high back treatments, there are those echoing a sleeve treatment or creating an overskirt, such as a surprise *apron* at back in several tiers ending at the floor; or a peplum can have a fringe or a flounce or a ruffle at or just below the waist. Design elements at the hips, such as a peplum, may wrap to form a *butterfly* back treatment, which is a diminutive, nondraping bustle as well as any number of bow treatments. A drop-waist sheath with a wrap overskirt in back or the lower trumpet skirt's *godet* (triangular panel) is often the point of departure for a cascading, multilayer tulle, ruffled flare, low-slung tulle swag, fluted self-fabric panel, or floral arrangement as its back interest.

A butterfly back treatment.

A butterfly back treatment.

A fishtail train.

Buttoned bustle-forming cones.

A traditional bustle.

A multi-tier ruffle.

A floral back treatment.

An illusion mock turtleneck effect.

A scoop neckline.

A wide-scoop neckline.

A set-away scoop neckline of *poi d'ainge* lace.

NECKLINES

The highest neckline, the *turtleneck*, is characterized by the bodice fabric being built up along the throat and folded over; a *mock turtle* is a curved single layer just brushing the chin, and a *cowl* is a single or double oversized layer left lavishly draped down the front or back. A *mandarin collar* stands up and slightly out perpendicular to the shoulders with a small slit in the middle, and a *ruched-edged* collar is formed by a series of pleats. The classic *wedding-band collar*, high and of upturned lace that encircles the neck, becomes a cameo neckline if a centered ornamental pin is included, and an *illusionary* if transparent silk tulle covers the shoulders in back and yoke in front.

The high necklines that are lower in front include the *Queen Elizabeth*, which closes in a V shape at the bust line, and the *Queen Anne*, which is sculpted to outline bareness at the collarbone and upper chest.

A standard *jewel* or high neck runs around or is dropped slightly below the throat and is rarely lace-trimmed. A *bateau* or *boat* neckline follows the gently curving collarbone from shoulder to shoulder in front and back; the two modified boat neck versions are straight across the yoke and lower in back or straight in back and lower in front. Closely resembling it is the *sabrina* collar, which is also straight but begins closer to the neck, about 2 inches from the shoulder seams. A *portrait* neckline stands away from the neckbones and shoulder caps to frame the face; if a decorative fabric or lace panel is attached, it forms a *bertha collar*. A *scoop* neck is round and low; a *square* neck is actually a half square; a *V-neck* is angled into a point; a *sweetheart* is an open heart shape; and a *keyhole* is an open teardrop, beginning 2 inches inside the shoulder line.

Most neckline styles can be fashioned into a *plunging* neckline; a deep plunge revealing cleavage is referred to as a *décolletage*.

A Queen Anne neckline.

A bateau neckline detail.

A square neckline.

A V neckline.

A jewel neckline.

A stylized portrait neckline.

A sweetheart neckline.

More than any other element, the neckline influences the image that a wedding dress or gown evokes, including its propriety at a religious ceremony. As a coordinated package of design lines, details, and focal points, the bodice expresses the bridal spirit, especially at close range on your receiving line. What's more, the lines around the throat set off and frame a bride's face, which is the most serious consideration for any bridal ensemble.

The closest related component to the neck is the shoulder fit or lack of shoulders. It prominently states the fashion direction and style, and reflects the wedding attitude and ambience. The waistline, which refers to the point where the bodice joins the skirt and not necessarily where your body nips in, serves to accent the body's natural curves while differentiating the upper from the lower portions of the silhouette. Any bride-to-be who wants the drama, pomp, and splendor of a formal silhouette with a snug bodice should bear in mind that wearing one is a far different experience from wearing an everyday dress. A structured bodice, whether strapless, sleeveless, or off-the-shoulders, corsets you in, constricting movement. Even a snug bodice with a full skirt is as restricting as a narrow, body-hugging sheath; each requires practice walking in a refined and delicate fashion.

The first considerations when selecting the neckline are whether the shape is harmonious with your face, whether its size is in proportion to your head, and whether the overall scale is balanced. This can only be ascertained by trying it on in front of a mirror. The neckline should highlight and enhance your particular look by pleasingly framing your throat and chin.

A scoop, sweetheart, or keyhole neckline is a gentle shape that opens up the neck and face, making an innocent visual statement.

Similarly, a peekaboo sleeve or the high, illusionary wedding-band collar has an innocent effect, especially with a romantic or feminine cuff ending. A square neckline's straight lines must be considered carefully because this neckline, if too high or loose, will appear matronly; however, a square can be very dramatic and quite sexy when low. A high neckline looks good only on a long neck; a plunging V neckline, while it frames the face, elongates the neck.

A covered-up or high-neck look—from a turtleneck to a high-back, low-front Queen Anne—is best on the tall bride who wants to appear shorter. "A heavy bride-to-

A seemingly unsupported, deep-tuck portrait neckline is executed by Scaasi with a silk-brocade fitted bodice and a bouffant skirt.

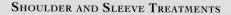

A sleeveless bodice.

A kimono-style sleeve.

Whenever fabric or lace is fitted to join at the neckline or on both shoulders, the effect is a *yoke* neckline; on only one shoulder, an *asymmetrical* yoke. The opposite styles, a bare neck and shoulder caps, are *off-the-shoulder*, which has set-away or dropped-bow sleeves; *spaghetti-strap*, with negligible vertical straps running over the top of the shoulders; and *strapless* or *bustier*, with fabric or lace beginning just above the bust line and curved. Wearing a jacket, stole, or wrap is an option with each style.

A *sleeveless* bodice has a slit-seam armhole. A sleeve can be *set in* that slit seam, running over the shoulder cap and under the armhole, or extended up and over the shoulder cap without breaking, referred to as a *cap sleeve*; the off-the-shoulder styles have a half sleeve. The common sleeve lengths are *skimpy*, covering the uppermost part of the arm only; *cap*, which is fitted, or *capelet*, which is softly flared, ending an inch or so above the elbow; *three-quarter*, which ends just below the elbow; or *long*, which extends just above, at, or below the wristbone. A traditional *fitted* sleeve is long with little or no fullness; it is a *draped* sleeve if the fabric is folded or bias-cut. When fabric or lace extends along the back of the hand forming the letter V, it is a *pointed* or a *gauntlet* sleeve.

The most exotic sleeve treatments are smooth at the shoulder cap and set in under the arm. This either forms a *kimono* sleeve with fabric hanging down from the armhole and draping to the wrist, or a *dolman* sleeve with fabric extending down in an exaggerated fashion and creating a capelike effect before tapering to a fitted wrist.

A *melon* sleeve is rounded from the shoulder to the elbow, ending in a cuff or band; a *puff* is gathered from shoulder to elbow in a smaller rounded, balloon shape; a transparent puff called a *peekaboo* sleeve exposes the skin underneath; a *petal* sleeve has epauletlike, layered panels that form short or skimpy sleeves.

The *leg-of-mutton* or *gigot* is a generous, fully rounded, loose sleeve from the shoulder cap through the elbow with a nipped-in wrist; the *bishop*, derived from a medieval cloak, is full through the forearm and gathered as a wide cuff at the wrist; the *Gibson* is full at the shoulder and fitted at the wrist; the *bell* or *pagoda* style gently flares from shoulder to wrist; and the *poet* sleeve is pleated at the shoulder and full to the cuff.

A set-in sleeve.

A leg-of-mutton sleeve.

A gauntlet sleeve.

A Gibson girl sleeve.

A melon sleeve.

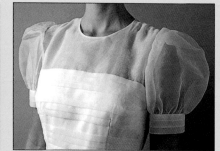

A puff sleeve.

A poet sleeve.

be especially should consider a low V neckline first," says talented bridal-wear designer Ron LoVece. "And a small bride-to-be *must* open herself up at the neck. The more flesh she shows, including a sheer illusion yoke, the more she dominates the dress.

"Any bride with ample breasts must have an open-neckline gown as well. The layered look, portrait collar, and bertha collar's added panel, for instance, ameliorate a disproportionate or flawed upper torso by hiding a large bust or making a small bust line appear larger; also, flowers or a bow and sheer covering around the shoulders, upper arm, or sleeves can compensate for width as well. A boat neck's horizontal lines are better to widen narrow shoulders than an off-the-shoulder neckline, unless a portrait collar effect is included. For extremely narrow shoulders, the sabrina neckline, which begins closer to the throat, works very well.

"The advantage of the scoop or sweetheart is that it moves the eye across the bust. A V neckline moves the eye up and down; however, it appears more matronly as well. A square neckline and any décolletage style are very chic and instantly connote a fun-loving atmosphere when wide and low, but they both require wonderful shoulders and cleavage. An asymmetrical neckline can be a balancing or design enhancement for the face, but it has little effect on the body's proportion."

Any neckline lower in front and higher at the nape, ranging from an innocent sweetheart to a regal Elizabethan-style ruffle, is suitable morning, noon, or night; a shallow scoop or square, standard jewel (T-shirt–like), mandarin (perpendicular and slit), mock turtle (curved, single layer built up along the neck), turtle (folded over), or cowl (lavishly draping) is more suitable for a daytime wedding, but any one can easily be adapted for the evening as well. The higher the sun, the less bareness is correct, front or back; so deep-plunging necklines, necklines standing away from the shoulders, and all shoulderless styles, except for tank tops, are reserved for the late afternoon or evening.

Except when necessary for religious reasons, today's wedding gowns no longer have high necks and long sleeves. In fact, every shape, size, and style of shoulder and sleeve treatment, even bare shoulders and skimpy

A petaled duchess satin cap sleeve forms artichoke epaulets.

A dropped waistline.

A princess waistline.

A stylized princess waistline.

WAISTLINES

A waistline is categorized in relation to where it falls: above, at, or below your natural waistline. Only when the bodice and skirt join at the torso's narrowest point is it called a *natural* waist.

The highest a waistline can be placed is called a *blouson* effect, because fabric is draped from the shoulders and armholes with its greatest fullness gathered and fastened above, at, or below the natural waistline. The *Empire* skirt begins just below the bust line; the *raised*, 1 inch above the natural waistline. A *cinched* waist is any sashlike panel that extends above, through, and just below the natural waist.

An *antebellum* waistline begins at the classic natural waistline, dipping 2 or 2¹/₂ inches and ending in a pronounced point. A *basque* begins 2 to 3 inches below the natural waistline, remains parallel to the ground, or forms a gentle U shape or a sharper V shape at center front.

An *asymmetrical* waistline is angled and dropped on one side only; a *dropped* waistline begins anywhere from 3, 4, or 5 inches up to 14 inches below the classic natural waistline; and a *princess* waistline is straight with no waistline whatsoever.

lines achieve a widening effect, any puff or drop appears wider than a flat, high set-in sleeve; on the other hand, vertical designs, such as dolman sleeves, lead the eye down along your body, creating a slimmer illusion.

The variables when determining the right scale or degree to exaggerate a sleeve treatment, especially the leg-of-mutton, Gibson, or bishop, are many. The proportion and sleeve size depend on the bride's size: a tiny bride looks longer with a focal point at her neckline, but big puffy sleeves appear overpowering, unless they are sheer. A big bride looks bigger with fullness at her shoulders: the bigger the shoulder and sleeve treatment, the bigger you look; moreover, a long, fitted straight sleeve creates a narrower look—its vertical lines break up a bulky appearance. Knowing which sleeve treatment is most appropriate can be a complicated matter and may require the help of a professional.

While the traditional bridal gown has volume to impart importance, it must also look sexy. A fitted bodice or beaded lace jacket with jeweled neckline may be enough to look modern and sexy; however, a bride always looks more regal in an enlarged shoulder treatment, long sleeves, and an important neckline. These components of a bridal gown's design, when left to modern fashion masters, become an extravagant part of the silhouette, which further removes the gown from the everyday. Two masters of the incredible neckline and shoulder/sleeve treatment are James Bradgley and Mark Mischka, a recently formed design team who are on fashion-conscious minds. "Our bridal gowns are extraordinary confections," they claim with excitement. "Because instead of reinterpreting the leg-of-mutton sleeve or jewel neckline, our philosophy is for a gown to combine ready-to-wear–inspired fun with the sophisticated fantasy of old Hollywood movies and period

sleeves, is worn. The barest styles exposing the shoulder and arms require a sophisticated attitude, good bone structure and proportions, as well as wonderful upper arms, bust line, and shoulders. To compensate for narrow shoulders or a wide waist, a puff or flowers on the sleeves can be added.

The balance and proportion of the sleeve treatment, which begins at the shoulders, remain vital to the overall design lines. The amount the sleeves taper in relation to the waist and to the overall length is crucial, and the effect on each angle in front, side to side, and in back can be equally difficult for a bride-to-be to gauge properly herself. For example, because horizontal or exaggerated fashion photographs. We re-create and re-vise the traditional bridal characteristics, for example, scalloped tulle draping from the neckline or along the sleeve or an Empire silhouette with reembroidered lace that plunges to create a back treatment."

The waistline is the midpoint and narrow-est portion between the chest and hips, and after years of the popularity of exercising, enormous emphasis has been placed on a tapering torso that ends in a narrow waist. Your gown's waistline, however, is the ac-tual intersection of the bodice and skirt, which immediately makes this point impor-tant. A snug fit or soft fullness highlights the waistline fit, but easy draping fabric subor-dinates it. A blouson effect or a high Empire

or raised princess line, for instance, hides a bulky midriff, while dropping the waist cre-ates an illusion of a slimmer waist by direct-ing pressure away from the midriff and contouring a bulky waistline to look smooth (however, this can foreshorten the skirt). A cinched waist covers just above and below the natural waist, perhaps with a sash em-bellished with a flower or draping streamers, which draws the eye to a slim or well-proportioned midriff.

Even a minute shift in the waistline place-ment will create a dramatic change. For example, both the antebellum (beginning at the natural waistline) and basque (beginning 2 to 3 inches below the natural waistline) elongate the torso when combined with large

Rows of pearl encrustation camouflage a simple, form-fitting princess-line bodice while the drop torso relies on exposed princess seaming for shape.

An illusion sweetheart neckline and long fitted sleeves create a fairy tale princess bride.

waistline and then flared, an overskirt effect is achieved; if fitted and with a dropped waistline, a tunic shape evolves; and if low and slim, this becomes the mermaid silhouette."

The exact number of inches to raise or drop the waistline above or below the natural waist is determined according to each bride-to-be's torso length, width, and her overall proportions. A short bride-to-be should stay with a natural or very slightly dropped waist. A tall bride-to-be can limit the illusion of height, to match her bridegroom's proportions if necessary, by including a natural or drop waist that becomes a full skirt.

A properly scaled waistline balances the other components of your bodice as well as creates the harmonious relationship you desire between the bodice and skirt; however, finding the right style, placement, and fit is not a pure science. The most important aspect is how the waist feels and that it is comfortable. What is more, one of the waistlines you prefer wearing every day is likely to be right on your bridal gown as well.

sleeves and a layered but sheer full skirt. The V-waistline antebellum, however, does not foreshorten the legs and skirt, whereas a similarly combined basque waistline, because it begins closer to the natural waist, does, and while a parallel waistline elongates the upper torso, the round effect does not look as long as a V or U.

"For an even longer, leaner look and to compensate for bulk, the waistline can also be varied," says Ron LoVece. "For instance, three or four inches above the waist in the center, sloping down at the side seam to a natural waist, and continuing to slope in back to a drop waist. If loosely draped to the

A wisely chosen outline with components and design elements that are well coordinated and scaled to one another will state who you are as a woman and bride. A perfectly balanced silhouette emphasizes your personality; scaling each component in relation to another pinpoints the characteristics you choose to highlight; and balancing the design elements with simple adjustments changes their degree of importance and expresses a different desired wedding spirit and ambience.

No one will sit you down and bestow every detail of this information upon you, and then help you to develop the necessary skills. An awareness of how to create the

look you have chosen comes by spotting it in photographs, and noticing that a silhouette, component, and a design element are being used together effectively. But only experimenting with different components and trying specific ones on gives you a hands-on instinct; essentially, the knack can be developed through self-instruction. Your own interpretation when combining components and design elements on a silhouette will ultimately result in an overall statement that is distinctly you. This does not necessarily require having on hand the actual bridal silhouettes you are considering or even seeing an element on a wedding dress: the same impression of size and shape in relation to your chin, throat, and shoulders can be construed from looking at yourself in a cowl-neck sweater as in a cowl-neck gown.

It is also possible to retain your gown's direction when transforming yourself from the participant in a solemn ceremony to the centerpiece at a festive reception. "A beautiful, storybook princess is the quintessential initial bridal presentation," says Jim Demetrios, chief designer and owner of Ilissa Bridalwear in New York City. His experi-

ence as the wedding-dress buyer for his family's bridal salon taught him what brides wish to express with their attire, and the how-tos of creating those bridal statements. "This is best evoked in a graceful, ball-gown silhouette, emitting a golden fairytale glow. Grand stature, but normal scale, is achieved by including an important, sheer jewel neckline and long sleeves, repeating and balancing the collar embellishment at the wrist, and by using a snug bustier bodice with a basque waistline that spreads into an airy, full skirt with a long, sheer, contrasting airy train to fulfill the fantasy spirit. Traditional romance, another bridal statement, is created with the same snug bodice, but with the use of an antebellum-style waistline, an off-the-shoulder neckline, and short, large-scale puffed sleeves, especially paired with an airy, larger-than-life full skirt—reminiscent of the widow

A deep-flounce shoulder treatment, narrow antebellum waist, and ethereal tulle skirt epitomize romance and innocence.

Delicately rolled, multilayer tulle hems on a bouffant skirt.

A demure, high V neckline and modified Gibson girl sleeve.

A blouson effect with batwing sleeves drawn from the hip.

Scarlett O'Hara dancing off in *Gone With the Wind*, albeit all in white. An imposing, regal presentation, a third popular statement, is instantly recognized as stature when overscale, wide shoulders (which enhance most face shapes), and sharply sculpted chest area are combined with a deep V neckline. The overall proportion promotes importance by combining equally exaggerated Gibson sleeves, scaled down to a small waist, and an elongated, cascading, deep-pointed flounce to balance a long, many-layered full skirt.

"Affluence, which is more than merely displaying finery, is not achieved solely with an overscale ball gown's lines. There is a scaled-down, understated classification as well; for example, a gathered, drop-waist, princess-line bodice flaring into a full skirt is unadorned chic, epitomizing class for many brides-to-be. On the other hand, to achieve importance and a sophisticated aura, an all-white, narrow A-line column with one generous detail—perhaps a long train, gently draping from a wide butterfly back treatment, then flaring and trailing behind—with an overall proportion that creates a thin line, all combined and set off in a world-class hotel, whispers minimal chic."

Modesty can evoke innocence with a demure, high, opaque neckline, including either a shallow, conservative V or jewel and narrow, square or scoop neckline with a moderate puffy shoulder and sleeve treatment. Likewise, a yoke neck that covers the shoulders can be modest, but it can also inspire the opposite aura, a bold spirit. A wedding-band collar throws innocence aside and becomes sophisticated when a generous, draping bodice, overlaid on top of a camisole or teddy, and wide dolman sleeves are included. This is restated by fitted forearms and wrists to blend with the collar and contrast with the blouson waist.

The bold spirit turns into a sexy spirit with a fancy, open back and busy full skirt, though a simple, unembellished straight sheath and train can say it just as clearly. Further vivaciousness requires a sleeker outline, a lower neckline, and a drop waist—the mermaid silhouette. The realm of good taste has been expanded and safe sexy can be employed with a provocative and seductive nude sheath lining that eliminates any trace of vulgarity. However, the neckline can plunge into a décolletage and the train burst and swirl around the ankles, which creates an overall harmony by adding a godet, for doing an enthusiastic hootchy-kootchy.

Informal and Contemporary Directions—The Experts' Broad-based Assessment

A bride-to-be choosing a traditional informal or contemporary bridal presentation generally has little desire to emulate a childhood fantasy bride, and wants to appear as she does for other special occasions in her life: at the theater, a fancy restaurant, or a very important party.

What transforms everyday attire into traditional informal wedding garb is the use of unmistakable but scaled-down bridal motifs. An informal wedding dress is all-white, smooth, and shiny, uses floral lace, has an important neckline, is often somewhat illusory, and includes a back treatment, particularly small buttons or a butterfly bow, as a bridal presentation at the altar. Other elements of bridal style—elaborate trimmings, embellishments, and the accessories, such as headdresses (perhaps a hat with tulle veil), and accents, such as lacy gloves and flowers—complete the ensemble and contribute to the undeniably bridal look.

If a traditional informal wedding ensemble is distinguished by its use of bridal motifs, then a nontraditional or contemporary wedding dress is best characterized by the absence or the extremely limited use of them, and the substitution of whatever elements of style are considered fashionable at the moment and may be a complete departure from or even defy conventional bridal motif use—for example, pearls embedded in denim or terrycloth with a tulle ruffle.

A traditional informal and contemporary wedding dress follows current fashion trends more than traditional bridal wear does. A bride-to-be choosing either can approach her selection with a better awareness of how to present herself. She knows which silhouettes will be most comfortable and appropriate because the scale of the components closely resembles her everyday clothes, whether casual and understated or dressy and flamboyant, in the country or in town, at home or in a private club.

The casual (underscale and unconstructed), everyday office-appropriate (moderate scale and lines), or dressy (larger, more luxu-

rious scale) commonsense parameters used daily as a dress code (as opposed to traditional wedding etiquette) can also be applied for both traditional informal and contemporary bridal wear. Generally, a tailored (shaped and built up section by section) silhouette is

A fluid skirt contrasts with a man-tailored jacket.

less dressy and has masculine overtones or design details, including a boxy or solid shape, whereas a dressmaker (cut and sewn) style is dressy and includes more feminine details, such as a flowing ribbon sash.

A bride-to-be wishing to use relatively small-scale components in unique combinations to create a focal point might wear a micromini that drops to a midcalf skirt in back with a sleeveless, wide portrait neckline, or a knee-length, body-hugging strapless sheath—the possible combinations are endless. A slim or slightly bouffant street-length dress, a dressmaker outfit (with or without a jacket), or a more casual man-tailored suit (jacket with matching or contrasting skirt or pants) is appropriate for a luncheon following a City Hall ceremony. A cocktail-hour ceremony and reception wedding is dressier when in a hotel, and would require a more form-fitted dress in a luxurious or unique fabric and a degree of bareness. A more carefree attitude would be expected on, say, a beach, where the bride might wear an airy cotton batiste dress with sheer sleeves. Evenings always connote dressier, more flowing, and larger-scale clothing, which would have to be more extreme at a party for five hundred guests than at an intimate, at-home celebration— for example, the neckline might be deeper or the shoulder treatment and skirt fuller.

In many ways the hemline's length is not as important a factor as scale in determining informal or contemporary attire. "In my opinion, length no longer makes a wedding dress dressy," says Hedda Kleinfeld, bridal wear's merchant princess. "At one time, a traditional informal bride would wear a scaled-down wedding dress that came to her ankles or was tea-length; an older, remarrying woman wore a street-length suit. But who am I to dictate to a bride-to-be who says, 'I'm having a very informal wedding, but I want a dress that comes to the floor'? If that's how she wants to appear, she should go for it.

"A great deal is in the eye of the beholder. Along with scale, a dressy informal bridal statement or a contemporary outfit depends upon the embellishment. For instance, a short white dress with handmade allover pearling is pretty darn formal, depending on how bare it is on top—which normally a wedding dress is not, unless you happen to be an actress or rock star, like Madonna, or want to be married in something that really shows off your cleavage.

"Personally, I don't think something that's got a lot of rhinestones is necessarily appropriate for an early morning wedding ceremony; usually they are reserved for very dressy dresses. Here again, this is a moment to do whatever she wants."

A midcalf or handkerchief hem represents the demarcation line when a formal traditional dress is construed as an informal dress. Traditional informal dresses are short, white, and appropriate to a small chapel and great big churches that have small chapels, the minister's study, the judge's chambers, or a friend's home. "A contemporary wedding dress's spirit is derived more from the setting and the bride's personality," says *Bride*'s magazine editor-in-chief Barbara Tober. "I love the word 'karma' to express the manner in which these brides handle their wedding day: how they see themselves and the entire ambience. The setting could be by the side of a river on a dock at a campsite—very rural and rustic—at sunset. That bride could dress in something quite interesting, quite unusual, perhaps short pants and a lace jacket. Or the river could be the Mississippi with a ten-column house on a knoll. The bride walks up a path in a wonderful front-buttoning, cinched-waist sheath, hanging to midcalf in back and just above the knee in front,

worn with a perky hat and veil. The outfit can also be contemporary because the setting and bride's aura suggest that quality."

TRADITIONAL INFORMAL ATTIRE

There is an immense range of appropriate traditional informal dresses. They are cut, sculpted, and embellished more in a ready-to-wear genre, and often are created as a simple white dress or festive pastel cocktail dress. Many have long skirts, but not to the floor, and very few have a train because this implies increased formality; though some have convertible skirts, others are high at the knee in front and low in back. Some of these dresses have overskirts opening on the sides to reveal an undertrouser; others have overpants or an overskirt that doubles as a wrap. Each creates a more relaxed statement that is ideal for many brides as the fourth bridal presentation during the reception.

"Actually, any pretty dress style or outfit can serve the traditional informal bride,"

OPPOSITE: A slim cotton afternoon dress with sheer blouson bodice.

An asymmetrical, three-tier waistline, silk taffeta, dance-length dress with matching ruffle-trimmed stole.

OPPOSITE: *A riot of sheer, flamenco-style rolled-bias ruffles emphasizes the mermaid's design lines.*

A simple, princess-seamed, drop-waist, ivory silk organza wedding dress with a gathered full skirt results in a schoolgirl quality.

Hedda Kleinfeld points out. "However, a traditional informal bride should never look overly contrived and lost, letting the dress take all the attention. And yes, she should be different, fresh, and imaginative! Informal dresses, in contrast to traditional, formal, floor-length, and train dresses, also offer a wider range of crisscrossing or diagonal tiers, detachable wraps, and use more pastel colors."

Award-winning designer Reuben Cruz explains, "Traditional informal wedding dresses are textural but soft, elegant but flattering to the body, and have limited design embellishments that accommodate a bride as if she were on the street, in a restaurant, or traveling. Whereas a traditional formal gown is inspired by history, such as Napoleon's Empire, nineteenth-century Victoriana, the antebellum South, Statue of Liberty, or an up-to-date Princess Diana, a traditional floor-or tea-length semiformal wedding dress is a somewhat understated version with fewer design embellishments. In some cases a young bride wears a short skirt or dress, which would be more appropriate at a small first-time wedding, or on an older bride at a second wedding.

"An informal wedding dress is often a package of simple lines and elements, but combined in an unconventional manner. Traditional informal brides-to-be tend toward more unexpected, out-of-the-ordinary touches, such as long sleeves with a revealing neckline. This requires balance between each element to complement the whole as well as each other. For instance, an asymmetrical shoulder might be bared to inspire beautiful jewelry or enlarged to create the stature befitting a bride yet not be too overwhelming for her face. Even a sensual informal wedding dress focuses its allure on only one body part, such as a bride's shoulders, waist, or hips, while maintaining her modesty. For ex-

ample, a slit running along the leg will give the impression that the leg may become exposed; it never does on a wedding dress, however."

"If the information concerning the type of wedding points to informal, the dress will be shorter, and the stockings and shoes are going to play a more important role in creating the total look. I visualize traditional informal dresses as either very bouncy or very slim," Monica Hickey says emphatically. As Saks Fifth Avenue's resident bridal-wear authority, she advises informal brides to look "exuberant like a firecracker, or simple yet rich. The classic ball-gown silhouette, a scaled-down bouffant skirt worn without a crinoline, and a straight silhouette are perennial informal favorites.

"A traditional informal second-wedding dress does not have to be old-looking. A sheath, reaching just above the knee, looks wonderful on an average figure, perhaps with an intricate woven pattern to give dimension and form a patchwork effect. If necessary, its severity can be modified by wearing an overskirt or peplum. A second direction is using a narrower flounce, which is repeated at the hemline without a dip, to create harmony and a lovely but special look.

"Although brides have worn pants at different stages of fashion evolution, they are definitely an informal approach and clearly contemporary. Certainly many French brides, for instance, wear white pantsuits. However, I've never recommended pants, even at their height of popularity, because they don't inspire romance for me."

Martin Price, president of the House of Sant' Angelo in New York City, says, "Many brides-to-be who come looking for an informal wedding ensemble are often drawn to a suit because they want a jacket's clean lines. It can be a solid-shaped, boxy, and

less dressy tailored style or softer, more feminine, perhaps, without a collar and with a blouson sleeve. An older bride should wear the very clean lines of a suit. I love seeing a very elegant, modern-looking bride wearing a beautiful ivory man-tailored suit—almost like black tie for a bridegroom. They are also perfect for any first-time bride as well, especially if she wants to be married in one thing, and still have a more formal feel about the way she's dressed for the cocktail reception. A spaghetti-strap blouse or dress silhouette under the jacket, for instance, is a wonderful idea for a country-club setting and very practical, too."

A Contemporary Direction

Any bride-to-be wishing to depart from conventional bridal attire by making an absolutely contemporary statement can choose freely or adapt from any number of extraordinary outfits and a wide array of wedding fashions from American and European ready-to-wear designers and fashion houses. These designers carry their distinct signatures over to afternoon dresses, suit styles, or cocktail outfits. For example, a white blazer with gold buttons with a pleated skirt, routine silhouettes by everyday standards, is very modern compared to traditional bridal-wear guidelines. However, a contemporary wedding dress shares the traditional ideals for high-standard finery.

A truly contemporary bride-to-be won't be afraid when she is shown something that is indeed a departure from tradition. Stylish attire best expresses the sentiments and spirit of either a young or old independent-minded bride-to-be not bound by tradition. "Today's bride-to-be," says Paula Varsalona, a fashion-forward bridal-wear designer who knows her market well, "has definite attitudes that are constantly changing. She

wants a sophisticated yet individual aura for her wedding dress—to feel unique and different from anybody before." In short, her wedding dress must be personal and state who she is even if it is merely a straight white sheath using asymmetrical scallops as its only design motif.

A woman's idea of how she wants to dress is changing and it is showing up in all aspects of her life, including her wedding day. With the ever-increasing dichotomy between a classic bridal ensemble and modern-day dress, the modern bride-to-be gives us a glimpse of how future brides may look. Bridal wear no longer exclusively looks to the past because today's young woman combines whatever clothes she wants as her personal style, and she will wear them anywhere. Wedding attire must change, however slowly fashions change.

Your contemporary wedding dress, like a traditional one, should have an aura of fantasy. This is true no matter how innovative or thematic the event. At the close of each Parisian couture runway collection, a bridal design is presented. "In any given season, we see brides escorting the designer down the runway to take his bows dressed in all-black, miniskirts, bathing suits, even in men's clothing," reports CNN fashion correspondent Elsa Clench. "Brides give a designer fancy, fertile ground in which to roam, but the finale bride is a good indication of the direction a designer's work—and fashion itself—will take. These fashionable bridal ensembles are wonderful creations for any cutting-edge-of-fashion bride-to-be to consider, and they can be ordered directly from the fashion house."

The fashion designers' visions run the gamut from sporty to very contemporary to frivolous to romantic to futuristic and absolutely outlandish; from bouffant dresses to culottes ending at the knee to slips covered

The right fabric and accessories turn an afternoon coat dress into suitable bridal attire.

in flowers to short skirts. There are several dresses suitable for a contemporary and second-time bride within each designer's collection as well. "They are designed, constructed, shown, photographed, and immediately become history. Few brides-to-be ever see them, but they can be inspirational," says Texas-born fashion designer Victor Costa, who began his illustrious career in bridal wear. "Even if it is her second or third wedding, every bride wants a special look. Usually, it is more fashion-oriented—a mirror of the times, a Chanel-looking suit or a portrait collar à la Scaasi—with her personality translated, perhaps, in a champagne or icy pink color choice. Wally Simpson, the Duchess of Windsor, who was a third-time bride herself, married the Duke, Edward, in a long crepe dress that was in the fashion of her times. Another choice is wearing something thematic in a more intimate garden gathering rather than an extreme costume, such as a medieval fantasy or Renaissance bridal gown."

Bob Mackie, couturier to Hollywood stars, gives three examples that demonstrate Costa's points. "Occasionally, a customer marrying for her second or third time wants a big gown. I have found that classic touches, not a Broadway-premiere aura, are often more comfortable for these sophisticated women, but if having fun is a priority, she may want a strapless sheath. Diana Ross is one example. She wore a diamond tiara, veils, and an antique lace bridal gown in a large Swiss cathedral. The important ingredient was that the dress suited her: she looked like a queen, and not an ingenue. When Diahann Carroll married Vic Damone, I fashioned a lace camisole under a heavy crepe jacket, and for Lynda Carter's second wedding, I made a peach satin gown with a turn-of-the-century embroidered bodice of bugle beads, silk flowers, and fringes to

create a lace feeling. It was both very beautiful and glamorous.

"I advise a bride-to-be to remain true to her everyday self. Of course, she must put her best face forward, but I always caution her not to adapt a look so digressive that it just isn't her," Mackie continues. To which Elsa Clench adds: "What every working woman has realized is the importance of wearing comfortable clothing. She must be comfortable in order to look good and be happy. As a bride, she is not going to change her mind about that."

A silk crepe cocktail dress goes anywhere, does everything!

The way to ensure that your wedding dress tells *your* story is to imbue it with your individual taste. Considering each aspect of the bridal embellishments and carefully weighing your decisions requires time. It is never too early to begin investigating all the delicious options to be found on a wedding dress. Take a few weeks if possible because there are plenty of pleasing possibilities to ponder, including the fabric and lace you like best and want to find a dress in. There is no telling how satisfied and happy your informed choices will make you on your wedding day!

The first practical step for a neophyte in this area is to get acquainted with the terms and expressions common to bridal embellishments, including a fabric's "hand" (textile talk for its distinct feel), bridal passementerie (unadorned to elaborate trimmings), the enhancement concept (how and where embroidery and beading pick out a design), and notions (fastenings, especially buttons). Next, expose yourself to the plausible and accessible alternatives. Familiarity with fabrics leads to an understanding of what makes one apropos for an ultraformal presentation and deems another better for an informal approach. Next, it will be helpful—as well as fun and interesting—to have an overview of the enormous variety and different properties of each available lace. The details, the finishing touches on the dress, are decided third; they include trim, enhancements, and notions, ranging from an invisible zipper to an important button back treatment. They should all compliment your figure and complete your gown, as well as confirm your wedding style (ultraformal to informal) and be harmonious with its ambience (large and lavish to small and simple) and compatible with its attitude (urban or country, indoor or outdoor) and its spirit (at-home, civil ceremony to catered, religious affair).

Your research should begin with photographs on costume design and fashion

Attention to Detail

fabric, lace, and embellishments

OPPOSITE: A heavily embroidered cutout silk with matching lining has raised, beaded appliqué rosebuds for three-dimensional focal interest.

The delicate lace appliqué rises above the wide, drop-shoulder neckline.

you. Get a hand for each fabric, for example, the slippery hand of satin, the crisp hand of taffeta, or the crunchy hand of crepe. Play with the swatches, lay them next to one another, interchange then until you come upon the harmonious combinations that you like best. Ask friends and relatives with sewing experience to look at your choices; explain the effect you wish to achieve and ask for their suggestions.

The decision concerning the trimmings comes last. Bridal trim should never be pedestrian: its very purpose is to create a special focal point—you as a bride! Go back through the photographs you have earmarked, looking at the details on the dresses you like. Make a photo collection of ideas to consider and pick up samples of the passementerie—lace, fabric, and nonfabric trim—you might like on your dress. Play with them, consider how you will use them. Think about the embellishment technique, if any, you might wish to employ: fancy embroidery stitching with exotic threads, raised embroidery treatments such as quilting, or reembroidery with beads and pearls, to name a few possibilities. Some prominent ornamental trim concepts include embellished necklines, particularly the illusionary wedding collar, standing ruched scoop, or ruffle-edged high neckline; reembroidered appliqués on panels falling from the shoulders; a bow-and-button back treatment; and lace trim on exaggerated, puffed sleeves, especially leg-of-mutton.

Every bridal gown Robert Work designs can be considered an excellent value, because Work conceives each gown with its cost in mind. He has observed that "brides-to-be—even those who would normally reject such thoughts—become voracious with detailing. It seems to take an older, more sophisticated, second-time bride," says Work, "to appreciate an elegant, high-quality

history, by leafing through bridal catalogs and tearing out pages in bridal and fashion magazines, by browsing around fabric, notions, or bridal shop windows, and by talking to experienced salespeople and dressmakers.

The fabric or lace on your wedding dress that makes the biggest impact requires your attention first. It is crucial to decide on the prominently featured fabric at the outset, either because it is seen most or it has a special quality that will stand out. Your first choice must be carefully coordinated with the second, which, perhaps, will be a simpler or flatter fabric used on the skirt or sleeves.

Collect swatches of fabrics that appeal to

fabric and understated, romantic lace trim. In short, subtle details speak more eloquently than busy, bejeweled embellishments and lavishly enhanced lace appliqués.

"Begin with a clean look. Then see if—and where—an addition is wanted. Most brides-to-be select a certain specific trim, such as satin, lace, or self-fabric rosettes. If that is the case, each rose should be treated with importance, set off beautifully, perhaps with embroidery for dimension, and placed on a wonderful scallop, ribbon, or soutache [braid] border trim." Work concludes on a cautionary note: "If the detailing is complex, more time should be allotted for the gown to be completed; in addition, time may be required for each layer to be altered."

Every aspect of your personal adornment, particularly each detail on your wedding dress, should be far more special, elaborate, and individual than on any everyday outfit you wear. No matter how appropriately your wedding-dress style harmonizes with your wedding ambience, or its components balance your physical proportions, the ingredient that creates the unmistakable aura

A contrast of lightness and density.

of a radiantly beautiful, happy bride is the special combination of fabric and lace, passementerie, a design concept for the enhancements, and notions.

The fabric, trimmings, and notions markets are your bridal gown's best resource—and what a choice of styles and colors they supply! What exists is virtually endless; what does not can be custom-made. While no gown needs it all—and many need very little—the wedding dress you purchase, even if understated, should have its unique, strategically placed focal points.

Fabrics—The Goods' Hand

Bridal-wear fabric cycles tend to be long. Silk satin, transparent net weaves, and lace, after all, have remained the bridal fabrics of choice for hundreds of years. Bridal-wear fabric production, however, has undergone a revolution during the past few decades. Prior to this, only a few changes have occurred since cavewomen formed crude needles to sew pelts together. The ancient Middle Easterners, primarily Egyptians, Persians, and Syrians, developed spun fibers and woven fabrics and introduced ornamental embroi-

A lace motif of pearls repeats itself on an elongated sheer sleeve.

Silk damask and Chantilly lace.

BRIDAL FABRICS

Fabrics for bridal wear are differentiated by their most distinguishable characteristics, which can include the weave—a smooth or textural quality; the weight—heavy to light; the luminous properties—high-luster (shiny) to deluster (dull); the thickness—one-ply (thin) to six-ply (thick); translucency—opaque, sheer, or transparent; and the pattern—woven or embossed, if applicable.

A simple twist in silk organza.

The ultratraditional bridal fabric is a pure silk (smooth and lustrous) weave, including the full-bodied and heavy *duchess* satin. There are also a softer, flexible *Charmeuse* and a backed satin, called *crepe-backed;* the stiffest textured satin weave, *panne;* and a dull, nubbed-surface *antique* satin. The second classification of traditional silk bridal weave is *taffeta* (smooth and glossy texture) along with the mellower *peau de soie,* a combination of taffeta and satin.

There are many less-used, though classic, Old World fabrics to explore, in addition to ultratraditional bridal weaves. These heavier-weight silk and wool weaves include *ottoman,* a shiny finish with a cord or ridges; *faille,* with equal thin ribs in the yarn; and *grosgrain,* a thicker, irregular, crosswise rib of cord. Other coarser, irregular raw silk or bouclélike (looped and knotted surface) silk weaves include *shantung,* with a slightly irregular shiny weave of raw silk or silk blend; the closely related but lighter *douppioni,* with threads of uneven size and weight spun together; *pongee,* an unbleached silk with a rough woven surface that requires an underlining for stiffening; *cloque,* a heavier, spongelike hammered texture; and *matelassé,* a springier, bubbly textured weave. And finally, there is a wool or cashmere *jersey,* which is fine-combed yarn plain-knitted into an elastic, ribbed fabric.

Velvet, originally a silk but now exclusively a silk and rayon blend, has a high sheen with a short pile that drapes loosely. The five most popular velvets are cut, which is soft, flat, and shiny, with a burned-out pattern; brocaded, which has an embossed pattern; panne (not to be confused with panne satin), which has an extra-high sheen with irregular watermarks; the heaviest of all, crushed velvet, with regular watermarks; and translucent velvet, which is lightweight, reflects light, and becomes somewhat iridescent. An all-cotton velvet is called velveteen.

There are several similarly woven silk, cotton, or blended patterned *brocades* with interwoven raised designs, including *damask,* with a lustrous, reversible figured pattern; the multicolored *Jacquard,* a lustrous and dull contrast, with a medallion pattern; and *moiré* silk taffeta with its smooth luster and waterlike patterns.

The lightweight linen, cotton, or silk weaves are *batiste,* a fine, often sheer cotton in a plain or figured pattern; *eyelet,* a pattern of regular, reembroidered holes; cotton *organdy,* almost transparent but

Heavy brocade with drop pearls.

crisply textured; its silk match, *organza,* with a soft or stiff finish, which can be reembroidered with a dot or a motif; and *gazzara,* a satin-faced organza with a plain weave.

Along with bridal *tulle* (sheer, stiffened mesh), there are repeat-pattern net fabrics, such as *point d'esprit, English net, Swiss dot,* and *French meshes* with large or small, simple or tufted dots, ovals, squares, or diamonds on a net or tulle background. There are also several *illusionary* (plain, fine, and transparent) fabrics, including *chiffon*—sheer cotton, with a soft or stiff finish, and the synthetic-fiber, chiffon-textured *georgette; voile,* which is lighter; and *gauze*—transparent, loosely woven, and lighter still; two-, four-, or six-ply *crepe,* lustrous and noted for its drapable, filmy quality; or the lighter, shinier, and smoother *crepe de Chine.*

Three tucks at an organza hem.

dery; then for one thousand years there were few changes, excluding new woven designs and far-reaching innovations with dyes. In the eleventh and twelfth centuries, elaborate weaves with gold and silver thread were created. The Industrial Revolution brought the single major contribution to cloth and fabrics for a bride as handspun natural fibers, including wool, silk, linen, and cotton, were inexpensively manufactured by machines into cloth blends.

More recently, modern synthetic fibers were introduced into the established cloth weaves and bridal fabrics were radicalized. While the quality of some 100 percent polyester or manmade fibers such as rayon, nylon, and acetate are far less desirable than the natural fibers they imitate, their use as a backing, as in rayon-backed silk-faced satin, provides a stronger, less costly, wrinkle-free alternative to natural fibers. Also, a low percentage of manmade fibers blended with natural fibers enhances a silk weave's qualities considerably—for example, a gown of slipper satin or polished taffeta, both silk and acetate blends, retains its shape like no other.

An array of modern blends is being used to create new and interesting fabrics that are subtly different from classic blend combinations and classic weaves in their texture and application. Rayon and wool yarns have been devised that are fine enough to create ethereal, airlike goods, unknown seventy-five years ago. Don't be afraid of a new or little-known novelty fiber, such as fibranne, used in tandem with silk, cotton, or wool; its qualities may be just what your wedding dress needs to be soft and supple enough.

Until recently, bridal-fabric formality was classified by its weave: supple, finely spun silk fibers were considered most suitable for evening wear, and thicker cotton, wool, or linen for less formal occasions. In the con-

temporary fashion sense, fabric use crosses the old formality lines and unique applications are common. For instance, denim, a coarse cotton devised a hundred years ago to endure hard labor, dirt, and strong detergents, is used today in both street suits and haute evening dresses, while chiffon, crepe, and tulle (the most nighttime of all fabrics) are worn casually and to trim sweatshirts. Almost without exception, though, the fabric of a contemporary wedding dress will be more deluxe, dressy, and intricate than any fabric worn every day.

A lightweight brocade is given added punch by running a silver Lurex thread throughout.

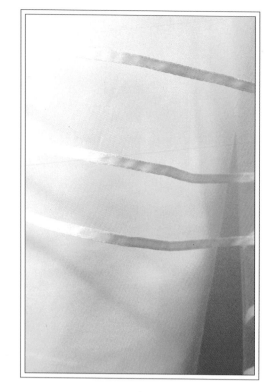

The Uses and Effects of Fabrics

The construction, the look, and the formality of a wedding dress are determined to a great extent by the choice of fabric. Generally, a smooth, luminous satin or taffeta is closely associated with formal, evening bridal gowns whereas a duller, textured fabric—say, organza or shantung—can be considered just as fancy but more compatible with a less formal afternoon wedding. Just as certain fabrics work better in a particular setting, they also work best on certain figures and for particular design concepts. For example, a flowing gown needs a fabric that drapes well, so a four-ply (fairly thick) silk chiffon, crepe, or Charmeuse would be used; a knife-edge look requires a crisp, silk taffeta or crepe-backed satin hand, although they wrinkle easily.

All fabrics, including the long-standing bridal gown staples (satin, taffeta, and tulle, or organza and organdy for summertime) are produced in every quality and price range, from an expensive pure silk or cotton to a mid-range natural and polyester fiber blend to a low-end 100 percent polyester with its unmistakable blue-white hue and high sheen. Heavier and more expensive fabrics, especially pure silk satin or velvet, are typically used for fall and winter, while lightweight, sheer fabrics, like crepe and gazzara, are more springlike. However, sophisticated air-conditioning and heating systems have almost eliminated seasonality, and while sheer allover organza may still be somewhat out of place in January, it is acceptable to wear tulle at all times. Less expensive transitional fabrics, which are usually natural and polyester fiber blends—say, georgette—can be worn year-round. This allows a bride-to-be who falls in love with a pure silk gown to substitute fabrics, bringing the gown into her price range.

Each season a few new and appropriate fabric concepts are introduced by bridal-wear designers as other fabrics fall into temporary disuse: jersey one year, douppioni the next, and so forth. Demand for these fabrics can reach a rage pitch, then brides-to-be are once again drawn back to the perennial favorite—smooth silk weaves. "Each ambience has to be treated differently," says talented bridal-wear designer Ron LoVece. "Whether I am creating a formal or less formal gown, I concern myself with the gown's design elements, but just as much thought goes into the right fabric. Often, more than one is used. Coordinating fabrics with a similar formality is one route, while combining a formal with a less formal fabric takes a gown into another direction.

"An off-the-shoulder neckline in organza, for example, sets off a semiformal bride beautifully at a luncheon following an early afternoon ceremony. The same dress with satin would be more in keeping at a small black-tie affair in a ballroom. For an informal ambience, I use cotton organdy and piqué eyelet. In the evening for a dressy wedding, tulle or reembroidered organza are well suited, even at a small gathering. But how the fabric is used is also a contributing factor. A great big bishop sleeve in reembroidered organza with a satin cuff is certainly appropriate in the afternoon; the bride would be reminiscent of Katharine Hepburn in *The Philadelphia Story* or Grace Kelly in *High Society*. The same sleeve in satin would enable the bride to comfortably wear the gown late in the afternoon as well as throughout an evening reception."

At an informal afternoon wedding, for instance, followed by a small civil ceremony and a lunch in the private dining room of a restaurant, either a linen dress coordinated with a cotton lace jacket or a reembroidered organza jacket, which is see-through, coordinated with a linen skirt would be quite appropriate. A completely esoteric and diametrically opposed example, appropriate only for a formal evening wedding, would be an all-tulle shadow ombre (graduated colors, ivory to white to blush) twisted, knotted, and wrapped around the bodice, draping to a full skirt and extending into a royal train.

Important considerations in choosing a fabric are its weight and capabilities. Duchess satin, the richest and most deluxe, tends to make a heavier bride even wider, because it is shiny and plain. So does chiffon, particularly on the hips, even though it is filmy and drapes beautifully. "Shantung, on the other hand, is like air and can be shaped into anything," advises New York couturiere Candice Solomon. "Any illusionary fabric, such as tulle, point d'esprit, dotted Swiss cotton, organza, or organdy, makes the body look smaller. A bridal gown's full skirt or snug, form-fitted, sculpted bodice quality can be created by overlaying one fabric or several fabrics as well. This gives form and

Heavily reembroidered ribbon lace with oversized, sheer, and drooping off-the-shoulder ruffle neckline and matching satin edge.

shape to a gown; moreover, layering fabrics also creates textural dimension without necessarily adding bulk.

"Combining two or more fabrics effectively is far more complex than merely placing one on top of another: only perfect mates can be placed together and create a balance," continues Solomon. "Each fabric should be equal in quality, though not necessarily the same color, weight, or weave. A see-through crinoline layered with tulle netting and lace skirt has an ethereal, dressmaker feeling; a bride literally seems to be floating into the church and down the aisle."

Using a novel fabric or layering more than one fabric is always a personal statement. Furthermore, it takes a bride with a unique personality to wear an unconventional fabric, and a developed fashion sense to pair it with a traditional one—for example, a rayon organdy camisole or cashmere camilla underneath a man-tailored baby wale corduroy or lace jacket, or a denim wedding dress trimmed in white lace. "Over the years, fabrics come in and go out of style," says Barbara Tober of *Bride's*. From her vantage point at the epicenter of the bridal world, she suggests three out-of-the-ordinary, contemporary fabric choices for consideration.

The extra dimension of layered lace with scattered crystal beads.

"There have been incredible jersey and linen wedding dresses. Yes, they wrinkle, but who cares? It could be heavy linen or handkerchief linen. Linen would probably be more appropriate for a morning or afternoon ceremony and jersey, which is slinkier and sexier looking, would feel more comfortable in a hotel ambience. And after umpteen years of exercise, there is now a demand for a third unique choice: see-through fabric, specifically designed for bridal wear. Obviously, not everyone can wear these—what is underneath has to be extremely appealing! But as harem-style pants with a jacket, the layers create an increasingly less see-through effect, but still, bareness remains on the arms and legs."

Laces—A Long-standing Tradition

Lace is a decorative openwork fabric created by looping, braiding, interlacing, knotting, or twisting cotton, silk, wool, nylon, or other type of thread to form a picture, design

motif, or floral pattern on a ground or back-ground. The motifs or patterns are joined by bars called, ironically enough, brides. Bridal lace employs the lacemaking technique referred to as needlepoint or point lace, where a single thread holds the design outline onto a background entirely worked with a needle; a bolder outline requires a visible, heavier thread, the cordonnet.

While many decorative embroidery, reembroidery, knitting, and crochet styles create lacelike fabrics, they are not considered lace because they were not created by a lacemaking technique; neither are knit or openwork fabrics made on a loom, such as reembroidered organza, fancy patterned meshes, or a brocaded gauze, however exquisite they may be.

The art of lacemaking could be said to have invented itself as thrift-conscious medieval women knotted a frayed sleeve or neck or hem threads together in order to continue wearing an older garment. Lacemaking developed further in Europe during the fifteenth century; what began as a cottage craft blossomed into prosperous commerce between the feudal city-states of the period. Each region, particularly Venice, Antwerp, and Brussels, had distinct techniques, specialties, patterns, or designs; but as the Italian and Flemish varieties became coveted as signs of affluence and symbols of power, lace was reserved exclusively for royalty and the clergy.

By the sixteenth century, sumptuary laws were passed in France and Italy limiting the quantity, size, and amount of personal adornment as well as restricting when and where commoners, merchants, and even the noble class could be seen wearing proper lace in public. Brides were excluded from these restrictions, so bridal or carnival lace (distinguished by its ciphers, crest, or armorial bearings) became a bridal tradition.

The Industrial Revolution brought a loom on which lace could be inexpensively manufactured, and demand immediately surged. Modern laces are copied from the original regional styles, employing similar patterns and lacemaking techniques. Except for very expensive imported laces, which are all cotton, most modern lace is made of nylon netting embroidered with a rayon and nylon blend cording and reembroidered with a rayon cordonnet for additional sheen. There are several widely used modern bridal laces with distinct properties, many regional fa-

Reembroidered alençon lace with tiny silk satin rosettes randomly scattered.

BRIDAL LACES

Laces are categorized by their design or pattern, whether flat or raised, the thickness of the yarn, and the method of manufacture. Certain laces are used as an allover fabric; others are ornamental braids, trims, or borders. Few modern laces are handmade or even of natural fibers; most are machine-made of rayon threads and nylon net.

The most common lace, *alençon*, is a mesh lace combining architecturally arranged swags, neat and precise classic bells, hearts, geometric, and floral designs. The shapes are outlined with a heavier cordonnet thread. Its elaborate pattern laid flat is sufficient to convey elegance and beauty, and it is often reembroidered over the cordonnet for further dimension.

By comparison, *Chantilly* is also flat, but softer and more pliable, so it drapes better. Its close association with love and romance stems from its elaborate patterns of scrolls and floral designs caught, as if suspended in air, by flowering ribbon bands. A popular Chantilly lace is *poi d'ainge*, face of an angel.

Venise is a heavy embroidery on a plain ground known for its draping, three-dimensional, repeated floral design. It is manufactured on metal looms and machines by punching sections out and weaving fine threads and thicker cording.

Guipure was originally made with bullion, threads of gold or silver. Over time, guipure became the generic term for the heavier tape or Venise laces with a mature-looking spirit.

Ribbon lace has large floral or swirling patterns formed by a coarse ground held together by interconnected threads, with narrow ribbon stitched along the repeated vermicelli, serpentine, and swirling patterns and designs.

Schiffli is embroidery on fabric with cord, made by continuously threading until a fine floral or medallion design is repeated. The patterns are traditional bridal motifs, such as swags, garlands, or scalloped edging. It is made on a schiffli machine, embroidered on a chemically prepared *plauen* lace ground, woven, burnt, and cut.

Lyon is a malines (gauzelike) lace, which is characterized by hand-run silk or mercerized (glossy) cotton outlining its floral design.

Brussels lace has a cordonnet edging on its pattern. Modern patterns have separated flowers, which are used as appliqués laid flat on top of the fabric, and as an allover lace.

Battenberg lace can be traced back to the Renaissance period. It has a floppy edge made of big loops of tape caught by twisted brides drawn across wide spaces.

Many embroidery and reembroidery stitches, knitting and knotting styles, are lacelike, although they are not manufactured by a lace-making technique. The similar handcrafted, ornamental openwork fabrics, though not on a ground or background, include *tatting*, which is threadwork; *macramé*, whose patterns are formed by knotting bunches and crosswise threads; and *needlepoint*, whose buttonhole and blanket stitches are sewn on a paper pattern.

vorites, numerous custom-made variations, and some unique varieties that have been temporarily forgotten. Although an undeniable difference exists in the quality, price, craftsmanship, and designs between an antique lace made by machine and new machine-made lace, modern laces created on old looms with new fibers provide a viable and reasonably priced alternative.

THE USES OF BRIDAL LACE

The true artistry and magic of a lace manifests itself when a designer transposes it onto a gown and makes a subtle, lavish, romantic, traditional, or unique design statement. Depending on its eventual use and placement, a sheer to opaque backing gives even the flimsiest lace strength for use as an allover fabric. Two complementary laces may be combined to highlight a design motif, or several may be collaged—harmoniously laid next to one another—to create a unique all-lace blend of texture, dimension, and hue. And nothing else reads "bridal" quite like lace when it is used as a trim—appliqués (sewn onto the fabric) and cutouts (the fabric underneath removed for a see-through effect).

From a background steeped in antebellum traditions, including an appreciation for handiwork, Pat Kerr began designing her dolls' clothing at five years old, then designed her first communion and confirmation dresses. As a teenager, she designed her school dresses and party dresses, which were followed by her prom and debutante dresses. Eventually, Kerr designed her own wedding dress. "I was always impatient and never wanted to look like anyone else," she admits. "A seamstress did the sewing, but I selected the fabrics and learned to cut them freehand, and I discovered that lace has a unique capacity to create a mood. Though

Beaded alençon(center), Venise(top left), schiffli(bottom left), Chantilly(top right), and alençon (bottom right) lace.

Silk moiré with pearl-enhanced floral lace appliqué.

partly religious, much of lace's aura is its connection with romance, expressed with lace hearts and flowers; tradition, with bells; luck, with horseshoes and four-leaf clovers; and fertility, with wheat. Nothing else comes close to giving a bride as glorious an aura or can surround her face as well as a handmade antique lace."

As a drawing, painting, and art history student, Kerr became fascinated with lace design, and was a serious textile collector by the 1960s. Developing a network of sources for handmade lace throughout London, the mecca of artistic lacemaking, Kerr searched for high-quality, handmade pieces at factories and estate auctions. "I bought the best examples I could find and incorporated these museum-quality laces into my own wardrobe, never putting a scissors to them. In the late seventies when I began my fashion collection, the laces were based around these incomparable nineteenth-century lace designs, which, of course, were high-end and custom-made," says Kerr about her inspiration—antique lace.

"The laces I combine on a gown cross both centuries and borders, to make a bride-to-be look fabulous," Kerr continues. "Even a low-cut bodice or sexy, see-through lace back treatment will allow a bride her allure; she always appears charming and gracious. Under the right circumstances, a skirt can have one hundred lace pieces and still remain simple if collaged to accentuate the positive or eliminate a negative aspect of a figure. I think of each design element on a wedding dress as a canvas on which to display the lace. The outside-to-outside points serve as a frame for the eyes, so a well-placed vertical line can visually reduce a wide torso. An opaque, overall dress fabric used as long sleeves tends to widen a bride, but a break at the elbow with alternate sheer lace sleeves has the opposite effect. A paneled bodice,

Matching lace embroidery and appliqués form a traditional wedding collar and illusion neckline.

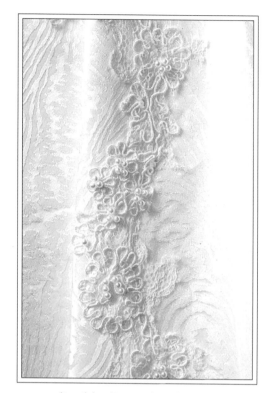

even a fitted bodice with collaged lace—in a vertical direction—reduces the body size further."

Bridal-wear experts estimate that 70 percent of all ready-made and custom-made wedding dresses sold are satin, about 10 percent are taffeta, and the remaining dozens of classic fabric weaves contribute another 10 to 12 percent. Only a small fraction of all bridal gowns are allover lace. Such a wedding dress is unique and will always be considered a very strong, sophisticated statement. As an allover fabric treatment, lace creates a beautiful and special wedding dress, though no more formal than a satin weave. A simple, A-line silhouette to the knee with a modest sleeve and neckline in allover lace seems fancier than an opaque fabric, as well as more festive. It would also be suitable as a semiformal organdy gown at an evening wedding, or as an informal organdy dress outside in the daylight. An allover lace dress can appear spunkier and perhaps sportier at a second-wedding ceremony, or it can give a sophisticated look for an older bride-to-be.

"Any allover-lace silhouette with a long skirt looks very formal," says allover-lace wedding-dress designer par excellence Mr. Butch. "Unless it is white or ivory, depending on the skin color of the bride-to-be, and includes another traditional bridal element or trim, such as a grand train or an embellished neckline, an allover-lace dress looks more like a special-occasion evening dress than a wedding dress. Every allover-lace wedding dress is backed with a fabric that gives the lace enough stability and body, yet allows it to retain its pretty, lacelike—fluid and filmy—quality without absorbing the characteristics of its lining. Yet a puffy sleeve should be able to stand up or out. If a backed reembroidered alençon lace seems too heavy or textural as a full-skirted ball gown, especially for a petite bride-to-be, a lighter, delicate Chantilly may prove a better choice. The most dramatic choice, even on the simplest bodice, moreover, is a reembroidered

ribbon lace with its interwoven, textural rosette pattern. Somewhat less dramatic are the vermicelli designs."

Most silhouettes and components are adaptable to an allover-lace dress. Prominent seams showing across the shoulder or at the neckline do not lend themselves to a scalloped edge, but an off-the-shoulder neckline with a bow or cap sleeve or an exaggerated leg-of-mutton sleeve is perfect for allover lace. "When any allover-lace wedding-dress construction technique is evident," Mr. Butch continues, "the dress appears far less elegant. Ideally, the lace and its lining should move separately. This construction technique requires extensive hand-stitching. A high-quality allover-lace wedding dress merely lies over its backing, each layer conforming exactly to the other; they are not stitched together, except where absolutely necessary—the neckline, armhole, or fastener only. A less expensive allover-lace wedding dress is stitched onto the backing, so two layers become one fabric. Every seam and dart on a better-made allover-lace dress is made separately from its lining. Finally, the seams and darts can remain exposed on the right side, or the seam allowance can be cut away and the seam concealed by overlaying small lace sections, such as petals on a floral pattern. An allover-lace wedding dress should appear as though it was continuous around the bride."

Trimmings—Fabric and Lace

Because so many traditional bridal gowns are satin or taffeta with lace trimmings, any bride-to-be selecting another fabric or combining and blending fabrics will immediately appear to be in a more personalized gown. A second creative option, though, is to develop a unique look with the trimmings you in-

A drop jewel neckline has the simplicity of a T-shirt.

Crystal-pleated, bias-cut ruffles trail asymmetrically.

Bias-cut fabric strips cage a shell of lace.

Swirling silk sewn on silk shantung.

Reembroidered organza with bugle beads.

BRIDAL PASSEMENTERIE

Bridal passementerie is the term applied to any prefabricated or custom-made trim on a wedding dress, whether of the same fabric as the gown (self-fabric), a coordinated fabric or lace (typically alençon, Venise, or schiffli), or nonfabric (a feather, for one).

There are four bridal passementerie categories. The first is an *edge* running along a seam or defining a boundary—for instance, a band separating the skirt or sleeve from the bodice. *Border trims* (technically an edge, they are placed where a fabric ends) are commonly referred to as a hem. The second category is *embroidery*, the art of elaborately decorating fabric with ornamental designs using a needle and colored yarn, floss, soft cotton, silk, or a metallic (bullion) thread, and reembroidery, which is fancy stitches over an embroidered surface. The third, *appliqués*, are any addition sewn—usually reembroidered, but iron-ons exist—to the gown. And last are *fabric treatments* directly on the gown fabric, using additional fabric or lace, or fancy stitches on the fabric, which is raised embroidery.

EDGING is either a narrow lace, cord, or woven band used to bind or outline a section of fabric. The styles include *piping*, a narrow strip of cloth or cording folded on the bias, and stitched along seams; *swags* or *garlands*, moldinglike, draping ornamental fabrics or entwined nonfabric materials; *fringe*, a pendant of twisted cords or hanging threads bound at one end to hang singly or in groups; or *tassel*, an embossed or flat-surface fringe usually found ending a belt zipper pull and occasionally attached as an appliqué. The woven band edgings are *braid*, silver or pearl frogs or Brandenburg cording; *coronation* braiding, mercerized cord that alternates between wide and narrow; *couching*, flat and worked with minute metallic thread stitches; *diamanté*, fake sparkling jewels sewn on strips of fabric; *embroidered*, tape with rosebuds or another motif at regular intervals; *hercules*, several braids used together; *ladder*, open cross-stitches or bars; *galloon*, any very narrow band, sometimes with metallic yarn or threads added; *gimp*, heavy yarn arranged in a raised pattern; *rattail*, a silk tubular shape; *rickrack*, several zigzag widths; and *soutache*, narrow flat border or allover pattern of mohair or silk.

A *border* trim gives a wedding dress its finished look. Each effect, whether at the cuff, neckline, or skirt bottom, makes a unique statement; it can add to an air of simplicity or increase the dress's formality. Unadorned *hems* are created by turning under the fabric, concealing the initial fold, and securing it with stitches. A *French* hem uses the wrong side of the fabric and a *rolled* hem, the right side; a *lingerie* hem creates a tiny puffed edge; a *marrow* stitch, prevalent on sheer fabrics such as tulle, organdy, voile, and chiffon, uses three threads; and a *shell* hem is a shallow, scalloped one formed by an overhand stitch at regular intervals.

Scalloped edges, a graceful series of curves, *fabric treatments*, and *edgings* are also used as a fabric or lace border treatment, and are then further enhanced—for example, a ribbon border, an appliquéd border, or ruffled-lace border. In addition, there is nonfabric border trimming of every description—fur, feather, fringe, braid, semiprecious or precious stone, and the like.

EMBROIDERY is a variety of fancy needlework techniques applied to fabric or lace. Embroidery stitches are also used to secure appliqués and cutouts onto a fabric (employing tiny *raccroc* stitches), to reembroider enhancements onto fabric and lace, and to create fabric treatment effects, for instance, *petit point*'s slanting *byzantine* stitch, which fills in the background canvas.

Wheat sheaves on a gathered bodice.

The decorative embroidery stitches most often found on wedding dresses include *basket weaves*—*basket* stitch, consisting of a diagonal needlepoint stitch, and the straight, long, parallel *satin* stitch; *crewelwork*—*bundle* stitch, resembling a small bowknot made by taking three or four loose stitches side by side, placing a stitch across at the center, then drawing them together, and *French knots*, in which embroidery floss is looped around the needle, which is then pulled through, forming a small ball of yarn at the surface. Also often used are *cross-stitches*—which are groups of stitches, including a *cable* and *chain* stitch forming connected links; *couching*, a long stitch with tiny tight stitches surrounding it; an *oriental* stitch, a long, straight series of parallel stitches with short diagonal stitches at the center of each; and the closely related *petit point* stitch, using paired threads. Also are *featherwork*—a group of stitches forming a distinct pattern, including *blanket* or *purl* stitches, which are a series of interconnected letter U's; *cross-stitches*, forming letter X's; *fagoting*, consisting of a double row of the letter V side by side (used to join two fabric edges together in an openwork effect); *huckaback* stitch, creating a zigzag border; *hemstitch*, which is parallel threads drawn and fastened together with groups of vertical threads, forming an hourglass figure; and the *honeycomb* stitch, resembling a row of diamond-shaped stitches.

A lace appliqué.

APPLIQUÉS, the third category, are any fabric or design form—a bow or garland is an example of each—that attaches directly onto the gown's fabric. The three most popular nonlace appliquéd bridal passementeries are *ribbons*, narrow fabric strips, usually silk with selvage (finished) edges to prevent raveling, that hang straight or are curved, referred to as sculptured; *bows*, narrow or wide ribbons knotted with a loop or loops; and *flowers* of every variety and size, both real and artificial. Ribbons, bows, and flowers can be fashioned from the gown's fabric or a contrasting weave—especially a crosswise rib called *grosgrain*; small thread loops and knots called *picot*; a cut-pile surface, *velvet*; and a smooth-faced *satin*. The alternative ornamental trims include a *medallion*, which is an oval or round design on fabric; *streamers*, which are several ribbons sliced into narrow strips that extend or flow; and a *cockade*, which is a ribbon rosette originally worn on a hat to indicate rank, office, or a form of military or civil service.

The perennial bridal favorite, of course, is lace appliqués. These narrow to wide designs and slim to broad sections have short net threads left hanging to be sewn directly onto the gown or to be applied onto shoes or a handbag. A lace cutout is any appliqué with the underneath fabric removed, creating a see-through effect to another fabric, underlining, or skin (the most beautiful accent for lace). The most popular lace appliqué motifs are a series of scallops or curves; circular segments, like one edge of a shell; cameo designs with a central motif surrounded by a symmetrical, outlining pattern; and medallions, a large subject set in a circular or oval frame or design.

Satin ribbon streamers.

A horizontally bias-shirred bodice.

A lace-enhanced bow.

A basket weave front-plate.

FABRIC TREATMENTS

Fabric treatments that use the gown's own fabric are the following: *folding* (turned back over itself), *pleating* (repeated folds), *plaiting* (braided folds), *tucking* (horizontal folds), *gathering* (drawn together), or *shirring* (parallel gathering).

Other fabric treatments create an effect with additional fabric and include *ruffles*—pleated or folded, sheer or opaque fabric strips gathered along one edge, or cut in a curve to produce a rippled or frilled effect; and *ruching*—a strip of silk, crepe, or chiffon, pleated or gathered at the neckline or waist and stitched through the center to form a ruffle on both sides. When ruching or a ruffle is used for a curved area, the fabric is cut on the bias—diagonally across the grain—to create the narrow strips or a flouncy addition. This gives the fabric added pliability when covering the raw edge at a curve, and allows the ruching or ruffle to cling closely along the neckline, for instance.

A *gimp*, another treatment, is any narrow fabric, lace, or other material with a wire or coarse cord running through. These fabric treatments are often used as borders on the hips (*furbelows*, if fussy enough), neckline (a *jabot*, if horizontal and biblike), waist (waistband, sash, or belt), wrist (a *gauntlet*, if covering the hand), skirt (gored, overskirt, pannier, or flounce), or panel (a *godet*, if adding fullness).

The last variety of fabric treatment is *raised embroidery*, which uses more than one fabric and forms a pattern by employing fancy stitches. These fabric-addition treatments are *quilting*, which uses fine running stitches or machine stitches made through two thicknesses of material with a lightweight padding between to give a raised or puffed effect, or to outline a background; and *smocking*, decorative stitching holding fullness in a regular square or diamond pattern after elaborate gathering of the fabric. This usually forms a honeycomb or diamond pattern.

Ribbon embroidery.

clude. The additional decorative elements may be made of the same fabric as your gown or of a coordinated fabric, lace, or any number of nonfabrics, such as feathers, flowers, and fur (considered the most chic bridal trim, worn by duchesses and countesses on their bridal gowns for generations).

Your trim, its size, placement, and textural quality, should enhance rather than detract from the wedding-dress style, create a focal point, and balance its overall proportions. There are several factors to consider when choosing the trimmings for your bridal ensemble: How are the proportion and balance of your wedding dress affected when a trim is added? Does the trim affect its formality? Do its style, color, and mood match your personality and wedding ambience? How will the trim work with the direction and spirit of your wedding dress? Will greater support for your gown be necessary to preserve its basic form? (There can be some degree of difficulty carrying a gown encumbered by heavy interlining structure, fabrics, and additional trim, so decide whether you want to forgo being carefree to appear in a very structured aura for the sake of trimmings.) Finally, if adjusting the trimmings on a ready-to-wear wedding dress, it is imperative that a prefabricated trim match its style and color.

WELL-WORN TRIMMINGS

Many elements, including style and fabric, affect a wedding dress's formality. The trim placement and luster will confirm any degree of formality while creating importance; the right trim will also balance imperfections in the shape of your silhouette—hips, bust, or overall proportions. This is not to say a very formal gown must have excessive or elaborate embellishments or that a perfectly simple dress with subtle detailing cannot be formal.

But the more a detail stands out, the more formal the dress becomes. Flat seams on a basque or princess waistline's two front seams, for example, are informal; a fancy embroidered cord piping would create a semiformal air; and a diamanté braid would give it a formal aura. However, if that degree of detail accentuates your hips too much, piping placed at the neckline or hemline instead of the hips would lend the formal effect and avoid that problem.

In general, the bigger an embellishment—say, a bow—the more formal it appears, as long as the bow remains in proportion to the dress and you; beyond that, the bow becomes fanciful. On a matte faille dress, a small self-fabric rosette is informal and a larger rosette would be somewhat semiformal because it stands out more; yet a small lustrous satin rosette would appear to be semiformal, and a cluster of small satin rosettes would be more formal. If self-fabric petals are picked out with couching stitches, the rosette would be informal; using embroidery on the entire flower would be more formal still.

The degree of formality can be reinforced by the type of trim, its placement, amount, and treatment. Adding a border can make a simple dress into something fancier; especially with a large border at the neckline and hem, the same dress can become quite formal. A deeper scallop will appear more formal than a shallow scallop; however, a shallower scallop with embroidery can be far more formal than any flat, deep scallop. Another commonsense matter is the effect size and color can have. A similar treatment can range from quiet and sensitive to fanciful or playful, depending on its color or size. A ribbon falling about your shoulders or placed at your waist becomes focal interest, moving the eye or creating an illusion of importance wherever needed. It can be decoratively em-

Beaded and formed self-fabric rosettes, lace cutouts, and appliqués trimming satin.

broidered; when a shimmering golden bullion thread is woven into a white fabric, it adds a formal but warm glow to your skin.

Finishing off your wedding dress with the right trim is essentially a question of objectives. Any fabric treatment, large or small, appliqué, bow, tucking, or quilting, will increase bulk to some degree, but at the shoulder it also adds stature. Adding a contrast nearer the neckline, perhaps a ruffle with a colorful edge, makes you appear taller (provided you have a long enough neck to accommodate it).

"Certain trim types and styles flatter some figures better than others," says Michel Piccione, the chief designer of Alfred Angelo and design supervisor for Dior bridal gowns. "Petite brides easily look encumbered; they are best carrying delicate, simple, and small-scale trimming, with limited embroidered details added. Likewise, a large bust should have minimal design or detail embellishments, and the same for a large waist and hips. In fact, the entire bodice to the hemline on a petite bride-to-be should be kept plain, keeping any focal interest points high, preferably at the neckline, shoulders, and sleeves. A small appliqué border at the hemline or cutouts along the train can balance a similar, larger, and higher focal point trim.

"The style trimming not only personalizes your wedding dress; when coordinated it also moves your entire ensemble further in whatever direction you desire. A bodice embroidered with ribbons and a point d'esprit skirt has a distinctly Spanish feel, particularly when the yoke

A dramatic, puffed melon-shape sleeve edged in lace cutouts.

edging includes orange-blossom passementerie appliqués; they complete that mood. Shantung, the most popular textured fabric, needs less trim, as do heavy velvets or brocades, whether used alone or in tandem with a lightweight tulle layer over them, because they make a statement by themselves. An understated bride may choose a heavy silk satin or taffeta bow as a butterfly back treatment with tiny buttons to the neck, delicate lace on the bodice, and none elsewhere. A grander spirit would require an embroidered appliqué at the hemline, train, and on the bodice."

While nothing reads "bridal" as readily as a lace appliqué, when coordinated lace passementerie is combined and properly placed on a gown, something soft and pure is created. A lace bodice and French mesh skirt give a bride a lift—almost physically elongating her. If applied in a flat manner on a fitted bodice or slightly flared skirt, the design pattern provides a romantic focal interest. On the upper bodice its light, airy feeling and extraordinary beauty around the neckline of a satin gown add a magical glow and give an aura to a bride.

Although the same laces are available to each designer, no two eyes ever see a piece of lace in the same way. Therefore, no two designers select, back, cut, arrange, or combine lace appliqués with the same concept in mind. A lightweight alençon adds to the comfort of a dress material, retaining its pliability, but a lace pattern usually continues through the trimmings without introducing or mixing two patterns. "While using an alençon lace appliqué is traditional, how it is used should seem somewhat unique," says Christos, a master craftsman at adorning bridal gowns with lace. "What works on a bodice does not necessarily look right on the skirt. I prefer working with matching appliqués. For instance, I will cut and place one and then surround it with pieces from its pair. This will enlarge an alençon floral design to resemble a textured fabric, while retaining the feeling of a traditional lace."

Eve Muscio is bridal wear's undisputed mistress of lace. She was a seventeen-year-old Fashion Institute of Technology student when destiny's hand led her to Milady Bridal Gown's door. She now designs each Eve of Milady wedding dress, and is the owner as well. She believes lace trim gives a bride instant recognition, and likens lace on a wedding dress to spices in a cooking dish: "The same ingredients can be used to achieve different effects. My first wedding dress was inspired by my mother's peignoir set, which I spotted hanging on the closet door," Muscio recalls. "I trimmed its neckline and hem with a lace far different from those used on bridal wear at the time. That wedding dress was an enormous hit, and gave me the enthusiasm and momentum to continue. My inspiration using lace has always been creating a fairy princess, whether the bride-to-be is short or tall. Also, the lace placement on a gown,

especially an entire lace bodice, can accentuate the fit and slenderize the lines of a bride-to-be's body, always within the bounds of good taste, though.

"My initial problem was that the more I looked at the available laces, the less I could tell one from another: they were too similar. Early on, my employers at Milady gave me the unique opportunity to design my own lace patterns. Over the years, I have collected antique pieces, because, after all, not that much has changed over hundreds of years. Now, every dress I create has my signature lace—designed, enhanced, and placed by me. For a gown with a silhouette and style taken from the grand tradition to look special, intricate lace appliqués can be placed in a mélange or combination that creates a theme within a theme. For instance—flowers with or without stems or leaves and scrolls with curlicues."

Enhancements— Flickering Finery

Since the beginning of civilization, beads have been used both as jewelry and as ornamentation for clothing. In the distant past, beads were regarded as magical and worn for both decorative and spiritual purposes. Beading and beaded fabric as an extension of embroidery have been used to embellish bridal finery since the Middle Ages. During the Renaissance, patterns with pearls and beads were created, and the Elizabethans added other small objects liberally. In many respects,

A simple, four-tier tucked bell sleeve contrasts with heavy decorative pearling and beading on the décolletage, peplum, and street-length skirt's hem.

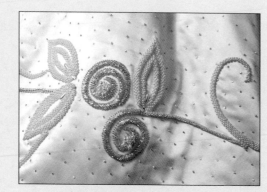

Three-dimensional glass and pearls.

Glistening rhinestone snowflakes.

Enhancement Concepts

An enhancement concept is any overall embellishment design that picks out a gown element with embroidery, and further highlights it with beads, seed pearls, pearls, sequins, rhinestones, crystal, or other materials. This can be done on a portion of the allover fabric, on a prefabricated lace or fabric appliqué, cutout, or border trim.

BEADS have a hole bored through the center of materials—such as glass, plastic, wood, crystal, or gems—and are strung on leather, cord, thread, or chain. Most are round, though some are cylindrical, square, disk-, pendant-, or oblong-shaped. The types include *aurora borealis crystal*, which is glass coated with a solution causing a rainbowlike reflection; *Austrian crystal*, which contains lead, is multifaceted and polished to reflect the full spectrum of color in both sunlight and artificial light, but may be coated on the back to reflect a blush color only, for example; *bugle beads*, which are short to long tubular-shaped glass beads, often white, gold, or silver; and *crystal beads*, which are carved out of genuine transparent quartz.

PEARLS are classified as gems. A genuine pearl used for beading is lustrous, translucent to opaque, and most often white, though faint ivory or pink are common. The four spherical pearl groups are *oriental* (natural), which develop in deep-sea oysters; *freshwater*, found in rivers and lakes; *cultured*—a tiny, artificially implanted mother-of-pearl irritant in the oyster causes a pearl to grow; and *seed pearls*, miniature, irregular-shaped genuine pearls. *Baroque* pearls, also known as chalk beads, are irregular, fan-shaped, white, freshwater pearls, but can be simulated, made of coated plastic or glass.

SEQUINS are small, shiny, iridescent disks of metal or plastic, pierced in the center and sewn on the appliqué or fabric to reflect light.

RHINESTONES are colorless, transparent artificial gems made of glass or paste, usually cut like a diamond and widely used as buttons and other evening ornamentation.

modern beading resembles these early imaginative embroidery designs. Even today in Arab countries a bride wears a single, blue talismanic bead to ward off any misfortune.

The most common bridal adornments—after lace—are pearls, followed by sequins, bugle beads, crystal, and rhinestones. Enhancing bridal lace with reembroidery was an early Victorian innovation which included pearlwork on panels. Beading, and especially crystal beads, became a popular trimming during the second half of the nineteenth century, but genuine crystal beads became so expensive by the 1930s that glass has been substituted since. Moreover, the use of pearls and seed pearls, short and long bugle beads, sequins, and teardrop pearls picking out a floral motif on a reembroidered bodice is very much a retrogression within the modern enhancement concepts oeuvre.

An enhancement concept, such as pearling or beading, can be executed either on the entire fabric, on a portion of an allover design wherever it appears, or on a section of the gown's fabric—the bodice or skirt, for instance. Or a lace appliqué can be enhanced and given dimension by a variety of delicate embroidery stitches, pearling, and beading that creates the illusion of a design individually placed rather than appearing as one element within a continuous pattern.

A heavily enhanced lace appliqué may have an additional three-dimensional quality, achieved by a bugle-bead fringe (referred to as a lampshade). Some lace appliqués are meant to be individually applied or collaged on to a wedding gown. These have a left and right side, a medallion design or pattern side. There are also fabric appliqués, like fabric ribbons and small rosettes, that do not weigh down a gown. For added dimension and appeal without disrupting the flowing aura, however, it is best to forgo lace and substi-

tute reembroidered organza or gazzara that has been superimposed with a piece of lace or fabric on top of its existing embroidery.

Less-embellished lace is more appropriate in daylight, whereas heavily encrusted lace immediately connotes an evening ceremony and a large reception. At a given point, a simple, daytime lace slip dress encrusted with pearls, bugle beads, and diamond adornments around the neck for emphasis, and random pearls on the skirt to prevent it from becoming too unwieldy, becomes more appropriate worn in the evening. If you want a very lavish dress with a lot going on, a great deal of enhanced lace can be used. For an informal or less rigid look, only a modest amount of less-adorned lace need be used on the bodice, and none elsewhere on the gown. The type of beads matters as well as the quantity when differentiating a semiformal from a formal enhancement concept, and on a contemporary bridal gown's dressiness as well, which ranges from very dressy to dressy to casual. Rhinestones can be worn in the morning or the evening on a formal or very

Exceptionally heavy patterned beading is reminiscent of a medieval doublet.

Schiffli embroidery fagoting effect embellished with bugle beads and pearls.

Artfully inserted alençon lace bodice panels (below) with antique gold thread, beading, and pearling create the impression that lace and fabric are united. The same beading technique occurs on the exaggerated overskirt's triangular, lace appliqué panel (right), again on floor-length lace cutouts, and where an enhancement concept is best seen: the set-in pyramid and cutout border of the detachable royal train (opposite).

dressy gown, but fewer would be worn in daylight or as a semiformal or dressy cocktail-like presentation. Delicate allover beading can be semiformal or formal, although heavy adornment in a single area is always quite formal. Elaborate beading on a gown is always formal, especially with any allover embroidery motif, such as enhanced rosettes.

"A daytime wedding ceremony often begins in late afternoon and continues into the evening. This calls for special consideration," says Jim Hjelm, who is referred to as Mr. Traditional Bridal Gown Designer. Hjelm believes that "as the princess on your wedding day, the same tasteful beading worn only in the evening is expected for the bride." However, he points out, "dangling beads and reflective rhinestones at a morning ceremony or reception are few people's idea of finery."

There are easy-to-apply guidelines to help you decide how much enhancement you should use. The first relates to quantity—the more it shines, the less you need; the second, to size—big wedding, big dress with more enhancements; small wedding, less of everything. Still other factors influencing an elaborate enhancement concept are the wedding party size, the number of guests, and the ambience of the ceremony and reception site. For a small wedding, when a best man, bridesmaids, and handful of guests are invited to an intimate space, a moderately ornamented cocktail dress might seem most appropriate for the evening; the same style of gown for a daytime ceremony and

reception might be embroidered with random low-luster pearls.

Christos, America's quintessential bridal-wear couturier, says, "In considering formality, a dress that I conceive as an informal presentation could become suitable at a formal wedding. The same unique placement for an alençon floral design cutout, for instance, could be on an informal outfit and reembroidered for a semiformal dress. In the evening under candlelight, if the bride wants to stand out, that same lace with a subdued pearl and sequin flower appliqué would do it, but adding crystal beads would be needed for her to stand out among five hundred guests. Personally, though, I prefer a toned-down enhancement concept to glittering embellishments.

"Another consideration is whether the trim lace is supposed to lie flat, give a fitted look to a bodice, or emphasize a draping quality. Adding beading, embroidery, or embossing increases the weight and stiffness. A heavily enhanced shoulder or sleeve acts like armor. A bride who wants a very elegant dress can opt for simple alençon trim, which has a rich pattern that does not detract from the gown's material or its ability to keep the shape and which minimizes the overall weight while giving a sumptuous air of sophistication."

Martin Price of the House of Sant' Angelo advises brides not to "fear color or extravagant beading. There is nothing wrong with it; however, you must know how to do it. This entails understanding and being able to spot—from experience or instinct—proper balance and proportion, so that everything is where it should be." He believes that "when a bride both understands her fashion statement and wants to look very much like a bride, she can really go all the way with an enhancement concept: silk flowers, bows, lace, and beading—whatever makes her happy and feel beautiful. She's the princess, but when the adornments are just saying 'bride' without an overall concept governing what, why, and where all this goes on the gown, it can be campy!

"There must be beautiful shapes underneath, and a reason for the encrustation. Then, when everything else is put on top, it hangs beautifully and the effect is complete. For example, if the heaviest encrustation lies at your bust line or higher, with everything else flowing, diminishing, disappearing, and flickering out at the borders, your dress has a visually upward lift. A border, because it is at the bottom, should have more beading, not necessarily the same type or amount—too little and it will fade away. A twinkle and highlighting that sparkles look beautiful in a photograph, too."

The most formal ornamentation concepts include sequin-covered areas enhancing pearls and reflective, aurora borealis areas highlighting teardrop stones. These adornments are reserved for important trains, back treatments, hems, or necklines. But the most

complicated enhancement concept by far coordinates an embellished bodice with a three-tier skirt and royal train. One of New York City's foremost lace merchants, Frank Senna, gives an illustration: "The beading concept could begin with an allover gold and pearl beading with bullion thread on a floral, scroll, and curlicue patterned bodice. On the midcalf apronlike overskirt, a graduated, embellished, appliquéd border picked out with pearls and bullion threads leads the eye to a central cascading cutout pyramid with randomly placed enhancing crystals. Underneath, peeking out on the floor-length tier, is a coordinated cutout border with only the flower blossoms picked out with pearling. Finally, on the royal train—where an encrusted design can be appreciated—its cutout border and larger appliquéd pyramid can be given further dimension with pearls and bullion at each flower's perimeter, and with crystals and gold beads picking out the buds."

Candice Solomon of One-of-a-Kind Brides in New York City's SoHo district, apprenticed in her mother's fashion-as-art shop revamping antique fabrics and appliqués into intricate evening-wear designs. She chose to specialize in classical wedding gowns because of the drama and attention to detail involved. "The extra weight of a skirt hem reembroidered with tiny beads allows the dress to move with the bride, and creates a magical feeling derived from the swaying, swirly swish emanating from that beaded hem—which may be heard only by the bride and her escort walking down the aisle."

Notions—The Closing Story

All clothing was initially loosely draped and held together by a belt, cinch, or pins. The first sophisticated closings consisted of leather thongs or cords, which were laced or passed through a series of slits or eyelets. Buttons, or secured disks or bones which were forced through the slits or buttonholes, led a steady progression toward modern notions, including snaps and hooks, culminating in the 1890s with the zipper, and Velcro, a twentieth-century innovation.

Notions should be considered when determining your dress's trimmings. The appropriate fastener allows a gown to fit properly and has the strength needed to hold the material closed: delicate illusion requires something different from heavy duchess satin. Hooks are used exclusively for dresses with back closings, and snaps are employed only where very little strain exists. Although it is customary for a bride to have attendants to assist, getting in or out of a wedding dress should be hassle-free. Whether to conceal a zipper to be almost invisible or to embellish the surrounding seam depends on the particular dress, the desired mood, and the overall trim concept. It is commonplace to include both a zipper for fit and decorative buttons, even numerous small ones, which have an allure as an important accessory.

Zippers, in general, create a smoother closing than buttons, snaps, or hooks. Zippers come in varying lengths, widths, and strengths of fabric, metal, and plastic. When covered by fabric, only a seamlike line with a small *pull* piece at top is seen. A decorative touch, such as a *tassel*, can be attached to the standard pull. Any wedding dress that has been dry-cleaned should have a *zipper stick* applied. This lubricates the zipper's teeth and prevents catching the fabric when it closes.

Buttons are usually placed in rows of every conceivable number, size, shape, and face or side coverings. The choices are virtually unlimited: old and new designs, shiny gold, dull pewter, white seed pearls or blush baroque pearls, big diamonds or small green emeralds. Textured, embroidered, crocheted, and beaded buttons can be used as well.

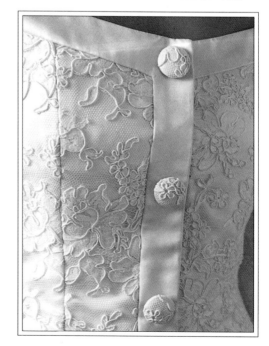

ABOVE: Self-fabric satin buttons and silk loops with a cascading lace appliqué.

❦

ABOVE RIGHT: The zipper seam disappears into an embroidered floral pattern.

❦

RIGHT: Tailored silk placket and neckline highlighted by contrasting lace-covered buttons.

A *thread* or *fabric* button has a ring, mold, or disk of thread or cloth that covers the face. When the button's face has a design cut or carved in relief, it is called a *cameo* button. The most common motif is a *flower* button made of ivory, ceramic, porcelain, or enamel. A *metal* button is either gold, silver, pewter, or gilded brass, and a *picture* button is a dull brass or white metal alloy.

Any clear or colored-glass, semiprecious or precious-stone button is a *jewel* button. These include an iridescent *pearl* or *mother-of-pearl* button, ranging from a white or pink hue to a darker color, used as an accent; a *shell* (deluster) button is either sculpted of abalone or lorry, which are off-white and ivory. Jewel buttons are set in the center with a metal rim and come in three size categories: *waistcoat* (the smallest), *Victorian*, and *Gay Nineties* (the largest). A *paste* button is glass prepared to resemble a semiprecious or precious stone; and any sparkling paste is a *strass* button, named after its inventor. They are backed with foil or metallic paint to reflect light.

Buttonholes, the openings for a button to pass through, are classified as *bound*, which are nonfunctional and purely decorative, or *worked*, which are finished by a machine-made buttonhole stitch or embroidered by hand with similar stitching. The buttonhole types are *eyelet*, round and used for buttons or laces; *piping*, which has a decorative edge; or *tailored*, with one rounded end, toward the edge of the garment, and a bar at the other end.

"Throughout the eighteenth century, young women collected 999 buttons on a string, called a charm string," say Millicent Safro and Diana Epstein, the owners of Tender Buttons, New York City's premier button emporium. "The lore surrounding the craze was that when the collection was complete, the girl would marry. All Victo-

rian buttons, but especially small genuine pearl balls, have remained a bridal tradition.

"The most common bridal button treatments of all, however, are lace-on-lace and self-fabric buttons, which blend in rather than diverting attention from the gown. In addition, a row of small buttons can be concealed by an edge coordinated to the trim, such as passementerie braid or piping.

"Large gold or jewel buttons make the grandest statement as a special contemporary accessory on a Dior suit, for instance; a row of cream or pink enamel background buttons with a painted floral design create innocence; antique porcelain buttons have a charming aura; and for romance, a miniature glass paperweight button has a built-in rosebud as its center."

A severely tailored princess-line suit with a Queen Anne collar set off with jewel buttons, a glittering detail.

A heavy taffeta ball gown with a double row of decorative crystal buttons alongside an invisible zipper.

$\mathscr{B}$efore deciding which approach will lead you to the perfect wedding dress, you must familiarize yourself with the available resources. A bridal ensemble at the opening of the twentieth century was made to order; today, a varied range of emporiums offer the bride-to-be an astounding array of choices, so having a general overview of retail bridal wear is important.

Bridal salons are specialized clothing stores and may be your first stop; the alternate routes include such retail establishments as department stores, boutiques, and antiques, rental, or costume shops. There are seamstresses, dressmakers, and designers to consider as well. Each path has its advantages. Of course, availability may be limited in your area if you live in a small-town or midsized market. The diversity in

Finding Your Good Provider

service offered is enormous too, ranging from a gruff discounter's bark of "What you see is what you get!" to the polite carriage-trade response to your questions: "Is there any more I can do for you?"

Start by defining the type of wedding dress you want: old or new. New wedding dresses and gowns can be purchased at a bridal salon, where bridal consultants assist while selecting from among manufactured and designer wedding dresses, or at a bridal rental salon that stocks wedding dresses of which dreams are made; they can be dressmade by a dressmaker or seamstress, or even a friend or relative experienced with working from a pattern, or created by a couturier (fashion designer). When choosing an old wedding dress, there are three options: an heirloom, limited by the availability of a relative or close friend with a wedding dress in the style you want to wear; an antique, which includes a wide range of authentic, handmade lace dresses and satin period gowns; or a rental, from a costume house.

Your wedding dress should not be treated as an everyday outfit worn directly

retail

bridal

wear

OPPOSITE: On a customized bridal gown as many special details as you wish can be added, such as those on this lace and pearl set-in wedding collar.

off the rack without alterations. For one thing, the blouse cannot be tucked further into the skirt. Also, if the dress is too tight it will create wrinkles; if too loose, it will drape and look like a borrowed dress. Every wedding outfit, dress, or gown must fit properly. As a bride-to-be, you need not understand each nuance of a good fit, but your dressmaker or seamstress must. A dress may be too narrow, your back too broad, or your bust too big; an experienced dressmaker or seamstress will understand which combination to alter and how much to adjust the seams, darts, or fasteners—buttons, hooks, or zippers. Beware of any dressmaker or seamstress who says, "I can do anything," since no one can do anything with the wrong-size dress. A good seamstress will tell you when something is impossible or won't look right.

Before trying on a dress, examine it to see if it is well made and that care was taken to finish it off nicely. For all intents and purposes, the insides of a $100 dress or $1,000 dress can look equally finished. (An $8,000 dress, however, should look perfect inside and out.)

On the outside (right side), each thread, button, and buttonhole should be secure and no sequin, bead, or pearl left hanging from an appliqué. It is especially important to peruse chain-stitched beading for pulled threads: one thread affects an entire row of beads, possibly on another section of the dress. Also check any area with embellishments for a lining, and be sure that hand-finished seams are perfect. Lack of either can cause unwanted irritation on your wedding day.

A well-fitted dress barely touches all the body points—bust, waist, hips—and feels good on. An overscale gown's weight and pressure should feel evenly distributed in the front and back and on the shoulders. A long hem or train should not feel as though it is pulling you backward, and a peplum should not cinch you in.

It is immediately obvious when a dress fits poorly: a portion does not lie flat and smooth or its movement is too constrictive. Each curve—convex or concave—should appear to have a gentle flow, not taut or pulled over, and should crease only slightly as you move. This is crucial at both the bust and waist.

The bodice or skirt should not pull excessively. The bust-line contour and shape should not pleat, gather, fold, or crease to the waist, a result of incorrect dart and seam placement and size. If you prefer a tight waist, be sure the dress is snug without preventing moving or walking. Both shoulders should sit well and be balanced (unless the design is asymmetrical); the sleeves should look fine and crisp at your sides, but allow forward and sideways mobility (this means at least 100 to 110 degrees of movement).

There is an easy test to determine whether the fit is proper. Raise and lower one arm, then twist your trunk a reasonable amount to the right and left as you raise your arm again. If either movement causes the bodice to pull from the armhole diagonally across the bust to the hip, or the hem to lift off the floor, the dress does not fit. The hips should feel comfortable to you—neither too full nor too tight. The precise overall length, however, is a matter of personal choice and current fashion styles.

It is important to remember that every dress style, construction, and size cannot be altered to fit every body. Adjusting the sleeves and hem length can only help to create a sense of proportion—so it is imperative to purchase a dress that suits your shape.

OPPOSITE: A contemporary Victorian-style cameo neckline, draped cotton, and lace bodice trim create an afternoon wedding dress; the gentle sweep adds a greater degree of formality.

Something Old . . . Restoring an Heirloom or Choosing an Antique

Trying on your heirloom satin wedding gown indicates how that gown looks on you as well as whether the seams are secure and the detailing intact. After years in storage, however, a worthwhile fabric condition—within *your* acceptable-to-wear range—can only be accurately assessed after a professional dry-cleaning. Though deterioration from age is apparent to most people, the eye of a qualified restorer is required to evaluate whether the gown needs more than alteration—replacing panels of fabric, a minor revamping, a major renovating, or modernizing.

Allow six months to restore your heirloom properly, so that it will hold up as expected on your wedding day. "With replacement fabric, virtually anything is possible, but rarely are minor alterations all that an heirloom wedding dress needs," says Susan Lane. Thirty years' experience designing for Country Elegance in Los Angeles has taught her to caution consumers about the results. "Cleaning up the fabric, restoring the embellishments or trim, and making seam adjustments are one thing," she says. "Entirely revamping the dress or adding new details can be very tricky. Extensive altering requires opening up the dress, and only an experienced seamstress can do that. It is quite complicated to reopen the gown, take it apart, match a panel from its train, replace a stained underarm, or lengthen the sleeves."

Modernizing an heirloom through extensive alterations and additions is even more difficult, and more care has to be taken by the seamstress. Technically any dress can be modernized or remodeled, but many are ruined in the effort. This means supervision by a designer, dressmaker, or seamstress who is comfortable working with patterns, changing trim, and reconstructing a dress to blend with your personality and wedding characteristics. It is imperative to find a seamstress or amateur capable of doing the job to your satisfaction; the trick may be finding one at a reasonable cost!

ANTIQUE WEDDING DRESS, VINTAGE BRIDAL GOWN

If a nostalgic antique or period wedding look is your heart's desire, but you don't have an heirloom from a friend or relative, the next option is shops that sell antique dresses and vintage gowns. Along with being an affordable alternative and a unique bridal look, an antique dress in good condition is an investment, a commodity with intrinsic value. However, before looking, it is best to be reasonably sure what styles or periods please you and how an antique dress will fit into your wedding ambience. Tracking down that perfect antique wedding dress in your size requires time scouring antiques shops extensively with a decisive shopping attitude; any hesitation whatsoever and the gown you are considering may be snapped up by someone else. Needless to say, an antique cannot be reordered; instead, your search continues. Shopping for an antique or vintage dress requires an understanding of quality and a good eye for spotting it. Seek out the reputable antique clothing dealers with extensive inventories or one willing to work with you to find the right wedding dress.

Vintage gowns vary and reflect the spirit of their day; some are demure, others are made of satin, taffeta, or raw silk in belle-of-the-ball styles. There are 1950s cinched-waist and bouffant skirt taffeta bridal gowns, '40s wedding dresses and suits in silk satin with padded shoulders, and '30s fitted-

A reproduction gown creates a traditional mood.

shoulder outfits (not originally bridal gowns), which work as semiformal bridal gowns in sophisticated settings. A 1920s drop-waist, satin wedding gown in "worthwhile" condition would be considered near to museum quality and prohibitively expensive. Unfortunately, the supply of extravagant Battenberg lace clothes or authentic Edwardian blouses, skirts, and dresses worn on special occasions as separates has completely run out.

A dress made before 1905 would be considered a costume today. They were small and narrow, heavily constructed, and cumbersome with high armholes, restrictively tight shoulders, puffy sleeves, and bustles, but a comfortable reproduction can be rented from theatrical supply houses. Fifty- to eighty-year-old antique dresses, however, are softer and less awkward on, and the bustle and puffy sleeves had gone out of

fashion by then. An antique wedding dress isn't likely to scream from across the room. Its appeal is the attention that was taken with its detailing—sophisticated handiwork and diminutive-scale craftsmanship on high-quality fabrics that are no longer available.

"There are cotton dresses from the turn of the century that did not shine or glitter, although they were intricately embellished with white-on-white or cream-on-cream reembroidered insertions and appliqués of handmade laces," says Jana Starr, proprietor of the East Coast's largest antique dress shop specializing in wedding dresses. Starr often suggests appropriate styles for a bride-to-be shopping for an antique wedding dress. "After hemlines rose off the floor, a train from the shoulder or waist was made to detach. These are suitable for many informal settings. By the 1930s, the shape and fabric were more important than an embellished surface. A self-fabric flower placed asymmetrically on one shoulder or a glass-bead–encircled neckline was more typical of the embellishments of the period.

"A hand-embroidered, sheer batiste cotton or lace is washable and easily restored, and makes a sophisticated, simple but elegant semiformal statement under a tent, for instance, although they were originally worn for Sunday afternoon tea. When worn without a crinoline, they drape beautifully and end in a sweep-length train trailing gracefully behind. Entering from a staircase or walking down the aisle in a handmade Irish lace gown embellished with couching detailings (minute gold thread stitches) worn with a full crinoline and the appropriate veil and jewelry creates the impact of an empress's wedding, and few of today's formal bridal gowns can compare."

Something New...Something Borrowed...

The wedding outfit, dress, or gown—whether traditional or contemporary—featured on a garden bench in a recent bridal magazine advertisement or editorial spread is just one of what can only be described as a limitless choice of styles, colors, fabrics, and details. Every imaginable wedding dress is available at either bridal boutiques, salons (which offer a wider range of services, such as etiquette advice for invitations), and department or specialty stores. There is also an array of original and imported copies of designer wedding dresses to be found at discounters, which are open-rack, warehouse-style retailers, and at rental bridal salons and period costume houses. The wedding dress you want can be located by a bridal-gown broker—in a process similar to mail-order.

There are three types of wedding dresses and alternate sources for each. A ready-to-wear wedding dress is bought off the rack—the same shopping style as all everyday clothing—at a bridal salon, specialty store bridal department, discounter specializing in bridal wear, or your favorite clothing store or boutique.

A made-to-measure wedding dress—a special order cut from a manufacturer's standard pattern that has been adjusted for your measurements—is selected by trying on a sample (exact replica in a standard size 6 or 8) with the assistance of a bridal consultant. When your choice is made, a fitter takes your measurements for the manufacturer. There are also specified modifications available to "customize" your bridal gown with the help of your bridal consultant, who then places your order with the manufacturer. An alternative is consulting with a bridal-wear designer at a trunk show (shop talk for a personal appearance) arranged through your bridal salon. The final option in new wedding dresses is a dress-made gown, either pattern-made, executed by a dressmaker or experienced seamstress (who may be you), or choosing a one-of-a-kind couturier or fashion designer original, which is made to order.

A common retail bridal-wear practice is to be seen by appointment only; your bridal consultant will bring a selection out for you to view rather than having you browse. The wedding dresses and gowns are heavy and cumbersome and made of expensive, light-colored fabrics, and most are kept in storage bags. So this is the most efficient way for you to look through their inventory. Naturally, a designer or dressmaker only sees one bride-to-be at a time. Start with a list of the salons, stores, shops, and alternate routes you wish to pursue. Head your shopping list with friends' and relatives' suggestions, include the establishments mentioned in magazine advertisements, and consult your local Yellow Pages, too.

READY-TO-WEAR: TRADITIONAL AND CONTEMPORARY

Before embarking on your first appointment, it is wise to have a clear idea of price range and a styling concept, because the first question you will be asked is "What type of wedding dress are you looking for?" Prepare a statement that includes the time of year and time of day of the wedding as well as the site and size of the ceremony and the reception. Merely saying "I want a high-neck gown" is far too vague and will lead to a long, protracted search.

Your wedding gown cannot be pattern-made or customized in time for a fast-approaching wedding day, say, less than three months away. If shopping for a reasonably priced wedding dress is paramount, any made-to-order gown will be out of your budget. Therefore, a ready-to-wear wedding dress sold off the rack is the best route when speed or cost is a factor: it is already made, and you need only find the one you want—and the best seamstress money can buy to alter it! Any wedding dress you have seen in a magazine but are unable to locate can be found by calling the manufacturer directly. They will tell you the authorized dealer (a bridal salon) nearest your hometown.

An exciting and somewhat offbeat choice for the right bride-to-be is to ask bridal designers and manufacturers about the one-of-a-kind, often out-of-the-ordinary wedding dresses made exclusively for their runway shows. These samples are model-size, 6 or 8. Write or call any designer whose wedding dresses consistently draw your attention, ask if these dresses may be purchased, and if so, find out how and where. You may also want to explore any bridal-wear retailer holding a sale of samples no longer needed for the salon's inventory, or seconds (slightly damaged). These wedding dresses and gowns often hang on racks in great abundance. A bridal boutique, department, or salon will provide a fitter and seamstress at your expense to make any necessary alterations.

Another possibility is a bridal-wear discounter operating in a similar manner to any other warehouse operation. You can look through a vast choice of styles and silhouettes, and try on and purchase the dresses "as is." A discounter generally does not provide expert assistance or alterations, and very little help is available to coordinate your ensemble's accessories; each is left for you to complete independently.

A bridal-gown broker will locate for a fee a nationally advertised dress or a sample gown at a discounted price. Your broker does the legwork, making calls around the country to find where the wedding dress or gown you want is available. With your approval, the dress is ordered and sent directly to you. The entire transaction is conducted over the telephone, and is similar to an 800-number catalog purchase. Purchasing your wedding dress without trying it on is far from ideal, however, and working with a bridal-gown broker requires extreme caution. While investigating which broker to choose, there are specific things to consider. Be certain that you are speaking with someone reliable, capable, and with enough experience to deliver what he or she promises. Find out how much it will cost (if anything) for the broker to conduct the search, if there is a charge if the search proves unsuccessful, and whether there is a return policy—or is the dress yours, satisfied or not?

Brokers are independent middlepersons with unregulated business practices, including how high the fee can be. Before placing

In small doses, good advice goes a long way!

your order, it is imperative that you be very clear about each step in the process. Ask if you will get a written receipt with the delivery date on it and if a down payment is necessary. If so, how substantial will it be? Can your dress be paid for COD? You must also determine whether you are comfortable with the broker's ability to work within your upcoming date. Leave yourself enough time to avoid a last-minute panic pursuing other paths. Lastly, how well does the broker compare with others in your region? Do his or her references check out? A call to your local Better Business Bureau or Office of Consumer Affairs is in order as well.

There is still one more option to consider that may be the quickest and most inexpensive of all. Ready-to-wear wedding dresses and bridal gowns are also provided by rental costume houses, which a wedding consultant can help you locate, and there are rental bridal salons for traditional and contemporary wedding dresses. For approximately half the purchase price, some rental salons offer recently purchased designer bridal gowns in their inventory. You may be the first to wear one, but it is not for keeps. Renting a wedding dress may be out of the question for many, yet for some it provides a unique solution. This is a growing choice among brides-to-be, and is quite common in some cultures, such as Japan.

Judith Stone, the proprietor of Island Brides on New York's suburban Long Island, has watched the idea ignite and spread in major metropolitan areas around the country. Regardless of the wedding gown, Stone believes, "renting offers an excellent alternative for brides-to-be in a rush, for remarrying brides unwilling to incur the cost or devote the time again, and for budget-conscious shoppers unable to afford the wedding gown of their dreams. The bridegroom, after all, has been doing it for years!

"We stock every imaginable style, size, and period wedding dress, although there are more formal, traditional bridal gowns in today's newest styles," Stone continues. "A rental bridal shop looks and operates like and provides the same service as a conventional bridal salon: a bride-to-be searches through the inventory with the help of a bridal consultant and tries on the possibilities before making her selection. That dress is then put aside or marked specifically for her. Nothing is ordered. A staff seamstress can alter the gown to fit each bride, even revamp it slightly for the fussiest bride-to-be, and virtually overnight. We also stock the matching veil styles."

A familiar store, the clothing emporium or designer boutique in which you normally shop, may hold the perfect wedding dress for you. For fifteen years Harriet Love, the owner of a SoHo boutique, was the premier force behind vintage wedding dresses. Recently, however, vintage special-occasion clothing in "acceptable" condition has become scarce and Love has adapted. She now stocks her shop with ready-to-wear dresses and separate pieces that are influenced by a vintage feeling—but not a copied pattern—with a bridal-wear point of view.

"There are any number of dresses that work as informal and semiformal bridal wear," according to Love. "A silk chiffon slip and top, slightly Empire-waisted, trimmed with beautiful lace and worn with a body suit, or perhaps an ivory silk, Dior-inspired, natural-shoulder shirtwaist, slightly drop-waist, worn with or without a belt. The skirt falls to the ankle, like a ballerina's, and it becomes a semiformal wedding dress. A definitely vintage-feeling bridal outfit for a statuesque contemporary bride is an ivory, ankle-length, shawl-collar silk Charmeuse dress; or a two-piece ivory velvet, dropped-scoop neck, drop-waist, and slit-to-the-thigh

A ready-to-wear, semiformal cocktail sheath with bridal accessories.

A portrait neckline trimmed in lace and a separate skirt with an extended lace hem make an appropriate informal afternoon or cocktail-hour bridal suit.

skirt with buttons forming a hobble skirt. A gorgeous pearl-beaded lace triangle scarf that drapes down to the waist as a yoke is a nice touch for the contemporary bride."

Informal bridal outfits—contemporary, fashion-forward, and avant-garde, closely following current trends, do not have to be a one-piece dress; the separate-component sportswear concept definitely can be applied to bridal wear. "The bride only needs a parallel attitude to wear pant suits, harem pants, or lounge wear," says master fashion designer Mr. Butch. "A lace jacket, satin bustier, and linen skirt or a full skirt of tulle, for instance, combines with a decorative white bustier and a hot evening wedding dress is created. A chiffon skirt can be worn with a lace bustier or lace camisole with beading; during the ceremony the lace jacket covers the sexier look. Or for something far less formal, a linen skirt paired with a motor-cycle jacket and a lace blouse for a fashion-forward bride-to-be. Linen coordinated with a dressy fabric takes on a different look. For instance, organdy, organza, or cotton lace combines well for an informal afternoon wedding dress. Bought off the rack, any beautiful linen dress could have a separate ribbon lace jacket to wear over it. Second-wedding outfits are also more practical, often reusable, and sometimes sexy: a lace bodice with reembroidered soutache under a jacket, which is suitable for a civil ceremony, perhaps in a country club or restaurant setting, or at home with a bridegroom wearing a suit."

BRIDAL SALONS AND YOUR BRIDAL CONSULTANT'S FUNCTION

Many retail chains, department stores, and specialty shops have bridal boutiques. The term "bridal salon" is commonly used by retailers for the department that carries bridal wear; however, a full-service salon has an experienced sales staff, called bridal consultants, to assist while you look through their wide selection of contemporary and traditional ready-to-wear dresses and special-order sample bridal gowns.

Your bridal consultant's first and foremost function is to provide assistance in your decision making: to encourage freedom as you pursue your fantasy, and foster creativity as you fulfill your dream. Many a bride-to-be's first impression of what kind of dress to choose is rarely what she eventually selects; it is a known fact among bridal consultants that every bride with her heart set on a straight silhouette probably should not wear a sheath wedding dress, yet certain minor fitting changes could accommodate that sheath to many figures. Also, each salon and its bridal consultants have an individual selling style; most gladly let you take your time deciding, but some apply high-pressure sales techniques.

Your bridal consultant will show you the available selection within your budget. She will tell you if a particular dress you like is also available in other colors or fabrics. When you try on a dress, your bridal consultant will answer any questions you have about style and fit and will offer her opinion. If you purchase a ready-to-wear dress, it is your bridal consultant's responsibility to schedule the fitting times and see to it that the dress fits perfectly. Finally, she will help coordinate your accessories.

A special-order gown requires much more service from your bridal consultant. Here she is an important partner, because she can point out the modifications available to make the dress conform to your statement, ambience, and needs, and will ensure that everything continues on schedule each step of the way. For instance, she knows which manufacturers or gowns need more than the usual

four months to deliver and when the salon will need more than an additional month for the final adjustments. The salon's fitter or seamstress takes your measurements and your consultant oversees placing your order with the manufacturer, then follows through to ensure that the right wedding gown arrives—on time. She then schedules your fitting appointments, and coordinates further adjustments with the salon's seamstress.

The same wedding dress carrying a higher price tag at another bridal salon more than likely indicates that more services are free of charge or longer consultations or better alterations are offered. "It is important to ask why, because all the needed time and care should be taken to discover which dress is special enough to make you feel beautiful and important," says Nancy Vanderboorn, a bridal consultant at the Vera Wang Bridal Salon on New York City's Madison Avenue. As Vanderboorn views it, "Your salon choice, to a great extent, depends on the bridal consultant working with you. They should be able to understand your values and priorities and match them with what looks best on you. Most important, their taste level should parallel yours. The salon itself should be convenient and offer a wide selection within the style you want. Before deciding, I would suggest checking on a salon's reputation as well as the bridal consultant's record with brides they have worked with recently."

Discuss the ceremony and reception setting with your salon's bridal consultant, as well as the fashion direction and wedding-dress style you had in mind, along with the silhouette and components, fabric, color, and detailing you think are right for your build and proportions. Confide in your consultant; let her know your innermost thoughts, how you always dreamed you would look on your wedding day. Show your consultant any sketches or photographs

OPPOSITE AND BELOW: This spaghetti-strap patchwork lace dress and its matching jacket create a discreet, semiformal afternoon bridal look.

you have collected from magazines, and any heirlooms or gifts—perhaps from the bridegroom's family—you are considering wearing.

Your consultant's task is to understand what you need. She can make suggestions, tell you secrets, and show you tricks for creating any image you want—many you probably never imagined possible. But a bridal consultant should never be tyrannical or try to dictate fashion and style. When your bridal consultant knows the direction you are taking, she can pull out a selection of wedding gowns for you to view, and what an abundance there will be!

Foremost, the right bridal consultant will help get you started in the right direction when beginning the selection phase. At the world's largest bridal salon, Kleinfeld's in Brooklyn, New York, Hedda Kleinfeld presides. She has helped brides-to-be decide on their attire for forty years, and has observed that many of them need persuasion to express themselves. "It is very important to know when—or if—to push a bride-to-be just a little bit. Occasionally we steer her away from a boring or one-in-a-crowd choice by showing her something refreshing or innovative."

Kleinfeld has also helped prevent a busy, sophisticated bride-to-be from making a social error or inadvertently crossing the line of good taste. "For some, my advice is needed on a family matter, because the bride-to-be's mother is out of town. For another, it may be advice concerning religious traditions. Or it may be a practical matter. For instance, one customer wanted beautifully fitted sleeves. When I heard her saying to her friend, 'I'm going to dance my head off,' I looked at her in the gown and said, 'Not with those sleeves. Your arms will be pinned to your sides all day.' Needless to say, we immediately started to look for another gown."

"Problems can arise when a dress arrives late, damaged, or if it is not exactly as a bride-to-be envisioned," says Annette Gerhardt, owner of a Pennsylvania bridal salon and president of the Bridal Retailers Marketing Association. "Your bridal consultant will be able to make adjustments so you are ultimately pleased, whether it requires using the salon seamstress or even locating an outside expert to fix a dress properly. This would be a very difficult situation for a bride-to-be without professional assistance." In addition, your bridal consultant knows which modifications—however small and subtle—should best be made when the manufacturer is cutting and sewing your gown, which can be accomplished in the alteration phase, and what cannot or should not be attempted; however, every bride-to-be will benefit by understanding the exciting possibilities and striking transformation that modifying your gown can achieve.

Everyday undergarments, excluding pantyhose, are unnecessary under a made-to-measure gown; it is a petticoat, crinoline, underskirt, and built-in foundation of corsetlike stays (boning) that make the silhouette form-fitted and its skirt full and shapely. This complicates trying on many styles and requires more extensive fittings than a ready-to-wear gown. Even for the bride-to-be who occasionally attends fancy-dress balls, this will most likely be her first experience special-ordering a form-fitting gown with these atavistic foundations. While helping you select a gown, your bridal consultant points out how the underpinnings, perhaps your petticoat, could be layered beginning below the hips as well as shaped from the knee to ankle to make the silhouette look good on you.

Your bridal consultant will also provide whatever help and guidance you need to select your headpiece, veil, hairstyle, jewelry, and shoes. "When each item for the ensemble must be decided upon," Gerhardt continues, "it is the bridal consultant who can help most and who knows when to start looking. Although searching for a linen hanky or the right touch may be exciting or challenging, locating the right headpiece, veil, and foundations can become frustrating, time-consuming, and expensive. A full-service salon has everything you need under one roof, which is convenient shopping."

CUSTOMIZING AND MADE-TO-ORDER: THE DIFFERENCES SPELLED OUT

Any bride-to-be wishing to maximize the extraordinary opportunity of walking down the aisle in a bridal gown should understand what "customizing" a gown means, and what the advantages and limitations are, before making a final wedding-dress decision. It is important to know the difference between customizing the details on a made-to-measure gown and having a made-to-order gown created by a couturier or one custom-made by a dressmaker sewing from the pattern and materials you specify.

While a pattern-made gown may be too much responsibility for most brides-to-be, and a one-of-a-kind, made-to-order gown is feasible for just a few, familiarity with each type provides insight for any bride-to-be. A custom-made wedding gown is conceived by an interactive process between its creator and you. A pattern-made gown's design is controlled entirely by you, and it can be adapted to your tastes even further by the materials and detailing you choose. When a gown is customized, the designer's concept is modified by you in conjunction with your bridal consultant.

Aside from the cost difference between

A simple lace dance dress takes on a special look if made to your exact measurements.

a pattern-made or custom-made wedding gown and a manufactured made-to-order gown that can be customized—the made-to-order gown is the more costly—there are additional distinctions. A customized gown's measurements are taken at your bust, waist, hips, and length, to ensure proper fit. A dressmade gown is more precise. For her made-to-order gowns, designer Candice Solomon, of One-of-a-Kind Brides, in New York's SoHo, measures twenty-two distinct body parts, including the rib cage, neck, back, shoulder to waist, waist to floor, armhole, arm length, elbow, and wrist.

"My brides-to-be have three fittings on their gown," Solomon explains. "She tries on what appears to be the lining of the dress first—the muslin fitting. A one-inch leeway is enough to make the adjustments for fit. At this stage, changes can be made, such as making the back higher or lower or the sleeves longer or narrower. Once the dress is cut and sewn, radical changes are not made.

"After the dress is pieced together, there is a second fitting in the unfinished dress—there is no detailing, and its trim and embellishments are not in place. Any minor alterations for size, or minor changes concerning details, trim, and enhancements, can still be made.

"The final fitting is scheduled one month to one week before the wedding date. Most brides-to-be want to lose some extra pounds for the occasion. To be sure that their shape has not changed, the final fitting will be as last-minute as is possible. The hemline is checked one more time. If she is comfortable walking in a long skirt, the gown comes within one inch of the ground in the front so the shoe just peeks out, which is pretty, or the hemline can be raised one-half inch higher if she feels that would be nicer."

Every dressmade gown is created step by step, but a customized gown never includes a muslin fitting or a second fitting before the detailing is intact. Once your customizing changes are chosen and ordered, there will be no middle stages; your gown is cut, sewn, and trimmed according to your order. On arrival, your wedding gown is fitted by the salon's seamstress with the bridal consultant overseeing the final fitting, which is exactly the same for all dressmade gowns.

CUSTOMIZING YOUR WEDDING DRESS

The House of Bianchi was established as a custom bridal shop in the basement of Mrs. Bianchi's Boston home in the 1950s.

At the time, all retail bridal wear was either dressmade (designed and made to measure) or sold off the rack, with the store begrudgingly performing alterations. Bianchi approached Sophie Gimbel, Saks Fifth Avenue's in-house designer, and offered to make any change to the gown's sleeves, neckline, fabric, and beading a bride-to-be desired. A bargain was struck, the customized wedding gown was born, and bridal-wear retailing was revolutionized. A bride-to-be could now try on a manufacturer's wedding gown sample, make her selection, and modify it.

Each designer and manufacturer creates very particular looks dictated by the silhouette, the pattern-cutting technique, the fabric quality and variety, the use of lace, the trimmings, and the embellishments. "It just isn't feasible," explains Joseph Massa of the House of Bianchi, "for one bridal salon to have every design variation a manufacturer offers to show a bride-to-be. Some large manufacturers provide a photographed catalog, but your bridal consultant knows exactly what they are, in most cases, and can point out the subtleties and how best to utilize a change on a gown."

Customizing a gown is often viewed as merely increasing the cost by lengthening the sleeves or adding more elaborate laces, trims, or embellishments to increase the gown's formality; however, the process works another way as well. You can realize substantial savings when selecting a high-quality but lightweight fabric, for example. "A full ball gown takes up to ten yards of fabric," bridal-wear designer Robert Work points out. "A substantial savings occurs by not using a pure silk satin, for instance." Work has taken on the challenge of creating the look the bride-to-be wants at a reasonable cost. Her priorities determine where the savings are to be found. "If I were a bride-to-be having a cathedral ceremony," he supposes, "my choice would be a more dramatic back treatment leading to a breathtaking, beaded, lace-appliquéd train. While the fabric quality of the gown is very important, it does not necessarily have to be the most costly douppioni silk. After all, the silk never touches the skin; a polyester lining does."

During the course of each business day, bridal manufacturers are asked to accommodate a multitude of changes, so being service-oriented is an important function for each bridal-wear manufacturer. Your bridal consultant will have access to the designer as well; in fact, in most cases, she can call them directly to ask an opinion or to verify if they can accommodate a requested substitution. This service-oriented attitude has created another option, the designer trunk show.

At a prearranged appointment, a bride-to-be can consult with the wedding gown's creator and receive a wide range of advice. Paula Varsalona, the fashion-forward bridal-wear designer, describes the advantages of attending a designer's personal appearance. "I lend my expertise to a bride-to-be on every aspect of her ensemble—not just her bridal gown, but the flowers for her bouquet and a harmonious headpiece to coordinate with her wedding setting and scale. After a sample is chosen, but before the question of how to customize it is tackled, I can advise how the look can be altered if the lines *are* what the bride-to-be wants. I ask how she sees each component ideally—increasing the train, bustling its fabric into a flowerlike burst just below the waist, substituting the fabric, adding and deleting the gown's embellishments. Occasionally, when asked about customizing my design, the bride-to-be has moved so far away from my original design concept that I refer her to a dress from a past season. If that works better, then the bridal consultant and bride-to-be can take over from there."

When you alter a design element to bal-ance your body's proportions, include additional beading at the hem to increase the illusion of height, substitute sheer sleeves to reduce a bulky midriff, or enlarge the shoulders for additional stature, are you merely modifying or completely changing the style? The latter, for example, requires altering the gown's design lines. "The issue is where does accommodating an element stop and changing the style begin?" says Edna Forsyth, the sales manager for Forsyth Enterprises and Scaasi Brides. "There is no precise answer because the degree to which an element needs altering plays a big role. However, when the bride-to-be wants to drop the waistline, change the skirt's shape, or substitute a portrait neckline, she wants the designer's design changed. It is the bridal consultant who should realize that this particular bride-to-be needs a different wedding dress." If a manufacturer's line does not have a variation of that dress best suited to her, the prospective bride needs to consider a made-to-order or pattern-made dress.

Something (Windsor) Blue . . .

DRESSMADE, PATTERN-MADE

In 1937, for what was then to be the wedding of the century, Mainbocher created a made-to-order or custom-made wedding ensemble for Wallis Simpson, the American divorcée the Duke of Windsor had given up the English throne to marry. The designer fashioned a simple but fabulous jewel-neck, skimpy-sleeved, closely fitted, belted, crepe and wool wedding dress with small buttons from the neck to the waist. He also personalized the shade of blue (concocting Windsor blue) to evoke the mood of the time. Wallis Simpson wore a small, matching circular hat designed by Mainbocher as well.

Your dressmaker can add a small detail, like this silk tied-and-sashed apron, to personalize your wedding dress.

the restrictions of customizing a manufacturer's special-order gown by elevating you to the level of designer. As your own client and designer, you control the design of your dress each step of the way. You also control how your money is spent. Seeking the advice of others, especially your dressmaker or seamstress, is wise at every stage.

While bridal patterns are overwhelmingly traditional, a contemporary or remarrying bride can select an evening or cocktail dress pattern and then refabricate (choose an alternative weave or color for the suggested fabric) and embellish the pattern with lace and additional bridal details. The bridal gown patterns of renowned designers and celebrities, such as Victor Costa, Carolina Herrera, Caroline Kennedy Schlossberg, and Princess Diana, are available, and can be made at a fraction of the original cost. An additional personalizing step is to combine several patterns—the bodice from one pattern, the skirt from a second, and the detailing concept from a third.

Start to completion will take six months to a full year depending on the dressmaker, the pattern, and your organizational skills. In general, a simple silhouette with modest embellishments can be cut, sewn, and trimmed quicker and requires fewer dressmaking skills than an intricate gown. Your cost will be determined by the pattern, its design components, the quality of the materials used, and sewing time. A train, for instance, adds time and costs; a long, embellished train takes even longer and costs more. Tucks, pleats, and handmade appliqués are time-consuming and labor-intensive. If you're not careful, a dressmade gown can easily become as expensive as a store-bought gown, if not more so.

The first step for a pattern-made gown is to add the bridal section of pattern catalogs—available at fabric stores—to the bridal

If the dress of your dreams seems a dim hope, and enough time remains until the wedding day, an enticing option to explore is having one component or your entire wedding ensemble made from a pattern to your individual design specifications. "A bride-to-be seeking a dressmaker usually wants a more unique wedding dress that makes a statement about her personality and expresses her style. She is more of a risk taker," says Danielle Franco, a dressmaker in the Georgetown section of Washington, D.C. "She also has more of an imagination than a bride-to-be wanting to see each detail of her wedding dress in front of her before making a decision." The process of creating a pattern-made wedding dress eliminates magazines through which you are looking for ideas. As you do your research in these publications, pull or earmark or photocopy any page with an idea. File them by category—for example, fabric, neckline, beading—because you can combine elements from many patterns as well as adding your own thoughts for some components.

Before making a final decision and purchasing any patterns, be sure your dressmaker is experienced in working with the pattern, fabrics, and details you are including. Ask for any recommendations or alternatives regarding the design, fabric, and trims; identify where to save money, if that is a concern, and discuss your timetable carefully. Be sure she has plenty of time to finish before your wedding day. Danielle Franco adds: "Even a bride-to-be who has selected her wedding-dress pattern and fabric before I am commissioned to make it can need additional help visualizing what is suitable for her figure. Sometimes she wants to adjust the pattern's formality to be more or less dressy. Very often a bride-to-be is not too familiar with what is available, so I accompany her to the fabric and notions shops. We look at all the fabrics and trims, and I try to guide her toward the wedding dress she always imagined rather than just designing one for her. She then is the co-designer."

Once your dressmaker is chosen, order the pattern, or combination of patterns, and the fabrics, trims, notions, and all the detail and enhancement materials, such as beading, lace appliqués, or edgings. There are also accessory and accent patterns, for instance, a garter belt, ring bearer's pillow, or coordinated bow tie and cummerbund for the bridegroom. These patterns and materials should be considered now, even though they can be ordered a month or so later.

The step-by-step process is the same for every custom-made dress, so understanding the purpose of each fitting is crucial. A change after the muslin fitting will be costly, time-consuming, and may mean starting a section from scratch—new pattern, fabric, materials, and so forth. After the second fitting when the final adjustments are made, it is time to begin assembling the other ensemble elements. Start with your shoes and headpiece as the trim is being sewn. Approximately three weeks before your wedding, one last fitting will be needed to ensure everything is perfect for your wedding day.

Made-to-Order: The Phantasmagoric World of Couture

A custom-made wedding gown is conceived by an expert with you in mind and with your approval at every stage; it will be executed using the finest materials and handmade parts. Each couturier(e) has a preferred vocabulary of silhouettes, design elements, fabrics, trims, and enhancements, and each works in his or her distinct style to create the wedding gown right for you. For some designers the design concept begins with a sketch, others begin by draping a mannequin, but Monica Hickey heads a unique design team, including a dress and accessory designer, that collaborates.

Hickey was the quintessential bridal consultant before creating magnificent custom-made ensembles exclusively for Saks Fifth Avenue's flagship New York City store. She began in retail bridal wear thirty years ago at Henri Bendel, then moved to Bergdorf Goodman. "Every bride-to-be is quite different. I work with each as a particular person with her own circumstances, personality, and body type," she says.

Hickey has strong views on the communication that should take place at the initial appointment for a made-to-order bridal

Illusion climbs the throat, covers the shoulder cap, and disappears into a taffeta portrait neckline and decolletage bow.

gown. "There is no simple formula; the right wedding dress depends on that particular bride-to-be. The most crucial aspect is discovering what she wants to project as an individual that day. Absolute concentration is necessary when listening to the bride-to-be identifying her wedding: Where will it take place? What time of day? How many guests? Will it be catered, with dancing? Will a photographer be present?

"Meanwhile, my mind must search through the styles most appropriate for her," says Hickey. "After all, some are for daytime or small weddings and others are best at a large evening wedding. Every bride-to-be can be transformed by her wedding gown, so I begin by weighing what would be the most flattering and what won't work. All the while we talk, I'm thinking of each possibility, discovering where she needs help, or perhaps finding she doesn't need help at all."

Monica Hickey's rule of thumb is that a plain dress works well on a gorgeous bride-to-be and a plain girl is transformed into a beautiful bride by a very pretty dress. "It gives her a lift and lets her individual beauty shine through. I can't say, 'You are plain, my dear, you need a very pretty dress,' can I? But what I can do is highlight her most appealing physical attributes. For example, if she has a wonderful neck, upper torso, and lovely posture, I strive to make the most of it. And if her bosom isn't developed, we will use little devices, such as a snug bodice that comfortably holds in the midriff with boning. In general, I search for the silhouette that accents her positive points while eliminating the others."

The same standards and care are employed as every couture wedding gown is created. The results, however, are far different. America's foremost couturiere, Carolina Herrera, changed the direction of bridal wear in the mid-'80s with the simple classic lines she created for Caroline Kennedy Schlossberg's wedding dress. Herrera oversees every detail of her bridal collection, setting a very high standard indeed. She likes her dresses to be well fitted, well finished, and created with the best materials, workmanship, and details. "Simple, never flashy," is her philosophy. "I believe if you are going to wear white, do it properly, which means demure, innocent, and romantic; if it's to be sexy, tight, and open, then wear red or black."

Herrera's made-to-order bridal gowns are celebrated the world over, as is her step-by-step method for custom-making just the right bridal gown for a very nervous bride-to-be: "We first sit down alone and talk. I want *her* to decide, to tell me what she wants on her day. I know this is a very emotional time. Every bride wants to glow and be her best. For this to happen, she must be pleased with the way she looks.

"Every bride-to-be is a bit nervous, unsure of what she really does want. Inevitably, her first words are, 'I want a very different gown. I don't want to be like all the brides in the world—they all look the same to me.' In her own way she tells me if she wants embroidery, appliqués, bows, or ribbons. Then I start with a drawing of *her* wedding dress that she can study and live with and change."

Herrera also supervises the fit: a fitting in muslin takes place, then another before the gown is finished that includes shoes, headpiece, and bouquet, and then one last fitting in the finished gown.

"After the muslin fitting, when she comes back for the first fitting to see what her gown looks like, the placement of the embroidery, appliqués, ribbons, bows, or whatever she wanted, I hear 'I don't want flowers, I don't want tulle, I don't want a train.'

"A certain amount of psychology comes

OPPOSITE: A truly regal aura is possible when your couturiere creates a bridal ensemble to your specifications—for instance, stylizing leg-of-mutton sleeves, embellishing the lace, and then positioning a shimmering tassel; each element can be tailored to your liking, down to coordinated lace gloves.

OVERLEAF: Dramatic cuffed, strapless sheath beautifully offset by a petal headdress and a long veil.

into play; I will say, 'Yes, yes, of course! I'm going to take care of that,' and then in the fitting room we begin to change it a little bit . . ."

"At the final fitting, when the gown is ready, I have to say that each one looks at herself in the mirror and asks, 'Is this train too small? Didn't I say I wanted a lower waist? Are there enough appliquéd flowers?'

"I stand back to look, then I tell her just how beautiful and special she looks—which she does!"

Many but not all brides-to-be remain nervous about the dress until the wedding day arrives. Martin Price, president of the House of Sant' Angelo, who also creates lavish wedding gowns, concurs, but thinks some prospective brides need encouragement of a different order. "I have found that a bride-to-be is either very sure of how she wants to look, or very confused. Often she has seen too much and wants it all, and all at once, then doesn't actually want anything she has seen. I never dictate; I study how she moves, her coloring, her style, what strikes me and what could strike others.

"On the other hand, one bride-to-be arrived knowing exactly what would make her happy. She wanted to build her entire wedding around a very theatrical theme: 'I have to be a Camelot bride.' Every detail was worked out, including the wedding music, the fairytale setting, the flowers and food—no effort was to be spared. Why would I try to dissuade a bride-to-be who is very definite?

"If I was not inspired or the right designer, it would not have been right to work with her or to change what she wanted. *We* created the perfect tulle and gold lamé gown with glorious embroidered tapestries to match her fantasy theme. Her wedding day was complete when she marched out a radiant, happy Renaissance bride."

Part Two

Completing

Your

Ensemble

*B*ridal accessories and accents are the adjunct garments or items that complete a wedding-day ensemble. Down through the ages they have evolved and have been refined, and their symbolic value has been strengthened. Each accessory or accent can symbolize good fortune, health, everlasting love, peace, happiness, offspring—in other words, an abundant life together forevermore.

They also become part of life's memories, touchstones steeped in a rich tradition of lore and myth. Today's bride, on the wedding day and long after, cherishes her accessories and accents; they serve to make her feel as innocent, as happy, and as beautiful as they did for every bride preceding her.

The Crowning Touches

Furthermore, brides-to-be from different religions, countries, regions, and cultures have their own customs or "musts" to include, which have been passed down from one generation to the next. After these are incorporated into her ensemble, the prospective bride picks and chooses freely among the other traditional or updated accessories and accents.

There are so many options available that your first step should be to explore their length and breadth—then learn the handful of guidelines that will help you decide what accessories and accents look best, suit the occasion, serve your need.

Accessorizing a wedding gown is a challenge, however. The opportunities are limitless because only one rule holds: the gown, its fabric, embellishments, and direction (traditional, period, or contemporary) and style (ultraformal to informal), sets the overall statement, the characteristics to be followed through or picked up by each accessory and by each accent without exception. A white gown and its accessories are a unique ensemble; a step-by-step approach to completing it is required. But the selection order becomes moot when a gift, heirloom, or keepsake—

where to begin among related elements

OPPOSITE: A very contemporary hat-style headdress with flocked polka dots on transparent tulle.

especially a lace veil or large jewelry piece— is involved. It then becomes the major consideration when choosing the gown as well as each subsequent accessory and accent.

The elements that can relate an accessory to your ensemble vary and include a matching period piece; a design element, such as edges; a similar woven pattern—the common ones are floral, geometric, or medallion designs; a motif—such as fur, silk bows, or lace appliqués; an ornamentation concept— created of pearls, sequins, or beads; and color—whether pure white, off-white, a blush hue, or ivory.

It is critical, before embarking on your search, to understand the range of styles within each accessory and accent and to consider their possible advantages and limitations for you. As even a cursory glance in a mirror will reveal, certain styles, sizes, and shapes emphasize your particular beauty better, drawing attention to or enhancing bone structure and proportions, highlighting advantages and camouflaging flaws.

Your wedding day is an occasion to be at your best, and that requires careful coor-

Schiffli-embroidered organza appliqués form a corsage-effect hair ornament.

dinating and planning. No accessory or accent can be left to a last-minute or one-try-only settlement. Adequate time is needed to research, experiment, select, change, exchange, and adjust.

Almost every bride adheres to one convention: wearing something in her hair. So, as a practical matter, accessories are usually considered before accents, beginning with a hairstyle to frame your face, followed by a headdress to serve as a centerpiece, then adding color and shape with jewelry— always earrings and occasionally a necklace. The final accessory for your head and shoulders is a tissue-thin tulle, lace, or chiffon veil, carefully selected to counterbalance the other elements. The veil is a very important accessory when worn as an elaborate layered headdress to accompany a formal gown or as a simpler veil and headpiece to set off a semiformal dress. With an informal or contemporary outfit, little else can say "bride" as directly as a hint of veil, either on a hat or attached to hair ornaments. Flowers—whether carried as a bouquet or worn in your hair, on a garment, or incorporated with another accessory or accent—are important as a long-standing symbol of the earth's bounty, and the next accessory to be chosen.

In general, an overall beautiful form is sought, its focal point your face and its epicenter your eyes, nose, and mouth. The balance between your hairdo, headdress, jewelry, veil, and the upper bodice is so delicate that no part can be thought of separately. Harmony, of course, is the key, achieved when all elements are tied together and no part overwhelms the whole. Only after you are pleased with the image in the mirror have you arrived at the "right" presentation—otherwise, you will appear strange, uncomfortable, overdressed, or underdressed, but not at ease with yourself.

Accents must be selected as well, including all or some of the following: lingerie, hosiery, shoes, a makeup style, gloves, handbag, garter, handkerchief, and cover-up. These accompany and complement the whole, creating an individualized, finished look. Similarly, there are several optional incidental accents that are easily worked into any ensemble—sentimental touches, such as a Bible or a fan. An extra-healthy measure of common sense should prevail while you make these decisions, and extreme care must be taken to observe any nuance that makes a difference in the story—you!

Starting at the Top: Your Hairstyle

Experts universally agree that the most flattering hairstyle possibilities should be worked out with a professional consultant shortly after finding your gown.

This should take place even before setting out to find a headdress that integrates with your gown. With a fabric swatch and a sketch or Polaroid that shows the bodice clearly—its neckline and shoulders in particular—head for your hairdresser to discuss your hairstyle and headpiece. (If you don't have a hairdresser, begin asking for recommendations.) Allow extra time before the wedding day if you are contemplating a radical change, such as a different length or new style. At this point, the conversation can only be vague and practical—do not attempt to set in stone the hairstyle you'll wear. Ask the hairdresser's advice on which headdress shapes are complementary for your face; what size, height, and proportion are right for your head; and the preferred method for attaching the headdress and the best placement points, depending on your hair—thin, thick, curly, straight—and the headpiece's

size and shape. Bring any jewelry pieces you are considering, or a picture that shows the style and size. Be sure to ask for an opinion about the amount of veil around your face.

This gives you a framework and allows flexibility as well. To prevent a disaster and to be sure that your hair isn't cause for alarm on your wedding day, leave the decisions about a hairstyle's flourishes and adjustments to when you are looking in a mirror with your gown and headdress complete. From twenty years' experience preparing models for fashion magazines and bridal industry advertisements, and as a beauty consultant to private clients for their wedding day, Bobbi Brown has devised this simple hairstyle scheduling guide: "As soon as your headpiece is selected, return to your hairdresser with a Polaroid to work out the right hairdo, where the headpiece will sit, and how it will attach. Two weeks before your wedding day, which allows enough time for the trim to lose its stark look, bring the headdress, including the veil and jewelry you will wear, to have the hairstyle 'framework' you previously decided upon done. Go home and put on your gown or dress with your hair and headdress precisely as you'll wear them. Study yourself in the mirror. Live with the hairstyle for an afternoon or evening to see how it moves; watch for changes. Show your bridegroom, friends, and family, but only seek comments from those you trust."

There is no special hairdo for bridal headdresses. The same rule applies when selecting an everyday hairstyle: every woman looks best when her head appears lifted from the neck and shoulders with hair framing her face. These words of wisdom constitute the truism that Kenneth Battelle uses as a guideline for all brides. For decades, the House of Kenneth, his salon in New York City, has been a second home, a fashionable women's

Some headpieces require only a simple hairstyle.

"club," and a hair-design institution for his clients from all points on the planet. Kenneth is, and has been from his start, a celebrity and society woman's hairdresser-of-choice for her wedding. As he puts it, "When a woman wore different hats to shop in the morning, attend a luncheon, tea, or cocktails, and dine out in the evening, she didn't have her hair styled: it was laundered—cleaned and ironed! The very concept of a hairstyle, which arrived with the advent of hot rollers, killed wearing hats because hairstyles then served that function—softening and framing the face, creating shape and form, adding bulk and height."

In other words, a bride's headdress and hairstyle should combine to accomplish the

same effect as the right hairstyle alone would. If, for example, an elaborate headpiece will be placed on top, the less hairdo the better. "Ideally, if she has the length, I'd pull her hair back into a French twist, exposing as much brow and face as possible," says Kenneth. He also believes a bride should do nothing special to her hair color: "Except if she routinely adds highlights or touches," he continues, "which should be done later—several weeks before the wedding.

"There are few rules of thumb: daytime or evening is never really a factor, and more often than not, a formal bride wants her hair up or pulled back; down in back, up in front isn't 'special' enough, and down or flowing is too casual. If a bride is unsure about either her hairstyle or the headpiece, I will make suggestions as she is experimenting. From experience, I have deduced that a bride approaches her wedding day from one of two attitudes: a fantasy ideal—not to be herself; or the opposite—a beautiful version of herself. As her hairdresser, I must understand each bride's objective before I can satisfy her wish."

For every bride-to-be, the first step is deciding how much neck should show, then whether to wear her hair completely up, back off the face, or down. A good starting point may be your normal hairstyle. "A hairdo can be a great attribute and can give you a lift, but only if you're comfortable wearing your hair 'up' at special occasions; otherwise, there could be chaos in the making," says Bobbi Brown. "I've even advised sophisticated brides wearing a narrow, strapless sheath at a Saturday night, black-tie wedding to leave their hair down if that's what they are accustomed to. Even messy may be desirable under certain circumstances, but it must be under control. If the decision for your wedding day is not to have a hairdresser, either because your hair is short or

---

HAIRDOS: THE ONE RIGHT FOR YOU

A hairstyle and headpiece combine to accomplish what your hairstyle normally does alone. But a bride cannot treat her hairstyle differently from the rest of her ensemble. The possibilities should be worked out with a professional consultant shortly after you have made your wedding-dress choice, and before your search for a headdress begins. With a fabric swatch, sketch, or Polaroid of your upper bodice, and any jewelry pieces you are considering wearing, meet with your hairdresser. At this time discuss an overall look, and ask for advice on the style, placement, the method to attach your headdress, as well as the veil length.

Decide on a "framework"—not the exact hairstyle. It is crucial that your face—the central point—be seen clearly. There are any number of delightful hairdo variations—up, back off the face, or down—although your usual style may be the best starting point. The framework for your hairstyle is dictated according to your head's proportions; how much neck you want to show; your gown's bodice, neckline and shoulders in particular; and its overall silhouette.

After your initial hairstyle consultation, your headdress can be selected. Once the choice is made, return to your hairstylist to decide on the exact style and the placement for the headdress. (If you have decided on a large or dramatic one, be aware that little else can be near your face.) Go home wearing the hairstyle, and ask for opinions, especially from your bridegroom. Finally, several weeks before your wedding day, bring the headdress, veil, and jewelry to your hairdresser to make the final decision on style and cut, which allows enough time for the trim to lose its stark look.

it will be in a close-to-normal style, begin with clean hair.

Since every bride has a way of wilting, start the day with your hair a little fuller—just a bit more coiffed to be slightly glamorized. Short, straight hair usually dried naturally, for instance, can be blown out and sprayed very lightly to prevent it from appearing unkempt, especially in the photographs."

A bride should not treat the style of her hair differently from the rest of her ensemble; each element is part of the overall impression. Whether a floor-length gown or a short bouncy dress is being worn, its line will command certain proportions for your head. When a headpiece needs slight adjustments or to be placed differently to relate your head to the dress line and proportion, your hairstyle can best pull these elements together to allow the headpiece to work splendidly. For example: with an informal ensemble and a small headpiece seen minimally from straight on, such as a single flower behind the ear or a cluster of small buds, a modern hairdo framing the sides of the head becomes appropriate; with a country- or Western-style wedding dress and a decorated comb as the headpiece, loose hair flowing in back or wavy may work as well.

As the central focal point, it is axiomatic that your face be seen, which means directing your hair, if necessary, with a barrette or comb, allowing it to fall gently around your forehead and chin, but keeping it away from the temples and eyes. If you are wearing a large and dramatic headpiece, absolutely nothing else should be near your face. "It is a generality, but I've noticed that seeing more face makes sense with an all-white formal gown," continues Bobbi Brown. "Gowns and full dresses demand less hair around the head: they somehow seem to come together when the bride pulls back her

hair and the headdress catches it. Even when pulled back, a bit of height—rather than completely flattened to the skull—is in better proportion to bigger dresses; the tendency with headpieces and veils is to flatten hair further against the cheeks. This buries a face."

Kenneth agrees: "When a bride says, 'I've always worn bangs, I'm not comfortable without them,' I advise her, 'By all means wear bangs! Just clear the rest of your face—especially around your cheeks—by holding the remaining hair back, caught softly behind the ear to emphasize your face.' To me, there is nothing prettier, more classic and flattering, than a halo effect—whether very simple and striking or elaborate and extraordinary by combining real pearls, jewels, and flowers—if for no other reason than that every guest would like a glimpse of the bride's face as she walks down the aisle."

Wires of pearls and beads, delicately rendered as flowers and vines, frame a simple swept-back hairdo and add importance to a pouf veil.

Finding the Right Accompaniment: Headdresses and Ornaments

Wearing some form of headdress is an enduring and important bridal tradition that just about every bride-to-be decides to honor because it lends stature. In fact, bridal consultants universally echo a comment heard over and over again: "When I put on my headpiece I really do feel like a bride." As a controlled and contained accessory—like other aspects of fashion—a headdress joins your ensemble with a particular task: to complete the overall look and create harmony, making a personal style statement. It must be well thought out, but there are few hard-and-fast rules and fewer guidelines as to which headdress style is appropriate with which dress style.

There are, however, several important factors to consider. Each bride's outward demeanor, her personality and physical proportions, will affect the choice. Scale, too, affects headdress choice: after all, a cathedral and chapel or a restaurant and ballroom are entirely different physical and psychological settings. The groom's height and proportions, a father's fantasy, or a mother's wishes should also be taken into account. After the ceremony, in many instances, the veil will be detached and a portion of the headdress will remain throughout the celebration. It must still look complete, complement your features, and remain in proportion to both your head and silhouette. Finally, a gown's silhouette and length have everything to do with the wedding itself: its style (formal or informal), ambience (lavish or simple), attitude (urban or country), direction (traditional, period, or contemporary), and spirit (grand, romantic, bold) all affect the choice of headdress, and to ignore them, or worse, to deviate from them now, would be ill advised.

The embellished, set-back pillbox hat is a popular, easy-to-wear complement.

OPPOSITE: A delicately beaded tiara holds a mass of tulle ruffles spraying into a simple, lightweight veil with random pearls.

HEADDRESS FORMALITY, NEEDS, AND TASTE

Even before the try-on phase, a bride-to-be can begin examining and defining her options, ranging from the traditional, which translates into wearing a headdress and veil in either a formal or semiformal presentation, to a more informal approach, using a hat or hair ornament and "fun" veil, to the very contemporary, dispensing with the headpiece and veil entirely in favor of an up-to-the-minute hairstyle—a viable option even with an ultratraditional gown. While a gown is selected before the headpiece, the reverse is true when yards of lace for a veil or an inherited period headdress—that you love and that fulfills your every dream—is available. In this case, simply work backward by looking for a dress that harmonizes with that headdress's style, relates to its embellishments, and matches it in color.

The guidelines for selecting a flattering formal, semiformal, or informal headpiece are similar because the same headdress can set off far different gowns. Headdress does follow the gown's lead, but its shape can subtly change the feeling of that gown while giving the bride a completely different—if just as finished—look. "A pillbox, for instance, can create a casual look if coupled with a pantsuit, a tailored look when matched to a simple dress, or an elegant look with an elaborate lace bodice and skirt," says bridal headdress designer Elaine Vincent. After graduating from the Parsons School of Design in New York City, Vincent apprenticed in the sportswear arena, but it was while working on Arnold Scaasi's bridal line that she caught the bridal bug. "The demand was so heavy for elaborate headdresses and poufs that it was almost impossible to find a simple, well-designed headpiece to complement a bride's clean, modern hairstyle. That prompted me to create my own headpieces, which are designed to be customized.

"Size, height, adornment, and placement affect a headpiece's look as well: large, high, prominently placed pieces are quite grand, and small, flat, and low-in-back are less so. A regal diadem, stately coronet, and delicate wreath, for instance, are all worn on the bride's crown, but a more formal statement is created as the height increases. Similarly, the materials used as decorations can lift a headpiece shape into a more formal statement. Any tiara shape embellished with real jewels or pearls is ultraformal, while adornments such as gold beads or sequins are somewhat less formal, and Austrian crystals would push the same headpiece toward a courtly-period dress. Likewise, a self-fabric or lace bow, cap, and headband bedecked with silk ribbons, hand rolled and applied satin flowers, or pearl embroidery are formal or semiformal headpieces. Informal headdress is generally plain with fewer and more moderate decorations, such as a lace bow with monotone bugle beads, silk flowers with small sequins rather than large rhinestones, or an enameled barrette and comb combined with a ribbon. A picture hat, worn in the afternoon for a civil or religious ceremony, becomes a garden hat if a country-feeling band or sprig of field flowers is used as a decoration."

A bride's personal style is a major factor as well. An understated bride may choose a bun cap rather than a Juliet cap, a narrow satin bow or small silk flower placed at the nape of the neck rather than high on top, or a raised halo type of headband rather than a tiara. A bride uncomfortable with a traditional headdress or a cutting-edge-of-fashion bride in a simple dress might select a fabric headpiece, fresh flowers, or combs with a Russian veil (an open-weave netting) worn asymmetrically or at back. The popu-

A puffed headband.

A ruffled-tulle mantilla effect.

A macramé and pearl crown.

An afternoon garden hat.

HEADDRESSES, HATS, AND HAIR ORNAMENTS

There are limitless variations on each of the seven basic, elegant—though not necessarily elaborate—tried-and-true millinery creations functioning as bridal headdresses. *Headbands* are narrow, medium, or wide strips that follow the head's arc. When asymmetrical, they are referred to as profile headbands. *Wreaths, garlands,* or *circlets* are circles placed either at the back of the head, flat on the crown, or low across the forehead, and are composed of fresh or silk flowers and other organic materials. *Sprays* are patterns resembling branchlets, twigs, or flowers. *Mantillas* are lace or netting that frames the face and is raised by a wire armature and secured with an elaborate comb or an elegant pin. *Tiaras* are crownlike curves sitting on the head (a diadem) or above the brow (a coronet).

There are ten hat and cap shapes incorporated into bridal headpieces as well. *Picture hats,* which are large, have a wide brim and are made from straw and horsehair (actually interlocking basket-weave nylon); there are slanted-brim shapes, which are called *upturned* hats, and *half hats,* which cover only a small portion of the crown. The most often chosen brimless bridal hats are cone-shaped *toques,* bell-shaped *cloches,* round-crown *turbans,* which are small and close-fitting, and *pillboxes,* which are flat, close-fitting, and large or small geometric structures. The long-standing favorite bridal caps are the *Juliet* cap, which hugs the crown and is worn at the back of the head; the *skullcap,* a larger version—a sort of ladylike yarmulke; and the *bun cap,* which is jewel-encrusted or flower-covered, and designed for hair that is pulled into a chignon.

There is an endless variety of hair ornaments with numerous decorations and various methods of fastening them into a hairstyle, including the *caul,* a hairnet; or the *snood,* a netlike bag placed at the back to hold the hair in place; *barrettes* with bows; *combs* with ribbon streamers; and *florals*— porcelain, silk, or fresh.

A forward-placed headpiece.

The ever-popular snood.

A bow with an upswept hairdo.

Flowers complement a hairstyle.

lar accenting headpiece for second-time and modern brides is the flat, oval or round, self-fabric pillbox hat, 3 to 5 inches in diameter; for the more fashion-forward, there are WAC-inspired pillboxes, reminiscent of a 1940s servicewoman, designed to sit either high on the head or low slanted over one eye, and held in place by a rubber band or comb. A traditional informal headpiece for a second-time bride is a circlet of pearl lattice-work, silk rosettes, or fresh flowers placed nearer the nape of the neck; for a large reception, the same headpiece could be more crownlike if greater importance is needed.

For a young bride marrying at home, in a garden, or in the country, a simple wreath combining fresh wildflowers, natural tea roses, or silk flowers mixed with baby's breath, or a picture hat, is often selected. Francesca, the resident bridal milliner for Saks Fifth Avenue, began her millinery career when the Coty award–winning designer Adolfo wanted headdresses made to accompany his collection of fairytale organza dresses on the runway. Francesca of Saks Fifth Avenue has this cautionary word regarding a large-brimmed picture hat: "While they look very good in fashion photographs, unfortunately their advantages begin and end there! First, the guests and photographer cannot see the bride's face as she walks down the aisle; second, on the receiving line the hat gets knocked off with each kiss; and third, it is in the way while dancing. So, more often than not, a picture hat gets cast aside and replaced with a hair ornament, such as a small bow from the dress fabric, after the ceremony."

Hairstyling, especially its volume and length, comes into play immediately because all headdresses and hairstyles won't work together. Headbands, for example, look well with most lengths, but pillbox styles work better with short hair. All simple hair orna-

ments, such as a self-fabric bow, small fan, or bursting silk flower, placed at the top, center, or back of the head, and sophisticated tiaras, soft-looking floral wreaths, or ornamental combs, berets, chignon clasps, ribbons, or snoods, usually work better with longer hair. Asymmetrical bows or flowers must have a counterbalancing hair shape to be graceful. Depending on how your hairstyle falls, the bow or a flower can be embellished with small pearls that run across the head, or it can be built up onto the crown or scaled down to sit higher, forming a halo. In short, it has to be made workable.

WHAT THE EXPERTS SAY ABOUT HEADDRESS SELECTION

Wearing a headdress is not the norm for modern women—especially one convertible enough to wear during a solemn ceremony and a joyous reception—whether breakfast, lunch, cocktails, dinner, disco party, or celebratory ball. Its uniqueness in her life alone makes its pursuit a unique experience and an adventure for most brides.

There are several methods, however, for a bride-to-be to gather ideas about which headdress style to select, ranging from window shopping to attending bridal fashion shows, from studying costume textbooks to browsing in books on fashion, from leafing through women's magazines for current trends to tearing out bridal magazine pages as a visual reference. An expert in the know is Rachel Leonard, who garnered her vast knowledge of the field working as the promotion coordinator for bridal-wear advertisers before assuming the fashion editor's responsibilities at *Bride's* magazine. She suggests a starting point well worth considering: "Whenever you try on a gown you might consider buying, also try on the manufacturer's or designer's headpiece matched with that par-

A puffed headband encircled with pearl ropes pulled off the face creates the illusion of a higher and wider forehead, and supports a tulle pouf.

ticular gown. This allows you the opportunity to see yourself in bridal headdress, and it gives a more complete idea of how that gown will ultimately look on you. Besides, you are then tapping into the experience of someone whose design sense you respect. Almost every headpiece can be purchased separately, so keep any one you like in mind: returning to try it on again with the gown you eventually select is one more alternative."

Under ideal circumstances, every prospective bride would be able to rely on her bridal consultant for assistance in finding the right headdress and perhaps customizing it, but this is not always the case. A common misconception even among salespeople, not to mention brides-to-be, is thinking that if some

element is closely coordinated, such as silk swags, encrustations of pearls, or porcelain flowers, it constitutes enough to tie an ensemble together. A gown's fabric, color, formality, silhouette, and embellishments are far from the entire picture. The most significant consideration is whether the headdress is right for your particular facial bone structure and features. One headdress style looks good with a prominent nose, a high forehead, or close-set eyes; some work well with long, round, or square faces; and other styles are best with certain hair types, quantities, and lengths. You have not come upon the right headdress until it complements your bone structure and facial features, pleasingly frames your face, and works perfectly with your gown's neckline and shoulders to outline your head—which is extremely important for portrait-style (from the waist up) photographs.

More than likely, further research at bridal salons and department stores' accessory counters or millinery shops—the headdress specialists—will be necessary, since headpieces aren't easily returned and your gown isn't easily transported or necessarily ready yet. When shopping, if you find yourself without trustworthy guidance, begin with one style and experiment with as many other styles, shapes, and sizes as needed until coming upon the ones that are right for you. By carrying a Polaroid or magazine shot of your gown along with a swatch (fabric sample) as you shop, you can avoid making a disastrous mistake or straying too far afield. Wearing your hair in a similar fashion to your planned hairstyle framework—pulled back, loose and flowing, brushed to the side, or whatever—is imperative. Also, your gown's bodice design figures so heavily into the right shape, placement, and proportion of the headdress that it is far easier to visualize how a headpiece will look when wearing attire with shoulders and a neckline resembling the bodice of your dress. Notice, for example, when one headpiece shape works better with a high neckline or short sleeves and another outlines and exposes your face; what placements interfere with your hairline; and which proportions overpower your head, making it look more constrained than luxuriously framed. Keep notes of the designs and shapes, lines and proportions, that are complementary and benefit your features.

For a bride unaccustomed to seeing herself in hats or any bride who believes she doesn't have a "hat face," Elaine Vincent cautions against buying a headpiece merely because it looks good in a picture. Although a headdress must relate to both a bride and her gown's overall proportion, in general, Vincent suggests beginning with a scaled-down headdress because it will be less severe, more modern, and easier to wear. "Minor differences in fullness, height, or width make a big impact, and could prevent a headpiece shape from fitting the bill; therefore, try on as many variations of each headdress shape as you can find. For example," she continues, "the same bride could consider a large, flat-brimmed picture hat or a baby pillbox style; a large skullcap or a smaller Juliet cap; a large, traditional tiara or mantilla treatment or a small, dressy version of her everyday hair ornament, such as a headband, comb, or bow."

At least for the time being, put aside the concern of harmonizing, coordinating, matching, and blending your gown's fabric and ornaments—first, decide on the shape and proportion, size and height, of your headpiece. Once these factors are determined, your search can be confined to that style with the elements that fit your dress. Bridal headdress is embellished with the same trimmings found on wedding gowns themselves—lace, pearls, bows, beads, sequins, and silk flowers, in an endless range of colors. If all else fails, and you have not located the exact headpiece you want, these materials can be customized in order to complete your desired look. After extensive research, brides-to-be often come up with their own initial concept or design to have custom-made, which is one more reason to allow yourself time: the headdress may need to be put into the works far in advance.

SELECTION AND PLACEMENT ACCORDING TO FACIAL FEATURES

Since each bride's head is a three-dimensional object, with height, depth, and width as seen from straight on, in profile, and from the back, the same dress and headpiece change with each angle: one angle could be lovely, one less so, but occasionally the third is disastrous. Although a face shape cannot be changed, a change of headpiece shape, size, proportion, or placement can make every bride look more beautiful. As with any article of clothing, a vertical or horizontal line will create an opposite optical illusion: width is reduced by vertical lines and length by horizontal lines. "With only one overview, selecting a headdress to create elongated lines and a visually slimmer face—excluding those already too long and thin—would be far easier," Francesca of Saks Fifth Avenue advises brides. "Go with what is and soften that, rather than attempting to radically change your face shape. An oval face can take many headpiece shapes, whereas long, broad, narrow, or round faces are more limited. On a wide face, a headpiece across the crown, instead of lying flat, creates a slight rise at the center, serving to elongate the head rather than emphasizing its width. A small face, for instance, can be enlarged by placing a headpiece high instead of circling

A wide pearl crown balances the headpiece with the neckline and sleeve treatment.

the forehead, which only compresses the face into a smaller area. A headpiece placed in the back accentuates a long face, but cutting across the forehead with a flower circlet or adding fullness on both sides of the head, at the cheekbones and temples, places emphasis on width rather than length. A round face needs height, not another curve, but a square face needs several curves to soften the angles rather than lines that accentuate them."

Looking at yourself in a headdress style is one method for determining if that style relates well to your head size: it is the *only* way to be sure that it will camouflage a prominent feature or face shape. Similarly, seeing yourself in many headpieces is a sure-fire method to determine whether the one you choose should rest in back, go from ear to ear, rise from the brow, sit on top, or cross nearer your forehead. "Only when a headpiece is well placed and angled will the lines integrate gracefully, which allows the eye to be led from certain areas and guided elsewhere—perhaps from a high hairline to strong cheekbones," says Patricia Bomer,

the headdress designer at Bergdorf Goodman in New York. Bomer graduated from Parsons School of Design and has designed bridal headdresses ever since. "Assets—such as a beautiful chin, mouth, nose, eyes, or high cheekbones—should be emphasized, made to stand out, shown at their best. No part of the headdress should cover, come near, or interfere with an extraordinary feature; it should sit high on the crown or be fastened low at the nape of the neck. An average feature can be made compatible with most headpiece styles with slight adjustments to size, proportion, or placement; for example, a wider nose gets more height so the cheekbones become more prominent, or a narrow nose gets width added to both sides of the head."

Although there are several headpieces that will work with each dress or gown, every headpiece doesn't work equally well with every face. *Bride's* fashion editor Rachel Leonard's one cautionary piece of advice is "I unequivocally warn brides-to-be about sprays and wreaths with branches—fabric flowers strung on self-curling, monofilament fishing wire—crossing the forehead, like an Indian headband, or protruding from the ear, like a telephone operator: neither creates a flattering, refined look." A less desirable or overly prominent feature, which needs to be somewhat overwhelmed or obscured entirely, cannot work with all headpieces, either. "Prominent noses and chiseled chins with pointed headpieces, including dropped ornaments or even a headband placed too far forward onto the face, will draw attention rather than balance nature's imperfection," continues Bomer, "whereas slight curves, say, a circlet or a softer cap placed off to the side, will deflect the eye to the headpiece first and to the center of the face second, which softens or counterbalances the sharp chin. Small, close-set eyes should not compete for attention with a headdress, either. Greater volume at this point, furthermore, will create the optical illusion of width. Another alternative would be a simple headdress shape, perhaps a pillbox hat worn back away from the face, and a touch of color—a tinted or silver-backed crystal sequin on a flower—placed near the eyes to bring a vivid eye color into prominence.

"A high hairline causes a prominent forehead, which can be broken with a gentle beaded band or flowers across the forehead to replace the bangs expected to be there. Soft bangs can remain, but brush them across if your headpiece is placed slightly farther back. With a low hairline, nothing should be placed on the face or at the side of your head; height in front is needed to take the focus up off the brow optically, and to limit the sense of a constrained, small head. A small bow or curve of flowers can be placed high on the crown with some hair on your forehead; the remainder is brushed up and back. Another possibility is to pull all the hair back and place a cap or flowers in back. For a small chin, no detail should keep the eye hovering around the ear and jawline—so no small caps. The eye must be brought farther up, perhaps to the forehead with a soft curl or by placing a tiara, Juliet cap, or wreath farther to the back of the head."

FACTORING IN THE GOWN'S NECKLINE AND SILHOUETTE

The bodice-to-headdress relationship, such as a simple dress with a simple headpiece, is one matter for which common sense serves as a good barometer; matching the gown's color, fabrics, and silhouette is a second; and blending its trimmings or embellishments is a third. However, creating harmony—a curved neckline picked up by a circlet, for instance—must be based on good design principles, which begin with balance and symmetry from your neckline to the top of your head. The neckline should frame the bottom, the headdress the top, of a bride's face. Saks Fifth Avenue's Francesca is the first to admit that there are far too many contingencies to enumerate, but experience has taught her that the best shortcut is a comparison with the shapes that are *likely* to be complementary. "Only extremely simple, classic headpieces that closely pick up a gown's detail and fabric are interchangeable with any neckline.

"A plunging neckline, for instance, requires a tiara or headband to be placed high, directing the focus off the bosom and onto the face. However, if a pointed chin is a consideration, the curve needs to be emphasized. Another low neckline is the sweetheart, which is a romantic heart shape curving over the bust line to open and slant toward the throat; it needs a more open and airy headpiece to work, such as a wreath or spray, while a tailored or daytime look simply won't look as well. A mantilla treatment works with a scoop neckline by echoing the oval below, and a cap accomplishes a similar effect by adding a second, equally sculpted form. As for high necklines, a square neckline is formal and can be paired with either a high, courtly effect or a low, curved shape, such as a bun cap, snood, or bow; if additional harmony is needed, outlining the headpiece and neckline in the same crystals, beads, or pearls achieves this end. The bateau neckline is usually very simple but always horizontal, and looks well with a Jacqueline Kennedy–esque pillbox hat worn back on the head, for instance. A lace or chiffon illusionary neckline has a band around the neck that forms a tier, so a toque or mantilla treatment works equally well, as long as each has a common element: matching fabric perhaps. With a portrait and Queen Anne neckline, a Juliet cap or skullcap or a bun hugging the crown will relate the lines working up the neck and framing the back of the head; the opposite direction would be accentuating the almost regal aura with a delicate tiara or profile headband. Finally, an off-the-shoulder bodice can take any romantic headpiece—especially a delicate wreath placed off the forehead, or a mantilla if the gown has a fitted back."

With minor adjustments to size and placement, it is possible for several headdress styles to work with various face shapes and features; moreover, the most complemen-

tary proportion between your head and the gown's silhouette can be formulated by adapting the headdress shape, size, and placement. These decisions are best made visually. "Assuming that the narrowest point is around the eyes—a very common trait and therefore true for many brides—the proportion of a full-skirted ball gown can be balanced by adding dimension to the side of the head, accomplished by a headband, for example," says Francesca. "For an A-line skirt, a reduced amount of fullness is needed at the temple to optically eliminate a tight or long look, so I recommend a cap and hairdo; and for a pencil-thin sheath, just enough width is needed for the bride's head not to look like the dot above a lower-case *i*. If a bride-to-be loves the 1930s, she may select an elaborate crystal and pearl hair ornament as headdress; and a sexy and sophisticated bride-to-be in her late thirties might match it with a profile headband that frames the side of her face. The classic princess gown—skimming the waist and gently flowing into a skirt—could be balanced with a traditional crown if the neckline is low, or half-crown if it is high. For an Empire gown, which lends itself to a leaner look, all hair could be swept off the neck, pulled into a twist, and a minimal tiara or headband worn at the back of the head. A romantic, English-looking circlet of silk, organdy, or fresh flowers is popular with the French basque waist, because this is a very young silhouette with a scoop neck that encircles the torso, clinging to the rib cage, and ending at the waist in a full skirt."

COORDINATING THE DETAILS

So the adventure begins—but where? Deciding on the elements to reintroduce on a traditional bridal headdress—whether informal or formal, elegant or casual, urban or country, day or evening—is fairly straight-

Matching alençon lace on the bodice and the stiffened and wired hat's underside tie the ensemble together.

forward because your sense of style and taste, personality and idiosyncrasies, preferences and peculiarities, are evident and included within your gown, dress, or outfit. Merely looking at it gives clues concerning what detail, trim, or fabric would be a well-suited accompaniment on the headdress. Typically, the fabric is considered first: either it has or doesn't have a pattern; the luster is high or low; the texture is smooth, slubbed, or lace. Fabric is rendered inconsequential if your headdress is to be fashioned entirely of other elements, such as flowers, metal, crystal, pearls, or beads. The adornments are considered with the purpose of amplifying a motif or trimming that has already been chosen—or the lack of any. There are two possible strategies: balancing the gown or highlighting the headpiece.

For a dress that has silk roses as the predominant feature, continuing with self-fabric roses fosters cohesion and balance. Indeed, the headpiece component, such as beaded lace, further embellished by adding a more elaborate or intricate or colorful array of crystal, sequins, or rhinestones, could have a magical effect. Although it always works to match seed pearls with seed pearls, don't disregard other, secondary elements if they are flattering to your face; surprisingly, a contrast sometimes enhances an ensemble even more. An unusual idea is wearing a pastel shade picked up from the gown, which can be continued in other accessories or accents later. A second example of contrast is endowing a very simple bias-draped, scoop-necked white silk dress with dramatic impact by wearing a multicolored crystal or latticework tiara, a fresh flower, or a fur or marabou headband. A contrasting headdress can be a wonderful addition—especially on an ample woman with a beautiful face.

You are making subjective decisions in an unfamiliar territory, so don't dismiss a con-

A classic 7mm double-strand pearl necklace with diamond and freshwater pearl-drop earrings.

cept as unworkable without first trying it. Feel free to experiment with fabric as long as its lead is taken from the overall gown fabric; some fabrics will not coordinate because of their luster or pattern or density. As part of a silk shantung ensemble, for instance, a headband wrapped in silk shantung or a pillbox frame covered in it will always relate. If you've chosen an unadorned dress, an all-pearl headpiece might be the perfect complement; on the other hand, if the bodice has a bow motif, pearls alone may not work as well as reintroducing a silk shantung bow with a pearl border. Moreover, fabrics need not match; they can harmonize or blend—for instance, a velvet cap with mink trim harmonizes rather than matching heavy satin, and works very well. For a dress with beaded alençon lace at the neckline, beaded lace somewhere on the headpiece, though not necessarily perfectly matched, is enough to tie the ensemble together. However, if collaged lace is on the dress, and its patterns, side by side, have created a wonderful textural look, coordinating a harmonious collage motif on the headdress could easily be

A simple, wrapped satin headband can carry an elaborately shirred and ruched veil. For an Art Deco feeling, consider a triple-strand pearl bracelet with diamond bars.

too busy and too far over the top. Therefore, selecting one pattern that blends, or an all-pearl headpiece that harmonizes, may best complete the ensemble.

Coordinating an unexpected element into your headpiece entails a closely matched color or a blended texture as the harmonizing detail with the bodice. This could involve adapting the trimming, adornment, or even an ornament's proportion. However, the headpiece adornment tying a traditional bridal ensemble together may be as unique as you can imagine: there can be a seasonal relationship, or it can enhance the spirit, period, or attitude, ranging from feathers picking up a fantasy *Swan Lake* ballerina skirt or hand-painted ribbons on a semi-formal dress, to white ermine matching a muff's trim or intricate embroidery of rhinestones and seed pearls in a floral pattern on an ultraformal gown. The more complicated the headpiece ornamentation, the more difficult it can be to get it right.

On unconventional bridal hats, the elements must always appear as though they were designed specifically to be a part of an outfit. "As with a traditional bridal ensemble, you would not pair a coarse straw hat with a close-weave dress fabric: the hat follows the outfit's attitude, color, and line. The elements, however, can be included according to a bride-to-be's personality—straightforward, whimsical, or sentimental—as well as how she visualizes herself," says Victoria Di Nardo, a milliner in New York City's fashionable SoHo district. "I will customize a hat, because in many cases a bride-to-be wants something different, with only the influence coordinated, not necessarily bows that match bows. I find that a bride-to-be who is choosing to be contemporary often has a very clear idea of the elements she wants on her head. Some come in with only their jacket; a few arrive with swatches and a sketch to ensure complete and perfect coordination. A most memorable bride-to-be wanted a pillbox with flowers—but, strange as it may sound, she literally wanted the top tier of the pillbox to mirror the top tier of her wedding cake! What's more, the bride and bridegroom on top were to be removable and placed on her head, after the dessert."

A Lustrous Touch: Your Jewelry

As an accessory, jewelry harmonizes with the ensemble's overall statement, complementing yet never competing with the gown, dress, or outfit. Its primary role is to flatter your features—emphasizing your face, hairdo, and headpiece, which is likely to include a veil—and to balance the gown's neckline. Understated and simple, classic and conservative have remained the bridal standard, but so many brides-to-be possess a strong desire to display fewer, higher-quality pieces that bridal jewelry also tends to be more formal. A bride's choice has everything to do with the person she is, because background, heritage, the wedding style and setting, the time of day, and the type of couple you make determine what jewelry will be worn. Younger and traditional brides ordinarily wear simple jewelry to complete and complement their gowns; informal and country-style brides favor antiques, such as an heirloom cameo (a multicolored, layered design carved in relief) or a sentimental locket (a small case holding a portrait); older and sophisticated brides tend toward a conservative lavaliere (a pendant on a necklace); second-time brides are more daring; and forefront-of-fashion brides prefer a dramatic, larger piece or one with an air of fun.

The materials used most clearly define your jewelry's formality and style, from casual and trendy—plastic loops and feathers, for instance; to daytime and dressy—precious metals, particularly gold and silver, with gemstones sparingly added for the extra highlight that their sparkle and twinkle provide; to evening and conservative—all-diamond pieces or merely a strand of pearls, the long-standing mainstay. Elongated shapes, such as drops and pendants, or larger-than-normal sizes—to make a significant statement and remain in proportion with upswept hair—lean toward higher degrees of formality as well. This is not to say that every fine piece of jewelry must be intricate or large to be formal, nor is every bogus or costume-jewelry piece informal, regardless of size. The point is best illustrated by diamond or pearl studs and rhinestone earrings, because each will seem formal and dressy—no matter how small and simple.

While important jewelry is unnecessary for a bride, wearing a family heirloom piece given by the bridegroom's mother, say, should not be ruled out. Jewelry can be more important, however, when coordinating with the detailing in the dress, or with a little A-line dress if nothing else is going on. It is also true that for an afternoon wedding, discreet pearl buttons would seem more in keeping, whereas pearl drops encrusted and embellished with diamonds would be more appropriate for an evening wedding. At large, ultraformal weddings, great family diamond necklaces or exquisite pearls may be expected, but at small informal weddings a bride's jewelry should be simpler and less important—unless, of course, a carnival atmosphere or costume effect is desired. "After all, jewelry is a matter of taste and personal choice, not set by rules," avers Kenneth Jay Lane, who has created costume pieces for royalty as well as presidents' wives. "Anyway, there are none concerning what type or style of jewelry will be right or wrong for a bride. A wedding should be a joyous occasion for everyone, but it is the bride's day, so whatever jewelry she feels would be fun, give her pleasure, and make her happy is exactly right on her for that day.

A pearl-edged, wide-brimmed picture hat matches a convertible, double-strand, 7mm pearl necklace clasped with a decorative cameo encircled with diamonds and matching earrings.

"Yet the various jewelry styles do have different effects on which to capitalize. While some styles harmonize with almost any ensemble, others complete a certain look, adding to the whole. For example, understated pieces, such as diamond studs, foster an air of elegance; similarly, antiques add to the sense of tradition. For extra coordination, the jewelry style can be kept within the dress style: contemporary pieces blend with fashion-forward dresses; simply designed jewelry echoes simple dresses. Furthermore, an elaborate piece balances a heavily beaded gown, and a lavaliere counterbalances a train. If materials and shapes, like Austrian crystal and bows, are reintroduced in the jewelry, that can help an ensemble work better—for instance, coordinating the crystal from a bodice, on the headdress, and again in the jewelry, as opposed to, say, gold earrings and necklace, which may be borderline, or won't work at all."

Sticking with the Old Standby: Pearls

Few brides bother with a brooch or pin unless it is a family heirloom, and since everything centers around them or is taken care of by their attendants, brides seldom wear watches, much less concern themselves with the time. On the other hand, the single most meaningful jewelry piece, the wedding band—which is not part of the bride's garb at all—should be treated as an isolated case, because it will be a continuous accessory—for a lifetime. Although most bridegrooms want a plain round band, many brides want a band that has a special design, combines with her engagement ring, and can be worn every day. If it must fit these criteria—unusual yet adaptable—a wider gold or precious-stone band is always appropriate.

It is pearls, however, that remain a bride-to-be's number-one choice as bridal jewelry on this special day as well. It is partly because pearls are nature's symbol of purity—protected innocence, chastity, feminine charm—and of a perfect long-term partnership; and partly because pearls effortlessly tie together an ensemble—whether an outfit or gown, hat or tiara.

Always a bridal tradition, pearls are introduced and reintroduced as a fashion statement in both ready-to-wear and couture collections. The enormous popularity of larger-than-life, baroque, faux pearls has altered the classic bridal strand of pearl on fashion-conscious brides from small to much larger and has increased the use of such shades as pale pink, ivory, or yellow, with or without crystal and colored accents. "In fact, the first bridal arena for colors to be introduced was jewelry," recalls Janice Savitt of M. & J. Savitt, one of New York City's hottest jewelry designers. "The bride's coloring is a factor when deciding to wear colored, precious or semiprecious stones. For example, diamonds, like pearls, are always a popular accent because they combine with anything; they continue the all-white, pure-white theme, and a diamond probably is already present on her finger in the form of an engagement ring. The two most popular semiprecious stones are neutral yellow topaz and fiery red garnet. A topaz looks good on blondes and goes with yellow gold for a monotone effect; a garnet combines well with both brown and black hair and accents a deep red nail polish and lipstick. Green stones, such as emeralds, peridot, tourmaline, and tsavorite, are more of a personal decision, which is true for purple amethysts, opals, and so forth."

Denise O'Donoghue, who is *Bride's* beauty and jewelry editor, believes most brides already have in mind the piece of jewelry they'll wear. "Most likely it will be something she always pictured herself in on her wedding day, perhaps for sentimental reasons," she says. "In this case, keep in mind the portion of your dress or suit that must accept the accessory, because it will set the overall direction for your jewelry. The questions I am asked most frequently are 'Should I wear pearls and diamonds, or a diamond stud?' and 'Are drop earrings too important?' My answer inevitably is 'Wear what you want!' But I will remind each bride-to-be that any element surrounding her face can influence the appropriate jewelry piece, such as hair worn up without bangs, because more important earrings may be needed.

"I would not recommend wearing a necklace, and certainly not more than a strand of pearls at your throat, especially with high-necked gowns, without seeing it all together, including the headpiece. What I would suggest, however, is bringing a lavaliere along to the second or third fitting, when your final decision is made. The right choice may be that earrings alone are more than enough. The same is true for a pearl bracelet, which could be worn with a sleeveless gown, short sleeves, three-quarter sleeves, and even over tight-fitting sleeves and gloves: seeing your gown with and without the bracelet answers the question best. Furthermore, with many contemporary bridal ensembles, the expected can look wrong and the unexpected exactly right. With flowing hair, if ornaments will be worn, there are many jewelry pieces from which to choose, including an elaborate clasp, comb, parure of pins or barrettes, bejeweled cap, snood with shimmering threads, aigrette to hold plumes or a tuft of feathers; and gold chains or several strands of pearls can be woven, braided, or interspersed throughout the hair, inspiring a Botticellian innocence. For a hat, either a fancy buckle or whimsical hatpin or subtle

edging of pearls is a possibility as well. Many choices will work; however, each choice *must* be tried with the dress, with the headpiece, with the neckline, and with all of the above together, to know which you really like best. It is the only way."

Until quite recently, the perennial favorite and the *only* necklace considered appropriate for a first-time bride wearing white was a single strand of pearls paired with pearl button earrings, which remains very popular and basic to every wardrobe. Depending on her gown's neckline, many brides still choose from these classic lengths with one, two, or three strands of various-sized pearls, which include a dog collar, stacking up on the neck; a choker, which sits at the throat; princess, which falls to the bust line; matinée, which cascades over the bosom; and opera, which ends at the navel. Each additional strand adds another dimension—length and bulk; they can vary in diameter as well, for variety. Three strands of pearls are dressier than one strand; moreover, if the necklace clasp has a large rhinestone or diamond, it is dressier still. For graduated strands, where the larg-

Single-strand, 8mm, perfectly matched pearls.

est pearl is the centerpiece, the pearl on each side is matched for size as well as quality, color, luster, and so forth.

"As bridal gown necklines plunged, double and triple strands of larger, more important pearls became increasingly popular as well," adds Janice Savitt. "They are very beautiful when set off with interspersed diamonds or colored stones, and can be embellished with a clasp which serves as a focal point; or a rondure, such as a diamond disk, can hang off the pearls, serving as a motif in the center of the neck. Baroque pearls wrapped around the neck—even three or four times—look good as a lavaliere with a charm or pendant, such as a golden sun, hanging off the strand of pearls."

PEARLS

The three pearl categories are *deep-sea* pearls (known as oriental pearls), which are produced naturally by oysters; *cultured* pearls, the most common variety, which are produced through modern techniques of inserting an irritant into oysters, causing the pearl to develop; and *freshwater* pearls found in rivers and lakes, which are irregular, multihued, and possess an intense luster. Cultured pearls are virtually indistinguishable—except by X-ray photography—from their natural cousins, and benefit from a greater thickness, more concentric layers, and less likelihood of deterioration from contact with human body acids.

The six criteria for judging a pearl are its size, shape, color, luster, translucence, and surface quality; when coupled with other pearls, its match is also evaluated. Size is determined by weight and governs a pearl's value. Also, roundness—a perfect cultured pearl rolls true—is quite a rare quality and adds enormously to the value. A blemish or mark will detract from a pearl's value, but because a flawless surface is extremely costly, tiny natural imperfections are acceptable.

The natural pearl shapes include *spherical,* which is closely related to the classic bridal strand of pearls; *seed* pearls, which are very small—there can be as many as nine thousand per ounce!—and round, and are used for embroidery and trim on bridal gowns; *baroque,* which are irregular in shape with ridges, and often used as a drop; and *hemispheric* (known as blister or mabe), which are gentle mounds and particularly flattering for most face shapes and features.

The major color classifications of pearls are ivory, pink, silver cream, gold green, blue, and black. Because they flatter a complexion, pink, silver, and off-white hues are preferred by brides.

The pair of earrings you wear is a decision to approach with special caution, particularly regarding new and trendy styles, such as the shoulder duster dangling down alongside your neck. Anything of that kind is a very strong statement, whereas an earring close to the lobe, such as clusters or flower motifs with only a bare neck, prevents the jewelry accessory from taking over entirely. There is another factor that keeps brides-to-be away from anything ostentatious: fashion trends come in and go out constantly. Therefore, at various times in the future, looking at the wedding pictures or videotape, you will certainly appear to have been a very "with it" bride, but at other times you can look very dated. The designs and shapes of earrings are unlimited, ranging from clusters and sprays to florals and animal motifs, to geometrics and free-form designs. Larger button or round earrings accentuate a round face whereas a longer shape with a dangle, perhaps a pearl, widens a narrow face; near a short neck, an elongated shape, including an oval, works in the opposite manner. An angular face can be somewhat softened and enhanced if attention is drawn to the outside by a spray or cluster at the ear. A long face is cut by a square- or emerald-cut stone that focuses attention halfway down. "Large, spherical pearls are limited because they create very few earring shapes, but small seed and baroque pearls are not. They can form either an X shape with a feathered sweep that follows the contours of the jaw and ear naturally, or a cushion shape that is flattering when diamonds are clustered around or across," reveals Christopher Walling, whose one-of-a-kind, custom-made jewelry designs are referred to as art as often as jewelry.

"When budget is a consideration, it is far wiser for a bride to wear only a wonderful pair of earrings, and not mediocre earrings with a necklace to compensate. I am always extremely happy to see a pearl necklace of any length on the bare flesh of a bride, and perfectly happy to see an opera- or matineé-length necklace cascading over the fabric of a wedding gown; however, a necklace that just falls to the neckline—no matter what type—is a mistake. Likewise, the more naked the bodice, the longer the earring can be."

The renowned Parisian jewelry designer Mme. Belperron once remarked, "Brides are not buying their gowns off the rack, so why should they buy their jewelry without at least several hours' consultation with a designer?" An argument can be made for a bride-to-be customizing her gown to have one-of-a-kind jewelry as well, which, after all, will bring out her particular beauty and is instantly an heirloom. "I can design a piece based on her neckline, throat, or ear configuration; how she moves and her coloring are also important," reasons Christopher Walling. "Even an authority must compare one pair of earrings with a few alternatives. And a little-known fact is that an unassuming bridegroom, normally uncomfortable with fancy jewelry, will appreciate seeing his bride in a lavish jewelry piece as she walks toward him at the altar."

For fashion-forward and contemporary brides, both bracelets, with or without a sleeve, and pins, which are worn on the upper left-hand side of the chest or on a hat, should not be overlooked. "Two or three pins, whether buttons or jeweled flowers, that are equal sizes and relate to each other, or fresh flowers combined with a pin can be very chic," continues Walling. "And intricate filigree works with lace, as long as it does not conflict with the pattern. With a veil and upswept hair, I favor small earrings up on the lobe, but with a dramatic hat, a long dangling or a large on-the-ear earring may be

needed. As a case in point, I'll describe the jewelry that I would put with my favorite wedding dress, an Empire style by Givenchy. It is white velvet with the hem just below the knees in front, and the A-line skirt softly billows to form the train in back. To echo the gown, a white satin hat, trimmed in front with mink on a medium-sized brim, trails four feet down the back. For a bride wearing this dress, I would suggest long earrings, peeking beneath the hat."

The Crowning Glory: A Bride's Mantle

More than any single element, a veil sets the bride apart, lending stature, importance, and prestige, adding a special beauty and a touch of mystery to her ensemble. It is true for a second-time bride as well, though usually a more subdued veil treatment is selected, unless she eloped or had a very private first wedding. And a third- or fourth-time bride usually wears only a mere touch of tulle, which is incorporated as part of her hat or headpiece, unless as a late-in-life bride, she desires a more mysterious ambience or a more princesslike aura for her wedding day. Traditional veil presentations can attach to the headpiece and trail behind, stand out in back, burst on top, come forward to cover the face (symbolizing innocence, purity, and virginity), or any combination of the above.

In 1807 an Englishman, John Escoe, invented a knitting machine capable of weaving a silk net fine enough for an entire veil to be pulled through a bride's wedding ring. Although hand-rolled nylon tulle has replaced the fragile, costly, heavy, and cumbersome silk, the same infinitesimal, screenlike, crosshatch stitch, called "illusion," remains a traditional bride's first choice, because it engulfs her in a floating,

A wired-pearl, branch-design wreath and full puffed sleeves show through a translucent and wide-pouf veil to create an elegant bridal statement.

VEIL LENGTHS

The updated, informal veils are *birdcage*, falling just below the chin, and *flyaway*, brushing the shoulders. The semiformal veil lengths are longer, falling farther down the body, and include *fingertip*, touching the tips of the fingers; *ballet* or *waltz*, which falls to the knee; and *sweep*, which skims the ground. A formal presentation is a veil the same length as the dress hem or train, ranging from *court*, which extends 1 foot along the floor; to *chapel*, trailing 1½ feet behind; to *cathedral*, tumbling approximately 3 feet along the ground. An ultraformal veil—almost a *royal* bridal look—is an *extended cathedral* veil that cascades 5 feet along the ground.

A *blusher* or *illusion* length extends below the chin to the collarbone or as low as the waist. It is worn forward over the face to lie flat, puff out if held in place with wire, or stand out all around if circular-cut. "It symbolizes tradition, modesty, and virginity, and should not be considered a fashion statement," advises Barbara Tober, editor-in-chief of *Bride's* magazine. She also believes the veil has everything to do with the bride's presentation for her bridegroom's eyes only. "After walking down the aisle with her, the bride's father lifts the blusher, kisses her, puts it back, and brings her to the altar. He gives his daughter away. Symbolically, he is saying, 'I know you, and your husband will know you when this veil is lifted again.' After the ceremony, with an attendant's assistance the blusher is pushed back to create a halolike effect, as the bride and bridegroom walk back up the aisle together."

The veil's edge can remain raw or have a simple three-thread marrow-edge stitch, be hand-rolled or have a buckram, rattail piping, which adds elevation and fullness. Occasionally, a lace border, satin or grosgrain ribbon edge with colored bugle beads, pearls, marabou, or whatever corresponds to the dress trimming is incorporated. The blusher's tulle becomes smothering if extensively encrusted. However, interspersed gold or silver shimmering threads or modest embellishments, such as stitched dots, strategically scattered or randomly placed may further glamorize the tulle; anything more may block the bride's vision or fall unbecomingly on her face.

Another versatile veil is a *pouf*, which bursts from the nape of the neck or back of the head. A small pouf with small dots or spotted with crystal, pearls, or sequins often surrounds the bride's face. Poufs are worn alone, paired with a blusher, or combined with a blusher and a longer veil. A pouf rises approximately 6 inches and spreads out up to 9 inches. It is placed either low, peeping out of the sides, midway up to peek over the top, or high and visible from all angles. It can snap directly onto a headpiece, be grabbed by Velcro, or attach with a strong wide-toothed comb. Moreover, when a veil is removed after the ceremony, the pouf can detach as well or remain in place with the headpiece during the reception.

cloudlike, ethereal quality. Every bride does not wear tulle; in fact, among most European cultures, the bridal tradition is an oval lace veil or mantilla that graciously skims the shoulders or trails down to the middle of the back, the knees, or several yards along the floor. These mantles are great family treasures handed down from mother to daughter to granddaughter and loaned to relatives for their weddings as well. According to folklore, Martha Washington's grandniece, Emily Custis, was the first American woman to wear a lace veil: she wanted to make sure that the bridegroom would find her as attractive on their wedding day as he did when first spotting her behind a lace curtain.

Turn-of-the-century weddings were formal affairs by modern standards. They took place before noon or after six o'clock with a virginal bride in an elaborate gown, which had a long train with a veil to the floor. A short veil dates back to the afternoon "informal" weddings of that period when the bride's dress had a short train or none at all, and the veil fell proportionately down her back or to her shoulder. According to bridal consultant extraordinaire Monica Hickey, Saks Fifth Avenue's resident doyenne, "There was little change until the

OPPOSITE: A multitier inverted handkerchief veil.

A three-tier blue tulle veil is set back from an embellished pillbox hat to complement a formal bridal gown's multitucked bodice.

early 1970s, because milliners schooled in fashioning splendid, feather-light Brussels lace cloches or creating picture hats were abundant," she recalls. "Ten years later, the rage was less formal with simple veil treatments, such as very narrow borders of little bows or ribbons, which perfectly matched the then-fashionable short, informal garden wedding dress. Except to set off an ultra-formal gown with an important headdress, custom-made headpieces with veils lay dormant. All too often attention, emphasis, importance, was meted out exclusively on the gown. This oversight relegated the veil to an afterthought.

"Trends in veils do exist but they are reprises, so to speak—for example, nowadays every bride seems to want tiny roses. A bride wearing baby roses goes all the way back to the English Tudor kings."

Francesca Bianca finds today's brides have well-formed, specific fashion ideas, but even so, they treat their veil quite respectfully and somewhat traditionally. Bianca observes brides as Saks Fifth Avenue's designer of custom-made bridal veils. She is also the scholarly restorer and resident creator of accessories and accents, such as jewelry, shoes, and fans, that complete historic ensembles for the Metropolitan Museum's Costume Institute exhibitions. "Unbeknown to us they would double as wedding gowns," she recalls of her earliest bridal headdress experience. "The vast majority of young brides still choose romance—something from a childhood fantasy, perhaps, with a flashy, sparkling touch. A businesswoman in her late twenties or early thirties, who is a more tailored dresser, prefers a ladylike, simplified veil—nothing outlandish or way out. For extra simplicity, her gown's trimmings, such as silk flowers or delicate pearls, may be combined on the border."

A headdress can have abundant tulle for a cathedral wedding, less so in a chapel, and a tulle ruffle, bow, or streamer—but no veil per se—in a minister's study or judge's chambers. But with no tulle whatsoever, a bride's head can look tiny. Suzanne, a New York City milliner who specializes in both contemporary bridal hats and traditional headpieces, suggests that "for an informal or second-time bride's veil treatment, tulle and a hat work beautifully to connote a bridal feeling. On smaller hats, tulle with appliquéd roses can be wrapped around the crown or cascaded down one side for drama. For a large-brim picture hat, the tulle can be thrown over the head, held with a pin, and left to hang down in back or around the entire hat. Or it can attach with Velcro, be pushed back for the receiving line, and taken off for the reception. However, the tulle should balance the silhouette, bodice, and sleeves—for instance, long with a multiple-layer, handkerchief-point hem and short with a just-below-the-knee-length skirt."

Another possibility for contemporary brides is a fancy version of their everyday hair ornaments, such as a comb or clip with tulle. Eric Javits, a New York–based milliner whose easy-to-wear creations are sold at better specialty shops and department stores, has observed that a fashion-forward bride doesn't want a traditional headdress with a veil. "When braided satin headbands with pearls, silk camellias, cabbage rose blossoms, or bows appeared in bridal magazines," Javits recalls, "contemporary brides-to-be walked in and bought them, because they are dressy, available in shades of white or ivory, and they highlight, accent, and blend in or coordinate well with wedding dresses. Yet they are inexpensive, unobtrusive, and small. While tulle is unnecessary, of course, netting can be attached to

Opposite: A novel, inverted flowerpot-shape headpiece with stiff, openwork Russian net, worn rakishly, acts as a counterpoint to a symmetrically shaped dress and train.

a picture hat or eye-level mesh on a toque for something perky, festive, whimsical, or charming—remaining less than rakish, though."

VEIL COLOR, SIZE, AND PLACEMENT FOR A BLUSHING BRIDE

The veil's color should blend perfectly with the gown and headpiece. Therefore, white is worn with a white dress and ivory with an ivory dress; however, standard illusion veiling ranges from pure white, which is blue-white, to diamond white, which is brighter, to silky white, which is near to white satin. Ivory, antique ivory, vegetable dyes, henna, or tea-staining are other options to match a blue, pink, or cream dress. But certain tulle colors offset a bride's skin better—for example, white-white washes out many skin tones, which makes diamond and silky white or blush and ivory hues far more common than blue-whites and white-whites. A bolder, more modern approach would be matching a gown's accent color, such as vibrant flowerbuds.

"Bolts of tulle are two, three, and four yards wide, so any degree of fullness is feasible," reveals Suzanne as she hand-blocks a fur felt bridal hat in her millinery shop on Madison Avenue. "The mesh size ranges from a standard tulle to a Swiss net, which is fine, soft, and silky, to a honeycomb weave, which is coarser and can stand in a fountainlike effect. There are also French nettings, which include a wide mesh with diamonds or a narrow mesh with random nubs. While chiffon is certainly sheer enough, it blocks air flow, causing the veil to become confining—especially indoors and in warm, humid weather. Seasonality plays a minor role as well—for instance, in the winter a thicker treatment may echo the gown better than a lightweight, airy treatment.

"The headpiece style, its placement, and the desired look dictate the right veil treatment as well as where and how it will attach. For instance, the veil can sit high and back with a circlet, or low and forward on the crown, or over or under a halo headband. A blusher looks graceful when it comes from the top or under a wreath, which is a decidedly Victorian look; it rarely looks right from an asymmetrical headpiece. A short blusher falls awkwardly and flat on the face from a cap worn at back, unless it is caged:

Pearl-enhanced handmade roses in a row support a small pouf and a trailing veil of pearl-scattered tulle.

cut in the opposite direction, lifted up, and then brought forward. With modern bouffant hairstyles, a comb with a cascade of tulle works well and can be plucked out of the hair and replaced with a second decorated comb or a pretty piece behind the head, such as a silk flower, self-fabric bow, or pouf."

Another important consideration is the veil's convertibility—the options a treatment offers—and your needs. Monica Hickey firmly believes that a crowning touch, even a vestige, should remain throughout the wedding day. Before making their decision, Hickey advises her brides to consider how they want the veil treatment to look for each presentation of the wedding day—down the aisle, at the altar, on the receiving line, and during the reception. "Just ask yourself, 'Will the veil look right pushed back while I am walking quickly back down the aisle? Will it be detached after the receiving line, photography session, and first dance take place?' Because of its bulk and weight, a veil is likely to be detached after the formality of the ceremony and receiving line as the socializing begins, to be replaced by a smaller veil picking up a similar theme. For the next hour, the replacement veil can be pushed back and attached with the same hair ornament, and just the ornament can remain during the fun and dancing part."

LACE VEILS: CREATING A FOCAL POINT

An inexpensive veil with a good dress—or, for that matter, with a lesser dress—often won't work. If a bride is working within a budget and cannot afford an expensive gown, Monica Hickey suggests buying a perfectly simple but lovely dress and a more extravagant veil. "What is more, it does not necessarily have to be standard illusion. It can be silk chiffon floating along a chiffon dress with flowers cascading down the back, or when everything includes golden touches, a veil with golden threads sporadically woven in and a narrow golden border." Ivory antique veils—whether a family heirloom or a precious find—were made of high-quality Battenberg, French, or Venetian rose point lace, and were rarely embellished. A bride occasionally chooses to incorporate her mantilla-style veil with a simple illusion blusher, creating her own pièce de résistance. In this instance, an unadorned, lightweight alençon lace trim is used. It allows the gown beneath—usually a simple sheath or column style without a distinguishing bustle, back neckline, or important bow back treatment—to be seen faintly and not completely obscured. When the veil is detached, an entirely different style emerges for dancing at the reception.

When a bride walking down a long, wide aisle wants her guests to behold a very theatrical effect, a breathtakingly embellished lace veil can have that impact, even from afar. Indeed, with any number of religious and cultural traditions, when a bride is required to be heavily veiled, a dramatic statement may be warranted. "Once," recalls Monica Hickey, "a Sephardic Jewish bride asked me to put together a heavily beaded gown with an enormous, royal-length train behind. Everything came together when a lace mantle was added. It was lifted off her brow by an armature, which is a wired structure, and attached with a Spanish comb placed high on her head. As if by magic, a transformation occurred. She looked magnificent!"

Adorning and ornamenting a beautiful lace bridal veil with elevated encrustations is time-consuming and labor-intensive. It is a difficult process, but it creates a unique definition by highlighting and adding a

An Old World, lace mantilla-style headdress.

dimension to the original lace pattern. The embellishments can take it in many different directions, which in trade talk are design concepts. These encompass the type of add-ons and their size, the areas to be highlighted and how extensively, and where and how often to reembroider. A modest presentation is small with nonreflecting adornments, such as pearls or bows; if larger beads, sequins, or crystal are used, the degree of sophistication increases. The places and ways to use adorned lace treatments are as wide and varied as a bride's imagination and taste, ranging from an understated $1/2$-inch border of scattered pearls, sequins, and beads to a hand-cut appliqué with gold stars forming a series of pyramids, to an overall pattern with an ornamented edge or a crystal-bead-encrusted fantasy of lace trailing for yards. As more design concepts form, less and less lace remains. When properly designed, the effect gives the aura of a princess. Furthermore, if properly executed, each element enhances the entire ensemble without overpowering any part.

Loosely covered silk organza and floral appliqués achieve a light and airy look; the five-strand pearl choker, heart-shaped clasp, and tiny pearl clusters at each ear balance the exaggerated brim of the hat.

FINALIZING THE VEIL: STYLE AND PROPORTION

To visualize which veil treatment creates perfect harmony takes years of experience, and is determined only when the gown and headdress can be seen from several angles. It requires a trained eye, because it is necessary to judge whether there is too much at the temple or too little at the neck, when the veil should end higher or lower, when the color is off, or when an adjustment to the edging is correct.

Monica Hickey reveals her secret: "A veil treatment surrounding the head is highly individual. Therefore, I look for faults, which requires a critical eye. Before a veil turns out exactly right, I have asked myself over and over again, 'What could possibly make this veil better?' I stop fiddling when I'm satisfied that that veil best compliments the bride. Perfection is then achieved. Furthermore," she continues, "a key, to my mind, is never overdo, because the veil should further a harmonious relationship between the hairstyle, facial structure, and jewelry. It is a bride's hairstyle that gives her milliner the biggest clue to making it all work; therefore, knowing her hairstyle is crucial before considering the veil." It is so important that Hickey advises every bride to wear her hair as it will look on her wedding day when trying on veils with her headpiece and gown.

Every factor must be taken into account, but common sense is a very important ingredient. Although the veil length is known early on, how much veil—its fullness—is best left to the second fitting when the entire ensemble, including shoes for height, has been assembled on the bride. Hickey continues: "To judge the appropriate quantity of tulle, one must consider the wedding size, the scale in which the veil will be seen, the wedding style, the time of day, train length, and formality—or informality. Here, I search for harmony with the gown's silhouette, because the most important factor is always whether the size, shape, and length of the veil are right for the gown's magnitude and volume—that is, in proportion. For example, a big dress looks better to the eye, even if untrained, with more veil; the same rule follows for a small dress: a big veil will appear overpowering. The veil's length or the pouf's height can offset the fullness of a ball-gown skirt, so that a bride appears neither topheavy, cut off, or too closely cropped; in the same way, long, narrow veils relate to slim dresses and sheaths."

The right proportion need not be accomplished with a single veil. A single blusher tier is an informal presentation, but it can be part of a more formal, three-tier treatment as well—for example, a cathedral- and street-length veil with the blusher as the uppermost tier, covering the face. When five to ten varying lengths are combined, a layered look is created: the pouf on top, the blusher seen in front, and any additional veil lengths worn trailing behind. As the pouf increases in size and shape, its importance does too and it becomes a bigger factor in relation to the dress. The blusher length—to the waist rather than the shoulder or elbow— and its shape—full or encircling the head, not flat and forward—will also change the proportion. Generally, a tall, slender bride can add a pouf to a flowing veil treatment whereas a petite bride would resemble a snowball and an ample bride would not appear taller.

Customized Headdress

No one would argue that finding just the right headdress, headpiece, or hair ornament is an easy task, especially for a bride-to-be inexperienced with wearing hats for other than warmth. Many brides have a long-standing vision of themselves in a veil or have fallen in love with a magazine photograph, but have difficulty adapting it to their look or gown. For these brides, and any bride lacking the knack of accessorizing herself, it is wise to seek an expert's opinion before deciding on the hairstyle, headdress, jewelry, and veil. A custom headpiece designer can guide a bride-to-be—without dictating—by suggesting possibilities along the lines of her first choice, or can find an alternate direction that suits her features better.

Custom headdress is created with each detail taken into account: the headpiece is designed and the veil shape is created to work on you. When seeking a milliner's services, bring a magazine photograph, Polaroid, or sketch of the dress for the overall proportions and style, swatches (fabric samples) for the weave properties and color values, or photocopies for the lace's characteristics. The designer needs to be informed about the formality of the wedding dress or gown and about the spirit, ambience, attitude, and direction of the wedding ceremony

and reception. This governs the scale: a cathedral, for instance, begs for a long veil, a chapel asks for a simpler treatment, a field wants a straw hat with wildflowers, and a riverbank whispers for a different hat altogether. The hairstyle determines how a headpiece is anchored. The jewelry options, including gifts, an heirloom, or a sentimental or good luck piece, must be seen and coordinated as well.

While the cost is higher, the chance of being satisfied is far better because, if need be, headdress designers will lend their expertise and help in coordinating every element—hairstyling, headpiece and veil, jewelry, or makeup—to ensure an impeccable accessorized look.

A wreath secures the multiple miniature tulle poufs that create this rich, full, and long formal veil, which trails down the back of an impressive dress.

From prehistoric tribes to sophisticated societies, various dainty, sweet-smelling, or fanciful flowers have symbolized innocence, fecundity, and true love. Whatever the flower variety, it was given to a bride to wear or to hold in a prescribed manner, most likely without conforming to a recognizable design principle. Its presence was to ensure the bridegroom's faithfulness, the bride's fertility, and their long life together. By definition, today's equivalent, bouquets, are bunched flowers; by design, they are a combination of color, texture, and line forming a harmonious unit of rhythm, proportion, scale, balance, and contrast. By convention, a bride's bouquet joins her gown and headdress to balance an ensemble's total look, and it adds a soft, feminine glow that says "alive." It is symbolic, moreover, to have and to hold an object from the earth itself that pervades the air, however subtly, with its delicate fragrance, spicy aroma, or rich perfume. Therefore, each bridal bouquet's overall visual, tactual, and olfactory elements must be carefully considered in order to combine satisfactorily with the bride's attire, personality, and scent.

Florescence

carrying and wearing flowers

OPPOSITE: Consider flowers in a color that complements your complexion.

Any flower variety included in the bouquet makes a statement that is meant to last a lifetime, such as roses to connote the suitor's ardent love or orange blossoms to represent the bride's loveliness. Whichever flowers are used in the bouquet also directly affect its rhythm—rigid or flowing, subtile or coarse, dynamic or static—in a repetitive design or by combining, harmonizing, and contrasting the colors. The flowers and materials, including foliage, bows, ribbons, streamers, and such, govern the line or shape as well, whether long and slender, short and compact, a cascading free form, a focus-drawing pyramid, a symbolic pedestal formation, or a sexually suggestive mound. In addition, the components dictate the volume, scale, size, and proportion, which can vary from very full and large to quite small and narrow and everything in between.

Both a variety of harmonious colors and monotone flowers, with their subtle petal variation, can produce a light, bright, festive spirit to a dark, strong, and powerful mood when included as a bride's accessory. In each case, the bouquet's compositional balance, contrast, or focal point is derived by using the hues and textural varieties. For instance, identical ruffle-edged, blush-pink carnations positioned equally on either side of a central line creates an aesthetic symmetry, whereas an odd number and size or contrasting light and dark varieties achieves a sense of counterbalance; also, a single, flat flower with a dark area—say, a daisy—placed as the compositional center emphasizes dominance and brings the eye back to the bouquet. Most of all, each detail concerning the bouquet's elements, including the type of flowers, must compliment you while playing its part in your ensemble.

Personal Preference: The First Guideline in Selection

After months of decisions concerning the hall, caterer, and music as well as the gown and accessories, the wedding day is your moment to shine. As the centerpiece of all this attention—there will be more than enough flutter—your bouquet should be a personal statement that seems natural and not just something extra to carry. It should also serve as a calming object adding confidence, beauty, and importance. Therefore, the first consideration when contemplating the flowers to carry is *your* desire and predilection—you may know that a special lily carried as one simple, sublime stem or favorite roses in a big colorful bundle or an elegant spray of orchids or a basket of fresh garden flowers will make you happy and best express your emotions and personality.

OPPOSITE: A modest mum bouquet reflects a less formal and a more personal point of view.

Even a bride-to-be experienced with flowers often considers herself incapable of selecting those for her bouquet. Yet each bride-to-be, if she tries, can add some degree of her taste, personal style, and lifestyle. "Overselling and going overboard with the flowers for the bouquet is a disservice to the bride," says Bill Kenon, the longtime manager of Flowers by Beatrice Mann in New York City's Hampshire House, "because the ultimate goal is to discover what would be her most appropriate floral accessory." Kenon has been designing bouquets for forty-nine years. He claims to have lost count of the bouquets he has designed. "Perhaps I've worked with five thousand brides in my day, but the important factors remain for each bride: what she wants and can afford. For obvious reasons there is no formula.

"As a professional florist, I begin making flower suggestions according to her gown's color, style, length, and formality—whether formal, semiformal, or informal—as well as her height and weight. Her size is one element never to be overlooked; ample brides look better carrying symmetrical, slim flowers because large or round ones only accentuate her width; tall brides with a form-fitted gown and full skirt look sensible and in proportion with fuller or longer flowers; also, the flowers should be modified for the lines of a street- or cocktail-length dress—regardless of her girth. I can compensate on the bloom size and stem length—to a degree—when gathering the materials on the wedding day."

Flower Varieties

There is an enormous range in the overall effect that the flower or flowers you carry or wear can accomplish, owing in large part to the wide variety from which to choose.

Numerous variations in the color, size, shape, texture, and petal number or density have been developed, and new kinds are constantly being introduced through hybridization. If the decision has been reached to combine several types of flowers, it is important to remember that certain ones simply combine better with others—visually as well as scentwise.

This abundant choice is not available only in major cities, because on-the-spot florists or designers anywhere in the country can tap into the enormous international flower market. Furthermore, when given enough notice, a bride-to-be's flower choice can be located during any season and in whatever hue is necessary. Naturally there are a few exceptions, such as peonies and saintpaulia, which only exist in warm pinks and reds. However, even these flowers can be dyed to match a dress or blend into a color scheme. Some variations are easier to find than others; you may need to check several months beforehand—with your florist or designer as well as flower catalogs, greenhouses, or nurseries—to find exactly what you want.

Color, Texture, and Shape

Traditionally, all-white bouquets are carried and worn at formal weddings and colorful flowers at informal weddings; exotic-colored flowers are reserved exclusively for second-time brides. This formula is now somewhat passé, although white and delicate greenery with flourishes of bows, streamers, or ribbons of velvet, satin, and silk adding color remains a very popular choice for brides. As you discuss with a floral designer the most appropriate flowers and colors to include in your bouquet, remember that many elements speak for themselves. And your hair, skin, and eye coloring as well as how you plan to do your makeup are also important in defining the bouquet's color.

A bouquet falls into one of three basic color schemes. The first, a monochromatic plan, features dark and light shades of the same color or color family—yellow, ivory, and cream, for instance. A reciprocal plan, the second possibility, blends similar colors or those nearest in the color spectrum—violet and red or orange, for example. The third, a complementary plan, contrasts two or more colors; a strong contrast combines opposites, like blue and orange, and a soft contrast integrates purple, red, and orange, perhaps.

Any intrinsic fabric texture, including an airy illusion, soft satin, or stiff taffeta, can be heightened, simulated, or contrasted by placing specific flowers and foliage nearby—for instance, femininity is accented by sweetheart roses, mums, violets, or stephanotis; froufrou weaves are enhanced by touches of forget-me-nots or hyacinths; and the crispness of a dotted swiss cotton is increased with daisies. An intricate floral lace or geometric pattern can also be coordinated according to its design elements by carrying a quiet or soft arrangement of Queen Anne's lace with parts of hyacinth or tips of larkspur; these tend to harmonize and emphasize

OPPOSITE: Personal preference can dictate sprays of white and pink orchids to complement a pale pink gown.

Satin stitches on a bugle-beaded and ruched self-fabric rose are combined with floral appliqués to create an extraordinary effect.

the lace rather than contrasting with it. This is true whether the bouquet is held forward or it lies flat, like an addition to the fabric.

The composition of certain flowers matches components of the dress. Many flowers have a free-form or floppy shape, giving a soft impression, while others have a definite geometry, such as flat, layered, or circular. Stiffer dress fabric would dictate using a more defined flower shape. On the other hand, the petals of roses, tulips, and orchids have a definite glow, whether a shade of off-white nearly pink, or an off-white closer to beige. So a muted French rose, for example, will echo the low luster of white duchess satin, because the variations blend somewhat as light hits them both, creating an additional depth within each.

Naked flowers are rarely carried—not even as a single stem—so that many forms of ferns and ivy are combined in a bouquet to create a focal point and a flow, and to define the pattern or color scheme. The type of greenery and how much to use depends on the budget, although stretching the dollar by using greenery or other embellishments is not suitable in every case. One notable exception, perhaps, is a posy's lace collar. A second, beautiful option is streamers, which correspond to the flower selection, color, and texture, the gown's style and color, and the bride's height. A wide selection of antique, wired, or pleated ribbons exist in an array of colors and fabrics. Bows are a wonderful third touch as well, especially moiré or grosgrain. A fourth choice is flat or folded matching fabric, such as lace, tulle, or satin. Including a fabric, however, is a personal preference usually reserved for the most traditional bouquets. They tend to become messy, often like trying to wrap a napkin around a few flowers, unless the floral designer and, in turn, the bride know what they are doing.

Determining an Appropriate Bouquet Design and Style

Very formal bouquets require the most planning. They are classically constructed with wire or tape, and placed in a container to control each stem and blossom. An informal arrangement is simpler by far, yet it is still a thoughtful floral and foliage presentation. A semiformal presentation is a formal concept played down or with the informality played up, so to speak, and more or less combines elements from both formal or informal bouquets.

Over the past decade Marie McBride Mellinger, *Bride's* magazine's contributing editor for floral features, has watched many hard-and-fast rules concerning bridal bouquets wilt to loose guidelines with very soft edges. "First of all," she advises, "the

An all-white peony and lily of the valley presentation complements a statuesque bride as well as her three-tier lace dress with train.

A traditional bridal snowball of pale roses held in place by a hand grip; the bridegroom wears an identical rose in his lapel.

bouquet's size and its formality is an often misunderstood concept. Big does not mean formal: needing a wheelbarrow or someone to help carry the bouquet will be too much." Mellinger is an expert on personal flowers, and bouquets are her focus. Listen to her as she outlines a few up-to-date parameters on a subject she knows best: "When selecting a bouquet style, don't merely feel obliged to take a rule and follow it to the letter. Your taste, personality and ideas have gradually begun to matter most, so take everything into consideration. Work within the lines, spaces, and angles involved; also, evaluate what will work regarding your individual circumstances. While the design and shape indicate—but do not dictate—direction and formality, in many ways, less is now understood to be more: when beautiful flowers are placed together in a beautiful way, they can say a great deal."

While common sense can now guide what you carry, any floral treatment that is well-proportioned, carefully composed, and in a specific design—whether large, small, muted, bright, overpowering, or subtle—will create a more sophisticated spirit than carrying an arrangement that is loose and carefree. Any bouquet within the middle ground becomes a semiformal presentation. The formality of the bouquet varies according to several variables: whether the flower's self-foliage remains on the stem and if the stems show or not (lush self-foliage and exposed stems are very informal, sparse self-foliage with braided stems are less so, while incorporating only the flower head is the most formal choice); how the flowers are held together (short, hand-tied ribbon streamers are more informal than a wide satin bow trailing down, while enveloping all the stems in lace is very formal); the type of container (a basket or bascade—covered handles—is informal, while a carved wood or metal holder is

semiformal; only flower heads or petals and greenery is a formal floral presentation).

Plenty of thought and numerous discussions are expected to take place before the right inspiration comes—even though the execution can then be either simple or complex. Every bride-to-be's ensemble and situation is different, but the bouquet must harmonize with the wedding style. For example, bunched wildflowers in a wicker basket blends well with a shirtwaisted, gingham check dress, and a mound of flat orchids in a carved ivory scepter would complement a flesh-tone silk medieval sheath best. If a wildflower arrangement is your choice, the flowers must be selected, picked, bundled, and then placed in a holder. The orchid bouquet requires more extensive prepara-

A formal bouquet held in place with a hand piece and trimmed with satin ribbons and streamers.

FLORAL PRESENTATIONS

Nosegays, small, pretty bunches of flowers—
for the nose.

A traditional bouquet is chosen from among the following styles: A *classic sheaf*—containing one, two, or three varieties of long-stem flowers gathered, then covered with flat lace or tied with a ribbon. A *nosegay*—consisting of bright, tightly compacted, mixed flowers; wide is considered more formal than narrow. (There are two standard varieties, the *posy*, which is an initial, symbol, or a message woven in the "language of flowers," and the *Biedermeier*, which has intricate, concentric layers of tips.) A *duchesse rose*—fabricating hundreds of individual rose petals into a large rose shape. Any *geometric shape*—forming regular lines, curves, or angles. These vary from one to many types of blossoms and are characterized as *colonial* (round), mound, or globe, pear- or heart-shape; *lover's knot* or *fan*, triangle or pyramid; and square or *muff* (rectangle). A *cascade*—comprising a single variety or various flowers gently spilling out and down; the size, shape, scale, and drama vary both vertically and horizontally according to the length and shape of the bride's gown. A *spray*—combining several large, long, flat floral branches tied and arranged by either a large lace bow, ribbon, or streamer.

The most popular country mood or informal bouquet choices are a *winter bouquet*—incorporating dried flowers (heather, lavender, goldenrod, or such), grains, berries, or nuts; a *bouquet garni*—blending herbal garden flowers, grasses, or straw; and a *garland*—attaching flowers, foliage, and organic materials together as a band to be carried as either an open-ended, boalike length or in a loop to create a swag or scallop, which can fall to the floor. An unusual variation to a garland is tying the ends loosely into a group of circles that hang freely.

The most common informal floral choice is, in fact, not a bouquet at all but a small *corsage*. Wearing a corsage has Victorian roots and is an idea gaining in popularity; flower heads are thrust to one side or upward, held together by wire, and embellished with gewgaws—ribbons, bows, or streamers—of satin, lace, or silk. A bridal corsage may be held for the vows and attached to either the wrist, waist, shoulder, or used as an accent afterward.

tion: removing the flowers from a spray, adding ivy or moss, and sculpting the form.

Design Principles and Concepts

An experienced floral designer should be consulted and contracted, even if a possibility is gathering flowers for your bouquet from someone's cutting garden. This in no way precludes your input and influence regarding each detail! Keep in mind that most bouquet designs are nothing more than personal interpretations from such sources as

florist trade magazines, floral design books, bridal magazine photographs, and works of art, or they are adapted from another type of floral arrangement.

Seek out visual references; study the overall composition and carefully examine the details within—you will find elements in some to single out and become part of your bouquet. Note what draws your attention, whether it is the flowers, color, texture, shape, or style; perhaps it is the big picture or concept itself. When you see a bouquet that you like, sketch—or trace—the outline but draw in detail any element that you want;

you can eliminate or even rearrange parts of the composition if you choose. Remember, you are not attempting an exact copy, just enough to indicate your ideas to a bona fide designer. You will begin to recognize what holds possibilities for your bouquet and—perhaps more important—what does not.

"To my mind," Marie Mellinger explains from her years of experience, "the most practical design is the nosegay, which is a beautiful form, easy to carry, and versatile, because its personality and shape are workable for almost every flower and style. For example, all-white roses, tulips, and orchids are formal; less serious flowers, such as daffodils or tiny carnations, are informal; mixing colors and textures is semiformal;

and hand-painted gold edges on the ivy or galax is very formal. Variables can be added to change the effect and they work for all sizes as well—a little larger or a little smaller, depending on the bride. Moreover, most floral designers feel comfortable with the form."

Strict adherence to rigid formulas is passé and, what's more, license has been granted to break any convention or rule once held as steadfast. Take advantage of this new freedom: you are the only person to please and the bouquet can be your statement and creation. But there are some very general pointers to keep in the back of your mind.

First, the overall character of a bouquet has a great deal to do with the manner in

A classic sheaf of calla lilies tied with a broad silk ribbon—just the right finish for a soft, elegant lace and chiffon formal gown.

which the flowers are used. For example, the closer the flowers are to their natural growing state—on their stem, with leaves, and so forth—the less formal that bouquet will be; this is especially important for semiformal treatments.

Second, there are flower varieties that do not lend themselves to each style of bouquet, for instance, soft-petal orchids, peonies, lilacs, or lily of the valley. On the other hand, simple garden flowers such as of bachelor's buttons, long-stemmed daisies, or mixtures of tiny flowers are used more in an informal bouquet. Semiformal bouquets contain a mixture of sophisticated flowers and less serious ones—the ratio depends on the desired degree of formality or informality.

Third, all *self*-foliage is removed from the flower stems in a formal bouquet. Combining different foliage only adds to that formality; it does not lessen it. A duchesse rose bouquet with ivy or galax, for example, is both more luxurious and outrageous in this transposed state; therefore it is now more formal. The same principle applies to informal wildflowers or a simple daisy in a bouquet: only it now becomes a semiformal bouquet, not a formal bouquet.

Fourth, it does not always follow that *stiff* is equated with formality and *loose* with informality. A sheaf (bound stems) of roses, as elegant as they are, can be informal, semiformal, or formal. For instance, if the roses are barely tied and only the tips are exposed, the sheaf is formal; bound like a quiverful of arrows with the foliage spilling out of the top, the sheaf is semiformal; and if the stems and leaves are tightly braided, it is informal.

Fifth, the blossom size is not relevant to formality, because it is often altered by removing the tips or the entire bloom before being fabricated into a bouquet design. In a cascading bouquet of long-stemmed roses, for example, only the tips are shaped and hand-tied before they are placed in their ribbon or lace-wrap holder; in the case of tiny orchids, the individual blossoms within a spray are assembled into a larger composition and will no longer appear to be small. Extremely large flowers, such as calla lilies, are usually carried without any other flower lest the bouquet appear too heavy; roses, on the other hand, call for a filler of stephanotis or baby's breath or miniature orchids.

Sixth, if sophisticated flowers are arranged as an informal concept, say, in a bascade, the result is a semiformal bouquet; similarly, wildflowers arranged as a formal concept, such as a colonial bouquet, result in a semiformal presentation.

SIZE AND SCALE

Once the style and design of your bouquet are decided, the most complementary size and scale can be addressed. On the whole, a bouquet should be thought of as an accessory. It is not what walks down the aisle to be married—the bride is. The larger the bouquet, obviously, the more prominent it becomes; an oversized bouquet may look somewhat out-of-bounds in a living room, but would not in a cathedral; a small bride carrying a bouquet half her size will be ungainly.

The important factors to weigh include your head size, face shape and features, the dress—especially the bodice, neckline, shoulder, and sleeve treatment—and trim proportions as well as fabric pattern or floral motif size. "My initial impression forms after hearing a bride's input on design concepts, knowing her flower preferences, and looking at her color scheme; but seeing the bridal ensemble is the most important factor. I can then go to my work space and begin the initial sketches," says Abigail Goldman, the

floral designer and horticulturist. "There is far more to the overall design decision than merely calculating the proportion between her height and dress; as a rule, this won't settle the issue entirely or necessarily make a happy bride. Nor does reapplying conventional wisdom, such as 'Simplicity is strength,' 'A small bride carries a small bouquet and a large bride a large bouquet,' or 'Tall brides can carry cascading bouquets while short brides cannot.' Since I will custom-make her bouquet, the cascade could easily be scaled down to a smaller, stiff form instead of being too generous in a loose style, for instance."

There are additional factors to take into account before determining the appropriate size and scale for a bouquet, such as the wedding location, style, and ambience. Other factors will affect your decision to a lesser degree, such as the receiving line and the type and location of the reception—the bouquet, after all, is often put aside for this part of the celebration. If, for example, hundreds of guests are assembled to witness a long walk down the aisle of a church or synagogue, it is the designer's task to work within the bride-to-be's or bridegroom's means. One size and scale of bouquet will be more appropriate depending on whether the ambience is formal or semiformal; furthermore,

A romantic self-fabric corsage clasp.

OPPOSITE: Pink baby orchids give an informal look to this afternoon dress.

A large taffeta pouf is held in place by matching silk flowers and shiny antique green leaves.

different flowers would be selected. Here, seasonality is important; while hothouse varieties can be found, they will inevitably be more expensive, making large quantities prohibitive. Also keep in mind that a more labor-intensive design is going to cost more, so an alternative of fewer dramatic flowers, such as calla lilies or very long-stemmed roses, in an over-the-arm sheaf might work just as well.

If an intimate wedding is planned in a chapel or on a mountaintop, the spirit could range from quite sophisticated to very innocent. For the traditional chapel wedding a delicate, quivering, cascading bouquet of only orange blossoms may seem appropriate, while in the rugged setting a large basket of wildflowers could fit the ambience better. After either ceremony, looser, branchy flowers at the reception could work, too. A small garland laced with jasmine may seem more suitable at a rural church wedding; the garland could be carried and the informal theme punctuated during the reception as tea sandwiches are served out back in a garden. If a country-club wedding is planned, a tight nosegay of freesia, tuberoses, and bouvardia, perhaps, with the bridegroom's initials woven into a posy, would be in keeping at both the ceremony and the reception. At civil ceremonies, whether in City Hall, a judge's chambers, or your home, a corsage that converts from hand-held for the ceremony to worn during a restaurant luncheon is always apropos. A very formal wedding can be held in a cathedral at noon with a tented champagne breakfast to fol-

low or in a grand ballroom with a midnight supper reception. Exactly the same globe bouquet of all-white sweetheart roses and stephanotis could be right for each, but with the personality altered with golden or metallic touches and shimmering fibers in the fabric streamers for the evening.

Alternative Formal, Semiformal, and Informal Floral Uses

The concept of using flowers for personal adornment is hardly a recent one. Garlands—bands of flowers, branches, grain stalks, or leaves entwined with other materials—bedecked ancient Egyptians, Greeks, Romans, Hindus, Asians, and South Sea Islanders, in the form of laurel crowns or as personal accessories worked into a pattern, such as a necklace. They can be fashioned into a swag, which loops and adorns a gown—for instance, at the shoulder as an epaulet, at the bosom as a bursting brooch, at the waist as a sash—even as the bridegroom's cummerbund!—or at the hem as a border. In addition, a garland can decorate the objects a bride carries to the altar, including a family Bible or prayerbook, a scroll with handwritten vows, a fan, or a handbag; it can also adorn the ring bearer's pillow.

A small garland is, of course, a well-established headdress for a bride—interchangeably referred to as a wreath, coronet, chaplet, or circlet. Another method of wearing flowers in the hair is a single blossom or blossoms attached to a chignon, glued to clips and clustered behind the ear, or sprinkled around the head. "A more recent innovative floral use is fashioning a small garland made entirely of miniature flowers, perhaps Italian roses, to use as a garter with a short dress," says Bobby Wiggins, an established New York bridal floral designer, who is frequently asked to contribute his considerable services to magazines.

"A similar band could be worn at the neck or wrist. However, with the current rage to personalize the wedding, special uses for flowers—many rarely tried before—are being seriously considered as well." Wiggins expounds on these unique floral statements: "Certainly wherever hand-rolled fabric flowers embellish a gown, fresh-cut flowers can be used, including on the border of a neckline, collar, décolletage, and a bustled train. Still another wonderful place for fresh flowers is in the veiling, either at the crown with sprigs (ornamentation using a sprout) or as a series of individual flowers interspersed and diminishing down along yards of illusion.

"A simple but unusual touch is to clip a large, delicate rose onto the toe of a plain white pump, then outline the opening with a garland of smaller roses. I find that only a very daring bride, however, will wear a blossom at the nadir of a plunging back, and an outright adventuresome spirit is needed for a fresh-flower bodice or bolero-style jacket, for instance. The mechanics of these unusual uses require careful planning, and replacing the flowered garment with a nearly identical garment in fabric after the receiving line is a wise idea."

If properly conditioned, flowers—even a delicate lily of the valley or gardenia—will hold up for quite a long time, but bouquets have a water holder incorporated into the design, often hidden in the lace or satin wrapping. However, under no circumstance should the water container be entirely ignored and left exposed. When the flowers selected are extremely delicate or are not expected to last four or five hours, the bouquet, accessory, or accent should be duplicated or even triplicated. Additional precautions may be necessary on very hot summer days, if the environment will change dramatically (for instance, if the ceremony is far from the reception), if the photography session is scheduled an hour or more before the ceremony, and, of course, whenever fresh flowers are employed in a unique fashion.

One last thought: a few days prior to your wedding, place a sachet filled with the same petals used in your bouquet near your gown in the closet. This will allow a trace of your bouquet's fragrance to surround you throughout the ceremony and reception.

A lace fan floral treatment.

While today's bride can fulfill every desire by wearing anything she wants, she can also personalize her ensemble to create a statement about herself. In 1839, lights went off as Victoria became the first English queen to be married in a white gown, and white instantly became a bridal tradition. But perhaps the strong bond that an accent has for the bride may be better understood through a secondary aspect of Queen Victoria's bridal ensemble: in her bouquet were orange blossoms, which were planted at Windsor Castle shortly after the ceremony. These cuttings grew into the orange blossom trees from which both Princess Diana and Sarah Ferguson, the Duchess of York, had their wreaths fashioned, their use symbolizing an unbroken chain.

Adding Accents

Many traditional accents within a bride's ensemble represent merriment, virginity, and abundance, including a chivalrous garter, an heirloom brooch of innocence, or a proverbial buckle—never buttons, which are unlucky—to fasten her shoes. While visual symbols, such as ribbons, entwined streamers, and sheaths of wheat had their origins in good wishes, fidelity, and fertility, many items are age-old amulets to ward off an evil eye or spirit. These superstitions require such remedies as the bride possessing garlic or wearing a man's cloak. To promote good fortune, secure a penny in a shoe; to symbolically take your past along, fasten a worn-out corner of an adored childhood smock to a petticoat. Each sentimental touch, meaningful symbol, or valued garment that you have had in mind, such as a favorite aunt's handkerchief to catch those joyful tears, the family Bible for spiritual guidance, or a fan purely for additional decoration, should be gathered for inclusion with your ensemble.

A bride-to-be must think of accents not only as sentimental in nature but as necessary items and functional extras as well. The necessary accents are chosen first, and these include foundations—underpinnings (petticoat, bustier, all-in-ones)

the
final
flourishes

OPPOSITE: A velvet dress accented by a fur muff and hat is wonderful for a holiday-time bride.

or lingerie (bra, panties, slip); hosiery and shoes—both coordinated closely with the gown or dress as well as with each other; and makeup—in a suitable style. This is a necessity because, as the center of attention, you will continuously greet and be photographed with the guests. Second, consider the options you may want to include: gloves, handbag, handkerchief, and cover-up (if one is needed).

Necessary Niceties: A Story Goes on Beneath

The task of a foundation is to slightly revise a body's shape, figuratively speaking; the task of an underpinning is to support a dress; but the sole purpose of lingerie is to provide comfort and a feeling of femininity and glamour.

Custom-made gowns and more expensive ready-made dresses—cocktail, sheath, and informal silhouettes excluded—are designed with four or five fabric layers over an inner structure molded to fit the contours of your body. During the fitting process of an inexpensive dress, a bridal-salon seamstress will sew whatever is needed—bra or bustier, petticoat or slip—into the lining. In either case, any additional undergarment, other than panties, is unnecessary. But an exact shape and fit begins with panties that fit snugly but comfortably, never creating ripples or lines, yet firmly supporting your stomach and flattening your rear. Special cotton or cotton and Lycra blend panties should be bought for this occasion; moreover, treating yourself to a flattering yet durable style, perhaps high-cut with little or nothing in back, or with a hint of a bridal motif, such as lace or colorful bows, is equally important. If support pantyhose alone are insufficient to give you a perfect figure under a slim silhouette, panties can be found with a wide stretch waistband or a slip-girdle

combination, beginning 2 inches above the waist and ending at the knee.

Which foundations to combine depends on the demands of your gown or dress style, construction, fabric, and weight of trimming and enhancements, as well as your figure. A brassiere needs to be very structural with built-in boning or inserted stays to create shape and provide lift and support; any multiple-layer gown with encrusted ornamentation, elaborate trimming, long train, or hem is going to be heavy and tend to flatten, rather than remain up and in place. A strapless bustier or a long-line (bust to hip) strapless bra, occasionally with a slip attached, is needed under gowns without enough built-in padding for support and to enhance a small waist, giving a beautiful line to the figure. In addition, push-up cups—with padding on the bottom half—can be used to lend additional lift, or bust cups to keep the shape if needed. The increasing popularity of sheer and nude bodices, plunging low-cut fronts or backs, and off-the-shoulder gowns has heralded the return of an updated, romantic, and sexy white lace and ribbon, low-back, cutaway strapless "merry widow"—without a band across the back. For some brides-to-be, creating a lean line requires an "all-in-one," which is a girdlelike foundation with underwires from panty to brassiere, and is bought in a shop specializing in foundations. Any bride-to-be who knows the bra style she must wear, or who is considering a bare, off-the-shoulder gown, should have that brassiere or strapless bustier along when shopping for the gown or dress. Your bridal consultant or a seamstress will also point out whether a particular style of foundation will make the dress fit better while exactly compensating for your figure.

"Petticoats are constructed in three parts—a nylon lining that prevents the stiff,

A lace hanky will catch your tears of joy, but for fun, fling a garter; the one you wear can still be a cherished keepsake, if you substitute it with another for the toss.

starched, sized netting from scratching or ripping a stocking or irritating a leg; the fabric cover also protects the gown material," says Michael Raskin of Sidney Bush Inc., which is a major supplier of underpinnings to bridal salons and manufacturers. He continues: "Either a petticoat or slip is worn under every bridal gown, from formal bouffant to slinky sheaths. A slip, which is actually lingerie and not a foundation, does not give any form or shape to the gown but serves to line the dress, eliminate static electricity, and prevent the dress from rubbing on the stockings. They can be as feminine and frilly as you like. Petticoats are made of an open-weave net and meshlike, buckram cotton material (known as crinoline—originally horsehair and linen), often with a scallop, ruffle, or ribbon border, bows or streamers, swiss dot, and eyelet or lace appliqués that can peek out while you are climbing a step or on the dance floor. The purpose is to lift the dress out to match the silhouette of the gown and to hold the details out to show off heavy enhancement beading or trimming layers. Therefore, petticoat lines follow the standard bridal silhouettes and do not change with fashion trends."

Standard shaping begins at the knees and continues on down. Furbelows—particularly panniers or cagelike hoops—are no longer popular, because a bride-to-be seldom wants to accentuate her hips. Old-fashioned hoops or circular petticoats with plastic-coated wire (referred to as bones) and ruffles, which were a bridal tradition, have also fallen out of favor, because they are awkward for sitting and for getting in and out of cars. They have been replaced by big, three-ruffle petticoats with netting, but without wires. The petticoats can be customized in layers to create a desirable proportion without adding unwanted bulk; for example, a 40-inch-waist bride does not want netting at

her hips. However, demand is somewhat regional, because the Southern belle still wants to rustle down the aisle in an enormous antebellum skirt, for instance. There are also bustle-back slips, characterized by an A-line, no ruffles, straight up and down, and very little fullness. They are created by shirring net to the back, built up in tiers all around to give a full look in back yet be flat in front. They can also be built in when the gown is manufactured, sewn in during the fitting stage, or selected separately and worn as one, two, or three layers.

Petticoats are sized according to the number of wires—for example, one, two, four, and six wires, each adding to the circumference at the bottom and gradually decreasing to the waist. These multilayers can be adjusted to create the proper proportions and circumference. At the extremes are mermaid trains when a slip that flares at the bottom is worn, and bouffant skirts when an A-line petticoat is used.

SHEERLY FOR YOURSELF: HOSIERY

Although stockings are not an important bridal accessory, a bride-to-be rarely walks into the corner drugstore and buys the same stockings she wears day after day. She will most likely take the time to look for her hosiery in a department store or specialty shop. In every instance, stockings are selected according to her gown's statement—especially its color and fabric—as well as for comfort. Under a formal gown, the stockings' sole purpose is to make the bride feel more glamorous, elegant, feminine, pretty, and sexy; as a fashion accessory with an informal dress, a bride-to-be has a wide range of choices.

For hundreds of years women wore stockings either of wool or cotton—blended with a clinging, stretchy fabric, such as silk—

The wispy innocence of a back-tied, silk-chiffon hankerchief dress contrasted by vampish seaming, matched by lustrous nylon stockings, and complemented by tiny satin bows at the heels.

ranging from highly lustrous to matte, or nylon, a manmade fiber and until recently considered the most practical, beautiful, and luxurious choice. These fabrics are still widely used, but they lack vertical or horizontal elasticity, and never return to their original shape. Currently, the most popular and practical manmade fiber is Elestan, a form of rubber known as Lycra. It is a smooth, soft, stretchy fiber that holds its shape.

Brides-to-be choose their stockings according to size, which varies by leg length—tall, regular, or petite; by waist or garter style; by weight, which can be sheer or transparent to opaque or solid; by color—the range of hues, shades, and tones is unending; and by pattern or texture, which is knitted into the fabric, glued, or appliquéd. Stockings are also manufactured either with a seam in back or seamless. For the most part, stockings are tubular in shape or designed to conform to the leg, foot, and heel shape; these are referred to as full-figure or full-fashion. The mesh—hole or background size—and knit change with the fiber. Every fabric lends itself to a different knit, which affects its comfort, fit, and look.

Formal brides almost exclusively wear white, sheer stockings even if they will not be seen, except when they are seated or during the traditional removing and throwing of the garter. Brides-to-be can choose from several styles, which include built-in panties—a lacelike bikini, satin low-rise, open-weave, or wide hip-band—which acts as a girdle, or an all-in-one garter belt and stocking combination. There are also thigh-highs—with a silicon-backed elastic band to prevent slipping—or the more traditional stocking style worn with a separate garter belt. An individual's figure, needs, and personal preference dictate the right style, but under no circumstance should the stocking create a line or a layered look.

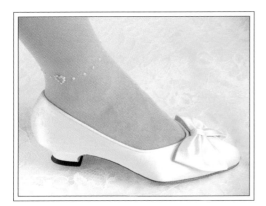

Most styles can be found in almost any fabric, and the available weights include ultra, daytime, or evening sheer. The sheens range from dull to slightly glistening to shiny, or opaque, which are tights. Every fiber reflects light differently; the larger its surface area, whether four-, six-, or eight-sided, the more luster: a round fiber creates a matte finish, and a triangular fiber sparkles. There are unlimited shades of white, including pure white, icy white (leaning toward gray), off-white, and creamy white, as well as various shades of ivory. To gauge the right shade, be prepared with your fabric swatch and shoes and keep in mind that everyone's skin tone affects the gradation of white differently. It is imperative, therefore, to try each pair of stockings on, or place them next to the skin, to be sure they are exactly what you need.

"While a bride-to-be dressing in a formal gown almost exclusively asks for white or off-white stockings, many ask to see the available alternatives as well," says Marijke Masquelier, manager of Fogal, a for-legs-only specialty shop on New York City's Madison Avenue. "For a short dress, whether informal or for cocktails, it is wiser to match the colors of skirt, shoe, and stocking; otherwise, the stockings will seem to cut a bride off at her knees. A taller bride can wear a contrasting stocking color, such as an ultrasheer hose with a silver shoe; a shorter bride, however, should stay with the dress color to create an elongated silhouette. In the autumn, winter, or early spring, when a shoe is dyed to match the dress or if a black patent leather shoe is selected, the dress color should be carried through in the stocking as well. With a light or airy shoe, a stocking color close to your skin tone, but still within the dress tone, looks better than a nude shade. Neutral colors, like cocoa brown on black women, appear more natural than flesh tones. Nude or suntan shades are usually somewhat less appropriate—unless a great deal of skin shows elsewhere, such as a bare back or shoulders."

Aside from overall patterns, there are ankle treatments, back treatments, and leg treatments. Many designs run down both sides of the leg, some are on one side, others on one leg only, and still others run down the seam from the calf to the heel in back. There is a wide variety of colors and design directions for dots, bows, stripes, bells, and geometric shapes or colorful bouquets, rhinestones, and sequins; the latter are worn in the evening, not with a daytime cotton dress.

The most popular overall patterns are heavy-mesh and micromesh lace, random bird's-eye dots, or a repeated dot pattern, perhaps with one small accent, such as a butterfly or a bow or a swag of ribbons placed on the ankle or top of the foot, but rarely at the back of the heel. "Bridal stocking patterns follow the lead of ready-to-wear fashion," says Susan Keller, who follows the hosiery market for *Bride's* magazine. "For example, the resurgence of the 1960s look

A traditional low-heel pump with a heart-shape and chain design pressed onto the hosiery.

OPPOSITE: Pairing scattered lustrous pearls on your stockings with a street-length polished taffeta and sequin dress makes a sophisticated statement.

A high vamp opera pump accented by a pearl loop and bow cluster is further set off by scattered-pearl stockings.

A sling-back shoe.

Clip-on ornaments.

Rhinestone accents.

A pancake-heel pump.

A Victorian bridal shoeboot.

has brought back fishnet stockings, with smaller holes which resemble tulle.

"The hosiery pattern, design, or texture is matched to dress details. For instance, with a dress that has appliqués with pearls, the stockings should have pearls, not bells. With a plain dress that has no frills, both overall patterns and ankle treatments can add a design touch or even wit, whereas coordinating a textured or patterned stocking with a frilly lace or patterned gown is a possibility, but may be more difficult. At a black-tie cocktail reception where a fancy beaded dress is worn, a simple sheer stocking is appropriate, and a subtle ankle or back accent can be wonderful as well. Aboard a yacht, when a moderately decorated short dress is worn and the leg will definitely be seen, a subtle—never garish—bow or nautical motif, such as multicolor triangular flags, would be fun.

"The stocking sheen should blend and complement the gown's fabric," she continues. "A dull finish is the most elegant look with a sophisticated silk dress which has its own slight sheen. The shiny stocking may detract from the silk, but it would complement a matte silk crepe or chiffon dress; sparkling or glistening stockings blend and work well with highly decorative sequin or rhinestone dresses."

"Stockings, which inevitably run, are a problem at best, but there are a few helpful hints. Always have a second pair handy. To prevent a premature hole, put your hosiery on with gloves, because a rough nail, hangnail, or even dryness can cause a run. And never walk around without shoes." Keller concludes.

The Bottom Line: Shoes

Too many brides-to-be underestimate the importance as well as the difference the right shoe can make. A shoe should never be treated as an isolated accent, whether you are wearing a full-length traditional gown, period dress, or short informal or contemporary outfit. The time to look for the right shoes is after the first fitting; they should be tried with the dress at a second fitting.

If your shoe selection is left to the last minute, you compromise your opportunity to have a perfect matching color, heel, height, or style; in short, everything about the shoe may be wrong. For Francesca of Saks Fifth Avenue, the dress and shoe style should be carefully coordinated into a unit that completes any bridal look, "because your feet are seen again and again and again: when stepping from the car and walking up the church steps, with every step down the aisle, and while taking the first dance steps too."

Usually a pair of shoes is bought for its color or look—its fashionwise aspect can often make a contemporary outfit work. This, however, is not the only purpose of the right bridal shoe. A bride's shoe should be selected for comfort first; comfort cannot be compromised. "So never buy bridal shoes unless they feel great and fit right," says Stuart Weitzman, who is consistently the leader among America's shoe designers. "If you're going to be standing, dancing, or walking all day, a hurting toe can spoil a happy occasion. Moreover, your wedding is not the time to try something completely new to you; don't make an exception on the overall style, the heel height and shape, or the toe shape. And if possible, look for natural materials, including uppers (any part above the sole), its front (the vamp) and back (the quarter), as well as a genuine leather lining and sole. Stay away from either synthetic fabrics or plastic insides and soles: they can cause a burning sensation after hours on your feet."

Many bridal shoes are incorporated from

another collection by adapting the designs in a textured white ivory lace or smooth satin, or silk. Weitzman, a shoe manufacturer as well as a designer, advises every bride-to-be "to look for a similar type of shoe as she is used to wearing on a day-to-day basis or for special occasions—plus beautifully decorated for her wedding day. If cost is a factor, immediately after the honeymoon any fabric shoe can be tinted or dyed—for instance, a lace or silk satin shoe can become black, green, or red and be worn with another evening outfit. This allows a bridal shoe, when it meets the comfort test, to be worn for many months before the style will change. What's more, a bride-to-be wearing a white dress who wants to add color can choose ruby red shoes."

Along with the traditional bridal satin and lace there are silks, such as peau de soie, faille, Jacquard, moiré, and damask; toes that vary from square to round, or no toe at all; heel shapes that go from razor-thin to courtly curves; and height ranges from ballerina slippers to 4½-inch heels. The overall patterns (floral or lace), glitter just on the heel, back, throat (opening), or toe (diamonds, rubies, sapphires, or emeralds), embellishments (scattered freshwater pearls, assorted seashells, sequins, or beading) or trimmings (seed-pearl borders, lace appliqués, satin bows, or hand-rolled silk roses) are drawn from the bridal gowns themselves.

Tying the dress and shoe together can be easy, freer and much looser than many bride-to-bes think. Your desired look can be accomplished with the shoe's design rather than its fabric or embellishments. So begin the shoe selection with the style, direction, or spirit of the dress, not necessarily by matching its fabric and texture. A shoe can also take its lead from your personality. For example, with a simple, pure white, off-white, cream, or ivory satin gown without

trimming, the look can be continued with a barely decorated pump, while slightly more embellishment to accent the gown is an equally correct choice.

"If you have a peau de soie gown, you don't have to have a peau de soie shoe," says Renee Scheffly, *Bride's* shoe editor. "It often looks better to have a contrasting fabric. With a suit, which is usually worn during the day, a plain, medium-heel white leather, lustrous leather, or black patent leather would work—unadorned or embellished with a simple button or bow or pearl treatment, since neither sequins or jewels are appropriate during the day. A shoe does not have to be shiny in order to be a little more special. Raffia or straw or lace with a bow and a low, curved heel gives a more country look, and a sling-back pump with a bow in back is understated and very acceptable at a daytime or civil ceremony.

"A fashionable short dress looks great with vinyl shoes, and a romantic and Renaissance dress looks best with, perhaps, a damask shoe with a curved court or Louis heel. Brides often decorate a white or ivory satin pump with handmade or fresh flowers around the throat of the shoe as well. But if you have a heavily decorated dress, a heavily decorated shoe could be too much, so a sleek, pointed toe, elongated front, or higher heel can add extra sophistication. And to be spicier, such as at a cocktail-hour reception, sequins, more pearls, or a decorated floral treatment in roses is peppy. In any case, the embellishment can be clipped on or attached directly to the shoe.

"While the guidelines for informal, semiformal, or formal bridal footwear are the same, an ultrasophisticated bride wears a more toned-down, understated shoe: a plain, peau de soie, 2½-inch heel, closed and therefore tailored, with the slightest embellishment, maybe a covered button or one little

Classic bridal footwear.

An oval-toe pump.

A medium-high pump.

An Edwardian theater pump.

An asymmetrical sling-back.

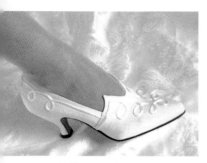

Silk rattail trim.

A closed-toe sling-back.

A high-heel sling-back.

A pointy-toe sandal.

A classic sling-back.

rhinestone rather than overall embellishments. It is usually younger brides wishing to be seen 'bride-y' who tend toward more elaborate decorations, such as pearls, bows, ribbons, or lace appliqués."

Peter and Linda Fox are a Vancouver, British Columbia, husband-and-wife shoe design team who create a decadently romantic, sophisticated line of shoes with a bride in mind. In four years, their signature boot has become classic bridal footwear. It has a sculpted quality with a narrow shank (the section between the sole and the heel) that is high at the arch and low at the ground. Peter Fox describes the inspiration behind his boot design as part of an entire silhouette. "When lace boots were first worn at the turn of the century, the ankles were never shown; they were considered an erogenous zone. In my design, I carefully regarded this 'proper' ankle shape, which creates a beautiful fit, and I retained the original Victorian version of a concave, curved Louis heel that evokes the eighteenth century. For a boot, rather than merely covering the inner structure with embroidery and beads, I try to keep its shape and use fabric, such as fine lace, brocade, a moiré look, silk Charmeuse, satin, or a high-luster, pearlized leather that looks like satin. On a pump, any embellishment, such as pearl buttons, little rhinestones, a fabric iris, or a classic bow or fan, should be delicate, following the design rather than appearing to be stuck on."

Linda Saro manages Peter Fox's New York City store, which sells bridal footwear exclusively. From her experience dealing directly with brides-to-be, Linda finds her customer knows the heel height she wants, whether white or ivory is needed, the fabric that would work best, and if simplicity or heavy embellishment is called for. Linda often cautions her customer to consider whether it will be warm on her wedding day

even though she is shopping when it is cold; to remember to scuff the bottoms or to adhere an oval sandpaper piece, available at most shoe repair shops, to prevent slipping, but not to put a rubber sole on until after her wedding day because a rubber bottom will interfere with dancing. Linda also reminds each bride-to-be that "a shoe will soften, but if a shoe is not comfortable in the store, its comfort level will not improve before the wedding day because fabric-covered shoes do not stretch with wear. To rationalize spending a large sum for a better shoe, I remind bride-to-bes that a fabric shoe can be accurately dyed according to a swatch and redyed afterward.

"While trying different lasts [shapes] and sizes for comfort, I've watched any number of brides-to-be slip on a shoe—not in the style they had in mind—fall in love with it, and walk out completely satisfied. I've also noticed that a bride-to-be planning to wear a long dress is more indecisive than her counterpart looking for a shoe with a knee-, midcalf-, or tea-length nontraditional dress. Here the shoe is a more integral part of her look and therefore its style is more critical. To assist in closely coordinating a shoe style with a dress style, I listen for directives and clues, such as a plain top, slender heel, Victorian, or not modern. Occasionally, a bride-to-be has always wanted to wear a wedding boot; they walk out very pleased, only to find at the next fitting that the dress can't take a boot. And the reverse takes place as well: women come in to look at shoes with two or three dresses in mind, but are unable to make a final decision on the dress. When they find a shoe they love, they select the best dress for the shoe—but this is not the norm."

For most brides-to-be, it seems easier to match rather than find the complement for elements. Even though the fabric match can be quite flexible—as long as the contrast is not too sharp—it is always wiser to have a swatch of your dress on hand when seeking a close match to it. "When there are complications, like blending the color as well as the ornamentation, it takes some brides-to-be three visits to reach their decision," continues Saro. "While embellishments do not have to match exactly, they should be in the same relative family; for instance, bows seem to cause little trouble and are usually similar enough; seed pearls blend easily with large pearls, even though they are not the same size or color; however, a dress with bows and pearls cannot accept sequins introduced on the shoes—unless the headpiece or veil has sequins as well."

Another alternative is to consider custom-made shoes, styled or ornamented specifically for your gown. The decision to wear a classic white pump or period shoe must still be addressed before color or its accent. "Style is the important criterion," says Francesca of Saks Fifth Avenue. "For instance, a bride-to-be with a high-neck, long-sleeve Victorian dress can tint a plain, classic pump cream to match her dress and add a Victorian bow embroidered with pearls or decorated with a piece of lace from her dress, but the modern shoe is the wrong accent.

"For a Victorian look, I would fashion a higher vamp—which is seen first by the guests and by the bride as she looks down. In fact, any traditional, moderately rounded, closed-toe, 1½-inch-heel T-strap shoe, and even a pancake-heel ballet slipper covered in silk satin, peau de soie, raw silk, or lace, can be custom-embellished to accommodate the theme. Many brides-to-be are open to a unique suggestion in materials, such as her grandmother's antique buckle, a fresh lace bow, an item from a friend, her initials in pale blue, or a small coin for luck. After all, the adage is actually 'Something old, some-thing new, something borrowed, something blue . . . and a penny for your shoe!'

"Before deciding on a custom treatment, I look at the bride-to-be and the shape of her foot; for example, if it is wide, I will make an elongated oval, which is a flattering shape, by angling the design inward, so when she walks the effect is sharper. I look at the dress to pick up a motif, from seashells on a lace medallion to feathers to hand-painted flowers or fans, to soften her look. Over the years, I have adorned a shoe's vamp with everything from an antique ribbon tied at the ankle that ran up the bride's leg for a more romantic mood, to pearls and crystal beads; and with a short, sophisticated, modern dress, which requires a five- or six-inch heel, I have taken a plain white satin shoe and embedded rhinestones all over the heels as the only decoration, so while that bride walked down the aisle, her heels were all sparkles."

This see-through vinyl pump, with silver-leather heel piece and sole, has an acrylic high heel set with rhinestones.

A Bride's Patina: Her Makeup

Your upcoming wedding is a wonderful opportunity to try new makeup products, skin-care treatments, and salon services, including massages, facials, and manicures. The latter is important because the wedding band will be shown off all day. Eight weeks before the wedding day is the time to begin experimenting. The task of makeup is to enhance your natural glow and to bring out a somewhat romantic aura. Ultimately, most brides-to-be feel comfortable looking elegant and refined, but not so totally different that they appear to be someone else. It is the quantity, color, and application that govern the outcome, but an important element is how the makeup is blended.

A makeup style is *never* decided on the wedding day itself; its look and the colors should be worked out well in advance. As the centerpiece of the "court" with a photographer to document your bridal ensemble in photographs that you will see for years to come, don't allow your makeup to compromise the effect. The guideline regarding makeup is to use enough to glow under the bright photographic lights, yet still to appear natural, look fresh, and hold up through the entire occasion. The right amount—not too much but not too pale—is difficult for an

Cerise lipstick gives an individual look, though few faces can carry such a strong color.

amateur to gauge. Bobbi Brown began working for bridal ads and magazines with such models as Suzy Blakely, Maud Adams, and Jennifer O'Neill and as a hairdresser at the House of Kenneth. She considers the most common mistakes made by brides to be using too much makeup, trying new products at the last minute, and seeking an unfamiliar side to themselves. "It makes sense to spend the engagement time researching and experimenting, looking at magazines, asking for advice at cosmetic counters, and going home to re-create what is appealing," says Brown, "then show your fiancé for his opinion. By your wedding day, the makeup used should be familiar, and applied extra carefully, which often means lighter, not heavier. A bride-to-be should try to look like an ideal version of herself the day she is married. Nobody should say 'Who's that?' or 'What did she do to herself?' Rather, they should think you look extraordinarily beautiful—but as yourself."

The quantity of makeup a bride uses can alter the overall effect of her wedding day. A bride's makeup statement is taken from her innate sense of style, her gown, the time of day, and the formality and size of the wedding. Only at larger weddings, which by their nature are more formal and involved, are drama or glamour carried to a bit more of an extreme. But even at very large receptions, the guests and the bride are never far from each other and everything can be seen. At intimate, family, or afternoon weddings, a bride should look fresh and simple, and her best features brought out or highlighted. In a more informal setting, let's say, outside for a small afternoon wedding with a lot of fresh flowers, a bride's makeup should be very "natural," which means only touches of makeup are applied to enhance the face; no telltale makeup signs are seen, except when one looks extremely closely.

No dramatic changes should be attempted, either. This means using only the absolute minimum foundation to cover blemishes; a soft-colored blush; matte-finish lipstick—perhaps a pale peach or mauve liner over Blistex—to keep the lips from looking dry; a light color shadow, such as taupe, around the eyes; and a little eye shadow if they need shaping. A touch of mascara adds length, size, and sparkle to lashes. For a more formal wedding, it is still appropriate to look demure and to glow. To increase the makeup's formality, add just a little more, such as lining the lips with a natural color that is not harsh. For a little extra punch, false eyelashes can be sparsely applied in small clumps.

One foolproof way to perfect makeup and to limit the pressure on you is to hire a beauty consultant to be on hand. Though it will seem obvious in retrospect, never hire a makeup artist without a practice session to find out if you will be satisfied with his or her work and if her or she understands the look you want. When a beauty consultant is not available, there are endless ways to learn makeup application. The most common method is to take lessons from a professional makeup artist. Qualified beauty consultants can be found through most beauty and skin-care salons and department stores. Very often, the professional works on one half of your face, then watches and guides you on the other half. This process allows you to copy the style afterward. During these sessions, sort through your makeup kit, separating the products you use all the time from those never used. To achieve your best look and the one right for your needs, such as softness in natural light or stronger eye shadow and lip lines at night, your beauty consultant should know your overall wedding statement as well as the style, spirit, ambience, and time of day.

During this demonstration, remember that one key to good makeup is discovering the colors that look great on you. The bride's nails usually remain close to natural, using either a lacquer with almost no color or a very delicate shade of pale pink. Moreover, within every cosmetic line there are products in a shade appropriate for every bride. A proper, personalized color match for your foundation, base, powder, eye shadow, and lipstick is critical, considering that most brides are draped in white or pastels from head to toe. While white makes most women look and feel washed out, adding a rosy glow, for instance, does not always work on a darker complexion. Too often, the immediate reaction is to use stronger makeup colors which may look too harsh, obvious, and bright. This does not make a bride look vibrant and beautiful.

A bride does not need heavier makeup under a veil because it is lifted off the face after the ceremony when people are close enough to see her. If the light is harsh and unnatural, which includes photographic light, use a little more color but take care to ensure that your makeup looks natural to the eye. The skin should not be covered, only evened out with foundation until no little red patches are visible and the skin under the eyes is perfect. Before beginning a photography session, your lip color and blush should be a bit more vibrant because the skin tones will be bleached out by the light. Also, a strip of brown false eyelashes, only a bit longer than your own, to make your eyes stand out, may be just the ticket.

Soft, natural-style makeup in colors complementary to your skin tones is highlighted by blush around the hairline and outside the perimeter of the face, under the eyes, and in the central nose area.

OVERLEAF: Opera-length kid gloves, always formal, appropriate, and correct.

The Functional Necessities

GLOVES

Historically, nobles, patricians, prelates, and even Tutankhamen wore gloves of one form or another, woven of fabric or leather, intricately embroidered or elaborately adorned. Gloves remained a male status symbol until medieval times when Catherine de' Medici changed all that by wearing gloves at her marriage to Henry II of France. Kidskin was introduced into court finery during the reign of Elizabeth I of England. Hand- or machine-knit gloves of wool, silk, cotton, or manmade fibers have only been popular since the industrial age began. A Victorian innovation, a crocheted mitt—created in dot, scallop, or floral patterns by interlacing strings or threads with a needle—has remained a classic and popular bridal glove.

The Old World method of measuring a glove's length is to count the number of inches above the thumb, which are referred to as buttons—for example, a two-button glove stops 2 inches above the thumb; a four-button, 4 inches above. All bridal gloves cover both the palm and back, have forks for the fingers, and extend up the arm. The five most common lengths are the shortie, one-button gloves that stop below the wrist; the gauntlet or wristlet, two-button gloves that come to the wristbone; six-button gloves that reach to just below the elbow; eight-button gloves that reach all the way to the elbow; and opera length, sixteen-button gloves that reach to the top of the arm. Most opera-length gloves are worn crushed or gathered, and have either elastic or Lycra blended into the fabric to help keep the glove up.

Deciding which length of glove is right with a particular dress follows common-sense guidelines. With bare shoulders or a bustier-style bodice, the sixteen-button-length glove works well; with short or mid-length sleeves, a six- or eight-button glove is appropriate; and with long sleeves, a two-button is beautiful.

"According to conventional wisdom, an ultraformal glove has an extension that passes the elbow, ends at the top of the arm, and is made from soft kid leather," says *Bride's* magazine accessories editor Elizabeth Rundlett. "At the other extreme, at a daytime spring ceremony in the country, a cotton wrist-length glove is more appropriate; the same glove in a color will accessorize a luncheon outfit or tailored suit for a civil ceremony. The fabric is selected according to the time of year, but in fact, suitable gloves can be found in many fabrics, such as leather, cotton—with an added benefit of absorbing perspiration—or satin. Many brides-to-be feel on a warm summer evening, even though leather is more formal, that an informal cotton crochet or lace would be more practical with, say, an off-the-shoulder gown. In this instance, the bride-to-be could instead select an opera-length, thin, all-cotton eyelet, satin, silk, or lace glove—either sheer or lined with satin, silk, or cotton—which is to say that neither length nor fabric alone dictates style."

The more ornate the dress, the less ornate the glove. The reverse is true as well; a simple dress can be accented by a more ornate glove. Therefore, an ornate sixteen-button lace glove is very popular with a simple, unadorned, organza or linen dress. "A crochet glove, however, is more versatile," says glove designer and manufacturer Carolina Amato. "It tends to be less visible on the hand and blends rather than distracting or interfering with most dress detailing. We manufacture gloves with embroidered trim of every possible variety, such as moiré, pearl, or braided borders, wreathlike lace

appliqués, and sheer vine cutouts; each is classic and always tasteful and popular.

"The long-term bridal classic is sleek, elegant, and simple white kid gloves, although overall patterns and lace are always an option. For a time, high-quality white kid gloves were impossible to find, and in came stretch fabrics. But gloves are back and they are being embellished with marvelous, wonderful bridal motifs that are works of art. The variations on the ornamental detailing are broad and vast—for example, cuffs—from sheer to thick lace borders; scattered or patterned pearls, rhinestones, and Venise or alençon lace; buttons in mother-of-pearl, pearl, satin, or self-fabric; bows of every description; fagoting—tied cross-threads; and enhancements—thick stitching with delicate beads, crystals, sequins, or even tinsel."

Most often when a bride wears a long-sleeved dress, a pair of gloves is eliminated entirely, whether her wedding is formal or informal. If gloves are worn during the ceremony, they are removed for the receiving line. Short gloves are removed before eating; higher gloves are unbuttoned at the wrist and folded under, thus exposing the hand while the arm remains covered. A fingerless glove that comes to a V at the fingers is meant to facilitate slipping on the ring. Any glove—high or low, cotton or leather—can be slit beforehand along one seam and resewn later to be worn again.

HANDBAGS

Though it is never carried down the aisle, a bride-to-be debates what shape, size,

An unadorned small clutch handbag.

❧

The floral wreath headdress and neckline treatment are carried over to a duchesse rose handbag.

fabric, and color purse to include with her ensemble, because her handkerchief, perfume, lipstick, make-up, and brushes must be kept on hand by the maid of honor or her mother. This usually calls for no more than a coordinated or accenting handbag; however, a matching handbag can be custommade. While a shoulder-strap design is rarely considered (except with a tailored suit or minidress), any constructed, geometric shape, such as square, rectangle, or round, is always in character. One traditional bag style for

Classic Chanel accessories: squared-off-toe and curved-heel shoes with handbag.

a bride is called a reticule, which is a soft white satin half-moon or pouch shape. "Big is unnecessary, clumsy, and less formal," says Elizabeth Rundlett. "Therefore the handbag that most brides bring along leans toward an unobtrusive evening size or clutch purse.

"It is the fabric's luster that determines the formality. A daytime formal handbag fabric is a high-luster white, ivory, or pastel, decorated with a subdued seed-pearl or lace trim. A formal evening handbag is a similar fabric or a metallic—silver, bronze, copper, and gold—but more heavily ornamented with sequins, beads, and jeweled buttons, clasps, or handles.

"A glossy straw or leather has a definite country feeling or informal look. A lower-luster fabric such as ottoman, satin, silk, faille, or linen, decorated with small pearls or lace, is appropriate for a semiformal daytime wedding; and the same bag becomes appropriate for a semiformal evening wedding when jewels or gold or silver accents are added."

The handbag's fabric can match, blend, or mix with the gown. An allover lace gown does not require a lace handbag—in fact, it could be too much—but a satin handbag could set off the lace; likewise, a satin dress could benefit from a lace handbag. The type of embellishment is coordinated with the dress in some way; for example, by an embroidery style or with rhinestones, if they are on the dress. Quite often a hand-me-down or antique purse is selected to fill the tradition of something old, borrowed, blue, or new. For good luck, put a penny in the purse!

HANDKERCHIEFS

For a bride to have an initialed hanky on hand to catch her tears of joy is a practical security measure as well as an age-old custom. It is often a bridal shower gift from a friend or favorite aunt that will be cherished and kept forever. The color is always white or ivory. They are made in cotton lace or with a linen, cotton, or nylon center and a border of lace, which is occasionally embellished with pearls; their size ranges between 8 and 12 square inches. Many brides prefer to carry an antique linen or silk hanky with a delicate alençon or filmy Chantilly lace edge or an embroidered border.

GARTERS

According to one legend, in the middle of the fourteenth century King Edward III of England returned a lady's garter that had dropped and this act of chivalry spurred the medieval custom of the groomsmen removing a garter from the bride's leg. Another version is that a medieval bridal game, "flinging the stocking," which took place after the couple was escorted to their chamber by the wedding guest, evolved into a bride throwing her garter to the groomsmen, with the winner marrying next. Today's bride's garter is a 3- or 4-inch-wide elastic band covered with satin or lace, often with an embroidered border decorated with bows, ribbons, pearls, or lace—and it is still thrown to the groomsmen. A long-standing bridal superstition says that no harm can befall a bride wearing blue, so very often a bride selects either a blue garter or one coordinated with her bridal party colors.

COVER-UPS

A wrap is needed by a formal bride for only brief moments, such as getting in and out of a car; usually the gown's multilayers of fabric are sufficient protection from the elements. However, in the evening, during the winter months, or when inclement weather is expected, a loose-fitting, matching or coordinated jacket, similar-color cape, cashmere scarf, shawl, or fur stole can be borrowed or rented and is carried by an attendant. Another suggestion for warmth is a removable portrait collar or stole, perhaps fastened with a decorative brooch, which can be made by the designer, manufacturer, or bridal salon from the same fabric as the dress. This can also be used for a religious ceremony, where bareness is inappropriate. A dressy coat should be on hand, even though it is unlikely that the guests will see an informal bride arrive.

A short, peplum-pointed satin jacket has set-in bead and pearl lace appliqué forming a peek-aboo opening.

Pampering Yourself: Achieving a Total Look

There are unsurpassed thrills as the day draws near: the pieces you've worked so hard on begin to fit together, the elements in your ensemble combine beautifully, and there is much to look forward to. Unfortunately, there are also times when tension levels soar. The endless succession of fittings, myriad details, hairdresser visits (including a final cut two weeks before the wedding date), facial, manicure, pedicure, and makeup sessions as well as other appointments to keep, pickups and returns to arrange, and decisions to make can cause stress. As time passes, it all shows on your face. It is important to relax, to slow down and pamper yourself. "If you enjoy facials and massages, they are in order. Certainly manicures, pedicures, or both should be considered to make yourself feel good. Don't forget scalp treatments, too, because tension and anxiety often show up there first," advises Georgette Klinger, who is the quintessential American beauty and skin-care consultant. "It is also important to realize early on, though, that general health and personal care needs must be heavily emphasized during the months, weeks, and days preceding your wedding. Certain procedures may be necessary to correct problem areas, such as outbreaks or dandruff, which could take two or three months.

"Every bride is beautiful—there is no doubt about it. But a bride who wants to look her best throughout her entire wedding day requires that little bit extra—let's think of it as being as vivacious or having the same vitality as when she first appears—while greeting her guests on the receiving line, as she mingles, drinks, dines, and dances. Reducing stress with regular exercise, getting restful sleep, honing your skin-care procedures, eating nutritious foods, not skipping meals, and limiting alcohol, nicotine, and caffeine will result in a bride who is surrounded by a happy, healthy-looking glow."

Your goals should be reasonable. Strive to reach your very best approximately six to ten weeks before your wedding day or the time of your last fitting, and then maintain it. Thinking through what areas to improve and then seeking professional expertise is a good starting point. A personal trainer's services, for example, are available. In one session they can give you an idea of what to work on and how to do it, then you can go on your own from there. Last-minute efforts simply won't work as well. The results over several weeks, for instance, of eating a normal diet with light exercise is a toned body; running five miles a day for one week results in sore muscles.

Trying to lose weight too rapidly—and few among us won't panic about it at some time—will inevitably cause problems. An unrealistic diet begun, say, two weeks before the wedding day will drain your energy level and can cause sudden or unexpected reactions on your skin as your metabolism shuts down. On the other hand, taking weight off slowly at, perhaps, the rate of half a pound per week is both healthier and more likely to be permanent. A nutritionist can be consulted to find the right balanced, low-fat, high-fiber, diet, one in which the vitamins you need are derived through a variety of foods. Massages, experts say, can help a great deal in weight reduction and toning muscle.

Considering your family's wishes, pleasing future in-laws, and catering to perfect strangers' needs—so as not to offend anyone—is wearing on every bride-to-be. One antidote is setting aside time for yourself. A second solution is regular exercise, which boosts natural chemicals in your blood and gives a quick pick-me-up. The third solution is to treat yourself well! This keeps the pressure to please from overtaking you, and includes beginning a new skin-care regimen, having facials, and consulting a dermatologist as well as testing makeup products and fragrances three months before the wedding. Your skin takes time to adapt and adjust. If needed, there are similar body treatment processes that will remove dry, flaky, or sunburned skin, which is important for bare necklines and short dresses.

Communication with your partner, the bridegroom, also helps you to be in control and free of stress. Sharing responsibilities makes you comfortable working together and helps you accomplish more. Finally, since no one looks her best when tense and tired, every bride-to-be should take the day before her wedding to relax, drift, bathe, and be

Get the works: pedicure, manicure, facial, and a massage. Many health spas offer beauty treatments and figure-adjusting regimens; however, they must begin far in advance of your wedding day.

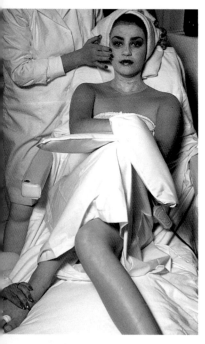

cared for and pampered with a facial, body and scalp massage, manicure, and pedicure.

When Your Big Day Arrives

The first thing to do when you get up on your wedding day is to have breakfast, because the remainder of the day will become increasingly hectic, with limited time available to grab a bite. A second pointer is to begin your final preparations with a luxurious, warm mineral or oil bath, which takes about twenty minutes for total relaxation. It will make an enormous difference during the coming hours. Pamper yourself, to be sure, but don't use a different solution or unguent or fragrance you have not pretested. There will be enough anxiety without an unwanted itch or irritation. Set aside a comfortable, private place and a realistic—almost leisurely—schedule for your preparations.

Of course, when to begin depends on the ceremony time, but several hours or more—at the least—will be needed to get ready. Plan on the better part of an additional hour for your hair—depending on its length and your hairdo—and just about as much time for your makeup. Your makeup should be done first—yet not so far beforehand for it to fade. If you are scheduling appointments at a salon, go early so as not to be rushed; but if the hairdresser and makeup consultant are coming to you, leave two or three hours, depending on your hairstyle and headpiece.

Getting dressed in all your finery is easiest when each garment is laid out on a flat surface, such as a bed or dresser, or hung up together in a dressing-room closet, with your hosiery, shoes, foundation, lingerie, and accessories—except the fresh flowers, which should be kept in a refrigerator nearby. Somebody, either your mother or an atten-

dant, should be on hand to help you each step along the way. "The order of dressing is to put on your bra and underwear first, then your stockings (with extra pairs on hand in case of a run) and garter. The dress should wait, so it doesn't wrinkle before you walk down the aisle—especially if it is a big gown," says *Bride's* magazine's fashion editor, Rachel Leonard. "It is wise, furthermore, to step into your gown rather than putting it on over your head: traces of makeup can rub off, your makeup may get smeared, and your hair messed. When this is not possible, a piece of gauze should be placed over your head. Your slip is placed into the dress without the other unattached underpinnings; they are put on under the dress, after it is on. Often, because of nerves, placing the headpiece and attaching the veil requires an extra pair of hands. Try sitting on a stool or on your petticoats so as not to crush the gown's back, which will face the guests during the ceremony. Next comes the jewelry. Here you may have a final decision to make, so try each alternative until you are absolutely satisfied with your choice. Place any personal good-luck charm or hanky in place. Finally, slip on your shoes.

"For big gowns, practice walking around unassisted, and then, with an attendant's help, practice getting yourself situated, attaching and detaching the bustle, fluffing out the train, and holding out the gown to dance. If the gown's material wrinkles easily, a hand steamer can be brought along to the ceremony site. Don't forget to put your handkerchief, makeup, and brushes into your handbag, to pick up your bouquet, Bible, or fan, and to put on your lipstick and a splash of your perfume while glancing in the mirror for the final inspection."

Now that everything is perfect—a testimony to careful planning—you are ready to sally forth and walk down the aisle.

OVERLEAF: A romantic, Victorian-style cotton country wedding dress with lace and trim and satin ribbons worked into an afternoon confection.

Part Three

Dressing the

Bride...

and Bridegroom

$\mathcal{W}$hether your big day is one year, six months, or only weeks ahead, the most effective tool for organizing each aspect of a bridal or bridegroom's ensemble is a properly prepared, chronological checklist.

For the bridegroom, there will be three simple stages: deciding the style—formal, semiformal, or informal—shopping and purchasing the elements, and making the final preparations. For the bride-to-be, there are four phases to selecting a wedding dress and assembling accessories. In the first phase, define your statement, determine a budget, and research the options. In the second, shop to find the right bridal-wear retailer, designer, or dressmaker, and a seamstress to alter an heirloom, vintage, or ready-to-wear gown. In the third phase, make your selection, purchase the dress, and accessorize it. Fourth and last, pull it all together: a haircut or trim, coloring, manicure, facial, and massage, and one final check that everything is just right.

Although some stress is inevitable, having a master plan and sticking to it allows you to make logical decisions with a minimal amount of stress. It also helps you if keeping to a timetable is important, and eliminates uncorrectable mistakes when making your purchases. Bear in mind that finding the right dress, headdress, and accents probably requires attention to detail that you take for granted or are unaccustomed to applying. Throughout this exciting period of discovery, reveling in the possibilities and accumulating the elements will be half the fun, but your sweetest reward will be walking down the aisle as a bride who looks and feels her best.

It is important to consider each step somewhat in order and not get too far ahead of yourself. This helps coordinate the numerous elements, prevents last-minute chaos, and acts as insurance against a disastrous oversight. One piece of advice: finalize your major focal point—the dress—then assemble your accessories by beginning with your headdress. Of course, there are exceptions. Wearing an

L'envoi

reviewing your situation

OPPOSITE: *An off-the-rack cocktail dress has draped sleeves from shoulder pads, in a leaf motif that echoes the wedding-day setting.*

important accessory, such as an heirloom lace veil or matching diamond earrings and necklace, as a primary focal point means your dress must accommodate the accessory. With a period or a contemporary street-length dress, the accessories can make an outfit work, so the shoe style, handbag, and flowers should be coordinated as one unit, not separately.

As you go along, collect any items definitely designated for inclusion, say, the corner of a cherished childhood smock to pin on your petticoat; and feel free to purchase any secondary accents, such as a lace handkerchief, as you happen upon them. This will save you running out for a similar item at the last minute. One cautionary note to remember as you establish a schedule: high demand, especially in the springtime and at certain holidays, like Valentine's Day, may cause unforeseen delays. Plan on this ahead of time, and compensate by allowing additional time between purchasing your dress and your wedding day.

Before assembling her ensemble, the bride-to-be should map out her path carefully. List all the ensemble components, then order them in steps or according to categories. Leave one column for reminders to yourself, with enough space to write down the names, telephone numbers, and addresses you collect. Reserve a column to keep track of miscellaneous information for each item: appointments, pickup and delivery dates, and cost, if you are so inclined. Be certain, next, to create a realistic, week-by-week schedule. Enter all your appointments. Write down when you need each item to be ready. Use color codes, highlighters, dividers—whatever pleases you.

Additional time will be needed to investigate many of the items in your ensemble.

Some things require extensive shopping time. Most custom-made components may have far-off delivery dates; they will require your attention sooner rather than later. Most likely, as you start moving through your list, it will be necessary at times to put an item on the back burner temporarily while you work on another aspect of your ensemble.

PHASE ONE:
DEFINING AND RESEARCHING

Before beginning to look for outfits, the bride and bridegroom must mutually agree on their overall statement: the expression of how they see themselves demonstrated by attire. Whatever the impression a couple wishes to create, their ensemble's character is governed by their sense of style and their presentation's formality. Its direction or mood—whether traditional, period, or contemporary attire, in keeping with a religious or a civil ceremony—is one important consideration, as is the spirit, which can range from innocent to sophisticated, grand to understated, romantic to classic.

The other important factors to consider are the overall wedding ambience, ranging from small and simple to large and lavish, and the framework, which controls the attitude—either urban or country setting, indoors or outside, in a public space or at home. Cumulatively, these decisions indicate the essence of a bride and bridegroom's ensemble, which your guests will grasp and the photographs capture.

While the budget is being discussed, start your research by brainstorming ideas with friends and relatives to pinpoint what to include in your ensemble, and select a companion to accompany you. Gather ideas from photographs in fashion and costume books, recent bridal magazines and catalogs, maybe even an acquaintance's photo album. Clip the photographs or make photocopies of any element that catches your eye. Keep a separate notebook or a section of your date book devoted specifically to ideas, such as any shade of white or pastel, or a complementary color scheme you fancy. File the

OPPOSITE: The bride's wedding dress sets the tempo for her bridal ensemble, the wedding party's attire, and, in fact, the entire wedding day.

EASY-REFERENCE GUIDELINES TO ESTABLISH YOUR TIMETABLE

There is no right amount of time to spend on any step of your ensemble, because every bride-to-be approaches each element from a different point of view. A bridegroom, however, must wait until his bride's dress is ordered before he sets out to shop for his entire ensemble.

Five or six months' lead time is the minimum needed for a bride-to-be to discover the options, thoroughly explore them, purchase a gown dressmade, or order customized touches. Any time over six months allows for a more leisurely schedule. Four months before your wedding day you should purchase your dress, since four to twelve weeks are needed to order a headdress. Approximately two weeks will be needed for the final preparations.

Working within a three-month schedule allows three weeks to weigh your options and three weeks to shop for your wedding dress. This leaves four weeks to assemble your ensemble and two weeks to prepare yourself. Your choices are limited to a ready-to-wear dress, sample clearance sale, or a rental; more than simple alterations to an heirloom dress may be difficult to complete on time. Your accessories, such as a headpiece or shoes, can be customized, however.

With less than two months to the wedding day, your decision-making phase must be deliberate and focused, your shopping quick and carefully executed. Everything can be accomplished on time, but your options are limited to ready-to-wear items.

photographs in categories, perhaps according to the silhouette or trim, and jot down any interesting leads for resources.

Since the wedding dress sets the tone for each setting—down the aisle, at the altar, on your receiving line, and at the reception—as well as for the entire wedding party, it is your primary concern, but you must also look for promising headdress, jewelry, flower, and accent choices to investigate firsthand later. Study and critique each photograph, and decide on the elements to include and those to eliminate as you go along. Ask recent brides to recommend bridal shops and shoe stores as well as consultants, seamstresses, hairdressers, milliners, florists, and makeup specialists. Try to line up and reserve time with the experts, especially a hairdresser, beautician, and florist, you are sure to want involved. By all means have preliminary discussions and benefit from their wealth of experience, but leave finalizing what each will do until the proper time.

PHASE TWO:
COMPARISON SHOPPING

After defining the statement that you wish to make, and conjuring up an overall dress concept (preferably sketched), with the budget for the ensemble in mind, you are ready to shop for a wedding dress. It will soon become clear which path is your best route. This early stage, meanwhile, is an excellent opportunity to try on the astonishing array of ready-to-wear wedding dresses and made-to-measure sample bridal gowns. It is never too soon to restore an heirloom or to look for the perfect antique or vintage wedding dress, which can be difficult to find in the size and style you want. If a pattern-made bridal gown interests you, begin looking for patterns and the right dressmaker to work with you. And if your budget's scope allows

for a made-to-order designer ensemble, set out immediately to discover the bridal-wear couturiers whose wedding dresses you admire most, narrow your choices down, then make an appointment to talk with a few designers.

A visit to several bridal salons, rental houses, department stores, or a stop at discounters to browse gives the best indication of the resources available to you. Weigh each emporium's style sense to discover the one with a large, varied selection close to your concept, needs, and taste; also, look through their headpieces, veils, shoes, and foundations to decide if you can complete your ensemble under one roof, especially if time is limited. Determine how helpful the salon will be, and meet with the bridal consultants. Ask yourself one crucial question: Is this someone I want to work with?

Get an idea of the time needed to order, fit, and accessorize your ensemble. Inquire about any additional costs, such as fittings, and if their sample dresses can be customized for you. Keep detailed notes, including the style number, color, and ordering time of any gown that impresses you. You may want to consider having a loaded camera ready during these visits to reference the dresses you are considering. Before time runs out, plan to investigate a few suitable alternate routes—a bridal broker, a boutique with components you can mix and match, a dressmaker for a custom-made wrap.

PHASE THREE:
THE STEPS TO AN ENSEMBLE

When you are prepared to purchase your wedding dress, call your chosen broker to order a manufacturer's sample in your size; return to a discounter or boutique to select a ready-to-wear dress, which requires finding a seamstress; schedule a bridal consult-

OPPOSITE: A heavyweight worsted wool swallowtail evening suit is worn with a white, wing-collar, "boiled front" (unpleated bib) shirt, a white piqué bow tie and waistcoat, and a white rose on the satin-faced lapel.

ant or rental salon appointment; or begin shopping for a pattern, fabrics, and trimmings as well as engaging a dressmaker or couturier's services.

The first step in selecting your wedding dress is to determine the best design line, the silhouette, including the upper portion, a bodice, and the lower portion, a skirt or, in rare instances, trousers.

Second, decide on the skirt length, and whether to include a design element, such as a train, back treatment, and any addition at your hips, like a peplum.

The third step is to coordinate each component, particularly the neckline, shoulder, and sleeve treatment, and its scale.

Fourth is embellishing your wedding dress, beginning with the fabric and lace. Once the primary fabric or lace, whichever stands out the most, is selected, then choose a complementary fabric or lace, if you want another texture.

Fifth, decide on the details: its trimmings, enhancements, and notions. Ideally, you should be able to sketch free-hand, trace the elements, or describe each component and detail of your dream wedding dress in a few sentences.

After your bridal gown, dress, or outfit has been ordered, it is time to complete your ensemble, and to let your bridegroom know immediately that he can start on his attire. The bridegroom should complement his bride, not draw attention to himself, yet he should still express his personality and demonstrate his individual sense of style. A bridegroom's attire is clear-cut and simple as ABC when broken down into three stages. First of all, each decision made by the bride in the initial stage dictates what the bridegroom wears, so knowing the appropriate formality is his stage one.

While the bride's dress style governs her bride-groom's attire, the ceremony time is also an important element. The bridegroom wears either formal attire, morning clothes, or full dress in the evening; a semiformal approach means a morning coat and striped trousers or dinner suit in the evening; and an

ABOVE: A white turned-down collar, flat-front dress shirt, and black batwing bow tie are worn with a red carnation boutonniere.

❦

RIGHT: A European look is achieved in a double-breasted, high-notch lapel, rose-colored gabardine suit with a paisley tie, solid polished-cotton pocket square, and a boutonniere.

❦

OPPOSITE: An unbleached cotton afternoon wedding dress with a long, apron-effect overskirt is complemented by a boxy, poplin sharkskin sack coat and trousers, a white shirt, a floral bow tie, and a yellow boutonniere.

informal milieu translates into a conventional suit jacket and matching trousers, with a darker color usually selected for the evening.

Along with a sack coat and matching trousers, the bridegroom's ensemble always includes specific and carefully coordinated accessories, a white shirt, tie (bow or four-in-hand), pocket handkerchief, boutonniere, and spit-shined shoes. Finding a reputable men's clothier or rental emporium is stage two. Shopping for an ensemble begins approximately three months prior to the wedding day for a custom-made suit, and two months for a ready-made suit or to reserve rented formalwear. The final preparations, stage three, include the final fitting, and checking that all the various elements are gathered. This begins at least two weeks before the wedding day.

❦

While certain key elements among the bride's ensemble should be addressed in order, particularly your hairstyle before your headpiece, holding fast to any order will be problematic. An accessory or accent that relates to the dress only can usually be considered independently, and those that relate to each other as well as the dress should be considered together. Items such as shoes and stockings depend on one another; flowers, on the other hand, can be tackled separately and out of order, but with regard to the whole.

The first and second fitting schedules govern when many of the remaining elements must be selected, purchased, and on hand. For example, your shoes (at least the heel height) will be needed for the first fitting, the headpiece and veil by the second, and all the jewelry possibilities at the final fitting. As soon as possible, make an appointment to meet with your hairdresser, beautician, and floral designer to finalize your bouquet.

Step six consists of accessorizing, starting at the top with your hair, headpiece, jewelry, and veil. Before looking for a headpiece, discuss and investigate the most flattering hairdos with your hairdresser. Set up another appointment for two weeks before your wedding to have a final haircut, trim, or coloring and to finalize your headdress placement; also, book your hairdresser for the wedding day, if you want him or her on hand.

The purpose of the headpiece is to frame your face, balance the entire ensemble, and match your personality; moreover, your accessory statement requires carefully coordinating the jewelry, including earrings, necklace, perhaps a bracelet and brooch,

and a veil presentation, which attaches to the headpiece. These crowning touches lend stature, create mystery, and set the bride apart. One additional consideration is your headpiece's convertibility when removing the longer, cumbersome portions after your receiving line for the remainder of the wedding-day celebration.

Although wearing a hat is hardly a unique experience, donning a headdress probably is. The selection process, therefore, is an adventure into uncharted territory for most brides-to-be. Isolate the best style, size, and shape first, and then the fabric and trim. Many experts suggest getting a feel for the right headdress by putting one on with each likely wedding dress; some advise stopping by a well-stocked department-store millinery counter; and others recommend going to a specialty shop. Whichever route you choose, you've come upon the right headpiece when it flatters your facial features and complements the design line and proportion of your ensemble. If the right size and shape headdress cannot be found in the color, fabric, and trim that are closely coordinated with your dress, your entire headpiece can be ordered and custom-made.

Step seven, your bridal bouquet selection, can begin soon after your dress is purchased. Look, smell, touch, and select the flowers to include. Regardless of the colors, variety, design, and size you choose, the bouquet relates directly to your dress. Bring a swatch, your sketch, or a snapshot to the floral designer. Finalize together how this focal point is to echo your overall statement, add rhythm and beauty, and punctuate the formality of your ensemble. Ask about the numerous unique ways to include flowers as personal adornment, such as a swag at your hemline, clusters in your hair, or by incorporating flowers with another accessory you will hold.

During step eight your bridal ensemble is completed as the necessary niceties—a fancy slip, comfortable shoes, coordinated stockings, and a special makeup style—are included. There are several functional necessities to coordinate as well, for instance, gloves, handbag, handkerchief, garter, and wrap. There are optional items that may be meaningful to you, such as a lucky charm, or perhaps a symbol of the lifelong relationship you are entering. They can be gathered as you go along, and completed as your wedding day approaches.

PHASE FOUR: TYING IT ALL UP

The last phase involves tying up any loose ends. One week before your wedding day, collect all of the items that will be taken with you to your dressing area. Have your dress pressed and prepare a makeup kit and safety pouch in which to keep pins and needles, thread, scissors, tape, steamer, extra hairpins, and a few pairs of stockings—just in case. Go over your checklist one last time to be certain that nothing has been left out.

Now is also the time to wrap up any regime that was undertaken to help you look your very best. Avoid a last-minute, panic-induced urge to crash-diet or to begin a skin-care treatment: they can be less helpful than harmful. As your wedding day approaches, don't skip meals, do get restful sleep, and treat yourself to a few small indulgences, perhaps manicures, pedicures, facials, massages, and long, soothing baths.

But the most important element to ensure a stress-free environment is maintaining an open line of communication with your partner, the bridegroom. Soon you, the radiant bride of your dreams, will walk down the aisle to meet him.

Good luck!

OPPOSITE: Heavily reembroidered lace and tulle floor-length gown for the bride and a velvet dinner jacket worn with black, lightweight worsted trousers with satin banding, wing-collar dress shirt with black bow tie, and a rose boutonniere for the bridegroom.

A quintessential Christian Dior formal bridal ball-gown silhouette is paired with classic morning clothes for the bridegroom.

A Sampling of Bridal Salons
Around the Country

ALABAMA

June's Brides
404 Riverchase Village
Birmingham, AL 35244
(205) 987-1888

Southern Bride
9021 Parkway East
Birmingham, AL 35206
(205) 836-7385

Nathan
1402 Beltline Road SW
Decatur, AL 35215
(205) 350-2000

Almeda's Bridal
2410 Fairway Drive
Mountain Brook, AL 35213
(205) 879-7733

ALASKA

Rose & Thistle
330 Wendall
Fairbanks, AK 99701
(907) 425-4011

ARIZONA

Kory's
243 Marley Avenue
Nogales, AZ 85261
(602) 287-2550

Axteca Plaza Bridals & Formals
1010 E. Washington Street
Phoenix, AZ 85034
(602) 253-2171

Bridal Couture of Scottsdale
8120 North Hayden Road
Suite E 106
Scottsdale, AZ 85258
(602) 991-3207

Wedding Elegance
7119 East Shea Boulevard, #111
Scottsdale, AZ 85258
(602) 991-7062

Brides & Proms Wedding and Party
    Center
5420 East Broadway, #254
Tucson, AZ 85705
(602) 748-9080

ARKANSAS

Low's Bridal & Formal Shoppe
109 North Main
Brinkley, AR 72021
1-800-338-9054

Formally Yours
1823 N. Grant
Little Rock, AR 72207
(501) 663-7508

CALIFORNIA

Marry Me Bridal Formalwear
5701 Santa Ana Canyon Road
Anaheim Hills, CA 92807
(714) 998-9110

Brides House
1002 Wible Road
Bakersfield, CA 93304
(805) 397-0440

Renee Strauss for the Bride
8401 Wilshire Boulevard
Beverly Hills, CA 90211
(213) 653-3331

The Bridal Suite
1807 El Camino Real
Burlingame, CA 94010
(415) 692-8500

The Unique Bride
1209 Howard Avenue
Burlingame, CA 94010
(415) 347-7001

Bridal World of Southern California
250 3d Avenue
Chula Vista, CA 92010
(619) 426-2100

Mon Amie Bridal and Formal
Countryside Center
355 South Bristol Street
Costa Mesa, CA 92626
(714) 546-5700

Rhapsody in Romance
560 South Hartz Avenue
Suite 102
Danville, CA 94526
(510) 838-2953

Luftenburg's Bridal
909 Fulton Mall
Fresno, CA 93721
(209) 237-3496

Mary Linn's Bridal & Formals at
    Lovers Lane
1823 W. Glenoaks Boulevard
Glendale, CA 91201
(818) 241-3159

I. Magnin
8637 Villa La Jolla Drive
La Jolla, CA 92037
(619) 455-7111

I. Magnin—Wilshire
3050 Wilshire Boulevard
Los Angeles, CA 90010
(213) 382-6161

Special Days Bridal & Formal Wear
3330 Oakdale Road
Modesto, CA 95355
(209) 551-3297

The Bride
230 Newport Center Drive
Newport Beach, CA 92660
(714) 760-1800

The Classic Bride
2245 East Colorado Boulevard
Suite A201
Pasadena, CA 91107
(818) 792-0366

Style Bridal
4150 Railroad Avenue
Pittsburg, CA 94565
(510) 439-5578

Bridal Nook
2638 El Paseo Lane
Sacramento, CA 95821
(916) 483-5733

Bride 'N Formal
2808 Marconi Avenue
Sacramento, CA 95821
(916) 482-8267

Miss D's of San Carlos
1179 San Carlos Avenue
San Carlos, CA 94070
(415) 593-2323

Here Comes the Bride
7610 Hazard Center Drive, #701
San Diego, CA 92108
(619) 688-9201

Bridal Galleria
1 Daniel Burnham Court, #10
San Francisco, CA 94109
(415) 346-6160

I. Magnin
135 Stockton Street
Union Square
San Francisco, CA 94108
(415) 362-2100

New Things West
410 Town & Country
San Jose, CA 95128
1-800-766-GOWN

Clarissa Bridal
1821 Mt. Diablo Boulevard
Walnut Creek, CA 94596
(510) 930-0214

Bridal Images . . . Simple to
    Sophisticated
22540 Ventura Boulevard
Woodland Hills, CA 91364
(818) 999-0083

COLORADO

Bride's Boutique
13698 E. Iliff Avenue
Aurora, CO 80014
(303) 337-3128

A Formal Affair
1441 Arapahoe
Boulder, CO 80302
(303) 444-8294

Brides Gallery, Ltd.
4740 Table Mesa Drive
Boulder, CO 80303
(303) 499-6052

Montaldo's
3000 E. First Avenue
Cherry Creek, CO 80231
(303) 750-1073

A Wedding Showcase
90 Federal Boulevard
At First Avenue
Denver, CO 80219
(303) 935-2444

Bea's Bridal Nook
2800 E. 6th Avenue
Denver, CO 80206
(303) 333-4588

CONNECTICUT

Marie's Bridal Shoppe
2337 Black Rock Turnpike
Fairfield, CT 06430
(203) 372-5712

Chatelaine
140 Glastonbury, #167
Glastonbury, CT 06033
(203) 659-2313

Bridal Couture
120 Elm Street
New Canaan, CT 06840
(203) 966-8122

Harold's Formalwear
19 Elm Street
New Haven, CT 06510
(203) 562-4156

Julie Allen Bridal's
97 South Main Market Place
Newtown, CT 06470
(203) 426-4378

The Bride's Maid
452 East Street
Plainville, CT 06062
(203) 793-0883

Mariella Creations
2192 Silas Deane Highway
Rocky Hill, CT 06067
(203) 529-8558

Lucy Baltzellshop
36 LaSalle Road
West Hartford, CT 06107
(203) 233-1203

The Plumed Serpent
136 Main Street
Westport, CT 06880
(203) 226-9868

DELAWARE

Simon's Bridal Shoppe
215 W. Loockerman Street
Dover, DE 19901
(302)678-8160

Bride & Grooms
4627 Stanton Ogle Town Road
Newark, DE 19713
(302) 368-9007

Bridal Fashions by Frank Bernard Ltd.
925 Philadelphia Pike
Wilmington, DE 19809
(302) 762-6575

DISTRICT OF
COLUMBIA

Marie Coreen Ltd.
5300 Washington Ave. NW
Washington, DC 20015
(202) 537-1461

Rizik Brothers
1100 Connecticut Avenue NW
Washington, DC 20036
(202) 223-4050

Royal Formal and Bridal
1328 G Street
Washington, DC 20005
(202) 737-7144

Woodward & Lothrop Bridal Salon
1025 11th & F Streets NW
Washington, DC 20013
(202) 347-7275

FLORIDA

Chic Parisien/Frances Novias
118 Miracle Mile
Coral Gables, FL 33134
(305) 448-5756

Coral Gables Bridals
366 Miracle Mile
Coral Gables, FL 33134
(305) 445-5896

David's Bridals & Formals
1515 E. Las Olas Boulevard
Ft. Lauderdale, FL 33301
(305) 463-1773
(15 locations)

Patricia South's "The Bride's Formals"
4066 W. Broward Boulevard
Ft. Lauderdale, FL 33317
(305) 791-6007

Sue Gordon Bridal Salon
721 E. Las Olas Boulevard
Ft. Lauderdale, FL 33301
(305) 522-8200

Victoria's Bridal Couture
825 E. Las Olas Boulevard
Ft. Lauderdale, FL 33301
(305) 522-1678

Queen's Fancy Bridal Salon
1937 Suwannee Avenue
Fort Myers, FL 33901
(813) 936-8074

June's Bridals & Tuxedos
6099 Hollywood Boulevard
Hollywood, FL 33024
(305) 987-0525

Bridal Elegance by Bea
2431 West State Road, #434
Longwood, FL 32779
(407) 788-6969

Alegria's Brides #1
1974 NE 163d Street
N. Miami Beach, FL 33162
(305) 949-8174

Beverly's
902 Lee Road
Orlando, FL 32810
(407) 628-2960

A Flower Mart & Bridal Fashions
10041 E. Colonial Drive
Orlando, FL 32817
(305) 277-6670

Erica Loren
3101 PGA Boulevard
Palm Beach Garden, FL 33410
(407) 624-8214

Brisch's
525 Brent Lane
Pensacola, FL 32503
(904) 477-5683

The Main Event
8008 North Armenia Avenue
Tampa, FL 33604
(813) 935-3161

The Collection
521 Park Avenue South
Winter Park, FL 32789
(407) 740-6003

GEORGIA

Anne Barge for Brides
3209 Paces Ferry Place NW
Atlanta, GA 30305
(404) 237-0898

Bridals by Lori
6022 Sandy Springs Circle
Atlanta, GA 30328
(404) 252-8767

Bride Beautiful
Perimeter Mall
Atlanta, GA 30346
(404) 394-2177

Impressions
2460 Galleria Mall
Atlanta, GA 30305
(404) 841-6202

Impressions Bridal Salon
99 West Paces Ferry Road
Atlanta, GA 30305
(404) 953-9545

Saks Fifth Avenue
3440 Peachtree Road NE
Atlanta, GA 30326
(404) 261-7234

Regina Bridals
2100 Pleasant Hill Road
Duluth, GA 30136
(404) 476-7398

Brittany Leigh Bridal
5475 Chamblee-Dunwoody Road
Dunwoody, GA 30338
(404) 551-0989

Here Comes the Bride
5370 Highway 78
Stone Mountain, GA 30087
(404) 469-6552

HAWAII

Liberty House
91-262 Oihana Street
Ewa Beach, HI 96706
(808) 945-5819

Deanna Bride N' Fashion
320 Ward Avenue, #107
Honolulu, HI 96814
(808) 538-1344

Island Romance
615 Piikoi Street, #106
Honolulu, HI 96814
(808) 538-7555

IDAHO

Sanders Sweetheart Manor
10205 McMillan Road
Boise, ID 83704
(208) 376-3264

ILLINOIS

Beautiful Brides of Arlington
835 E. Rand Road
Arlington, IL 60004
(708) 577-0774

Victorian Bridals at Wolsfelt
1025 S. Lincoln Avenue
Aurora, IL 60505
(708) 896-7166

Carson Pirie Scott
1 S. State Street
Chicago, IL 60603
(312) 641-7475

Carson Pirie Scott
36 S. Wabash, #1200
Chicago, IL 60603
(312) 686-8891

Eva's Bridals & Fashions
3339 North Harlem
Chicago, IL 60634
(312) 777-3311

Exclusives for the Bride
311 West Superior, #216
Chicago, IL 60616
(312) 664-8870

Marshall Fields
111 N. State Street
Chicago, IL 55440
(312) 375-3210

The Ultimate Bride
106 E. Oak
Chicago, IL 60627
(312) 337-6300

Margies
6440 W. 95th Street
Chicago Ridge, IL 60415
(708) 599-7700

Margies
445 W. Ogden Avenue
Clarendon Hills, IL 60514
(708) 325-7035

Bridal Suite
3433 Rupp Highway
Decatur, IL 62526
(217) 877-0577

House of Brides
1184 Roosevelt Road
Glen Ellyn, IL 60137
(708) 629-4040

Margies
1075 Golf Road
Hoffman Estates, IL 60172
(708) 882-1444

Volle's Bridal Boutique
53 S. Old Rand Road
Lake Zurich, IL 60047
(708) 438-7603

Eva's Bridals & Fashions
16711 S. Torrence
Lansing, IL 60438
(708) 474-8844

The Bridal Shoppe & Boutique
404 Robert Parker Road
Long Grove, IL 60047
(708) 634-2550

Margies
5645 W. Dempster
Morton Grove, IL 60053
(708) 966-7000

Elise Bridal & Formals
804 S. Route 59, #111
Naperville, IL 60565
(708) 369-9929

Eva's Bridals & Fashions
Ogden Avenue at Royal St. George
Naperville, IL 60540
(708) 717-8800

Eva's Bridals & Fashions
4811 W. 95th Street
Oak Lawn, IL 60453
(708) 422-5599

Margies
11010 S. Cicero Avenue
Oak Lawn, IL 60453
(708) 423-1013

Eva's Bridals & Fashions
305 Orland Park Place
Orland Park, IL 60462
(708) 403-3334

Margies
7401 W. North Avenue
River Forest, IL 60305
(708) 771-6600

House of Brides
1209 E. Golf Road
Schaumburg, IL 55555
(708) 605-1700

Maggie Lee
4132 West Dempster
Skokie, IL 60076
(708) 679-5080

Colleen's Bridal Collection
466 E. 162d Street
South Holland, IL 60473
(312) 596-1224

INDIANA

Bridal Boutique of Carmel
2160 E. 116th Street
Carmel, IN 46032
(317) 844-1780

Brides of Carmel
472 E. Carmel Drive
Carmel, IN 46032
(317) 843-2928

Marco Bridal
517 S. Green River Road
Evansville, IN 47715
(812) 479-5095

Posie Patch
586 S. State Road 135
Greenwood, IN 46142
(317) 888-1380

Diana's Bridal Boutique
8029 E. Washington Street
Indianapolis, IN 46219
(317) 898-5171

Elaine's Bridal Estates
8605 W. 400 North
Michigan City, IN 46360
(219) 872-6419

Potpourri Bridal Salon
100 North Main
Zionsville, IN 46077
(317) 873-5614

IOWA

Schaffer's Bridal Shop
300 8th Street
Des Moines, IA 50309
(515) 288-0356

KANSAS

Margie's Bridal Shop
Bridal Plaza
Overland Park, KS 64304
(913) 642-8108

Beverly Brooks for the Bride
3955 W. 83d Street
Prairie Village, KS 66208
(913) 381-1060

Alkire
1912 S. Oliver
Wichita, KS 67218
(316) 684-3693

KENTUCKY

Cherished Moments
3199 Nicholsville Road
Lexington, KY 40503
(606) 273-9313

Ruth's Bridal Shop
153 Patchen Drive
Lexington, KY 40502
(606) 253-0900

Greenups Belles & Brides
838 South 4th Street
Louisville, KY 40203
(502) 587-1749

Abbington's Bridal House
1531 Frederica Street
Owensboro, KY 42303
(502) 684-4547

LOUISIANA

Bridal Boutique of Baton Rouge
8750 Florida Boulevard
Baton Rouge, LA 70815
(504) 925-1135

Chez Lilly
2525 W. Park
Houma, LA 70364
(504) 868-3874

Jay Charles
One Galleria Boulevard, #746
Metairie, LA 70001
(504) 836-5944

Just For A Day
4312 Veterans Boulevard
Metairie, LA 70002
(504) 888-5711

Linda Lee
3029 Veterans Boulevard
Metairie, LA 70002
(504) 834-4180

Pearl's Place
3114 Severn Avenue
Metairie, LA 70002
(504) 885-9213

Abdalla's
133 West Main
New Iberia, LA 70560
(318) 364-4116

House of Broel
2220 St. Charles Avenue
New Orleans, LA 70130
(504) 522-2220

Saks Fifth Avenue
301 Canal Street
New Orleans, LA 70130
(504) 524-2200

MARYLAND

Annapolis Formal
954 Bay Ridge Road
Annapolis, MD 21403
(301) 268-3806

Leo Amster, Ltd.
1300 Goucher Boulevard
Baltimore, MD 21204
(301) 296-8383

Claire Dratch Bridal Salon
7615 Wisconsin Avenue
Bethesda, MD 20814
(301) 656-8000

Royal Formal and Bridal
5115 Lawrence Place
Bladensburg, MD 20710
(301) 779-0707

Robinson's Bridal & Formalwear
8 Mountain Road
Glen Burnie, MD 21060
(301) 766-4600

Laurel Bridal and Gown
14234 Baltimore Avenue
Laurel, MD 20707
(301) 725-4600

Arthur Liebman/Mark Daniels
115 N. Washington Street
Rockville, MD 20850
(301) 762-7577

Marian Bridal Shop
8780 Georgia Avenue
Silver Spring, MD 20902
(301) 587-7347

Gamberdella
30 W. Pennsylvania Avenue
Towson, MD 21204
(301) 828-7870

MASSACHUSETTS

Christina's Bridal
63 Park Street
Andover, MA 01810
(508) 470-3956

Allegria
285 Belmont Street
Belmont, MA 02178
(617) 489-1449

Jordan Marsh
450 Washington Street
Boston, MA 02205
(617) 357-3913

Mary Burns Bridal Shop
11 Newbury Street
Boston, MA 02116
(617) 247-3205

Sumner Charles Inc.
16 Newbury Street
Boston, MA 02116
(617) 638-8966

Bridal Corner
720 Memorial Drive
Chicopee, MA 01020
(413) 534-7828

Manhattan Bridals & "Tux" Shops
   at Rotary
283 Washington Street
Dedham, MA 02026
(617) 329-6664

Nikki
328 Worcester Road
Framingham, MA 01701
(508) 875-1727

Gowns by Jane Bridal Boutique
148 Washington Street
Norwell, MA 02061
(617) 878-2050

Terry's Bridal Shop
599 Washington Street
Norwood, MA 02062
(617) 769-2262

Laura's
1235 Furnace Brook Highway
Quincy, MA 02169
(617) 479-1233

Weddings, Inc.
Route #1
Saugus, MA 01906
(617) 233-1844

Yolanda's
355 Waverly Oaks Road
Waltham, MA 02154
(617) 899-6470

MICHIGAN

Alvin's Bridals
249 Pierce
Birmingham, MI 48010
(313) 644-7492

Boulevard Bridal
1095 S. Hunter
Birmingham, MI 48011
(313) 642-4110

Jocabson Stores
336 W. Maple Avenue
Birmingham, MI 48012
(313) 644-6900

Alvin's Bride
249 Pierce Street
Birmingham, MI 48009
(313) 644-7492

Sue Gordon
708 N. Woodward
Birmingham, MI 48011
(313) 642-1112

Arena Bridal Salon
16890 E. Eight Mile Road
Detroit, MI 48205
(313) 839-2203

Elizabeth's Bridal Manor
402 S. Main Street
Northville, MI 48167
(313) 348-2783

Lina's Bridal
570 S. Main Street
Plymouth, MI 48170
(313) 455-1100

Dayton, Hudson, and Field's
21500 Northwestern Highway
Southfield, MI 48075
(313) 443-4164

Blaga's
13426 Fifteen Mile Road
Sterling Heights, MI 48312
(313) 795-8505

MINNESOTA

Dayton's
Box 644
700 on the Mall
Minneapolis, MN 55402
(612) 375-2179

Rush's
927 Nicollet Mall
Minneapolis, MN 55403
(612) 339-0581

Schaffers Bridal Shop
1000 Nicollet Mall
Minneapolis, MN 55403
(612) 338-6464

Mestad's Wedding World
1171 6th Street NW
Barlow Plaza
Rochester, MN 55901
(507) 289-2444

Wedding Shoppe
1196 Grand Avenue
St. Paul, MN 55105
(612) 298-1144

MISSISSIPPI

Betty Ann's Bridal
631 Brookway Boulevard
Brookhaven, MS 39602
(601) 833-3516

Waldoff's
Cloverleaf Mall
Hattiesburg, MS 39401
(601) 544-8511

The Bridal Path
4465 I-55 North
Banner Hall, #104
Jackson, MS 39206
(601) 982-8267

Deedy's Dress Shop
Highway 90-1072 Thorn
Ocean Springs, MS 39564
(601) 875-2011

MISSOURI

Margie's Bridal Shop
1305 West Main Street
Greenwood, MO 64034
(816) 537-6968

Jones Store
1201 Main Street
Kansas City, MO 64105
(816) 391-7192

McDaniel's Bridal Shoppe
901-05 S. Glenstone
Springfield, MO 65802
(417) 869-7331

Maiden Voyage Bridals
1125 Cave Springs Boulevard
St. Charles, MO 63303
(314) 928-1108

Blustein's Bride's House
1010 Locust Street
St. Louis, MO 63101
(314) 621-1833

Neiman Marcus
100 Plaza Frontenac
St. Louis, MO 63131
(314) 567-9811

NEBRASKA

Sassis at the Wedding
2530 O Street
Lincoln, NE 68510
(402) 475-3741

Crossroad Bridals
340 North 76th Street
Omaha, NE 68114
1-800-732-8136

Suburban Bridal
345 North 72d Street
Omaha, NE 68114
(402) 554-8522

NEVADA

Celebrations
4760 Sahara Avenue, #28
Las Vegas, NV 89102
(702) 878-3888

NEW HAMPSHIRE

Julie's Timeless Traditions
49 E. Pearl Street
Nashua, NH 03060
(603) 889-8980

Marry & Tux Shoppe
100 Daniel Webster Highway
Nashua, NH 03083
(603) 883-6999

Miller's
80 West Pearl Street
PO Box 1388
Nashua, NH 03061
(603) 882-7171

Madeleine's Daughter
100 Spalding Turnpike
Portsmouth, NH 03801
(603) 431-5454

Bridaloft
Route #28
Salem, NH 03079
(603) 893-0020

NEW JERSEY

Chez Vinette Bridal Galle
708 Broadway
Bayonne, NJ 07002
(201) 858-3888

Belmar Fashion Corner
1001 Main Street
Belmar, NJ 07719
(908) 681-3000

Arlene's Bridal & Formal Salon
606 Bloomfield Avenue
Bloomfield, NJ 07003
(201) 743-9056

Milena's Bridal
37 N. Dean Street
Englewood, NJ 07631
(201) 567-0074

La Belle Boutique
154 Danforth Avenue
Jersey City, NJ 07305
(201) 434-4143

Rene's Bridal Chateau
1200 River Avenue
Route 9
Lakewood, NJ 08701
(908) 370-9393

Country Way
400 Route #38
Maple Shade, NJ 08052
(609) 235-1556

Something Old Something New
2020 Asbury Avenue
Ocean City, NJ 08226
(609) 399-9340

Bridals by Roma
Plaza 17
Route 17 South
Paramus, NJ 07652
(201) 445-3377

Roses at Bergen Mall
Route #4 East
Paramus, NJ 07652
(201) 343-2696

Gwili Ann
20 Beechwood Road
Summit, NJ 07901
(908) 241-0505

Vera Plumb
210 Bellevue Avenue
Upper Montclair, NJ 07043
(201) 746-5706

Park Avenue Bridals
341 Pompton Avenue
Verona, NJ 07044
(201) 239-7111

Bridal Garden
104 Main Street
Voorhees, NJ 08043
(609) 751-9099

Sophisticated Brides
363 Paterson Avenue
Wallington, NJ 07055
(201) 939-6677

Helen Bohn Bridals
647 Pascack Road
Washington Twp., NJ 07675
(201) 664-8677

NEW MEXICO

The Empress Shop
1809 San Mateo NE
Albuquerque, NM 87110
(505) 255-1323

Helen's Wedding Belles
3225 Central Avenue NE
Albuquerque, NM 87108
(505) 255-6677

NEW YORK

M. Solomon Brides
Colonie Center
Albany, NY 12205
(518) 459-9070

Saymel's Bridal Salon
30-46 Steinway Street
Astoria, NY 11103
(718) 728-2260

Lillettes
861 Merrick Road
Baldwin, NY 11510
(516) 546-5660

Botticelli Boutique
29 Park Place
Bronxville, NY 10708
(914) 337-6384

I. Kleinfeld & Son
8206 5th Avenue
Brooklyn, NY 11201
(718) 833-1100

Lestan Fashion Headquarters
1902 Ralph Avenue
Brooklyn, NY 11234
(718) 531-0800

Rose Salkin Bridals & Fashions
2274 East 16th Street
Brooklyn, NY 11229
(718) 332-0682

Bridal Reflections at Carle Place
80 Westbury Avenue
Carle Place, NY 11514
(516) 742-7788

La Couture Boutique
169 Main Street
Cold Springs, NY 11724
(516) 692-4577

"The Bridal Plaza"
1444 Hempstead Turnpike
Elmont/Nassau, NY 11003
(516) 775-0489

Martin Trencher
860 Franklin Avenue
Garden City, NY 11530
(516) 746-0795

Peggy Peters Ltd.
213 Middle Neck Road
Great Neck, NY 11021
(516) 466-8480

Bridal Boutique of Manhasset
1695 Northern Boulevard
Manhasset, NY 11030
(516) 869-8455

Elephant's Trunk
111 Main Street
Mt. Kisco, NY 10549
(914) 666-2612

Jo Marie's
396 Broadway
Newburgh, NY 12550
(914) 561-9261

Saks Fifth Avenue
611 5th Avenue
New York, NY 10022
(212) 753-4000

Vera Wang Bridal House, Ltd.
991 Madison Avenue
New York, NY 10021
(212) 628-3400

Pepi's Bridal Boutique
232 Genesee Route #5
Oneida, NY 13421
(315) 363-7612

The Bridal Paradise
210 East Main Street
Patchogue, NY 11772
(516) 654-5020

"The Bridal Plaza"
59-35 Myrtle Avenue
Ridgewood, NY 11385
(718) 366-9656

Bridal Hall
Greece Towne Hall
Rochester, NY 14626
(716) 225-3500

Jacqueline's Suburban Fashions &
  Bridal Salon
1788 East Avenue
Rochester, NY 14610
(716) 473-5000

Gianine's Wedding Shoppe
6 Franklin Square
Saratoga Springs, NY 12866
(518) 587-5017

Lace Bridal & After Five, Inc.
44 Main Street
Sayville, NY 11782
(516) 563-8888

Fontana
678 White Plains Road
Scarsdale, NY 10583
(914) 472-1441

NORTH CAROLINA

Mecklenburg Bridal
162 South Sharonamity
Charlotte, NC 28211
(704) 365-0877

Poffie Girls
5639 Central Avenue
Charlotte, NC 28212
(704) 563-0072

Enchanting Moments
132 South Fuquay Avenue
Fuquay-Varina, NC 27526
(919) 552-6393

Poffie Girls
512 South New Hope Road
Gastonia, NC 28054
(704) 866-0198

Josette's Boutique
500 State Street
Greensboro, NC 27405
(919) 272-6832

Mordecai Bridal & Tuxedo
707 N. Person Street
Raleigh, NC 27604
(919) 832-6447

NORTH DAKOTA

The Bridal Shop
101 Broadway
Fargo, ND 58102
(701) 235-0541

Moments to Cherish
301 North 3d Street
Grand Forks, ND 58201
(701) 780-9717

OHIO

Matina's
2101 Richmond Road
Beachwood, OH 44122
(216) 464-1288

Toula's Bridal
4373 Boardman Canfield Road
Canfield, OH 44406
(216) 533-2967

Bridal and Formal
300 West Benson Street
Cincinnati, OH 45215
(513) 821-6622

Laura Salkin Bridals
20235 Van Aken Boulevard
Shaker Heights, OH 44120
(216) 921-2500

Pat Catan Southern Plantation
12878 Pearl Road
Strongsville, OH 44136
(216) 238-6664

OKLAHOMA

J J Kelly Bridal
12325 North May Avenue, #107
Oklahoma City, OK 73120
(405) 752-0029

Ruth Meyers Inc.
6471 Avondale Drive
Oklahoma City, OK 73116
(405) 842-1478

Beshara's Formal Wear & Bridal Salon
1660 E. 71st, Suite C
Tulsa, OK 74136
(918) 492-4100

OREGON

Divine Designs
333 South State Street, Suite H
Lake Oswego, OR 97034
(503) 635-5909

April Showers Wedding Boutique
6809 Milwaukee Avenue
Portland, OR 97202
(503) 232-3515

Brass Tree, Inc.
PO Box 25465
Portland, OR 97225
(503) 626-6581

PENNSYLVANIA

Kaufman's
1301 11th Avenue
Altoona, PA 16601
(814) 942-5719

Suky Rosan
49 Anderson Avenue
Suburban Square
Ardmore, PA 19003
(215) 649-3686

Golden Asp
2438 Neshaminy Boulevard
Bensalem, PA 19020
(215) 752-4990

Bell Bridal in Bristol
420 Pond Street
Bristol, PA 19007
(215) 785-5622

Pat Morgat's
2210 Dogwood Road
Dover, PA 17315
(717) 292-2997

Sigal's Bridal Gallery
344 Northhampton Street
Easton, PA 18042
(215) 250-9373

Donecker's
409 North State Street
Ephrata, PA 17522
(717) 733-2231

Bridal Elegance
930 West Erie Plaza Boulevard
Erie, PA 16505
(814) 459-4241

Once in a Lifetime
3442 Germantown Pike
Evanburg, PA 19521
(215) 489-4781

Anne Bailey's Bridal & Formal Shop
Route #313 & Ferry Road
Fountainville, PA 18923
(215) 345-8133

Susan K
1350 Harrisburg Pike
Lancaster, PA 17601
(717) 392-5255

Bridals by Sandra
30 East Lawn Road
Nazareth, PA 18064
(215) 769-5156

The Cinderella Shop
62 West Main Street
Palmyra, PA 17078
(717) 838-5861

Anne Bailey's Bridal & Formals
   at Mirrow's
7053 Castor Avenue
Philadelphia, PA 18923
(215) 745-3484

John Wanamaker
1300 Market Street
Philadelphia, PA 19101
(215) 422-2991

Keren Rose
9985 Bustleton Avenue
Philadelphia, PA 19115
(215) 464-6200

Silverman's Bridal Shoppe
532 South Street
Philadelphia, PA 19147
(215) 925-8819

The Bridal Beginning
450 Cochran Road
Pittsburgh, PA 15228
(412) 343-6677

The Bridal Lane
952 Greentree Road
Pittsburgh, PA 15220
(412) 922-3232

Carlisles of Pittsburgh
409-11 East Ohio
Pittsburgh, PA 15212
(412) 321-2421

Jacklyn Lace and Promises
Boukse Shops
2101 Greentree Road
Pittsburgh, PA 15220
(412) 429-1011

Linton's
5863 Forbes Avenue
Pittsburgh, PA 15217
(412) 421-9700

Pat Morgart's Bridal Shop
2094 Carlisle Road
York, PA 17404
(717) 767-4864

RHODE ISLAND

Nina's of Park Avenue
678 Park Avenue
Cranston, RI 02910
(401) 781-5577

Belle Bridal
574 Main Street
Pawtucket, RI 02860
(401) 723-4144

Your Bridal Shop
952-954 Mineral Spring
Pawtucket, RI 02860
(401) 725-9080

The Wishing Well
333 Newport Avenue
Rumford, RI 02816
(401) 434-4600

Something Old Something New
   Bridal Boutique
1719 Warwick Avenue
Warwick, RI 02889
(401) 737-3166

House of Brides
203 Pond Street
Woonsocket, RI 02895
(401) 762-1772

SOUTH CAROLINA

Jack Krawcheck
311 King Street
Charleston, SC 29401
(803) 722-1777

Sharpe's Brides & Grooms
701 Harden Street
Columbia, SC 29205
(803) 788-9230

The White Room
706 East Washington Street
Greenville, SC 29601
(803) 232-5778

SOUTH DAKOTA

"The French Door"
1821 S. Minnesota Avenue
Sioux Falls, SD 57105
(605) 332-8841

TENNESSEE

Pamela, Inc.
10001 Kingston Pike
Knoxville, TN 37919
(615) 693-9399

Velma's De'Cor & Bridals
539 Myatt Drive
Madison, TN 37115
(615) 868-1312

Ballew
4864 Poplar Avenue
Memphis, TN 38117
(901) 767-0920

Goldsmith's
4545 Poplar Avenue
Memphis, TN 38117
(901) 766-2305

Memphis Bridal Gallery
3558 Hickory Hill Extension
Memphis, TN 38115
(901) 366-5097

Arzelle's/Nashville
2926 West End Avenue
Nashville, TN 37203
(615) 327-1020

TEXAS

Serendipity Bridal
1610 West Avenue
Austin, TX 78701
(512) 499-8908

Bridal Circle
138 Preston Valley S.C.
Preston & LBJ (southwest corner)
Dallas, TX 75230
(214) 386-6289

Bride 'N Formal
(The Village on the Parkway)
5100 Beltline, #728
Dallas, TX 76021
(214) 788-4482

Mockingbird Bridal Boutique, Inc.
5606 E. Mockingbird Lane
Dallas, TX 75206
(214) 823-6873

Neiman Marcus
(downtown store)
1618 Main Street
Dallas, TX 75201
(214) 741-6911

Bride 'N Formal
5000 S. Hulen, #104
Fort Worth, TX 76132
(817) 346-6455

Affair to Remember
7651 De Moss
Houston, TX 77036
(713) 777-GOWN

Bridal Salon of Houston
2500 Westcreek Lane
Houston, TX 77027
(713) 621-0898

Bride 'N Formal
7807 S. Main Street
Houston, TX 77030
(713) 791-1886

Bride 'N Formal Grand Salon
7555 Westheimer
Houston, TX 77057
(713) 781-7555

Louise Blum — Galleria II
5085 Westheimer Road, #3775
Houston, TX 77056
(713) 622-5571

Mary Ann Maxwell for the Bride
3331 D'Amico
Houston, TX 77019
(713) 529-3939

Saks Fifth Avenue
1800 S. Post Oak Boulevard
Houston, TX 77056
(713) 627-0500

Ventura's Bridal Fashion
102 N. Loop End Yale
Houston, TX 77008
(713) 880-2364

The Brides' Shop
1217 S. 10th Street
McAllen, TX 78501
(512) 686-1212

The Bridal Salon of San Antonio
2150 East Hildebrand
San Antonio, TX 78209
(512) 828-7931

Eastman's Bridals/Formals/Tuxedos
6999 Blanco Road
San Antonio, TX 78216
(512) 342-5151

Exclusives for the Bride
7959 Broadway, #106
San Antonio, TX 78209
(512) 829-7888

UTAH

Seven Oaks Bridal
6775 South 900 East
Midvale, UT 84047
(801) 566-1100

The Bride's Shop
430 E. South Temple
Salt Lake City, UT 84104
(801) 322-4324

Z.C.M.I.
2200 S. 9th West
Salt Lake City, UT 84137
(801) 321-6637

VIRGINIA

Gossypia
325 Cameron Street
Alexandria, VA 22314
(703) 836-6969

Hannelore Bridal Boutique
155 North Pitt Street
Alexandria, VA 22314
(703) 549-0387

Tiffany's Bridal & Formal
2131 Coliseum Crossing
Hampton, VA 23666
(804) 827-0390

La Reve Bridal
525A East Market Street
Leesburg, VA 22075
(703) 777-3757

The Bridal Shoppe
7833 Sudley Road
K-Mart Shopping Center
Manassas, VA 22110
(703) 368-0694

Jeanette's
10386 Festival Lane
Manassas, VA 22110
(703) 369-1998

Tiffany's Bridal & Formal
17 North Sycamore Street
Petersburg, VA 23803
(804) 861-4140

Lady L. Bridals, Formals
    & Tuxedos
8006 West Broad Street
Bridal Square
Richmond, VA 23229
1-800-486-5084

Montaldo's
Bridal Department
6235 River Road
Richmond, VA 23229
(804) 285-0705

Scruples
512 Maple Avenue West
Vienna, VA 22180
(703) 255-1323

WASHINGTON

Bellevue Bridal Boutique
827 Bellevue Way NE
Bellevue, WA 98004
(206) 451-1041

Belle Bridal & Formal
201 West Holly Street
Bellingham, WA 98225
(206) 734-1213

Elaine's of Edmonds
610 Main Street
Edmonds, WA 98020
(206) 778-1814

I. Magnin
601 Pine Street
Seattle, WA 98101
(206) 682-6111

Victoria's
524 East Olive Way
Seattle, WA 98122
(206) 329-1218

The Wedding Connection
15200 Aurora Avenue N.
Seattle, WA 98133
(206) 362-7777

Bridal Collections
120 North Stevens
Spokane, WA 99201
(509) 838-1210

Touch of Silk
10411 NE Fourth Plain Road
Vancouver, WA
(206) 254-8982

WEST VIRGINIA

Ginger's Apparel
418 Adams Avenue
Fairmont, WV 26554
(304) 363-5195

Elizabeth's
3151 Main Street
Weirton, WV 26062
(304) 748-3476

Victorian Traditions
751 Main Street
Wheeling, WV 26003
(304) 233-9333

WISCONSIN

The Bridal Event
2415 N. Richmond
Appleton, WI 54914
(414) 730-8321

Margie's
17300 W. Bluemound Road
Brookfield, WI 53005
(414) 821-5500

Edith's of Fond Du Lac
9 S. Main Street
Fond Du Lac, WI 54935
(414) 921-2420

Vera's House of Bridals
7857 Big Sky Drive
Madison, WI 53719
(608) 833-6006

Eva's Bridal Center
1229 W. Mitchell Street
Milwaukee, WI 53204
(414) 645-5698

Zita, Inc.
211 East Silver Spring
Whitefish Bay, WI
(414) 276-6827

Other Purveyors

DESIGNERS

House of Bianchi
(212) 730-1764

Bradgley-Mischka
(212) 921-1585

Broudé, Inc.
(212) 921-8081

Mr. Butch
(212) 563-7414

Carmi Couture
(212) 921-7658

Christos
(212) 921-0024

Victor Costa
(212) 719-1460

Reuben Cruz
(212) 736-8811

Jim Demetrios, Ilissa Bridalwear
(212) 967-5222

Forsyth Enterprises
(212) 302-7710

Carolina Herrera, couturiere
(212) 355-3055

Jim Hjelm
(212) 764-6960

Pat Kerr
(901) 525-5223

Priscilla (Kidder) of Boston
(617) 242-2677

Susan Lane
(818) 765-1551

Ron LoVece
(212) 840-3172

Bob Mackie
(310) 657-4360

Hanae Mori
(212) 472-2353

Eve Muscio, Eve of Milady
(212) 302-0050

Michel Piccione, Alfred Angelo
(212) 277-6199

Martin Price, House of Sant' Angelo
(212) 529-8100

Rose Marie Rousell
(212) 421-8477

San Martin Bridals
(213) 257-5333

Arnold Scaasi, couturier
(212) 755-5105

Candice Solomon, One-of-a-Kind
  Brides
(212) 966-8678

Lora Van Lear
(212) 764-7500

Paula Varsalona
(212) 221-5600

Vera Wang, couturiere
(212) 737-5200

RETAILERS

Francesca Bianca (*costume restorer/
  milliner*)
(212) 753-4000

Monica Hickey, Saks Fifth Avenue
(212) 753-4000

Hedda Kleinfeld, I. Kleinfeld and Sons
(718) 833-1100

Harriet Love of SoHo, New York
(212) 966-2280

Millicent Safro, Diana Epstein,
  Tender Buttons
(212) 758-7004

Frank Senna, Sposabella Fabric and
  Lace
(212) 354-4729

Jana Starr, Starr Antique
(212) 861-9256

Judith Stone, Island Brides
(516) 681-5816

HAIR AND MAKEUP

Kenneth Battelle, House of Kenneth
(212) 752-1800

Bobbi Brown
(212) 924-6760

SKIN CARE

Georgette Klinger
(212) 838-3200

MILLINERS

Patricia Bomer, Bergdorf Goodman
(212) 753-7300

Eric Javits
(212) 869-7530

Suzanne of Madison Avenue
(212) 593-3232

Elaine Vincent
(212) 768-2063

JEWELRY DESIGNERS

Kenneth Jay Lane
(212) 868-1780

Janice Savitt
(212) 869-5228

Christopher Walling
(212) 242-6885

FLORAL DESIGNERS

Creative Florals of Salisbury,
  Maryland
(410) 860-5112

Abigail Goldman (*horticulturalist*)
(212) 222-3000

Bill Kenon, Flowers by Beatrice Mann
(212) 757-1790

Marie McBride Mellinger
(212) 869-8798

Bobby Wiggins, Flowers by Bobby
  Wiggins
(212) 627-1412

Gramercy Park Flower Shop
(212) 475-4989

ACCESSORIES

Carolina Amato (*gloves*)
(212) 532-8413

Dyeables (*shoes*)
(914) 878-8000

Peter and Linda Fox (*shoes*)
(212) 431-7426

Stuart Weitzman (*shoe designer*)
(212) 582-9500

FOUNDATIONS

Marijke Masquelier, Fogal Hosiery
(212) 759-9782

Michael Raskin, Sidney Bush, Inc.
(212) 633-0620

MENSWEAR

Alan Flusser (*menswear manufacturer/
  author*)
(212) 422-3100

Joseph Gilhooley, A.T. Harris
  Formalwear (*rental*)
(212) 682-6345

Lou London, Smalls Formalwear
  (*rental*)
(215) 692-6624

Ken Merlow, Dunhill Tailors
(212) 888-4000

Jerry Zeller, Zeller Formalwear
  (*rental*)
(212) 688-0100

$\mathcal{P}$hotography $\mathcal{A}$cknowledgments

As photographer, it is fitting to begin with saying thanks to my friends master photographers Tom Palumbo, Bert Stern, and Peter Beard, for their encouragement and initial ideas on how I could illustrate my own text. The concerted effort of many talented people helped me to photograph this book; therefore, I am especially indebted to my fine production teams for their services and assistance, and for allowing me virtually unlimited access to their expertise. The four other photographers who assisted me must be lavishly thanked: James Egbert, for teaching me his masterly head-shot lighting techniques; Alex Marchiac, for giving me practical advice on fashion photography; Rory Francis, my natural-light assistant; and Eddie Sun, for enduring a mind-boggling process—documenting details on one hundred dresses. All bridal fashion coordination was overseen by Myraslawa Prystay, and styled with the assistance of Natalie Prystay and Nina Wells; and all the dress and gown details, the headdresses, jewelry, and shoe detail shots, were styled by Shelly Suzanne Saxton. Special thanks to Monique Goudailler of the Cultured Pearl Association and the Aaron Faber Gallery for the jewelry in New York City and Montauk; Cornelia Spain of Luray Caverns; and for the production coordination in New York City and Montauk, I am especially indebted to Helene Leskin.

I would also like to express my gratitude to hoteliers extraordinaire Anne Merrigan of Ruffner House, Luray, Virginia; Lorraine Luccia of the Morrison-Clarke Inn, Washington, D.C.; Mr. and Mrs. Monte of Gurney's Inn, Montauk, N.Y.; Marshall Coyne of the world-class Madison Hotel in Washington; and Richard Wilhelm of the renowned Plaza Hotel in New York City. I am eternally grateful to my good friend Hedda Kleinfeld for granting me and my photography crew access to her entire bridal emporium inventory. Without her insightful suggestions and her staff's assistance while choosing each example, the detail shots included throughout this book would have been far less complete and useful to my readers. Many thanks to the publicity department at Dyeables, Inc., for providing shoes for the location shots; Creative Florals, Inc., of Salisbury, Maryland, for lending bouquets, headpieces, and jewelry used on location; and Fogal Hosiery for providing all of the stockings. The range of bridal gowns could not have been photographed without the cooperation of Mrs. Muscio, Eve of Milady; the faith of Edna Forsyth of Forsyth Enterprises and Scaasi Brides; Sposabella Bridal Headpieces for lending the ensemble for my test shots; my niece, Sydney, for modeling; my friend Bijou, for styling and her makeup artistry; and Sebastian Petricek, color photocopier supreme. My thanks to Hanae Mori, the first to participate, and Ilissa Bridalwear, the last major bridal-wear manufacturer to join in my efforts, as well as to Ralph Lauren, Donna Karan, and Escada for rounding out the contemporary wedding fashions; and to Georgette Klinger, the Spot, and the House of Kenneth, whose beauty advice was crucial. The bridegrooms included were graced with fashionable and always perfectly tailored garments loaned by Neil Fox of Sulka Tailors, Lou London of Smalls Formalwear, and Joseph Gilhooley of A.T. Harris; I am also grateful to each for furnishing the necessary formal-wear capes, canes, and suchlike accouterments.

The photographs' success is also due to the numerous men and women who freely gave their time and creative effort. I would like to acknowledge the gracious assistance and support from the top model agencies and their bookers, including THE and Star Talent (Tamarra) of Washington, D.C., and Bookers (Tim), Avenue (Ed Feldman), Zoli Men (Vicky), Click (Frances), Name (Sarah), Elite Runway (Ellen Harth), Metropolitan, Paris USA, Cameo, Company, and Ice Men and Women, of New York City. The model brides and bridegrooms included Kate, Rachel, and Sydney Goldman, Myraslawa Prystay, Ashley Avilson, Richard Gollub, Mr. Kay, Craig Linden (Zoli Men), Paul Leahy, Mark Tardio (Zoli Men), Ray Smith, Rich, Geo, Kathleen, and Sonja (Avenue Models), Chris (Bookers), Vanessa Branch (THE), Maria Matijasevic, Bill Boettcher (THE), Tina James, Tina (New Models), Cory Davis, Natalie Prystay, Hera Pappnichail, Christine Ames, Belinda O'Neill, Christina Saddlick, Jennifer Blair, Jennifer O'Connor, Dawn Foester, Maryanna Taglienti, Elena Russo, Sophie (THE), Stacey Brady (Star), Sandy Lober, Osewega (Star), Steven Marry, Shelly Speed (Company Models), Karin (Company Models), Sara (Ice Women), Camilla (Ice Women), Mel Gorham, Lilly Coy (Name Agency), Kim Verback (Metropolitan Models), Alena (Elite Runway), Belinda Sawyer (Ice Women), Jill Gilbert (Elite Runway), Masha (Click Models), Carina (Click Models), Glena (Click Models), Maranda Todd (Paris USA), Brian B (Cameo Models), Keith Bullock (Click Models), Tony Kurz (Click Models), Jason Savas (Wilhelmina Men), Susan Camden and Jill Saari (all detail shots), Olivia Maxwell, Elizabeth Carlisle, Monique Goudailler, Eve Muscio, Mrs. Faraday, Reuben Cruz, Victoria Maxwell (actress), Cassandra Gava (actress), and Tracy Brooke Swope (actress).

As for hairdressers and makeup artists, a very special thank-you to James Egbert of the James Studio of Falls Church, Virginia, for his overall makeup direction. Also to Kenneth (the House of Kenneth); Stacey Ross (the Spot); Gillary (the Spot); and Susan McCarthy (hair); Hiromi Kobai (makeup); Sonam Kashner (makeup); Christine (makeup); Susan Schacter (hair and makeup); Eric Spearman (makeup and hair; of Alexandre de Paris Salon of Arlington, Virginia); and Helios de Souza.

Photography Credits

(BY CATEGORY)

ENSEMBLES
MANUFACTURER AND DESIGNER GOWNS, DRESSES, AND OUTFITS

Alfred Angelo, Inc.: *23, 34, 95, 146 (left), 154*
Lila Broider: *169*
Carmi Couture: *36, 64*
Oleg Cassini: *96, 174*
Christos: *13, 18, 46 (top center left), 48 (row 3, left), 77 (center), 101, 112, 143*
Country Elegance: *10, 90, 92, 150, 176*
Ursulla D of Saks Fifth Avenue: *144*
Demetrios Group: *37 (right), 39, 43, 45 (bottom center right), 104, 107, 117, 131*
Christian Dior: *80 (top), 152, 184*
Eleganza Italiana: *37 (left), 51, 53 (right), 139*
Escada: *60*
Eve of Milady: *79, 132, 166*
Faraday Bridal Salon, Manassas, Virginia: *154*
Hannalore's Bridal Salon, Georgetown: *56, 167 (bottom)*
Jim Hjelm: *40, 46 (row 3, left), 53 (left)*
House of Bianchi: *27, 34 (attendant), 49, 115, 136*
Joelle: *44, 54 (bottom), 126, 146 (bottom), 158, 168*
Laurie Kabali: *32, 69, 97, 181*
Donna Karan: *146 (bottom), 157*
Pat Kerr: *45 (row 2, left), 66 (top left), 70 (bottom), 77 (bottom), 93, 118 (row 2, left)*
Ralph Lauren: *55*
Fred Leighton: *20*

Ron LoVece: *22, 26, 45 (row 4, right), 48 (row 4, right), 62, 108, 124, 133, 135*
Sister Max: *24*
Jessica McClintock: *25*
Hanae Mori: *8, 61, 105, 122, 127, 147, 153*
Rose Marie Rousell: *41*
San Martin: *59*
Van Lear Bridals: *2, 16, 33, 46 (row 1, left)*
Paula Varsalona: *14, 30, 52, 98, 99, 167 (top)*
Vera Wang: *29*
Robert Work: *15, 57, 140, 149, 183*

DETAILS
GOWNS, DRESSES, AND OUTFITS

Abeira: *46 (row 3, right)*
Blake: *46 (row 2, right)*
Diamond: *45 (row 1, left; row 4, left), 74 (right), 76 (top), 78 (top)*
Fielden: *21, 66 (bottom left)*
Floranna: *75 (left)*
H. Forsyth: *74 (left)*
Gainville: *48 (row 3, right)*
Glascow: *45 (row 1, right), 46 (row 4, right), 50 (center), 78 (center left), 86 (left)*
Haynel Forsyth: *35 (left), 80 (left), 81, 82 (top), 83 (bottom), 88*
Herrera: *38, 48 (row 2, left; row 4, center), 50 (top and bottom), 58, 66 (top right and bottom right), 68, 71, 75 (right), 77 (top), 78 (right), 82 (bottom), 86 (top), 87 (bottom)*
Katsura: *48 (row 1, right)*

Kleinfeld's: *172*

Lenain: *46 (row 4, left), 65 (bottom), 76 (bottom)*

Jose Luis: *45 (row 2, right), 80 (top)*

Molina: *70 (top), 86 (bottom)*

Priscilla: *46 (row 1, right), 48 (row 4, left)*

St. Pucchi: *46 (row 1, center right), 54 (top)*

Scaasi: *45 (row 4, center left; row 3, right), 46 (row 4, center), 47, 65 (top), 67, 83 (top), 145, 151*

Solomon: *35 (right)*

Vicky Tiel: *87 (top)*

Tomasina: *78 (left)*

Valenta/Klsanovich: *45 (row 3, left), 48 (row 1, left)*

Victoria: *46 (row 2, left), 48 (row 2, right), 84, 85*

ACCESSORIES AND ACCENTS

Carolee, jewelry: *40, 115, 118 (row 2, left), 138*

Miriam Haskel, jewelry: *34, 113, 118 (row 2, left; row 1, right)*

Kenneth Jay Lane, jewelry: *13, 34, 116, 166*

The Pearl Association: *10, 18, 22, 93, 104, 107, 112, 117, 118 (row 2, left and right; row 3, right), 124, 125, 129, 165*

Carolina Amato, gloves: *61, 150, 166*

Boyd's of Madison Avenue, hair ornaments: *13, 58, 118 (row 2, right; row 3, right), 129, 165 (top)*

Brenda Bolling, headpieces: *116, 118 (row 3, left), 120*

Creative Florals of Salisbury, Maryland: *16, 33 (bottom), 43, 53 (top), 34*

(bottom), 64, 115, 118 (row 1, right; row 4, left), 120, 122, 127, 132, 147, 153

The Bridal Shop of Manassas, headpiece and muff: *95, 154*

Hannelore's Bridal Salon of Georgetown: *23, 167 (bottom)*

Suzanne of Madison Avenue, headpieces: *110, 138*

Victoria di Nardo, milliner: *113*

Elaine Vincent, milliner: *107, 117, 157*

Fogal, furnished all stockings on location

Les Belle Jambes, stockings: *159 (top)*

Givenchy Hosiery, stockings: *159 (bottom)*

Manolo Blahnik, shoes: *160 (top), 161 (center), 162 (second from top; second from bottom; bottom)*

Dyeables, all shoes used on location

Peter Fox, shoes: *159, 160 (second from bottom; bottom), 161 (second from bottom)*

Galo, shoes: *160 (second from top, center), 161 (bottom)*

Stuart Weitzman, shoes: *161 (top; second from top), 162, 163*

Chanel, shoes and handbag: *168*

Sposabella Fabrics: *1, 73, 137, 156*

Gramercy Park Florists: *148*

MENSWEAR
MANUFACTURERS AND FORMAL-WEAR RENTALS

Doneckers Department Store, informal suits: *25, 97, 174, 180, 181*

A.T. Harris Formalwear, rental: *93, 101*

Ralph Lauren, suits and blazers: *58*

Royal Brides and Formalwear: *184*

Smalls Formalwear, rental: *13, 22, 57, 183*

Sulka Tailors: *8, 61, 179*

LOCATIONS

Shadowbrook Mansion and Restaurant of Shrewsbury, New Jersey: *13, 61, 105, 179*

The streets, houses, churches, monuments, and parks of New York City: *18, 22, 44, 79, 101, 107, 143, 167*

Gurney's Inn and Spa, Montauk, New York: *15, 17, 41, 49, 56, 57, 64, 93, 149, 170, 183*

Petrossian Restaurant, New York City: *74 (bottom)*

Plaza Hotel, New York City: *20, 33 (top), 39, 43, 131, 144, 168*

Richard Golub's Town House, New York City: *24*

The Russian Tea Room, New York City: *23, 154*

Spirit of New York, New York City: *55, 58, 104, 117, 157*

Tatou Nightclub and Restaurant, New York City: *12, 36, 146*

Tavern on the Green, New York City: *51, 158*

Doneckers Inn and Restaurant, of Ephrata, Pennsylvania: *25, 32, 69, 96, 97, 174*

The Cloisters of Ephrata, Pennsylvania: *97, 181*

Luray Caverns, Shenandoah Valley, Virginia: *14, 53 (bottom), 139*

Ruffner House Inn, Luray, Virginia: *10, 90, 108, 133, 176*

The streets, houses, monuments, and parks of Washington, D.C.: *16, 33 (bottom), 34, 37, 135*

The Grand Hotel, Washington, D.C.: *40, 52*

The Madison Hotel, Washington, D.C.: *34, 146, 166, 184*

The Morrison-Clarke Inn, Washington, D.C.: *53 (top), 92, 98, 99, 150*

$\mathcal{I}$ndex

PAGE NUMBERS IN *ITALICS* INDICATE SIDEBARS.

$\mathcal{A}$ccessories and accents, 111–113, 125, 155–156, 175–176, 178, 180
  for bridegroom, 180
  cover–ups, *35, 48*, 113, 156, 169, 182
  flowers, *see* flowers
  foundations, 155–157
  garters, 113, 169, 182
  gloves, 113, 156, 166–167, 182
  hair ornaments, *see* hair ornaments
  hairstyles, *see* hairstyles
  handbags, 113, 156, 167–168, 176, 182
  handkerchiefs, 113, 156, 168–169, 176, 182
  headdresses, *see* headdresses
  hosiery, *see* hosiery
  incidental, 113
  jewelry, *see* jewelry
  lingerie, 113, 156, 157
  makeup, *see* makeup
  purveyors of, 197
  schedule and, *177*
  shoes, *see* shoes
  underpinnings, 42, 100, 155, 156–157, 171
  veils, *see* veils
Adolfo, 119

alençon lace, 71, 72, *73*, 81, 84, 124
A-line, *35, 38*, 124,
all-in-one foundations, 155, 156
Amato, Carolina, 167
antebellum waistline, *50, 51*, 52
antique dresses, 89, 92–94, 86, 175, 178
antique satin, 66
appliqué, 76, *77*, 91
  enhancement of, 81–85
  on veils, 137, 138
aprons, *45*
Art Deco, 126

$\mathcal{B}$ack treatments, *45*, 64, 179
  bustles, 42–43, *45*
  see also trains
Balenciaga, 27, 38
ball-gown silhouette, *35*, 36, 41, 53, 124, 138
barrettes, *118*
basque–style waistline, 23, *35*, *50*, 51–52, 124
bateau neckline, *46*
batiste, 66
Battelle, Kenneth, 113–114, *115*
Battenberg lace, *72*
beads, beading, 63, 64, 70, *73*, 81–85, *82*, 91
  bugle, *82*, 83
  extravagant, *85*

formality and, 83–84, *85*
  on headdress, 125
  on veils, 158
beauty consultants, 165
bell sleeve, *48*
Belperron, Mme., 131
bertha collar, *46*
Bianca, Francesca, 24, 119, 121–122, 123–124, *134*, 160
Bianchi, Mrs., 102
bishop sleeve, *48*
black, 28
blouson, *50*
blushers, *132*, 136, 137, 138–139
boat neckline, *46*
bodice, *33*, *35, 38*, 43–44, 52, 112, 128, 156, 179
  fit of, 91
  hairstyle and, 112, 113, *114*
  headdress and, 112, 113, 120–121, 123–124, 125, 126
  structured, 47
  see also necklines; shoulders; sleeves; waistlines
body shape, *33*, 36–38, 41, 44, 49, 51, 74, 91
  trimmings and, 79, 80
Bomer, Patricia, 122–123
border trims, 76
bouquets, 112, 141, 142, 145–146
  choosing of, 182

color schemes of, 145
design principles and concepts for, 148–151
determining design and style of, 146–162
foliage in, 150
formality of, 147–148, 149, 150–151, 152
style choices for, *148*
water holders in, 153
boutiques, 89, 94, 95, 98
bows, *45*, 79, 119, 121, 123, 136
bracelets, 129, 131, 180
Bradgley, James, 50
braid, 76
brassieres, 156
bridal consultants, 98–101, 178–179
bridal salons, 89, 94, 95, 98–101, 178
list of, 185–196
bridegroom
accessories for, 180
attire of, 31, 179–180, 182
bouquet and, 146, 152
jewelry and, 131
schedule for, 175, 177, *177*
stress and, 170, 176
veil and, *132*
brocades, 66, 80
brokers, bridal gown, 95–96
Brown, Bobbi, 113, 114–115, 164
Brussels lace, 72
bubble skirts, *35*
budget, 11, 13, 14, 24, 95, 175, 177, 178
bugle beads, 82, 83
bustiers, 150, 151
bustier style, *48*
bustles, 42–43, *42*, *45*
Butch, Mr., 75, 98
butterfly back, *45*
buttonholes, 87, 91
buttons, *45*, 63, 86–87, 91, 127
buying, 175, 178–179; *see also* retailers

Capes, *35*, 169
caps, *118*, 123
cap sleeves, *48*
Catherine II, Czarina of Russia, 23–24
Chantilly lace, 72, *73*

chaplets, 152
Charles, Prince of Wales, 25, 39
Charmeuse, 66, 68
checklist, *see* schedule
chiffon, *66*, 68, 69, 135
Christos, 81, 84–85
circlets, *118*, 124, 152
Clench, Elsa, 60, 61
cloque, *66*
coats, 169; *see* cover-ups
cocktail dresses, 61, 104, 175
color, 23, 26–29
of eyes, 28, 145
of flowers, 141, 145–146
of stockings, 159
of veils, 135–136
see black; pastel; pink; white
combs, *118*, 119, 121, 134, 136
contemporary styles, 11–12, 24–27, 28, 31, 32, 33, 39, 54–57, 60–61, 104, 126, 177
coronets, 152
corsages, *148*, 152
Costa, Victor, 61, 104
costs, *see* budget
couture, 60–61, 89, 94, 101–102, 105–107, 178–179
cover-ups (wraps), *35*, *48*, 113, 156, 169, 182
cowl necks, *46*
crepe, 20, 68
crepe-backed satin, 66, 68
crepe de Chine, *66*
crinolines, 38, 70, 157
crowns, 122, 124
Cruz, Reuben, 38, 58
crystal, 82, *82*, 125, 128
Custis, Emily, 132
customizing, 94, 102–103, 178
of dresses, 89, 95, 131
of headdresses, 139
made-to-order vs., 101–102
schedule and, *177*
custom-made (made-to-order) dresses, 95, 101–102, 105–107
couture, 89, 94, 101–102, 105–107, 178–179
customizing vs., 101–102
custom-made headdresses, 121

custom-made shoes, 163
cutouts, lace, 77, 80, 84

Damask, *66*
décolletage, 41, 46
Demetrios, Jim, 53–54
department stores, 89, 94, 98, 178
design elements and motifs, 19–27, 52–53, 179
detachable, 39, *42*
designers, 60–61, 89, 92, 94, 95, 96, 175, 178–179, 196–197
schedule and, *177*
trunk shows of, 103
design lines, *see* silhouette
detachable design elements, 39, *42*
details, 63, 64–65, 179
diamanté, 76
diamonds, 127, 128, 129, 130
Diana, Princess of Wales, 26, 39, 58, 104, 155
diet, 170, 182
Di Nardo, Victoria, 126
Dior, 38, 80, 87, 184
discounters, 95, 96, 178
dolman sleeve, *48*
dotted Swiss, 66, 82
douppioni, *66*
dressing, order of, 171
dressmaker vs. tailored, 12
dressmakers, 89, 91, 92, 94, 101–102, 103–105, 175, 178–179
schedule and, *177*
duchess satin, 66, 69, 103

Earrings, 112, 125, 127, 129, 130–131, 180
edges, 76
Edwardian style, 43
Elizabethan style, 20, 21
embellishments, 63, 64, 79, 91, 179
on antique dresses, 94
on gloves, 167
on handbags, 168
on headdresses, 121
on shoes, 163
on veils, 137

see also enhancement concepts;
    trimmings
embroidery, 63, 64, 71, 76, 77, *82*
    lacelike, *73*
    raised, *78*
Empire line, 23, *35*, 36, 38, 44, *50*, 58, 124
engagement rings, 128
enhancement concepts, 63, 65, 81–85, *82*,
    179
    guidelines for, 84–85
    see also beads, beading; embroidery
Epstein, Diana, 87
evening gown silhouette, 35
exercise, 170
eye color, 28, 145
eyelet, 66

*F*abric(s), 27, 31, 65–70, 102, 103, 104,
    179
    choosing of, 64, 69
    combining of, 70
    flowers made of, 79, 122, 145, 151,
        152, 153
    formality of, 61, 68–69
    "hand" of, 63, 64
    for headdress, 125
    synthetic, 67, 68
    treatments, *76, 78; see also* trimmings
    types of, 66
    uses and effects of, 68–70
    weight and capabilities of, 68–70
    see also lace
facial features
    earrings and, 130
    headdresses and, 120, 121–123, 124,
        182
    jewelry and, 126
    veils and, 138
facials, 163, 169, 170, 171, 175, 182
faille, 66
fashion designers, *see* designers
fastenings, 63, 86
    buttons, *45*, 63, 86–87, 91, 127
Ferguson, Sarah, Duchess of York, 155
figure, *see* body shape
finishing, of dress, 91
fit, fittings, 91, 99, 100, 101–102, 105,
    156, 180

floral designers, 178, 198
flounces, *35*, 42
flowers, 20, 23, 112, 136–153, 176, 178,
    180
    alternative uses for, 152–153
    care of, 153
    choosing of, 182
    colors, textures, and shapes of, 141,
        145–146
    design principles and concepts for,
        146–152
    fabric, 79, 122, 145, 151, 152, 153
    foliage and, 150
    as hair ornaments, *118*, 119, 123
    on headdress, 125
    personal preference and, 142
    size and scale of, 151–152
    style choices for, 146–152, *148*
    varieties of, 142–145, 150
formality, levels of, 11–14, 31–32, 177
    beading and, 83–84, 85
    bouquet and, 146–147, 149, 150–151,
        152
    fabrics and, 67, 68–69
    formal styles, 12, 14, 27, 28, 31, 33,
        39–54, 57, 58
    headdresses and, 116–119, 129,
        131–139
    informal styles, 12, 14, 31, 33, 39,
        54–60, 98
    jewelry and, 127
    makeup and, 164
    semiformal styles, 12, 31, 39–54, 58
    trimmings and, 79, 80
    ultraformal styles, 12, 31, 32, 39
    veil and, 138
Forsyth, Edna, 103
foundations, 155–157, 198
Fox, Peter and Linda, 162
Franco, Danielle, 104, 105
fringe, 76
furbelows, *78*, 157

*G*alloon, 76
garlands, 76, *118, 148*, 152–153
garters, 113, 156, 169, 182
    flower, 152–153
gauntlet, *78*

gauntlet sleeve, *48*
gauze, 66
gazzara, *66*, 68
georgette, *66*, 68
Gerhardt, Annette, 100, 101
Gibson sleeve, *48*
gigot sleeve, *48*
gimp, *76*, 78
gloves, 113, 156, 166–167, 182
godets, *45*, 78
Goldman, Abigail, 151
groom, *see* bridegroom
grosgrain, 66
Guipure lace, 72

*H*air color, 28, 145
hair ornaments, 112, 119, 121, 124,
    129, 134
    flowers as, *118*, 119, 123
    types of, *118*
hair salons, 178, 198
hairstyles, 20, 112, 113–115, *114*, 134,
    139, 171, 175, 180
    earrings and, 131
    headdresses and, 113, 114, *114*, 115,
        119, 120, 123
    jewelry and, 113, *114*, 126
    veils and, 113, *114*, 136, 138
handbags, 113, 156, 167–168, 176, 182
handkerchiefs, 113, 156, 168–169, 176,
    182
hats, 120, 121, 124, 126, 134
    earrings and, 131
    jewelry and, 129
    picture, 117, *118*, 119, 121, 127, 134
    pillbox, 116, *118*, 119, 121, 123, 125,
        126, 133
    types of, *118*
    see also headdresses; veils
headbands, *118*, 119, 121, 123, 124,
    125, 126, 135
headdresses, 20, 23, 111, 112, 115–126,
    128, 134, 135–136, 139, 171, 175,
    178, 180–182
    bodice and, 112, 113, 120–121,
        123–124, 125, 126
    bouquet and, 145
    choosing of, 116, 119–121, 182

headdresses (*continued*)
    convertibility of, 182
    customized, 139
    dress elements repeated on, 111, 112, 124–126
    facial features and, 120, 121–123, 124, 182
    flower, 152
    and formality, needs, and taste, 116–119
    hairstyles and, 113, 114, *114*, 115, 119, 120, 123
    jewelry and, 126, 129
    personal style and, 117–119
    schedule and, *177*
    types of, *118*
    veils and, 135, 136
    see also hats; veils
height, illusion of, 38, 41, 52
heirloom dresses, 89, 92, 175, *177*, 178
hems, *42, 56–57*, 76, 91
Herrera, Carolina, 104, 106–107
Hickey, Monica, 39, 58, 105–106, 132–134, 136–137, 138
Hjelm, Jim, 84
hosiery, 113, 156, 157–160, 180, 182
    color of, 159
    patterned, 159–160
houppelande, 21

Illusionary fabrics, *46, 66*, 69, 105, 131, *132*
informal styles, 12, 14, 24, 31, 33, 39, 54–60, 98

Jabot, *78*
jackets, 24, *35, 36, 38, 39, 48*, 55, 58–60, 98, 169
Jacquard, 66
James, Charles, 31–32, 38
Javits, Eric, 134–135
jersey, 66, 70
jewel neckline, *46, 75*
jewelry, 112, 125, 126–131, 139, 171, 178, 180
    formality and style of, 127
    hairstyle and, 113, *114*, 126

one-of-a-kind, 131
pearl, 127, 128–131
veils and, 138
wedding bands, 128, 163
see also hair ornaments
jewelry designers, 197
Johnson, Betsey, 25
Juliet cap, *118*, 121, 123, 124

Keller, Susan, 159–160
Kenneth, 113–114, 115
Kenon, Bill, 142
Kerr, Pat, 26, 73–74
keyholes, *45, 46*
Kidder, Priscilla of Boston, 38
kimono sleeve, *48*
Kleinfeld, Hedda, 28, 56–57, 58, 100
Klinger, Georgette, 170

Lace(s), 13, 20, 23, 31, 63, 64, 68, 70–75, 98, 125–126, 179
    alençon, 71, 72, *73*, 81, 84, 124
    as allover treatment, 74–75
    appliqués, *77*, 80–85
    combining of, 73
    cutouts, *77*, 80, 84
    manufacture of, 71, 73
    reembroidered, 81–85
    trimmings, 64, 65, 73, 74, 75–81
    types of, *73*
    uses of, 72–75
    veils, 136–137
Lalli, Cele, 43
Lane, Kenneth Jay, 127–128
Lane, Susan, 29, 92
leg-of-mutton sleeve, *48*
Leighton, Fred, 20, 25
length, creation of, 36–38, 44
Leonard, Rachel, 119–120, 122, 171
linen, 70, 98
lingerie, 113, 156, 157
Love, Harriet, 96–98
LoVece, Ron, 49, 52, 68–69
Lyon lace, 72

Mackie, Bob, 29, 41–42, 61
macramé, 72
made-to-measure dresses, 94, 100
    customizing of, 101–102
made-to-order dresses, *see* custom-made dresses
Mainbocher, 103
makeup, 113, 156, 163–166, 170, 171, 182
    bouquet and, 145
    for photography, 164, 165
    style and, 164
makeup specialists, 165, 178, 197
mandarin collar, 46
manicures, 163, 169, 170, 171, 175, 182
mantillas, 20, *118*, 121, 123, 124, 132, 137
mantles, *see* veils
Masquelier, Marijke, 159
massages, 163, 169, 170, 171, 175, 182
matelassé, 66
Medici, Catherine de', 166
medieval styles, 20, 21, 24, 83
Mellinger, Marie McBride, 146–147, 149
melon sleeve, *48*
menswear, 197
mermaid, *35*, 38
merry widow, 156
midriff, 44
milliners, 178, 197
Mischka, Mark, 50
mock turtle necklines, *46*
moiré, *66*, 74
Muscio, Eve, 81

Necklaces, 112, 125, 127, 129–130, 131, 180
necklines, 33, 43, 44, *45, 46*, 47–49, 54, 74, 75, 167, 179
    embellished, 64
    headdresses and, 123–124
    jewelry and, 126
needlepoint, 72
nettings, 66, 135
Nicholas II, Tsar of Russia, 23, 25
nineteenth-century design, 25
nosegays, *148*, 149, 152
notions, 63, 65, 86–87, 179

buttons, *45*, 63, 86–84, 91, 127
fastenings, 63, 86

O'Donoghue, Denise, 128–129
off-the-shoulder style, *48*
one-of-a-kind dresses, 95
organdy, *66*, 68, 69, 98
organza, *66*, 68, 69, 98
ottoman, *66*
overskirts, *35*, 36, 39, *45*

Pagoda sleeve, *48*
pampering, 169–171, 182
panels, *35*, 36, *45*, 64
panne, *66*
panniers, *35*
panties, 156
pants, 33, 58, 70, 98, 179
passementerie, *see* trimmings
pastels, 27, 125
pattern-made dresses, 95, 101, 103–105,
    178–179
pearl(s), 119, 125
    beading, 64, 81, 82, *82*, 83, 91
    on headdress, 125
    jewelry, 127, 128–131
    seed, 82, *82*, 125
    types of, *82*, *130*
    on veils, 137
peau de soie, *66*
pedicures, 169–170, 171, 182
peekaboo sleeve, *48*
peplums, *35*, 36, 42, *45*, 91, 179
period dressing, 19, 23–24, 177
petal sleeve, *48*
petticoats, 42, 155, 156–157
photography, makeup for, 164, 165
Piccione, Michel, 80
picture hats, 117, *118*, 119, 121, 127,
    134
pillbox hats, 116, *118*, 119, 121, 123,
    125, 126, 133
pink, 27, 28
piping, 76
planning, 12–14; *see also* schedule
poet sleeve, *48*
point d'esprit, *66*, 69

pongee, *66*
portrait neckline, 43, *46*, 47, 105, 124
poufs, *45*, 115, *132*, 136, 138–139, 152
Price, Martin, 59–60, 85, 107
princess line, *35*, 36, 38, 44, *50*, *59*, 124
puff sleeve, *48*

Queen Anne neckline, *46*, 124
Queen Elizabeth neckline, *46*
quilting, 78

Raskin, Michael, 157
rattail, 76
ready-to-wear, 94, 95–98, 175, *177*
redingotes, 23, *35*
remarriages, 25, 27, 28, 56, 58, 61, 98,
    104, 119, 127, 131, 145
Renaissance, 19, 21
rental shops, 89, 94, 96, *177*, 178–179
retailers, 89–107, 175, 197
    for antique dresses, 89, 92–94, 96,
        175, 178
    bridal salons, 89, 94, 95, 98–101, 178,
        185–196
    customizing and, *see* customizing
    ready-to-wear, 94, 95–98, 175, *177*
    types of, 94–98
    see also custom-made dresses
reticules, 168
retrogressive dressing, 19, 23–24, 177
rhinestones, 82, *82*, 83–84, 127
Rhodes, Zandra, 25
ribbon lace, 72
rickrack, 76
rosettes, fabric, 79
ruching, *46*, 78
ruffles, 78
Rundlett, Elizabeth, 167, 168

Sabrina collar, *46*
sachets, 153
Safro, Millicent, 87
sample sales, 95, *177*, 178
Sant' Angelo, Giorgio, 25
Saro, Linda, 162, 163
satin, *66*, 68, 69, 74, 79

Savitt, Janice, 128, 130
Scaasi, Arnold, 25–27, 47, 116
scarves, 169
schedule
    comparison shopping in, 175, 178
    creation of, 176–177
    dress purchase in, 175, 178–179
    easy-reference guidelines for, *177*
    seasonability and, 176
    statement definition and research in,
        175, 177–178
    tying up loose ends in, 175, 182
Scheffly, Renee, 161–162
schiffli lace, 72, *73*, 83, 112
Schlossberg, Caroline Kennedy, 104, 106
scoop necklines, *45*, *46*
seams, 91
seamstresses, 89, 91, 92, 94, 95, 175, 178
second weddings, *see* remarriages
seed pearls, 82, *82*, 125
semiformal styles, 12, 31, 39–54, 59
Senna, Frank, 85
sequins, 82, *82*, 91, 137
shantung, *66*, 68, 69, 80, 125
shawls, *35*, 169
sheaf, *148*, 149, 150, 152
sheaths, *35*, 38, 103, 124, 138
shoes, 113, 156, 160–163, 176, *177*, 178,
    180, 182
    choosing of, 160, 161, 162
    custom-made, 163
    dress elements and, 161, 162–163
    stockings and, 159
shopping, comparison, 175, 178
shoulders, 33, 43, 44, 47; *48*, 49–51, 179
    fit of, 91
silhouettes, 31, 33–39, *35*, 42, 43–44,
    52–53, 58, 106, 157, 179
    body proportions and, 33, 36
    components and design elements of,
        33, *35*, 36, *52–53*
    hairstyles and, *114*
    headdresses and, 116, 123–124
silk, 24–27, 68, 74, 125
skin care, 163, 169–170, 171, 175, 182
skin-care salons, 197
skin tones, 28
    flowers and, 141, 145
    veil colors and, 135

skirt, 33, *35*, 36, 41, 51, 52, 179
   fit of, 91
   fullness and length of, 41, 179
   width of, *35*
skullcaps, 121, 124
sleeves, 33, *48*, 50–61, 64, 179
   fit of, 91
   lengths of, 48
slimness, creating effect of, 38
slips, 156, 157, 171, 182
smocking, 78
snoods, *118*, 119, 123
Solomon, Candice, 69–70, 85, 101–102
soutache, 76
spaghetti straps, *48*
special-order dresses, 99
sprays, *118, 122, 148*
Starr, Jana, 93
stockings, *see* hosiery
stoles, 48, 169
Stone, Judith, 96
stress, 169–170, 175, 182
styles, 11–14, 31, 63, 95, 177;
      see also contemporary styles;
      formality, levels of; period
      dressing; traditional styles
suits, 58–60, 97, 178
supercotehardie, 9, 21
superstitions, 155, 169
Suzanne, 134, 135–136
swags, 76
sweetheart neckline, 46
Swiss dot, 66, 69
symbols, 19–29, 111, 131, *132*, 141,
     155, 182

*T*affeta, *66*, 68, 74, 105
tassels, 76
tatting, *73*
theater coat, 35
tiaras, 116, 117, *118*, 119, 121, 123,
     124, 125
tiers, *45*
timetable, *see* schedule
Tober, Barbara, 28, *57*, 70, *132*

traditional styles, 12, 31, 40, 41, 42, 74,
     92, 111, 177
   formal, *57*, 58
   informal, 12, 54–60
traditions, 19–29
trains, 33, 39, 40, 42, *42*, 43, 91, 179
   attachment places of, *42*
   bustled, *42, 45*
   detachable, 42
   length of, *42*
   shape and proportion of, 41
trimmings (passementerie), 24, 63, 64–65,
     75–81, 179
   body shape and, 79, 80
   choosing of, 79
   formality and, 79, 80
   on headdress, 127
   lace, 64, 65, *73*, 74, 75–81
   types of, 76–78
   see also embellishments; enhancement
     concepts
trousers, 33, 58, 70, 98, 179
trumpet skirts, 35
trunk shows, 103
Tudor style, 23
tulle, 21, *66*, 68, 69, 70, 80, 131–132,
     134, 135, 136, 138, 139
turtlenecks, *46*

*U*ltraformal styles, 12, 31, 32, 39
underpinnings, 42, 100, 155, 156, 157,
     171
underskirts, 35

*V*anderboorn, Nancy, 99
Van Lear, Lora, 42–43
Varsalona, Paula, 60, 103
veils, 20–21, 112, 120, 126, 131–139,
     153, 171, 182
   bouquets and, 145
   color, size, and placement of, 135–136
   convertibility of, 136
   earrings and, 131
   edges of, *132*

   formality and, 138
   fullness of, 138
   hairstyles and, 113, *114,* 136, 138
   headdresses and, 135, 136
   jewelry and, 126
   lace, 136–137
   lengths of, *132*
   makeup and, 165
   style and proportion of, 138–139
   see also headdresses
velvet, 66, 68, 80
Venise lace, 72, *73*
Victoria, Queen of England, 23, 155
Victorian style, 22, 23, 24, 59, 91, 136,
     162, 171
Vincent, Elaine, 116–117, 121
vintage dresses, 89, 92–94, 96, 175, 178
voile, 66

*W*aistlines, 33, 43, 44, 47, 51–52
   fit of, 91
   types of, 50
Walling, Christopher, 130–131
Wang, Vera, 28
Watteau trains, *42,* 43
wedding-band collar, *46*
wedding bands, 128, 163
wedding day, 171
Weitzman, Stuart, 160, 161
white, 23, 27–29
   color differences in, 27
width, creation of, 44
Wiggins, Bobby, 153
Windsor, Wallis Simpson, Duchess of,
     61, 103
Work, Robert, 64–65, 102–103
wraps (cover-ups), *35, 48,* 113, 156,
     169, 182
wreaths, *118, 122,* 123, 124, 136, 139,
     152, 167

*Y*oke neckline, *48*

*Z*ippers, 86